THE NEW IDOL

THE NEW IDOL

BY

GASTON LEROUX

TRANSLATED BY HANNAFORD BENNETT

WILDSIDE PRESS

CONTENTS

CONTENTS

THE NEW IDOL

CHAPTER I

A DRAMATIC SETTING

"LATE edition . . . Republic in danger . . . Dictatorship movement unmasked. Interpellation in the Chamber . . . Indictment of the accused."

The newsboys came into view at an angle of the grand boulevards and the Rue Royale. A number of Deputies lunching in a restaurant near by rushed outside as the boys came up and bought papers, returning quickly to their restaurant where groups of interested people gathered round them.

"So it is really to be this afternoon?"

"Why, I've already told you Carlier has proofs."

"Has he any names?"

"The names are on everyone's lips."

"I tell you Carlier will do nothing. It's more than a fortnight since he is said to have had proofs. He has nothing of the sort. Subdamoun and his gang are as clever as he is."

"They have not yet appeared before the High Court."

"They will be there within a week."

"Unless they are shot."

"Unless the Revolution has succeeded."

"All humbug. Do you believe in a Revolution? Do you think these things are worked in such a way? Look! Here's Mulot from the Ministry of the Interior. Well, Mulot, have you seen the Minister?"

The new-comᶧr had lived in a perpetual rage since nearly all his friends had joined the Ministry—a Ministry of the Extreme Left. Nevertheless he had complete control over himself though nothing could reconcile him to his exclusion from office. Thus he led Ministers a sorry life, urging them to adopt extreme measures, to take the most serious resolutions, accusing them of lack of zeal in applying their principles, and conveying to them the menacing orders of Carlier who held the Extreme Left in the hollow of his hand.

It was a far cry from the former policy, which none the less had raised a considerable amount of wrath and over which so many bitter fights were waged. That policy would have seemed very pale pink compared with that of the Hérisson Ministry.

Carlier furnished the Government with the names of the Deputies to be kept under observation, made charges against citizens without proofs, declaring that they should first be arrested and evidence would be forthcoming. According to him no time was to be lost seeing that the electors of the ninth district had replaced their old member, recently deceased, by returning to the House this young officer, Major Jacques. "Jacques I," or "Subdamoun I," growled those who already spoke of a dictator, recalling his uncomprising attitude before the Boundary Commission set up to delimit the frontiers of a French colony in Equatorial Africa. His attitude had brought down upon him official censure with the result that he had sent in his papers. During the War it so happened that he commanded a division

that made a name for itself—the Iron Division.
And since the peace he had never ceased to denounce
what he called "dissipating the victory"; and he had
thrown himself into political life as though he were
making an assault upon the trenches, ready to sweep
all before him. By degrees his extraordinary popularity made him leader of the malcontents, and they
were not a few!

He was an aristocrat by birth, heir to the name de
Touchais and a marquisate since his elder brother,
Bernard de Touchais, had met his death some years
before in the San Francisco earthquake, after more
or less ruining the family. His father's tragic end in
the fire at the Château de la Falaise, at Puys, a fire
in which the notorious Chéri-Bibi, of sinister reputation, also lost his life, still lingers in the memory.

Mulot at last condescended to answer young
Coudry seated beside him.

"Yes, I saw the Minister, and told him we had had
enough of it. Hérisson grasped the situation.
There's going to be the devil of a row! We should
have known all the ins and outs of the plot long
ago if that ass Cravely had been willing. But
Cravely is, it seems, both head of the Detective
Service and an honest man; he shrank from burglary. Think of the head of the Detective Service
having qualms of conscience when it's a question of
saving the Republic!"

Mulot winked at Coudry, a raging youngster
whom the last election had shot on to the Socialist
benches in the Chamber. He spent his time bark-
ing at the heels of every speaker, intercepting their
best periods when they happened to be not of his
own party.

"Do you know whom we've got to work with?"
went on Mulot after a pause.

"Lavobourg," returned the other in an undertone.

Mulot made an approving motion of his head.
Lavobourg was the chief Vice-President of the
Chamber.

"Clearly there's nothing but treachery all round,"
declared Coudry.

"All round."

"Then that's why they say that Subdamoun
spends all his time at the house of Lavobourg's mistress, the beautiful Sonia. It is she who must have
entrusted Subdamoun's papers to Lavobourg for
greater safety. The whole thing will come to a
head in a few minutes. Come, let's go. If Carlier
is to be believed everyone will be nabbed. There'll
be arrests in the Chamber itself. Oh, we shall see
what Subdamoun's gang think of it. And Major
Jacques will pull a long face when they march him
off to the Conciergerie Prison!"

At the moment when Mulot and Coudry were
about to leave the restaurant one of their colleagues
descended from a taxi and darted towards them,
eyes gleaming. It was Jolly the Questeur. He had
been lunching at the Presidency with M. Bonchamps, President of the Chamber, a true Republican and a stalwart, on whom the Revolution could
count, when Bonchamps suddenly put his hand to
his heart with a stifled groan and fainted and was
now dying.

"Bonchamps poisoned! Bonchamps poisoned!"
was the cry that spread swiftly through the restaurants in the Rue Royale as the guests poured out.

The frenzied company of Deputies crossed the Place de la Concorde and the bridge, being joined on the way by friends hastening to the Palais Bourbon. They at once learnt that the sentries at the Chamber had been doubled, and troops confined to barracks ready for any emergency. The friends of the Ministry could be easy in their minds on this score, since Hérisson had appointed M. Flottard, a civilian, as head of the military government of Paris, and without his signature the General, the Deputy Governor, could issue no order of importance.

Mulot, Coudry and the others tore like a whirlwind into the lobby and turned to the right towards the President's apartments, but were stopped by the door-keepers, who gave them reassuring news. The President was already much better; his indisposition was passing away. He himself had caused the rumor of poisoning to be contradicted. He hoped to be able to take the chair at the sitting.

"Whew! we have had a narrow escape," exclaimed Mulot, drawing Coudry to the Salle des Pas Perdus. "The position of President reverts by right to Lavobourg, and a warrant is about to be issued against him."

"Do you think his presence in the chair will embarrass us if Carlier turns informer?"

"We should see Carlier about that. But no one knows what has become of him since seven o'clock this morning when he left his house, so the President of the Council told me."

"He is not wasting his time. You know him."

"Here, as it happens, is Hérisson, and I must have a word with him."

As a matter of fact Hérisson, President of the Council and Minister of the Interior, was crossing the ante-chamber, his portfolio under his arm. To everyone who accosted him he said, without stopping:

"Have you seen Carlier? . . . Have you seen Carlier?"

But no one had seen Carlier, and the naturally stern and gloomy face of the little short man showed signs of anxiety. At last Carlier hove in sight, tall, bent, a snarling expression on his face. They made a rush on him like dogs eager for the quarry. But he shook off the pack, carrying his portfolio crammed with papers. He at once disappeared, taking Mulot with him. Just then the order, "Attention!" from the officer on duty rang out in the ante-chamber for the march past of the President's military escort.

But Bonchamps did not take the chair at the sitting. He had had a renewed attack of sickness and Lavobourg presided in his stead—Lavobourg, who strode forward between the two lines of soldiers as pale as though he were indeed walking to the scaffold which the Mulots and Coudrys spoke of erecting, as in the glorious days of '93, to chastize traitors to the Republic.

When Lavobourg was out of sight the general uproar increased. Rumor had it that the names of suspected persons would be read from the tribune. When members of the Conservative and Agrarian parties passed through the ante-chamber they were greeted with a regular outburst of hooting, and every throat cried, "Long live the Republic!"

The sitting promised to be an exciting one. The extremists made no secret of their purpose. "To prison with them!" they cried. If the Chamber did not shrink from its duty it would appoint a Commission of Inquiry charged with complete judicial powers. Coudry saw no other way of saving the Republic. Nevertheless to justify, even in part, such unwonted proceedings, Carlier would have to submit proofs from the tribune. Once more he had vanished, shutting himself up with Mulot. When Mulot appeared again he shouted to those who pressed round him:

"Let me be—I have nothing to tell you."

Coudry ended by getting him all to himself at the moment when his colleagues were bustling their way to the Chamber for the beginning of the interpellation. Mulot was shaking with nervousness. He had read Carlier's documents, the documents that had been filched from Lavobourg. That was something and yet it was nothing. Plans for a new constitution—everyone had a right to indulge in them. It was no crime to dream of revising the constitution. But evidence of an attempt to establish a dictatorship—where was it? And where was the incriminating list of conspirators? Carlier was still waiting for it. . . . Were they going to supply him with it? He swore they were! He was so utterly certain that he would not ask to be allowed to withdraw his interpellation. A withdrawal would have a disastrous effect. Moreover, with Lavobourg's papers he had the wherewithal to put off the Chamber while waiting for the list.

"Where is the list?" asked Coudry.

"Well," returned the other, casting a look round to make sure that no one was spying, "it was in the Major's possession, but it has disappeared."

"So that's why the beautiful Sonia looks so pale. I saw her not long ago. My dear fellow, she seemed like a statue."

"Oh, like her friend Lavobourg, she is trying to put a bold face upon it. But it's Subdamoun's face that we should see, and it will be long before he will show himself."

"Perhaps he has already escaped."

"You may ask Cravely that question. . . . Ah, there is Cravely."

A man of robust appearance in spite of his white hair was approaching, hand in pockets, his ferret-like eyes gleaming behind his spectacles. The chief of the Detective Service had risen from the ranks; and he still looked as if he were "on the track of some crime" as in those far-off days when he hunted down the most notorious criminals.

"Well, is the Republic to be saved to-day?" asked Coudry.

"Is it in danger?" returned the other; and then, going up to Mulot, "Have you seen Carlier?"

"Yes."

"Did they bring him the tempting morsel he expected?"

"Not yet. But how can you, the chief of the Detective Service, ask me such a question?"

"I came here to gather information."

He passed on whistling. Mulot shrugged his shoulders. They went into the Chamber to hear Lavobourg say in a tone of voice that was unrecognizable and scarcely natural:

"I have received from M. Carlier a request for an interpellation on the measures which the Government intends to adopt against the enemies of the Republic, against the conspirators whose avowed object is to overthrow existing institutions by revolution."

A storm of cries, uncontrolled laughter, humorous sallies arose from the Centre and Right while the entire Left stood up and applauded to the echo. Lavobourg struck his bell at brief intervals. He strove to appear calm, impartial, remote, almost indifferent. The truth was that he sat there like a man in a dream, his thoughts centred on the blow that was soon to be struck at him, for he knew not only that he had been robbed but, in particular, that the famous list at the head of which his own name stood had been stolen from the Major.

Although he tried hard he could not prevent his eyes wandering involuntarily to Sonia, the great actress, who had lured him into the mad adventure. She stood erect in her beauty, like a marble statue, between Baron and Baroness d'Askof, giving no more heed to Lavobourg than if he were not in the chair, addressing a word over her shoulder to a young man, no other than Jacques's friend, Lieut. Frederic Héloni.

But Jacques himself was still absent. And yet with what vigor he had that very morning calmed the most panic-stricken among his friends. "Nothing is lost," he declared, but he had not been seen since, and they all began to stare at his vacant seat. It was at the top, in the last row on the left, level with the President's chair. But he was a member of no party—not even of the independents.

The President of the Council rose from his seat and said: "The Government is at the disposal of the Chamber to discuss at once M. Carlier's inter-pellation."

At that moment Jacques came in. The Extreme Left received him with a hostile demonstration, shouting: "Down with Subdamoun! . . . To the High Court! . . . To prison with Jacques! . . . Issue a warrant!" while Coudry's piercing voice could be heard: "Guillotine him!"

An entire body of Deputies demanded silence, im-ploring these hysterical persons to hold their tongues and listen to Carlier, who had mounted the tribune. As to Major Jacques, he passed straight to his seat, thrusting aside gently but firmly the Deputies swarming in the hemicycle, and went up the steps to his place without seeming to hear either threats or insults.

He was of frail, almost delicate, appearance, but an indomitable will could be read in the dark eyes deep set beneath their straddling eyebrows, gleaming at times with a fire not easily withstood. His com-plexion was slightly tanned by the suns of Africa and the Far East. Hollow of cheek, his profile that of a Roman aristocrat, he was clean-shaven, with close-cropped upstanding hair. He seemed quite young. Of medium height, he was clad in a tight-fitting frock-coat of military cut, buttoned to the chin. An ardent spirit sustained him and manifested itself through its fragile envelope, throwing as it were a lustre over him.

"Gentlemen," snorted Carlier, whose stentorian voice secured silence more effectually than the Presi-dent's bell, "Gentlemen, I ask you to save the Republic to-day. A seditious faction, a mere handful, has sworn to overthrow it. . . ."

"Long live the Republic!' shouted Coudry. "I ask to be heard."

It was as much as Mulot could do to make him sit down. Carlier, in the tribune, folded his arms. Shouts from the Extreme Left greeted him: "Go on! Go on!" But it did not seem as if he were eager to proceed. He paused at the interruptions, waited for an impossible silence—in a word, seemed to wish to gain time. His reluctance was observed, and from every part of the Chamber impatient or perturbed voices cried: "Names! Names!"

He turned sharply to the left and rapped out: "I will give names. I shall not wait for the Commission of Inquiry. Moreover, you who demand these names know them as well as I do. You know the wretched individuals who, betraying the mandate received from the nation, are prepared to lay waste the country in order to achieve their monstrous dream of a dictatorship behind a seditious soldier whom the Army has dismissed from its ranks."

He had no need to point to Jacques, for every eye turned towards him. Were they about to hear his voice? Jacques did not move a muscle. So great an impassivity incensed even his friends.

"Answer! Answer!"

With a gold pencil he calmly took notes in a small notebook. Above him in the crowded public galleries the throng leaned forward. But in none of the galleries was the tension more acute than in one in which a woman had just taken a seat in the front row—a woman whose splendid white hair encircled a face that was still handsome and still retained its pristine purity of lineament in spite of her years. It was the Marchioness de Touchais, Major Jacques's mother, whom the people of Dieppe called the beautiful Cecily when she lived in the town of her birth, and whom the social world of Paris now treated with infinite respect.

Seated beside her was her companion, whom she called "my dear Jacqueline," clad in a semi-religious costume as befitted an ex-sister of St. Mary of the Angels, who had so greatly mourned her brother that terrible monster Chéri-Bibi. With the two older ladies a young girl of captivating charm had come in, and Sonia, seated in the gallery facing them, could not keep her eyes off her. It was Mlle Lydia de la Morlière, engaged, it was said, to Major Jacques who still continued to take notes. . . .

"Proofs! Proofs!" was shouted in increasingly loud tones.

Carlier opened his portfolio as though inviting the Chamber to have patience while he cast his eyes more and more frequently to the door on the left through which the decisive evidence would come. He had been told: "You shall have the list at three o'clock," and it was ten minutes past three. He began to feel uneasy.

"Gentlemen," he said, taking out a document, "passions alien to our constitution, opinions subversive to our present social order, memories of a hateful and ill-omened despotism have disturbed our minds . . ."

"No speeches—proofs!"

Suddenly an usher mounted the steps of the tribune and handed him a letter which he at once opened and read. His face beamed.

"I have proofs," he thundered, "but I have just received the most decisive of all. I ask for a ten minutes' adjournment."

His announcement was received with loud shouts and the banging of desks. Hérisson himself rose to his feet and asked the Chamber to agree to the adjournment. The majority was even now leaving the benches. Lavobourg put on his silk hat, but there was no need for him even to say, "The sitting stands adjourned"; and he descended the tribune, leaning on the bannisters as though he had already received his death-blow.

Carlier left the Chamber. Crossing the Salle des Pas Perdus and the lobby, he was seen to enter quickly one of those small office-parlors in which Deputies may shut themselves up with an elector, receive the visits of friends, and discuss private matters. He was soon joined by a man whom no one knew—not even Cravely who, as if by chance, was passing by craftily pursuing his own business— a big fellow of austere appearance in a long black frock-coat. This man, like Carlier, carried a morocco leather portfolio under his arm. The door closed after them, and the crowd waited in an atmossphere of excitement.

Impatience reached the point of exasperation when it became known that the mysterious messenger in the Quakerish frock-coat had left the room some five minutes, but that Carlier still lingered. He must be arranging his notes, making his last preparations for the crucial struggle. But it was felt that he was taking too long to collect himself, and one or two friends knocked at the door. There was no answer.

Mulot took it upon himself to open the door. He started back in horror. Carlier lay stretched on the table, his clothes awry, his waistcoat open, a dagger in his heart.

CHAPTER II

THE BODY IN THE TRIBUNE

THE rumor of the murder spread like wild-fire. A tremendous uproar, a wild struggle surged round the dead man so that a company of the Republican Guard had to be sent for to clear the approaches to the room. But it was to no purpose. Nothing could prevent Carlier's friends carrying the body of the victim to the Chamber, shouting as they entered, "Death to the assassins!"

Coudry, who supported the head and shoulders, and Mulot, who had made a grab at the portfolio to save its contents if possible, displayed faces distorted by a deep hatred. Shouts, clenched fists, rage on the one hand and consternation on the other formed a sort of mourning retinue to this sinister trophy which was laid on the shorthand writer's table at the foot of the tribune.

The dead man's friends pressed round the body, others in their delirium swore to be revenged. Pagès, who had maintained his presence of mind and ordered the doors to be closed, endeavored to restrain the confusion and exchanged a few words now with the Head of the Government, who had sent for the Attorney-General, and now with the Questeurs.

Mulot had opened Carlier's portfolio, but failed to find in it the papers stolen from Lavobourg. He at once joined Cravely in a corridor. Cravely assured him that not one of the accomplices would escape, and they would soon have the key to the mystery, for when the unknown visitor left the room he had put one of his best men on his track.

Lavobourg's friends advised him to remain in the background if he wished to avoid being stabbed in his turn; and under the pretence of keeping guard over him Cravely, in agreement with Jolly, one of the Questeurs on whom he could rely, placed detectives with the Vice-President of the Chamber and thus made sure of him.

It was then that an old man, who seemed at death's door and was held up by the ushers, said from the President's chair:

"Gentlemen, the sitting is resumed."

It was Bonchamps who, on hearing of the assassination, mastered the mysterious illness that was preying on him and drove to the Chamber to make sure that the President's chair should not, in such tragic circumstances, be left in the hands of the reactionaries.

This unexpected appearance, this splendid gesture, those impressive words, the supreme calm of the man upon whom death had already cast its shadow, had an immediate result, temporarily lulling the storm. The fury of a group of Deputies who had made a rush on Major Jacques, guarded by his friends and motionless, seemed suspended. And the Chamber in a body, appalled by the horrible crime, cheered the man who had at once restored to it a sense of its own dignity. But the cheering had

scarcely subsided when the Extreme Left turned
towards a particular seat, the seat where Major
Jacques still sat with folded arms, and Coudry's
voice could be heard above the others:

"There is the criminal!"

"I have never shed blood but on the battlefield. I
ask to be heard."

The words rang out like a clarion call. It was the
first time that that voice had been heard, and it
seemed to sound the rally to a distracted camp attacked by the enemy on all sides. A silence ensued,
during which another sentence could be heard uttered by Hérisson, already preparing to mount the
tribune:

"I withdraw my right to speak in favor of the
accused!"

The words struck home, and Jacques was seen to
grow pale while the Extreme Left cheered the President of the Council. Nevertheless Jacques strode
down the hemicycle with a buoyant step and in two
bounds was in the tribune. With hand outstretched
over Carlier's body he said:

"I swear on Carlier's dead body to discover the
assassin. If the Commission of Inquiry which you
are about to appoint does not elucidate this crime
which I abominate, I will do so myself. I swear
that if your commissioners and police are unable to
unravel the truth, I will not rest until I have brought
the criminal here with my own hands—I who am
not skilled in the use of the dagger and have never
wielded any weapon but the sword of France!"

At these words half the Chamber gave way to
prolonged cheers, and it seemed as if many of

Jacques's own partisans were relieved of an immense burden.

Mulot intervened:

"Carlier was assassinated for the purpose of stealing Lavobourg's papers, which are not in his portfolio."

"So, M. Mulot, you know that M. Lavobourg was robbed, and doubtless you know the thief," returned Jacques de Touchais. "Well, you are better informed than we are, for we know nothing of Carlier's murder. What the burglar's jimmy began the dagger has continued. But I swear that I and my friends have had no part in this disgraceful business. And I will tell you why. Because it is a matter of indifference to my friend Lavobourg and me whether a document in which we sketched out the model of a Constitution is read from the tribune or not. Is it unconstitutional to desire to revise the Constitution? All those of you who protest so loudly have been foremost in the past in seeking revision. Every good citizen demands it to-day."

"So as to overthrow the Republic!" shouted Coudry.

"What have you made of the Republic? What have you made of this France which has so valiantly recovered from the most terrible disasters? What have you made of this nation which astonished Europe by its steadfact prosperity and the splendor of its qualities?"

"And you—what do you wish to make of the Republic? Will you tell us that?"

"I wish to banish you from it."

The effect was tremendous. It was as though a

tidal wave had broken loose on the back benches of
the Extreme Left—a thundering wave whose raging
billows surged in the hemicycle and rolled as far
as the tribune amid uplifted fists, blows, contorted
faces, pandemonium, while in the public galleries
women screamed in terror. Jacques was borne from
the tribune as though he were a feather and found
himself below, clothes in tatters, blood on his face;
and assuredly he would have been torn to pieces had
not Lieut. Frederic Héloni and two sturdy fellows
suddenly jumped from the galleries like cats and
as it were scattered the assembly in a trice. The
impetuous rush of the invaders would doubtless have
been followed by not a few violent incidents had not
the strident voice of an usher risen above the din:

"Silence, gentlemen, M. Bonchamps is dying . . ."

Two men had died during that one sitting. It
was more than enough. But the death of these two
men had saved the policy and possibly the life of
the daring young Major. . . . He was allowed to
leave the Chamber accompanied by his bodyguard.

CHAPTER III

THE HOUSE IN THE MARAIS QUARTER

"Do you hear what I say, M. Barkimel? I will
never forgive you for keeping me waiting six hours
by the clock, as true as my name is Florent."

"My dear M. Florent," protested M. Barkimel,
"I give you my word that I would have come out
to you at once had it been possible, for in fact I was

longing to get away from the awful sight, but we
were held prisoners by the Republican Guard, who
would not allow us to move a step. That sort of
thing savors of revolution."

"Get out with your revolution! It was agreed
that the card admitting to the public galleries should
be used by us in turn, and you failed to keep your
word—that's all."

The two friends, two worthy and respectable citizens, retired shopkeepers, glared at each other as if
each wished to put fear into the other. Realizing
that their efforts were a failure, doubtless because
of former experience of this sort of quarrel, they
held out their hands in a spontaneous gesture.

"We are silly asses, Florent."

"We are, Barkimel."

"Ah, my dear fellow, what a cruel sight it was to
see that man being carried to the tribune with a
dagger in his heart! It was like an incident in a
revolution, I tell you. . . . I saw a scene that
happens in revolutions."

"You saw a mere item of news for the newspapers," returned Florent drily, for he was annoyed
at missing the episode and could not help belittling
it tormented by the thought of the success which
that confounded Barkimel would achieve that evening when he told his story.

"An item of news! Oh! of course the papers are
full of items of news like that every day!" said
Barkimel, shocked more than he could express.
"An item of news!"

M. Barkimel would never forgive M. Florent for
using such language.

"Bonchamps has been ill for some time," said

Florent in a calm but slightly sarcastic tone, "the poor man had to die somewhere. I don't see anything in that to get excited over. Clearly you don't know what a revolution is. I mean a real revolution like the one in 1792—in the time of Robespierre."

"Get away with your Robespierre! You won't admit that I have witnessed a scene from a revolution. And you take advantage of the fact that you used to keep a stationers' shop with a circulating library atached to it, to throw Robespierre in my face."

"We can't all sell umbrellas."

"Florent!"

"Barkimel!"

They glared at each other once more. They shook hands again.

"After all, are we so remote from Robespierre's time? From what I can gather manners in those times were pretty much what they are to-day. Just think. . . . Everywhere this mania for dancing, general corruption, public scandals, and on the political horizon a dictator."

"What nonsense! Let's talk of your dictator. He's not the first to give us a glimpse of the military tunic under his plain clothes. . . . Since we've been a republic we know to our cost what that sort of stuff means."

"Shut up, we're passing his mother's house, and you wouldn't talk like that had you seen him a little while ago."

The two friends while chatting and wrangling had crossed the bridge near the Hôtel de Ville, and reached the Marais quarter in which they lived. Before continuing their way they raised their eyes for a moment to the stately house which, after the terrible incident in the Chamber, must be the scene of considerable emotion.

"Where is all this going to lead us?" asked Barkimel with a shiver.

"Nowhere," declared the sceptical Florent, "or at least nowhere but home and a good supper and then a sound sleep."

At the corner of the street M. Barkimel said:

"Let me be. . . . I shan't be able to sleep tonight. I tell you that we are living in revolutionary times. And that's the opinion of my friend Hilare of 'Hilare's Up-to-date Grocery Stores.'"

It was in this one-time aristocratic quarter of distinctive architecture, where the houses were now for the most part given over to trade and commerce, that the Marchioness de Touchais lived after many years spent in mourning a happiness too quickly over, and bringing up in exile after her own heart, the son who was one day to be Major Jacques.

The house was never the property of the de Touchais family. It was the family mansion of the de la Morlières in which Cecily had taken up her abode after the death of Mme de la Morlière, whom she dearly loved and whose daughter, Lydia, she promised to watch over as though she were her own child. Lydia was extremely wealthy. Cecily was comparatively poor. She had barely enough suitably to maintain her rank, and the change in her circumstances was the result of the follies of her elder son Bernard.

Bernard had shown himself as a youth jealous of Jacques, so jealous that one day Jacques was found with his head cut open by a blow which Bernard

had given him in a fit of rage because Jacques had
opposed one of his whims. Cecily, already tried
greatly by her past sufferings, could not forgive him.
He was growing up, and she sent him to England to
finish his education.

Bernard always refused to return to his mother
on the ground that he objected to meet Jacques
again because of his exile, and when he became of
age he went to America. Here he committed in-
numerable eccentricities. He plunged into all sorts
of projects, signed bills for heavy sums, gambled on
the stock exchange, lost several fortunes, and com-
promised the honor of the de Touchais's. Cecily
paid his debts to the last sou, encroaching upon
Jacques's share which he generously surrendered
on attaining his majority. Notwithstanding the mil-
lions of francs thus wasted, honor itself might have
been wrecked had not the earthquake in San Francisco put an end to his career.

Cecily now had only one son, but she had a daughter in the handsome and charming Lydia whom she
had brought up with Jacques. Lydia was a little
girl when he was a big boy. In course of time they
fell in love with each other. But Jacques was a
poor man, and he wished to bring fame to Lydia as
his wedding present.

"We will be married when I have made a name,"
he said.

His fame had brought him to the present extraordinary pass which threatened to sweep all before
it and submerge them like wisps of straw. Lydia
grasped the significance of it during that tragic
afternoon so full of horror for Cecily and herself.

The two women were in each others' arms, Lydia

seeking to console Cecily, when Jacqueline came into the room to say that Lieut. Frederic Héloni had called.

"Show him in," they cried in unison, rising quickly in their eagerness to hear the latest news.

Héloni at once reassured them:

"All's well."

"What about Jacques?"

"A few scratches of no importance."

"You saved his life."

"It's not worth mentioning."

"Is he coming here?"

"Yes, for a moment before dinner."

"We don't know what happened in the Chamber after the incident," said Lydia, breathing quickly. "We left when we saw him out of danger. We hoped he would hasten back here."

"This is what happened and it was over quickly. After an adjournment, during which the bodies of the two dead men, Carlier and Bonchamps, were removed, the sitting was resumed. In five minutes the Chamber by an unanimous vote appointed a Commission of Inquiry. The Extreme Left succeeded in carrying a proposal giving the Commission the widest judicial powers. But these powers have to be ratified by the Senate, which will refuse to sanction them. We are certain of a majority in the Senate. In these circumstances it means so much time gained for us, and we ask nothing better for the moment."

"What about the assassination of Carlier?" asked Cecily after some hesitation.

"During the adjournment and after Jacques had departed Hérisson had a conference with the Attorney-General and the leaders of the party. It seems that as far as Carlier is concerned foul play is not absolutely proved."

"Oh, I am glad of that," said the Marchioness with a deep sigh.

"The dagger with which he was stabbed belonged to him, his waistcoat was open as if he meant to take his own life. Was it a case of suicide? Did he lose his head on learning that his visitor had not brought him the proofs which he had promised to lay before the Chamber? These are plausible conjectures. Moreover"—the lieutenant lowered his voice—"the papers stolen from him have been found."

"Where?"

"At Sonia's place . . . and that's not the strangest part of it. . . ."

"But don't you see that this man Carlier was assassinated to get back the papers," exclaimed Cecily in a trembling voice "and the assassin belongs to your party?"

"To *our* party—so we must keep silent, madame."

"Yes, yes a man of our party. . . . But this death . . . this assassination . . ."

"Oh, we are not responsible for that," exclaimed the lieutenant.

"This assassination frightens me," said Cecily with more agitation than she had shown during all this period so fraught with danger to her son.

"It merely surprises us. But since it helps us we have, as you may imagine other things to do than to waste time over it now. Events will move quickly. We must take advantage of Bonchamp's death. Honest but obstinate, he would have ruined the Republic in order to save the Constitution, and he stood in our way . . ."

"I may tell you that during that horrible sitting when I was not watching my son my eyes were on President Bonchamps, and seeing him in such pain, his labored breathing, I wondered if the rumor were true that he was poisoned."

"His doctor contradicted that odious rumor. And yet you, madame, repeat it."

"Oh, I dare not think about it any more."

"Our hands are clean. Jacques has said so," declared Frederic Héloni, "but we are no longer at the stage of the struggle when we can choose our friends or enemies."

"I thought, for my part, that I should go mad, and I should certainly have done so had you not rushed into the fray, my dear Frederic."

"Oh, I was not the only one," he said modestly.

"That's true. What have you done with your two men?" asked Cecily.

"They are in the kitchen. Jacqueline must be looking after them."

"Go and fetch them so that I may thank them. You don't mind?"

"Oh, they'll be delighted."

Héloni went out and returned with Jacqueline and the two men. They were two sturdy rascals with powerful necks and shoulders, standing on their feet as on bronze pillars. They twisted between their huge fingers their oil-cloth hats, such as children supposed to be dressed as sailors wear—hats that must have given them a singular appearance when they put them on.

Their faces might give rise to fear or laughter;

and yet they were neither grotesque nor vicious; they were worse—they were startling. They had deserted from the navy, so they said, because they were the drudges of a quartermaster who put them in irons every week. Thereafter they trudged about the world abandoning the idea of returning to France in spite of their immunity from arrest, for they had no relations. Frederic met them in Subdamoun when the expeditionary force was being formed, and they offered their services as carriers. During the local fighting they behaved like heroes, rushing headlong into the path of danger and acting as a bodyguard to Jacques, who returned unscathed.

One was called Jean Jean and the other Polydore. They were very nearly of the same height and same stout figure. That which differentiated them and disclosed their origin was that Jean Jean spoke with a Caux accent and Polydore with a Breton, and more particularly a Brest accent.

When the Marchioness congratulated them on their courage and thanked them for their devotion to her son, Jean Jean, who was the spokesman of the partnership, assured her that they had no other aim but to give their lives for the Major, who had brought them back to the path "of honor."

"Don't be afraid, madame, you can rely on Polydore and Jean through thick and thin."

"Good-hearted fellows," said Cecily after they had left the room.

"Of course they are," returned Frederic, "and though I don't know where they come from I couldn't put my hand on two pluckier fellows."

"Under their rough exterior," went on Cecily,

"they are as gentle as lambs, and have the hearts of children."

The lieutenant grinned. Cecily left him with Mlle de la Morlière.

"Tell me the truth," she said. "Where is Jacques? If you tell me where he is you shall be rewarded."

"Have you got anything for me?" he asked eagerly.

"Yes."

"Have you been to the classes? Have you seen Marie Thérèse?"

She showed him a letter.

"Give it to me!"

"Where is Jacques?"

"Why should I hide it from you," he returned, taking the letter held out to him. "Jacques is at Sonia Liskinne's with M. Lavobourg."

"I suspected as much,' said Lydia sadly. "He never leaves that woman now."

"You can't be serious, mademoiselle. You know that matters of great importance are at stake at the beautiful Sonia's."

"The beautiful Sonia's! . . . Yes, she is indeed beautiful. I was looking at her a little while ago in the Chamber. I can understand, you know, why she has turned so many heads. You could not leave her either. You were in her box . . ."

"Yes, with my two sailors hiding themselves at the back ready for any emergency. Oh, we were talking of anything but love, I assure you. There you have a woman worth ten men. Between ourselves, she is Jacques's most valuable lieutenant."

"Good gracious," murmured Lydia, turning pale. "Read your letter—I won't look."

She sat down dejectedly by a round table on which lay some illustrated papers and turned over the pages.

"Thank you, dear little postman," said Frederic when he had finished reading the letter. "Are you going to the classes again to-morrow?"

And he gave her a letter already written.

"This is a nice business you get me to do for you," she said, taking the letter.

"Oh, mademoiselle, you know I love Marie Thérèse as Jacques loves you—with the same deep and sincere love . . ."

Lydia rose to her feet and looked the lieutenant in the eyes.

"Frederic—you see I call you Frederic—I am going to talk to you like a sister. Do you think Jacques loves me as much as he used to do?"

"What do you mean? I am sure of it," he returned.

His obvious sincerity and the spontaneous nature of his answer seemed to allay for a moment her incomprehensible agitation.

"Thank you, you have done me good. Of course, I am a little beside myself. It is the result of all this strain, and then what do you expect, my dear Frederic," she went on with a forced smile, "since I have seen the beautiful Sonia I feel that if I were a man an insignificant little girl like me would mean so little compared with her."

"You do yourself less than justice when you say that. Look! Here is the major. I'll go and tell him."

"No, please don't say a word."

Jacques came into the room. Lydia ran up to him, crimson with an excitement which she made no attempt to conceal.

"Oh, Jacques, how glad I am to see you after that dreadful sitting."

"My dear Lydia!"

She began to cry quietly. Very pretty at all times, her tears seemed to make her adorable. When he saw those tears, which he was usually able to wipe away at once, he could not repress a gesture of irritation that did not escape her. And when he told her that he wished to see his mother because he had to return to M. Lavobourg—to Sonia Liskinne she thought—she uttered no word of complaint, and nothing in her bearing betrayed the acute disappointment that wrung her heart.

Nevertheless they knew each other so well, and Jacques's love for her was so sincere, that he intuitively grasped what was passing in that young and eager heart that beat only for him, and he availed himself of a moment when Frederic seemed engrossed in the examination of an old picture representing one of Lydia's ancestors at the battle of Marignan to take her in his arms and console her with a kiss and a few sweet words, at which she grew pale with joy and he reddened with remorse.

"My dear Lydia, I adore you."

It was true, but it was true also that at that moment he was thinking of the beautiful Sonia.

Cecily came in. She uttered a cry of joy. Mother and son embraced. It was not so much admiration or love that she felt for him as worship. In her inner consciousness she never despaired of him even

in crucial times, for she looked upon him as well-
nigh invulnerable. She had never attempted to dis-
suade him from his great project. But in her simple
heart, in which good and evil never became confused, she was still greatly troubled by the tragic
happenings which bore so much resemblance to
assassinations and so fortuitously and strangely
cleared the way for the hero on the war-path. It
was very different when Jacques told her the latest
news.

"Just think, Cravely had the mysterious stranger
followed after he left Carlier. Now this man managed to give the detective the slip for a time, but
he found him again."

"Well, what did the man say?" asked Cecil anxiously.

"He said nothing because he was found hanged."

"Hanged!"

"Yes, hanged to the sash of his window. Cravely,
it seems, is in a tremendous rage over it."

Frederic could not believe his ears.

"All the same," he said, "the day has ended for
us better than it began."

But they did not continue the conversation. When
they turned towards the Marchioness they observed
with alarm that she seemed to be gasping for breath.
They darted forward. Lydia held a bottle of smell-
ing-salts to her nostrils, and she came to herself
almost at once. She apologized for causing so much
trouble, kissed her son, enjoined him to exercise
greater prudence than ever, and expressed a desire
to go to bed. She went out on the arm of Jacqueline, who had been called in.

"Poor mother," said Jacques. "She must be

utterly exhausted, for she is not lacking in courage. Look after her, my dear Lydia; don't leave her during these all-important days, for I may not have time to come here even for a word with you."

"Rely on me, Jacques," said Lydia, stifling the sob that trembled in her throat. "Rely on me. . . And may you win through."

She clung to him. He gave her a last kiss, his thoughts wholly on her now, for he knew that if he were to fail he would probably never see her again; and he left, taking Frederic with him. They had scarcely passed into the street when two dark forms emerged from the shadow of the wall and followed them. But these forms were themselves pursued by two others, who began to talk in a low voice. . . .

"It is we now who are keeping an eye on the police. How times are changed!" said Jean Jean to Polydore. . . .

Cecily was worn out when she reached her bedroom and rejected Jacqueline's attentions.

"There are more urgent things to see to than nursing me when everyone round my son is being murdered."

"What do you mean, madame? I have seldom seen you in such a state."

"I will tell you. You will be able to give me good advice and perhaps help me because I want the matter cleared up, and I can't possibly remain any longer under the weight of the thought that oppresses me. . . . You remember the evening when we went with Marie Thérèse to the classical concert at the Comédie de l'Elysée?"

"Of course I remember it," returned Jacqueline. "It was the evening when, overcome by the heat, for the theatre was heated as if we were in the depth of winter, you wished to go outside for a while."

"Marie Thérèse remained in her place and you and I went outside. Do you remember what happened then?"

"Well, we had a stroll under the trees and then we went back."

"Don't you remember that the elections were on, and before going back we had to stop to allow a number of newsboys to pass who were selling an evening paper full of offensive remarks about Jacques?"

"Well no, I don't. What are you driving at, madame?"

"Don't you remember that as I was going back to the theatre I gave a silver coin to a poor old peanut dealer who for some little time had been pottering round us?"

"Oh yes, madame, I remember the poor old man. I was puzzled by him for some ten minutes. He looked so miserable, so bent with age, and so unassuming withal—and yet he never took his eyes off us. He certainly expected us to give him something. He spoke to you about Major Jacques. Oh, I remember him quite well . . ."

"Yes, that's the man. The poor old fellow knew who we were, and said—I am repeating his exact words—'God will repay you, madame. And besides, have no fear, the Government may do what it will, he will be elected. You may take this from me— it's all up with your son's opponent.' . . . Do you remember those words: 'It's all up with your son's opponent'?"

"Very likely."

"Oh, those words are still ringing in my ear; and they came back to me next day when the morning papers told us that Jacques's opponent had met with a motor-car accident the evening before, an accident from which he died a few days later."

"The old fellow had learnt who you were, madame, from words exchanged by people leaving or entering the theatre when we did. Your photograph, as his mother, has appeared in all the papers."

"He did not say, 'Your son's opponent has no chance,' he said, 'It's all up with your son's opponent.'"

"So you think he already knew about the accident? It's not impossible."

"It seems doubtful, for the accident happened pretty well at the same time."

"Newsboys were passing who would know about it, for it is easy to send a telephone message to a newspaper. It was important news, and the rumor quickly spread outside. He told you about it, the old fellow, delighted with an accident which pleased so many people."

"Don't talk like that, Jacqueline. It is not very charitable of you. Now I'm going to tell you something you don't know. I saw the peanut dealer again in the Champs Elysées. Next day, after I heard of the accident, I went back there on purpose to see him. What he had said aroused my curiosity. Besides, I had a longing to know—his pitiable figure haunted me . . .

"So next evening when it was dusk I ordered the chauffeur to stop for a few minutes at the corner of the avenue. I watched the passers-by for a while, when suddenly the old man appeared from

the darkness. He came up to the car window, looking more worn out than ever, and said in a weak
voice: 'What did I tell you yesterday?' I beckoned
to him to come nearer. He did so, trembling like
a leaf. 'Did you know about that accident then?'
I asked. At first he made no answer. I could not
see his face, for it was covered with a muffler.
Suddenly he straightened his back slightly. He
wore a pair of tinted spectacles through which,
Jacqueline, I swear I felt a look that scorched me.
I was afraid, and I ordered the chauffeur to go on.
Then the man, clinging to the window, said: 'In
case of any danger threatening Major Jacques, you
have but to return here in your car as you have
done to-night. Remain five minutes, and then drive
off again without leaving the car.' Having said this
much he disappeared. . . .'

"I thought that I had to do with some unhappy
madman, some poor maniac, and I did my utmost
to banish him from my mind. How can I explain
that it was of him I first thought when we learnt
that everything was discovered, and that Jacques
and Lavobourg's list had been stolen?

"Without saying a word to anyone I acted on
the peanut dealer's suggestion. I ordered the car
and drove to the spot suggested. I waited a quarter of an hour—half an hour. . . . No one came.
Then I remembered his exact words: 'Return here
in your car as you have done to-night. Remain five
minutes, and then leave again without getting out
of the car.'

"He did not say that he would come. My presence in the car for five minutes at this street corner
would mean that Jacques was in danger, so I argued

with myself, and I went back home. A few hours later I called myself a fool. . . . This peanut dealer is now, I confess, a nightmare to me. What was his reason for telling me to appeal to him whenever my son was in any pressing danger, and how is it that after I gave him the intimation he asked for every danger threatening Jacques was swept away so quickly and so tragically?"

"What is it you have in your mind, madame?"

"Jacques feared, above all, Bonchamps and Carlier," went on Cecily, growing more and more excited, "and they are dead. Jacques would have given anything to recover the stolen papers, and they are in his possession again as a result of this afternoon's tragedy. What is the secret of it all?"

"I am too unimportant a person to express an opinion in such terrible circumstances," returned Jacqueline, "but what surprises me most of all is that you should see any connection between the poor beggar and the incidents that are worrying you."

Cecily did not at once answer. She seemed to be deep in reflection, and allowed herself to be undressed without demur. But when she was in bed she said:

"Jacqueline, I want to know who this peanut dealer is. It can't be difficult to find him again. We've only got to look for him in the Champs Elysées in the evening, he told me. When did you see M. Hilaire last?"

"Oh, well, a good two months ago."

"Why doesn't he come here now? We are always pleased to see him. He may be ill."

"The last time I saw him it was, I confess,

madame, to find fault with him. I really had to complain of the week's groceries. I went myself to his 'Up-to-date Grocery Stores.' Virginie wasn't in the cash desk. He took advantage of that fact to accuse her of 'mistakes' in the delivery, and promised to see personally that they didn't occur again. But he seemed very annoyed, for he has a great deal of self-esteem, and looks upon himself now as a person of importance."

"He was very devoted to the late Marquis when he was his secretary, my dear Jacqueline, and I must say that after the fire at the Château du Puys[1] he would have made any sacrifice to do me a service. You must go and see him to-morrow for me. Of course, there's no need to tell him anything of this story, but you can give him a description of the peanut dealer, and say that I am interested in finding out what the man really is. You must tell him to keep the whole thing to himself."

[1] See *Chéri-Bibi and Cecily*, by Gaston Leroux. Translated by Hannaford Bennett.

CHAPTER IV

THE BEAUTIFUL SONIA

THAT same evening at eight o'clock—dinner was at nine—the blue drawing-room in Sonia Liskinne's house in the Boulevard Pereire was already thronged with guests. In the absence of the delightful hostess, who kept them waiting, but whom they excused since they were aware that she had come in late from the Chamber, they were received by Aunt Natacha.

Among the guests were the great Republicans Michel and Oudart, and Barclet, Senator and Member of the Institute, who firmly believed that the new idol was working for them; in other words, for the purification of the Republic. They held this opinion because they thought that in reality Jacques could do nothing without them.

The other guests who did not belong to their party shared the same hopes and perhaps the same illusions. That was why Baron de la Chaume, one of the most regular guests, who represented the old diplomacy, prudent and temporizing, whispered in the ear of whoso came up to him that if it were true the Jacques could begin nothing without the great Democrats it was equally true that he could complete nothing without the help of the great Conservatives.

Young Caze of the *Action Gauloise,* who would gladly have called de la Chaume an old dotard, made answer that he and his friends would decline to be the dupes of anyone, and that if the "new idol" delayed showing under which flag he was fighting they would make short work of him. It was said that the Empire party—for there was an Imperialist party—was represented secretly in Sonia Liskinne's house by the d'Askofs.

The d'Askofs were a singular couple. Baron d'Askof was much younger than his wife. She was a Délianof, of Russian Poland, and her first husband, Prince Galitza, was killed while wolf-hunting. She had one daughter by her first marriage, Marie Thérèse, now eighteen years of age, who attended the same classes as Mlle Lydia de la Morlière, Jacques's promised wife.

Where had Princess Galitza discovered Baron d'Askof? He was a tall, handsome, spare man, with a spreading golden beard, the only gold, it was suggested, that he had brought to the wedding. It was stated that he was of Hungarian birth, but no one could say for certain. The d'Askofs were unknown until the Princess produced her new husband from the heart of the steppes and thrust him upon the higher cosmopolitan society—a task which did not take her long.

She seemed to worship the Baron, her "handsome George," and was very jealous of him, which did not prevent him from making love to women in general, and Sonia Liskinne in particular. He was not the only one. Every man in the room was more or less attracted by the irresistible charm of the great actress; even the agreeable crank Lespinasse representing the Agrarian party, even Bassouf the Trades Unionist leader, even Lazare the Jew and principal shareholder in a great newspaper, even old Renard the scarcely civilized working man whom Sonia had contrived to lure to her house.

"We shall know through him how we stand with the trades unions," Sonia had said to Jacques.

To avoid the charge of devoting herself exclusively to politics, Sonia took good care to mix her guests. Among the number were Lucienne Drice of the Comédie Francaise; Yolande Pascal of the Grand Theatre, a little creature as dark as a plum, the mistress of the managing director of the Machinery Trust, a company with a capital of one hundred million francs, a considerable power; and many persons of importance in the industrial world.

So even in her relations with women Sonia managed to turn everything to account for the triumph of Jacques and, of course, Lavobourg. But Lavobourg seemed such a paltry figure compared with Jacques. What would Lavobourg have been without her? It was to her that he owed his political success, and even his position as Vice-President of the Chamber. He was well aware of it. Thus, as she told Jacques, the poor man never said a word when she rushed him into the obscure adventure without asking his opinion. Now came Martinez, the fop, sculptor, poet and dancer of the tango, greatly in fashion; and then Tiffoni the leading dancer of the Opera, representing in herself the moderate party.

All these guests at first thought that in the circumstances the famous Friday evening dinner-party would not take place; they telephoned to enquire, but were informed that nothing had been changed in the usual custom of the house. And so the regular frequenters had flocked in.

Some of them were impelled by an eager curiosity —those who had not witnessed the scenes in the Chamber. Others assumed an attitude of some reserve. Jacques's wonderful luck bewildered and, we must perforce admit, terrified them. Lespinasse, who always went straight to the point, was the only one to display unbounded enthusiasm. He repeated to Martinez Jacques's words—his cry in the tribune: "I wish to banish you from the Republic." And, turning to them all: "Why, I tell you he has only to offer himself for election in every constituency—it would be a plebiscite. And I know what

his idea is," he added, waving his arms and beating
a roll of the drum with imaginary drum-sticks.
"He means to revive the drum of Brumaire."

"And here is Our Lady of Thermidor!"

Sonia had, in fact, come into the room. A proud
murmur greeted her dramatic entrance. Martinez
dropped into poetry, declaring that Parisians had
never seen a more beautiful woman.

And, indeed, she had never seemed more beautiful, more radiant, more alluring. Was she
determined to turn every head, or, still more important, to win one particular heart? Rumor had
it, of course, that she was deeply in love with her
great man—they were not referring to Lavobourg—
and added that the great man lived for politics
alone and gave little heed to women.

After shaking hands with her guests she went up
to Lavobourg, who appeared in the doorway.

. "Good gracious, how pale you are!" she said,
adding with a deep-toned laugh slightly too reminis-
cent of the theatre, "Oh, my dear, you must pull
yourself together! You will outlive worse things."

Lavobourg, pale as he was, grew yellow, and,
concealing with some difficulty the grimace that he
intended as a smile, bent low to press his lips upon
those lovely hands that held him captive. When
he was able to say a word to her in private it was
to impart to her his terrible anxiety:

"What are we going to do? What course had we
better follow? The police are on our heels. This
house is under observation. I have heard that the
Commisison of Inquiry will sit to-morrow and adopt
exceptional measures . . ."

"Well, my dear, we know all about that, but still

they can't order any arrests on suspicion until the Chamber has suspended parliamentary privilege. They no longer have any proofs. Therefore the Commission will have to find or invent them—that will take a good twenty-four hours. . . ."

"I won't answer for anything after twenty-four hours. Hérisson has had an important interview with Cravely. It is commonly said that we shall be lodged in La Santé prison on Monday next."

"That is quite possible."

Lavobourg gave her a penetrating glance. As usual she knew more about it than he did.

"Yes, you grasp what I mean," she confessed, sinking her voice. "Either we shall be lodged in La Santé prison on Monday or *they* will be lodged there."

She left him gasping at the news, drugged by the incense of her personality. The best of it was that though he was aware that "it was to be on Monday" he still knew nothing of what was going to be done on Monday. No one knew—not even Sonia. Suddenly it occurred to him that since Bonchamps was dead the entire responsibility for maintaining order in the Chamber would devolve upon him, for he controlled the Republican Guard set aside for its defence, and could summon the Chamber specially in case of emergency if he thought fit. He dropped into a seat, for his limbs trembled under him. His power, suddenly glimpsed, overwhelmed him.

Sonia had taken a few steps when Baron d'Askof went up to her. He had kept his eyes eagerly fixed on her since she came into the room. Perceiving that the Baroness had allowed herself to be caught in the toils of a lady friend, he drew Sonia behind a screen, seemingly placed there for the use of those who wished to exchange a few serious and secret words in this drawing-room made for flirtation where politics alone were discussed. And, in fact, it was of politics that the Baron first spoke.

"Sonia, are you satisfied with your great man?"

"Why, yes, my dear sir. What a question!"

"Are you pleased with the turn of events?"

"It seems to me that I am beginning to live, and I don't forget that I owe that to you."

"That's very kind of you. You haven't forgotten that I brought Jacques here?"

"Of course I haven't."

"At a time when you were tired of everything?"

"Yes, at a time when life never seemed so dull, so little worth living."

"And do you remember what you said when for the first time I ventured to speak of my love for you?"

"Yes, I told you that I was tired of love as of everything else, and my heart would belong only to the man who would help me to fulfil a great task—a task almost beyond human power."

"And I answered that I would be that man. You thought I was boasting. That same evening Jacques was here. After he left I told you what I intended to do with Jacques with a woman like you to guide him."

"Oh, Jacques had no need of anyone," she returned quickly, beginning to scrutinize the Baron more closely so that he moved a little to one side.

"Jacques had no need of anyone!" he exclaimed. "Do you think so? Do you really think so?"

She saw his face set. She had no wish to offend

him, and above all to lose him at that critical moment, when Jacques more than ever needed all his
supporters.

"I tell you, dear, that Jacques is big enough to
shape his course unaided, but far be it from me to
forget all that you have done for him."

"And for you, that's the main thing. . . . It is
now no longer a question of Jacques, but of you
and me—simply you and me."

While speaking these last words full of audacity
and menace he took her hand, which she was careful
not to withdraw, and kissed the tip of her fingers
with great deference.

"You are a big silly," she returned, "and your
declaration has taken me by surprise. I think of
nothing but politics now. Let me get to know where
I am amid all these events, and wait until we have
won. . . . Why, of course, there will be plenty of
time to talk about all this."

She rose to her feet and was surprised to observe
that he was no longer looking at her, but that his
eyes were turned from her and fixed with unutterable hatred on the man who had just come in—
the new idol!

"Major Jacques de Touchias! . . . Lieut. Frederic Héloni!" announced the manservant.

The new-comers were at once surrounded, and
while the man of the hour was being congratulated
Sonia said to herself: "My goodness, they all hate
him. I am the only one who cares for him." But
Jacques strode up to her, and she was all attention
and smiles. Unfortunately he seemed preoccupied.

Frederic gave the Baroness d'Askof a summary
of the news in the evening papers which for some

time had been favorable to Jacques. Thus these papers stated without reserve that Carlier, unable to furnish the promised proofs, had committed suicide, and that the Extreme Left, furious at the death of their leader, had bodily made a rush on Major Jacques. Moreover, they completed the tragic picture by stating that Bonchamps, overcome by so much excitement, collapsed in the President's chair, never to recover again.

The man announced, "Dinner is served," and the guests filed into the dining-room.

Strange to say the Major seemed in lively mood. He told the story with amusing details of the scene of fisticuffs in which he had such a narrow escape.

"Oh, they might have killed you," exclaimed Lespinasse. "Remember, you had just said that you would like to clear them out of Parliament."

"It seemed that Pagès is preparing a great speech for Monday," said Jacques with a peculiar smile, "an indictment of that Republic which I spoke of banishing him from."

"And what reply will you make?" asked Caze boldly. "In politics Utopias begin where Kings leave off. . . ."

"I will meet you on Monday," returned Jacques somewhat curtly, "and you will be able to tell me if my reply pleased you. . . ." Then turning to Michel and Barclet, whom it was greatly to his interest to treat with consideration: "We are right, gentlemen, the Republic has been led astray from its destiny. The thing is to save it from these men and bring it back to the right path. The thing also is to effect this in such a way as to prevent it from relapsing into the same mistakes. What must we do to achieve our purpose? Add a few paragraphs to the Constitution which, on the whole, is excellent . . ."

The guests around him in their surprise stopped eating to listen to him. It was the first time that he had condescended to expatiate in public on this question, and each one strove to discern what it was necessary to accept or reject to understand "the Major's idea." In a clear voice, at times strident and masterful, he expounded his plan for the Constitution as he saw it, powerful and operative, in which the responsibility would be vested in the head of the State as the leader of the Government. He ended a long exposition amid a chorus of admiration.

Then he made a sign to Sonia to leave the table. He considered that they had been at dinner long enough. He had said what he wanted to say; and he knew that every word would be in the morning newspapers. Meanwhile he had no time to waste. These people no longer interested him. He bowed to the ladies and withdrew, followed by Sonia.

As they passed through the empty drawing-room she pressed his hand.

"Oh, my friend, she said, enveloping him with the irresistible look of love which she usually brought into play on the stage in her great dualogues, for even when she was sincere she never quite ceased to be the supreme actress, "how intensely I admire you like this. How fine you were in the Chamber. And how splendidly you spoke to them here. I think you are wonderful: you speak to soldiers like a great captain—you speak to politicians pure unvarnished politics. . . ."

"Do you mean that?" he returned bluntly. "I

imagine, Sonia, that you are not an expert in such
matters. I have just spoken to them like a corporal
speaks to his men. And that's what won them,
my dear."

"You are quite right again. It's I who am
silly. . . ."

"No, you are my most useful assistant. I could
do nothing without you."

"Then repay me. Give me a smile. You haven't
looked at me once this evening. Tell me that I
look nice and you like my frock. . . ."

"You are adorable. . . . Good-bye."

"Are you coming to work to-night?"

"Yes, I can't fit in a moment's rest for the next
forty-eight hours. Tell d'Askof. . . . Oh, by the
way, our poor Lavobourg seems to look as if he is
giving way. Tell him to show a more cheerful
countenance."

"My goodness, how unkind you are! You never
have a pleasant word for your real friends."

Just then the manservant brought the Major a
letter on a tray. He opened it eagerly, read it,
asked for a lighted candle, and burnt it. He had
become calm and smiling once more.

"All right?" she asked.

"Quite all right," he returned. "My old friend
General Mabel, in command of the garrison at Versailles, who has been slightly indisposed these last
few days, tells me that he is now perfectly well
again."

He turned on his heel without further words,
leaving her plunged in thought. She, too, was
somewhat terrified by this man, who seemed to
have the gift of striking unto death those who stood

in his path, and of restoring to health those of whom
he stood in need.

CHAPTER V

LITTLE BUDDHA JUNIOR

AT THE back of the Boulevard Pereire, within a
stone's throw of the railway locomotive repairing
station and the fortifications, stood a cabaret which
had received permission to remain open all night.

It owed its exceptional privilege to its proximity
to the repairing station where work never ceased,
and the whistle of locomotives could be heard at all
hours, while the sound of hammers on the anvil went
up in the darkness, pierced here and there by the
flashes from the fires in the forges. The tavern, of
unpretentious appearance, bore the sign: Little
Buddha Inn.

The clerks who had finished work at the offices
where the octroi was levied called at Little Buddha
Inn for a glass and a crust on their way home. On
the particular evening when we made acquaintance
with some of Sonia's guests the tavern was thronged
with customers. There was considerable smoking
in the room, but silence reigned. In short, it was
this silence which might have seemed strange, for
after all it would have been so natural for the customers to discuss among themselves the events
which had staggered all Paris. But they uttered no
word, worn out, apparently by the labors of the day.

The proprietor stood behind his bar with half-
closed eyes. He was a stout, sleepy-looking man.

He was as round as a barrel, still quite young, about thirty, and his figure, his violent and cruel temper under his simple exterior, were curiously suggestive of Little Buddha, his father, famous for his association in France with the terrible Chéri-Bibi, renowned throughout the world.

Little Buddha junior was born in a Paris prison, and his mother had brought up this scion of the gaol to admire the doughty deeds of his father, Little Buddha senior, a victim, of course, of the prejudices of society. She told him later how his father, after escaping from the penal settlement, had settled down under a false name as a publican in Dieppe, where they were to join him, but he had been murdered with some of his comrades in circumstances which were still shrouded in mystery.

Little Buddha junior had sworn to avenge his father, but it was to no purpose that he questioned the cut-throats with whom his mother still kept up some connection. They could give him no definite information. After his mother's death he continued to bear the name of Little Buddha as if in defiance of the community.

The son, as we have said, had every vice of the father, but he had another in addition, which was to save him from all the others and to which he owed his position in the world. After picking up a living by opening the doors of taxis, he became a barman in low-class pot-houses. He saved his money, and might have set up business on his own account long before, but the thought of drawing on his capital made him hesitate to embark upon the smallest enterprise.

It was then that an old fellow, whom he had

observed for some time selling olives and peanuts in the night restaurants and on the open front of cabarets, entered into conversation with him and spoke of his father, whom he claimed to have known well. He told him even that he knew how he met his death, and finally promised to furnish him with the means of obtaining a fine revenge if he would agree to join a scheme about which he would give him full particulars in due course. For the time being he would only have to set up as a publican and settle in a place which was to be had for next to nothing.

"Next to nothing! That sounds all right, but suppose I go bankrupt?"

"You won't go bankrupt. You will receive one hundred louis every month. And I'm the man who will pay them down to you."

"Shake!" exclaimed Little Buddha, holding out his hand.

"Only you mustn't be inquisitive," explained the amazing peanut dealer. "And whatever you do you mustn't pump your customers. You'll only have to doze behind your bar."

"That'll suit me."

"Oh, if by chance you express surprise a little too loudly at what happens in your place to friends outside, or to the police, for instance, I won't hide from you that I wouldn't give two sous for your skin."

"Whew!" said Little Buddha junior. "That's not very comforting. Look here, in these circumstances it will have to be one hundred and fifty louis a month."

"I agree to your terms," he at once returned,

"because I will take a room on the first floor which you must never enter. But you must allow anyone to go into it who places on your bar beforehand an agreed number of peanuts."

"How many?"

"The number will vary from day to day. Every day you will receive the pass number. Now here's another thing—after to-day never speak to me again."

"How shall I know the pass number?"

"You will see me at your place every day at one time or another. I will place on your bar the number of peanuts that callers must bring with them to pass in on that particular day."

"I see. What about the hundred and fifty louis?"

"Every month I will put down on your bar a paper bag of peanuts, and you'll find the three thousand francs inside."

Such were the extraordinary circumstances in which Little Buddha set up for himself as a publican. He had at first imagined that the peanut dealer was a go-between, whose business it was to discover in the cosmopolitan underworld of Paris an accommodating individual to keep one of these houses for the use of the light-fingered gentry. The room which the old fellow had taken on the first floor and furnished with a number of complicated locks, of which Little Buddha never had the key, was, in his view, to serve as a place of safety for the most debauched meetings. His astonishment was great on discovering that his cabaret was frequented only by honest workmen, railway servants, and inoffensive clerks from the octroi. Truth to tell he congratulated himself on such a piece of luck, for

his money was easily earned. Never any fighting
or quarrels or bad language!   Better still, his customers were as good as dumb!

As Little Buddha was contemplating the cheerful
sight of his prosperous cabaret, the door was opened
and a poor old man bowed down and deformed by
the weight of years came in. His head was so
near the ground that he seemed to be humpbacked;
he was miserably clad in a suit of threadbare velvet,
patched at the knees and elbows. One of his long
arms held a small wooden tub divided into two com-
partments, one containing peanuts and the other
olives.

A cap was pulled down over his bald pate. But
it was almost impossible to see his face, as much
on account of his stooping posture as the large well-
worn iron-grey muffler wound two or three times
round his neck. Now and again he slightly raised
his head, and above the muffler a big pair of tinted
spectacles could be seen which might have caused
fear. Strange to say all the customers that night
displayed a taste for peanuts, and he portioned out
to each a small packet for a few sous. On some
of the tables he placed in addition two or three or
five peanuts. When he reached the bar he laid
before Little Buddha seven peanuts. Then he left
the cabaret.

One night Little Buddha puzzled, impelled by a
feeling of curiosity to discover what it all meant
and where the amazing old man went after leaving
the cabaret, broke the terms of his agreement. He
sallied forth after the old fellow and followed him
cautiously as he walked up the Rue de Rome.
When Little Buddha reached the turning into the

Rue Cardinet he was set upon by a gang of vaga-
bonds who whipped out their knives. As luck would
have it the peanut dealer came up in time to rescue him:

"Leave him alone," he said. "This gentleman is
a friend of mine."

Next day Little Buddha was given an extra allowance of peanuts in a paper bag, and on the bag
itself he read the carefully typewritten words:

"Another time I shall let things take their course."

He acted up to the warning. . . .

After the peanut dealer left the cabaret some of
the customers went out.   Others settled down to
read the paper, looking now and then at the time.
At half-past two in the morning the door was opened
by a man dressed as an actor, his loose-fitting cape
flung back over the shoulder concealing in part his
face.   A soft felt hat turned down concealed the
other part.

He strode through the room, stopped a moment at
the bar, placed seven peanuts before Little Buddha, and entered the pantry. Here stood a spiral
staircase mounting to the floor above. The man
quickly clambered up, and found himself outside a
door whose three locks he proceeded to open. This
done, he entered the room simply furnished with a
round table, a cupboard, and several straw-bottomed
chairs. On the wall was a clothes-peg.

After lighting a small dark lantern he hung his
hat and cape on the peg. Then he went over to the
cupboard, opened the two leaves of the door and
closed them after him. He was in the empty cupboard, the back of which opened on pressing a
button. The man stooped and crept into a sort of

passage, closing the aperture behind him by means of a spring with which he seemed perfectly familiar. He at once made for the end of the passage, which was extremely narrow. Here, too, he had to open a door. He passed through, closed the door, put out his dark lantern, and stretching forth his arms, switched on the light.

CHAPTER VI

INCIDENTALS

THE man found himself in a most charming, luxurious and tasteful setting. It was the boudoir of the beautiful Sonia and the man was Jacques.

He at once sat down to his work at a Buhl table, between a large Coromandel screen standing before the door of the bedroom, and an elegant bookcase contrived in the old grey wainscoting in the Marie Antoinette style. The sight of this man working to overthrow the State by violent means in this lovely and exquisitely perfumed boudoir, a sanctuary of love transformed into a political laboratory, was no ordinary one.

Jacques drew from his inside coat pocket two long wallets and emptied their contents on the table. Here were some hundreds of sheets of notepaper bearing the heading of the Chamber of Deputies or the Senate. The notepaper contained a certain amount of printed matter, and Jacques proceeded to fill in the blank spaces with his pen.

Suddenly he looked up. He heard the sound of

footsteps traversing the next room and a key being put into the door leading to the boudoir. Sonia came in.

"I am very thankful to you for joining me so early," he said. "Will you lend me a hand? Where have you been?" And going on with his writing he asked: "What about the servants—your maid?"

"In bed. You have accustomed me, you know, to do without servants since you have taken to invade me here. But to-night, my dear fellow, before leaving you will have to unfasten sundry hooks."

He looked at her. She let her cloak drop, appearing before him as he had never seen her and yet as she had been all the evening—clad in a frock of great audacity that had created a sensation; but until then, in truth, he had been so utterly preoccupied that though appearing to see her he had not noticed her.

"Good heavens!" he said. "Dressed as you are I am surprised that you should need any help to take that frock off."

"Pleasant as usual," she said.

"I asked you where you had been. You must have achieved some success."

"Bah! people are thinking only of you. We went for a time to Magic, then on to the Bal d'Ispahan with Martinez and Lucienne Drice, and then we had supper in a dancing-hall. I wanted to feel the pulse of public opinion."

"I presume it is not too bad?"

"Excellent. Everyone is talking of your 'assassinations,' and they say: 'He is very clever. Nothing will stop him.' "

"I hope you don't believe in any of these absurdities."

"Well, dear, you can never tell. I know you so little."

She had drawn near him with her slow, queenly, graceful step and sat down beside him, her form brushing against him; and he felt irritated by the warm fragrance of this beautiful woman at a time when he needed all his self-control.

"Why are you frowning? Am I in the way?" she asked.

"Yes, you are really too beautiful."

"That is the first compliment you have paid me to-day. Now may I retire?"

"No, stay. I want you. And don't be a coquette for—for the next twenty-four hours. . . ."

"That's a long time! But what would I not do for you. Come, I will promise to be good. Let's talk business."

And straightway she showed him a serious face, of an intelligent and serene loveliness, encompassed by wonderful ropes of pearls that wound round her luxuriant golden hair, ran down from her ears, encircled her neck, and fell on her alabaster breast in sprays.

Her long hands, bedecked with rings clever at fingering bronze, ivory, silk, and such precious things, were clasped above the table. He slipped a pen between them.

"Write in these letters in the blank spaces as I am doing the words: 'This morning, Monday, at 5 o'clock.' As d'Askof is not here you will have to be my secretary. Why isn't he here?"

"Because I told him that you could not meet him

until half-past three this morning. I wanted to
speak to you of this man before you saw him again.
Be on your guard against him, my dear friend. He
hates you. . . . He hates you because he is in love
with me."

"I really don't see the connection," said Jacques
in a coldly evasive tone which wrung the heart of
the beautiful Sonia.

"Oh, I know, I know. . . . I know that you are
not in love with me. But he may imagine that I am
in love with you. . . . And he may imagine also
that you are in love with me."

"What next! My dear lady, you amaze me.
Baron d'Askof is aware that I have been engaged
for a long time, and he knows me well enough not
to do me the injustice of believing that had I aspired
to a person like you, Sonia, the most beautiful and
understanding of women, I would not have devoted
my life to you. Now my life does not belong to me."

He uttered these words quickly while continuing
to write. As he spoke of his engagement the pen
in Sonia's hand shook. "Besides," he went on without looking up, "has not my attitude always been
entirely correct?"

"Say rather utterly detached," she returned.
"When we are together we look like two business
men. You were not always so."

"What do you mean?"

"At the beginning of our friendship, when it was
a question of winning me . . . Oh, of winning me
over to your plans, of making me your slave with
the object of carrying out your aims—remember
how attentive, how assiduous you were. . . . My
dear man, others besides d'Askof might have thought

that you were in love with me—I most of all."

"What nonsense! Now you are jesting. For-give me if I seem a little . . ."

"Yes, a little brutal. . . ."

"Thanks, I deserve a different word, but you are far too superior a woman not to have grasped from the first that there could be no place in my thoughts for love at a time when they were so completely, so fiercely absorbed in these hateful politics."

"Well, I dare say you think me far more superior than I am in reality," she said, rising to her feet, shifting some books on the shelves, and thrusting her hand into a deep recess, "for when I received these letters I was simple enough to think you were in love."

She threw before him a perfumed sachet from which a number of letters slipped out. He glanced through them, smiled, and said:

"Still, it's quite true."

"So you were lying! There wasn't a single sin-cere word in all those pretty compliments."

"No, I was not lying. If you are absolutely bent on my repeating what I said here I will say to you again: 'Sonia, you are adorable!' And that is why I no longer write it to you. I was afraid of falling in love with you, my dear lady. That is the whole story."

"I saw Mlle de la Morlière in the Chamber to-day," she went on in a serious voice. "Do you realize that she is pretty—very pretty?"

Jacques did not answer. His brows puckered. She had the courage to ask him:

"You love her, do you not?"

"Yes," he returned bluntly, fuming.

Sonia remained motionless. Two tears coursed down her cheeks. Then she, too, began to write. . . . After a while she said in a voice that she strove to render firm:

"I see that it is to be Monday at five o'clock in the morning. You will win through, and either we shall be parted for ever or united in death, which is the same thing, for I have no wish to survive you. Life would be too boring after so much excitement. Forgive me, therefore, if before that tragic moment I wished to know . . . I shall not have to reproach myself with distracting you from your aim, and I say frankly that I shall be satisfied with our talk if I have succeeded in putting you on your guard against d'Askof."

"It was he who introduced us to each other," broke in Jacques, "and I shall be everlastingly grateful to him for that. It was he who conceived the idea of establishing communication between your house and the cabaret, and of placing a door in the wall of my flat in the Avenue de Jena so that while people think I am at home I am here quietly overthrowing the Constitution, assisted by the kindest and most devoted of secretaries. It was he, too, who contrived the scheme by which we could communicate with each other, thanks to the most amusing and unsuspected of pass-words—the peanut dodge."

"Oh, ever since that stolen list was returned in a bag of peanuts, your peanuts terrify me."

"Let's finish filling in these invitations, if you don't mind. Since we are agreed that we must beware of d'Askof it is not necessary for him to see them when he comes."

"But how will you get them delivered? You don't mean to trust them to the post?" returned Sonia.

"Not likely! I shall trust them to you. It is through your instrumentality that they will reach their destination. Only you and I know the exact time fixed by me for convoking this special meeting of the Chamber. My dear lady, you must get these forms signed by Lavobourg on Sunday. His signature will legalize to some extent this special summons and strengthen the waverers. But listen carefully: From the moment that Lavobourg signs these forms you must not allow him out of your sight. For then there will be three to know about them, and I consider that too many, though, strictly speaking, if Lavobourg does not leave you, and you continue to keep a watch on him, I shall be easy in my mind."

"I promise you it shall be done. Lavobourg will sign the forms and not leave me. But what must I do to make certain of their reaching their destination?"

"Did you see the man who came this evening from Versailles?"

"Oh, of course."

"Well, this man, a reliable friend of General Mabel's, will be at the Grand Parc ball with twenty soldiers from my old Subdamoun regiment, at present confined to barracks at Versailles. These men are devoted to me. They will be in Paris on Sunday in plain clothes. It is these men who, at the last moment, will deliver the summons to specified members of the Chamber and Senate after you have given them to their leader, the messenger whom you know. I have had a box reserved for you at the Grand Parc ball which begins at midnight. You will go there with a few friends and, of course, Lavobourg. At two o'clock in the morning the man will come up to you, and you will hand him the packet secretly."

"That's good."

"Oh, another important piece of work. When Lavobourg has signed the forms, you must yourself put them in their envelopes and carefully address the envelopes from the names on the list."

"Now tell me, Jacques—I think—I think I understand. But what you are going to do is very daring. So you are only summoning the Deputies and Senators mentioned on the list?"

"Of course."

"Well, what about the others?"

"We will give out that the summons failed by accident to reach them, or was delivered too late. I am holding these convocations in reserve, and I shall not have them sent out until everything is over, and then we shall be acting within the law. By that time we shall have voted for the revision of the Constitution."

"Where does the President of the Republic come in?"

"We shall leave him out of the whole business. He will know nothing until both Houses are at Versailles. He will not have to intervene. Neither himself nor his position will be affected, if I may say so. And as the law will not have been broken he will only have to let things be. His silence and non-interference are all that we expect of him for the time being."

"And what then?" asked Sonia eagerly.

"Well, this is how things will happen: At five o'clock in the morning the two Houses will decide on immediate revision and a meeting of the National Assembly for that same morning. The sitting will last ten minutes at most. Thereupon the Senators and Deputies representing the nation and arrogating to themselves the right to dispense in such a crisis with the useless and dilatory procedure of publishing the resolutions in the *Journal Officiel* will set out for Versailles. Motor-cars will be in readiness for them. At seven o'clock the National Assembly will hold a sitting and decide to begin the revision there and then; it will pass a resolution declaring the Government suspect; and it will nominate a provisional Government reduced to its simplest form— a duumvirate—to act while the revision is in progress."

"Who will form the duumvirate?"

"Myself and your friend Lavobourg. We shall be empowered, as the phrase goes, to dispatch routine business, to watch over the safety of the Assembly, and to protect its work."

"But do you think the Assembly will follow you in this course?"

"I am certain of it. Between now and then I shall have terrified them. They will do whatever I wish. The President of the Senate, to whom the Presidency of the Assembly reverts, will have signed an order in Paris giving General Mabel, commanding the army in Versailles, the task of defending the National Assembly. When the National Assembly arrives in Versailles it will rejoice to see all the troops at their posts and my famous regiment

in the courtyard of the Château ready to support and defend it, but, mark me, Sonia, ready
also to make it act if I give General Mabel the
order."

"Heavens, what you tell me sounds scarcely cred-
ible. . . . Why, as soon as the rumor of the morning's work spreads throughout Paris, and it is known
what is happening in Versailles, the Government,
which has at its disposal the whole forces of Paris,
will move against Versailles."

"You forget that it will then be acting against
the law."

"Well, my dear, don't let's juggle with words.
They will maintain that it is you who have violated
the law."

"No, they won't maintain that, for I shan't give
them the chance."

"How about Flottard? You are forgetting Flottard, the civilian head of the military Government
of Paris. He'll come on the scene with his troops."

"Why, but don't you follow me? I told you that
the Assembly will at once appoint a provisional
Government—a duumvirate—of which I shall be
the head. Within five minutes, you understand, of
my being entrusted by the legally constituted Assembly of the nation with its safety, I shall have
telephoned an order to arrest Flottard, every suspected member of the Government, and most of our
headstrong Deputies and politicians!"

"Cravely will never do it."

"Do you take me for a simpleton? Do you think
I need the services of that ass? It is the Prefecture
of Police that will do the work, my dear Sonia."

"I have always said that the Prefect of Police was a perfect gentleman."

"Oh, he will only act if we succeed. He will refuse to do anything until he receives a telephone message from Versailles; but then, protected by a spurious legality, he will be thoroughly with us. Up to then he will only be of use to us to separate those whom we wish to be rid of. Some of the telephone wires connecting the Ministries with the Palais Bourbon will not work after a certain hour! Oh, we have thought of everything. We shall nab those worthy gentlemen of the Extreme Left in their beds. Oh, we shan't hurt them much. They will have a surprising awakening—that's all. Now do you feel more confident?"

"What a wonderful man you are, Jacques! If you succeed, where will you stop?"

"But you forget that I am above all a good Republican."

They had finished their writing. Jacques made a parcel of the letters and wrapped them in a newspaper and gave them to her.

"Here you are. You hold the fate of the Republic in your hands."

He knew what he was about in relieving himself of the precious parcel and placing it in her possession. To begin with, though he might fear a last hesitation in the mind of the pusillanimous Lavobourg, he was certain that Lavobourg would not be able to resist Sonia, but would sign the letters either at her request or command; secondly, he knew that the venture was now launched, whatever happened.

Sonia accepted the charge with an inward joy that

knew no bounds. She came nearer him, scorching him with the eager look in her eyes. He could not withstand her when she took his hand and drew him after her.

"Come! I must show you where I am going to hide these letters until to-morrow night, in case any accident should happen to me. We must provide for every contingency."

She had already lifted the curtain and entered the bedroom. She let go his hand, switched on the light, seemed to pay no further heed to him, to be in no way constrained by his presence for the first time in this room prepared for her repose with such rare and disturbing luxury. And yet the soft and delicate fragrance in which this feminine privacy was steeped affected him as though he were a schoolboy for all his strength of mind, and even now he was scarcely conscious of her words.

He saw her graceful form pass lightly over the carpet on which lay the skins of wild beasts; he saw her mount a stool which served as a sort of pedestal; he saw her raise herself on tiptoe to reach the shelves of a small bookcase at the head of the bed.

"There, this is the place—behind this book. No one would think of looking here for them. I'll put them with the famous list. Do you know what else there is in my little hiding-place? See, the bag of peanuts, the pink paper bag that we found on the table in my boudoir with the list so strangely returned to me. Say what you like, it was very mysterious—and why these peanuts?"

"I suppose," returned Jacques, making an effort to say something, "they were intended to convey to us that the man who brought back the stolen list was one of our friends, one of those who sometimes come here in the evening to work with me, one who knew all about the peanut way, if I may say so, and had no wish to divulge who he was. What then? Why, my dear Sonia, don't let's trouble about these peanuts."

He uttered these words in a voice so new and strange that she gazed at him as she stood on the stool. He was quite close to her, and held out his hand to assist her. She took his hand and lightly stepped down. But the high heel of her shoes caused her to stagger for a quarter of a second.

A quarter of a second! Love or Death needs but a quarter of a second when it lies in wait impelled by Fate. In a flash Sonia fell into his arms. He clasped her to his breast. She sighed, and he kissed her. . . . And as the seconds, minutes, hours sped by . . . all else was forgotten! . . .

CHAPTER VII

BARON D'ASKOF

AT half-past three in the morning Baron d'Askof entered Sonia Liskinne's boudoir by the secret door. He sat down and waited for the Major, who, contrary to his custom, was late. The Baron was not a little surprised, and a quarter of an hour went by. He began to grow impatient.

His eyes fell on the table and observed a kind of Indian sachet which he had never seen before. What was that strange article doing there? Inquisitive, he took it up and opened it.

Letters? Yes, letters in the Major's handwriting. He read them. And as he read them his lips twisted in a wicked smile.

The letters dated from several months back:

"BEAUTIFUL SONIA,

"I have seen you in my dreams all night long, and yet I am not in love with you, but I will not answer for the future if you continue to display so much charm before such an unworthy object as myself. Forget that you are a woman and we may work together and, between us, accomplish great things. Try to please me by looking less beautiful. And above all do not dress as you did last night nor wear your hair as you did last night nor smile when you speak to me as you did last night. When you are with me endeavour to be the reverse of that which you were last night or I shall lose my head— my poor head of which I am so much in need. That is understood, is it not, my dear comrade?"

Another letter finished with the words:

"They are madly in love with you, and I do not wonder at them. I am not in love with you. It is something more than that."

Another:

"I shall never forget the two hours spent with you. You were the most wonderful of women this afternoon. How can I do without you?"

Another, making an appointment:

"To-night we will work for a couple of hours in our dear little boudoir. You may count upon me.

Yes, I have been thinking of you. You amaze me with your reproaches. You are never out of my thoughts. I can do nothing without you. I have a feeling of never-ending admiration for you. Did you receive my flowers?"

And on another only the words:

"Thank you. There's no one like you."

Baron d'Askof returned the letters to the sachet and placed it in his pocket. Just then he seemed to hear a murmur. He pricked up his ears. He was not mistaken. He caught the sound of voices in Sonia's room. He rose to his feet, went quietly behind the Coromandel screen, lifted the heavy curtain, and heard their two voices behind the door. Then he let the curtain fall and turned to his seat deadly pale. Suddenly he darted up and left the boudoir by the secret door.

A few minutes later a man wearing the kepi and cape of an officer in the octroi left Little Buddha's cabaret, walked up the street, crossed the railway bridge, and stepped into a closed car waiting at the corner of a narrow street at right angles. He told the chauffeur to drive to the Place du Palais Bourbon, and the car darted off at express speed. The man put his head out of the window and looked behind. He noticed that another car, coming from he knew not where, was following him at a like pace, whereupon Baron d'Askof, for it was he, withdrew to the back of his car, divested himself of his cape and kepi, lifted a cushion, opened a locker, drew from it a hat and great coat, put them on, and waited. Lavobourg lived within a stone's throw of the Chamber of Deputies, and it was to Lavobourg's house that the Baron was driving. . . .

He alighted from the car and rang the bell. Before the door was opened he was able, on the one hand, to perceive at the end of the street skirting the Palais Bourbon the car which had followed him and had now pulled up near the quay at a spot where it was easy to keep watch on the door of Lavobourg's house, and, on the other hand, to perceive at the corner of the Rue du Palais two figures which undoubtedly were those of men belonging to the detective service.

The door opened. D'Askof ran up to the first floor and rang the bell again. A manservant opened it.

"Tell M. Lavobourg that I must see him at once."

Just then the study door opened and Lavobourg himself appeared.

"What's the matter? Come in."

D'Askof hurried into the study. His face was still distraught.

"The matter is that you are being . . ." And he whispered a word, followed by details.

"What are you talking about? Why do you come here at such a moment?"

"Do you consider what I have just told you of no importance?"

"I don't believe you."

"Well, my dear fellow, go to her flat and we'll discuss it again when you come back."

"The Major! Why, it can't be. I know she has played the coquette with him, but he did not even pay her any attention. Hang it all, he has other things to do. . . . Who told you this?"

"No one. I have just come from the Boulevard Pereire and I overheard them. I went by the peanut way and found myself alone in the boudoir, and I heard them talking in the bedroom. They are still there. Go and see for yourself."

Lavobourg reeled. He could no longer entertain any doubt.

"Look here, Lavobourg," went on d'Askof, "my car is outside. You will find the octroi officer's kepi and cape in the locker. The pass number to-night is seven peanuts. Make certain of the facts and come back. I'll wait for you here."

"I'll go," said Lavobourg.

"Well, take my great coat, turn up the collar, put on my hat, and slip into the car. The detective officers watching your door will mistake you for me. . . ."

D'Askof heard the street door close and the car drive off. Then he returned to the empty study. He observed that when disturbed the great politician had been engaged in carefully ensuring his own personal safety. In the fire-place papers, doubtless of a compromising nature, were almost completely consumed.

Twenty minutes had scarcely elapsed when the door opened and Lavobourg came in seemingly no less perturbed than on his departure.

"I tried to get through but failed. Did you not tell me that the pass number to-night was seven peanuts?"

"Why, yes. I got through with that number."

"Well, when I put down seven the man behind the bar looked at me and, shaking his head, said: 'You can't go through.' I tried to continue my way. He made a sign, and two customers at once left their stools. I did not persist, and here I am back again. Oh, I had an intense longing to enter the house openly. It couldn't be helped. It would have aroused the other's suspicions, and I shouldn't have found him there. Besides, the house was being watched by the police."

"Oh!" said d'Askof, whistling. "Oh, how clever they are! How clever they are. They must have suspected that there was something out of the way in my hurried departure and changed the pass number."

"But who are *they*?" demanded Lavobourg excitedly. "Can you tell me, when all is said and done, for whom you and I are working? Can you tell me who is behind Jacques de Touchais? For, after all, seeing that you loathe him, a fact that I realized before to-day, there must be something which impels you to act. Whose tool are you? And whose puppet have I been up to to-day?"

At Lavobourg's appeal d'Askof rose and began to pace up and down like a wild animal preparing to make a spring and shatter the bars of his cage, but gradually his excitement lessened and he returned to his seat, the tension relaxed, almost calm.

"It's no use," he said in a strained voice, "I can't tell you."

"The party for whom we are working must indeed be powerful. Is it a political party—a financial party—a religious party?"

D'Askof shook his head.

"You are nowhere near it," he said. "It's something much more extraordinary than that. Besides, don't ask me. I can't tell you."

"Why not?"

"Because I value my skin. Listen, Lavobourg, there is but one point on which we can understand each other—it's about him—the Major. After all, it's entirely a question of that man. We both hate him."

"Oh, I hate him! I'd like to kill him. I shall challenge him. We will fight him."

"And he'll kill you. That won't improve matters. No, we can do better than that. And besides, I have done what I could by coming here to see you, by telling you how matters stand, and by enabling you to give vent to your feelings. It's for you to act now. You can ruin his adventure. You know that it is fixed for Monday. You can have him arrested between now and then. And when they have laid hands on him they will discover, in part, the secret."

"The assassination of Carlier!"

"Don't try to make me say what I must not say."

"Then what do you expect me to do—go and see the President of the Council?"

"What would you say to him? That Jacques is making his move on Monday? But what more? We still know nothing about it, you and I. He is the only man who knows—he and possibly Sonia. But I know he is relying on you. You are in the forefront of the scheme and will be informed at the last moment. Doubtless he will tell you to-morrow the part you are to play. Well, wait patiently until then. . . ."

Lavobourg stared at d'Askof.

"When you entered the boudoir were they in Sonia's room?"

"I have told you so."

"How long did you remain in the boudoir?"

"Over half an hour. Why, but, my dear fellow, what more do you want me to tell you? It was the sound of their kisses that warned me. . . ."

Lavobourg uttered a dull moan and swept his hand across his fevered brow.

"All right. . . . All right, you may count on me," he said.

"Then good-bye for the present."

"Shall I see you this afternoon."

"Yes, I suppose, in the house in the Boulevard Pereire, and if you don't see me to-day we shall certainly meet on Sunday where we have been invited to dine."

"I may know everything then. I shall have, perhaps, to make some sign to you. . . ."

"Well, my dear fellow, whatever you do, don't do that. You will have to act on your own. No one suspects you. I cannot move a step without having X's secret police on my heels. They saw me come to your place to-night. That doesn't matter, for it has happened several times, and they think that you are in all sincereity in the scheme. But if I were to try any startling or ambiguous move—set foot in Flottard's place, for instance—I should be dead before I crossed the threshold of his office. Oh, they are not trying to catch me unawares, they have warned me."

"But after all, forgive me for persisting now that

we have joined forces—who are *they*? Who is the mysterious X?"

"My dear fellow, were I to tell you I fear that the very walls of this house would come crashing down and bury the both of us."

CHAPTER VIII

MONSIEUR HILAIRE

"MONSIEUR HILAIRE, I beg of you to be good enough to drop your politics for the moment and attend to business. I'm sorry, gentlemen, to interrupt such an interesting conversation, but—don't you think so?—there are the interests of the 'Up-to-date Grocery Stores' to be considered as well as the interests of the Republic."

Thus in pompous and carefully chosen language Mme Virginie Zenaide Felicité Hilaire expressed herself, addressing first her husband and next his friends, three of the principal members of the Arsenal Club, a political club well known for its advanced views and influence in municipal matters, which had elected M. Hilaire as its secretary.

It was not, however, that M. Hilaire felt any very pronounced taste for the fleeting glories of public life, but the Mme Hilaire had sufficient ambition for both of them, and dreamed of being the wife of a municipal councillor. As usual, he gave way to her, for he had a holy terror of her. Mme Hilaire had a will of her own.

She sat enthroned in the cash desk—the word ˌenthroned is no exaggeration to suggest a picture of this massive and masterful dame perched aloft in the centre of the imposing paraphernalia of the cash and order desk in Hilaire's "Up-to-date Grocery Stores."

Virginie, the youthful maidservant at Le Pollet, had put on weight since she met the poor young man then called the Dodger.[1]—Hush, suppose the Dodger should hear!—and they both left their home in the Rue St. Roch . . .

"One tin of peas, one tin of good quality peas, one tin of extra quality peas," enumerated Mme Hilaire. "Oh, by the way, have we any of those Canadian apple rings?" . . .

"In any case I can assure you that we shall know where we stand at Carlier and Bonchamp's funeral. The funeral is on Tuesday. A state funeral," cried one of the most important members of the Arsenal Club, helping himself to a handful of almonds from a bag yawning beside him.

"M. Tholosée," said Mme. Hilaire, "will you go with your friends to the little café at the corner, for I am worked off my head. I will send M. Hilaire when I've done with him. Come, M. Hilaire, I asked you if we have any Canadian apple rings."

"What we want is 'wringed' necks!" exclaimed the big gawky-looking Tholosée, dragging his friends out of the shop and hustling two worthy citizens who drew back to allow him to pass.

"Come in, gentlemen. He's a big fool, but not a bad chap. Well, how are you, M. Florent? And you, M. Barkimel? You look out of sorts."

---

[1] See *The Dancing Girl*, by Gaston Leroux. Translated by Hannaford Bennett. (John Long Limited.)

"Mme Hilaire, you receive people here who will do you harm," ventured M. Barkimel.

"In what way?" asked M. Hilaire, riding the high horse as the phrase goes. "They are Arsenal Club friends of mine. They merely desire the good of the people. The proof of that is they have elected me secretary."

"To save the Republic!" said Florent, shrugging his shoulders.

"M. Hilaire is no bigger fool than other people," said Mme Hilaire ruffled. "And he is not the man to be dazzled by the stripes of a twopenny-halfpenny soldier. You can tell Subdamoun that from me."

"You are going a little too far," said M. Hilaire obviously embarrassed.

"Hold your tongue."

"Virginie, everyone is entitled to his opinion: we have our own, but there is no object in our losing the Marchioness de Touchais's custom."

"Let her keep her custom. Conceited thing!"

"Virginie, I wish you wouldn't . . ." exclaimed M. Hilaire. "You are forgetting . . ."

"What am I forgetting? What am I forgetting?" she shouted, descending from the cash desk. "Ah, M. Hilaire, we'll have this out once for all, and we'll see if in future you will use words of double meaning astonishing your friends. Will you do me the favor of coming into the dining-room?"

M. Hilaire did not wait to be asked a second time. The door was closed with a bang.

"He's going to get it hot," babbled M. Florent in consternation.

Mme Hilaire in the dark, damp dining-room let

herself go with all the impetuosity of her revengeful temper.

"What am I forgetting? That I was a servant girl at the Marchioness's? Well, yes, I am forgetting it, because it doesn't suit me to remember the time when though I was nobody you were merely an ass who submitted to every imposition."

"Virginie, I wish you wouldn't . . . People will hear you. Don't shout so much."

"I shall shout as much as I like. I never saw such a big booby with his 'Marchioness de Touchais.' How you like to mouth those words 'Marchioness de Touchais!' Oh, don't pretend to be indifferent. All said, I know what you think. It's all very well to pretend to be a democrat, but you would like nothing better than to return and black the boots of the Marchioness and her son Jacques —aping Bonaparte. It's enough to make one die of laughing. Be quiet! You've always had the soul of a flunkey."

"Virginie . . ."

Just then a knock came at the door.

"Some one wishes to speak to M. Hilaire."

Virginie went over and looked through the pane of glass, pushing aside the curtain an inch or so.

"There!" she said. "Here is the good sister, the Marchioness's companion, as it happens. I will see her—don't disturb yourself."

She went back to the shop, stood before Jacqueline, and said:

"What do you want, madame?"

Jacqueline seemed somewhat embarrassed at not seeing M. Hilaire.

"Well, I wanted some soap. . . ."

"Scented soap? What sort? We have . . ."

"Oh, just some soap for the washing."

"Very well, madame, but I could not guess that, could I? Boy, attend to madame." And she mounted the steps of her throne.

When she was served, Jacqueline took her courage in both hands, for this stout lady, who looked at her from the height of her desk in such majestic fashion, rather frightened her, and she ventured to ask: "Is not M. Hilaire in?"

"Yes, madame, he is in, but I must tell you he is very busy."

"I have a word to say to him."

"But, madame, I will pass it on."

"It's from the Marchioness de Touchais."

"It doesn't matter whom it comes from, I am Mme Hilaire. I must ask you to tell me what it is you have to say to my husband."

Just then the dining-room door was opened and M. Hilaire was heard to say in a firm voice:

"Will you please come into the dining-room, Mademoiselle Jacqueline?"

Jacqueline, startled, but glad of the unexpected intervention, hastened to take advantage of the invitation and escape the terrible Mme Hilaire. And the door closed behind her who formerly was Sister St. Mary of the Angels, and on him who formerly was the Dodger.

Mme Hilaire in the cash desk gasped for breath. Swallowing her confusion she began to add up long rows of figures, endeavoring to recover her composure. M. Florent and M. Barkimel had ordered a glass of port at the bar at the other end of the shop and turned their heads away so that she might think that they had not observed the incident. . . .

Let us return to the dining-room into which M. Hilaire had invited Mlle Jacqueline to step with an authority and resolution that surprised and, let us add, dismayed him, for he could not help thinking of the consequences of his sudden impulse.

"Thank you, M. Hilaire," said the old spinster. "I have come to ask you to do the Marchioness a favor."

"Out with it quickly," said Hilaire, his face turned towards the door, fearing lest his irascible spouse should appear.

"While out driving in the evening near the Grand Parc or coming from the theatre the Marchioness has on several occasions met an old man, bowed down with age, selling olives and peanuts. She would like to know who this man is, his exact circumstances, his name and where he lives; and she thought of you because you were so devoted to her until you took up with this odious politics."

"That will do, Mlle Jacqueline," cried M. Hilaire. "I won't allow you to say that I am no longer devoted to the Marchioness. I shall never forget that when we were living in Dieppe she became the godmother of our poor boy, who for that matter was not spared to enjoy such distinguished patronage, for he caught whooping-cough and died. Peace to his memory! . . . I will gladly do the small service the Marchioness asks. To-morrow, or next day at latest, she shall know what she desires to know. Tell her that from me."

He opened the door and they both went back to the shop.

"I assure you, Mlle Jacqueline," said M. Hilaire

in a loud voice, "I assure you that we can't reduce our prices. Trade generally is in a very bad way."

Thus he escorted Mlle Jacqueline to the street door and then returned to the counter. But Mme Hilaire said no word. She did not even look at him, continuing to add up her figures. It was the beginning of his punishment and he knew that it would be dire. He gave a sigh, but Mme Hilaire refused to hear it, for her affectation of deafness would be a part of his punishment. And that was not the only thing. To her deafness and silence she would add starvation—no less than that.

When luncheon-time came Mme Hilaire would declare that she was not hungry, and indeed would sit at table but refuse to touch anything. And at dinner-time she would likewise decline food, as though she were on hunger strike, so that at ten o'clock, not having had a bite all day, which was indeed rash for a woman accustomed to deny herself nothing, she would faint and collapse on the floor.

It was at this moment that M. Hilaire would rush up to his victim uttering cries of despair so that she would reopen her eyes and mouth. The eyes would be listless and the mouth would say in a lifeless voice: "Carry me to my room!"

The room was on the first floor, and Mme Hilaire weighed fifteen stone. That was why M. Hilaire sighed.

CHAPTER IX

DANCING ON A VOLCANO

THAT Saturday was particularly disturbing for M. Hilaire. Had his wife been in better humor he might have hoped to induce her to join him and see some dancing in one of the establishments in the Grand Parc, but after the scene between them he dared not think of it.

The news in the evening became so bad and the echo of rumors from the chief suburbs so threatening that M. Hilaire was in no way surprised when M. Tholosée entered his shop holding in his hand the latest edition of a newspaper, wherein it was stated once again that the Republic must be saved.

M. Tholosée had come to tell M. Hilaire that the Clubs in every district were being specially summoned to meet that same evening with a view of passing resolutions in support of the Government and the Commission of Inquiry and of forcing the hands of both, if necessary, to prosecute the assassins of Carlier and Bonchamps.

He advised M. Hilaire, as the secretary, to be at the Club in good time, not later than half-past seven, and then, in increasing excitement, went on to the Arsenal Club. But he left M. Hilaire in a state of elation.

On the plea of having to go to the Club to fulfil "unavoidable" duties, he would leave the shop early; and indeed he would be glad to substitute a night of pleasure, of song and dance, in the Grand Parc for one which promised first to be painful and then

entirely political. He would go to the ball with
his friends Barkimel and Florent, whose presence
would not prevent him from pursuing his inquiries.

Taking advantage of the message delivered by
Tholosée in his wife's presence, and calculating that
her fainting-fit usually occurred about half-past
eight, after dinner he said:

"I can't stay to dinner, you see, Virginie. Besides, like you, I am not hungry to-day. I'll be off
to the Arsenal Club at half-past seven."

But at half-past seven he was compelled to lower
his tone, for the shop doors having been closed, he
saw Mme Hilaire slip the key of the little door in
the iron shutter into her pocket and make for the
dining-room, where the maidservant had just laid
a smoking soup tureen.

Without seeming to be concerned by the appetiz-
ing odor of vegetable soup, Mme Hilaire sat down
and began to read the newspaper brought by M.
Tholosée. M. Hilaire watched her with a look of
consternation.

"Virginie, have you finished hurting my feelings?" he asked in his meekest and most ingrati-
ating tone. "You know I ought to be at the Club
at half-past seven. Why do you refuse to give me
the key of the door? I must be making a move."

Silence of Virginie.

"I shall be censured and got rid of, and a lot of
good that will do you, seeing you wish your husband to be a municipal councillor. Won't you eat
anything? Presently we shall have the usual trouble
again, for worn out by lack of food, overcome by
weakness, and a victim of your pride, you will col-

lapse to the floor, and once more I who adore you will think you are dying."

As a matter of fact Virginie suddenly let her head sink on her shoulder, opened her mouth as to breathe her last, showed her listless eyes, and then dropped to the floor with sufficient cleverness, however, to avoid breaking the chair.

"There! What did I tell you!" cried M. Hilaire. beside himself.

On this occasion he forbore to utter the usual cries of despair, but displayed every sign of intense exasperation. As ill-luck would have it a small barrel of treacle stood beside him in which lay the scoop used for serving it. He filled the scoop with a generous supply of the liquid and flung it with all his might at Mme Hilaire's inanimate face. End of the good lady's silence and her immediate resurrection.

"Villain! Scoundrel!" she cried.

"At last you have found your tongue."

Virginie, rising without assistance to her feet, spluttered forth insults mingled with treacle dripping down on all sides, and made a rush at her husband. But he still held the scoop in his hand, and calmly declared that he would not hesitate to sacrifice the rest of the barrel if she refused to come to her senses. Then, vanquished, she burst into tears. Mme Hilaire, weeping, her face covered with treacle, was no pleasant sight, but it softened her husband's heart.

"Come, Dolly," he said, more touched than he ought to have been at such a moment if he wished to reap the full benefit of his victory. "I see what it is—you want me to take you up to your room as usual." And he carried her up to the first floor, exhibiting a strength far beyond the ordinary in a man of his ripe years.

M. Hilaire did not descend again until he opened the shop next morning. On Sundays the staff was a small one, and the shop was closed at midday. Mme Hilaire appeared in her turn. She made her way to the cash desk with a look of satisfaction and careless grace that delighted them all, and not least M. Hilaire.

"In reality she is not a bad soul," he thought. "She never bears malice."

Just then Mlle Jacqueline came in, carrying her prayer-book in her hand. M. Hilaire looked cautiously around and then hastened to her and said in an undertone:

"I know nothing yet, Mlle Jacqueline. I couldn't get out last night, but to-night—you may rely on me. And he added aloud: "What can I do for you, Mlle Jacqueline?"

But suddenly he realized that his ruse was forced. On her side Mlle Jacqueline reddened. She stammered:

"I want some almonds, raisins and filbert nuts."

"At four francs a pound?"

"Yes."

As he served her he risked casting a glance in the direction of the cash desk. Mme Hilaire was adding up her figures. Presumably she had observed nothing.

"Quick—go!"

Jacqueline left the shop. M. Hilaire returned to the cash desk, hands in pockets, a look of unconcern on his face.

"If you like, my dear Virginie, we'll have a breath of fresh air this afternoon," he said.

Silence of Virginie.

"I suggest taking you for a drive."

Silence of Virginie.

"To-night we could go to the theatre."

Silence of Virginie.

"To the ball."

Silence of Virginie.

M. Hilaire could restrain himself no longer. He slapped his thigh, folded his arms and cried:

"So you're at it again, are you?" And in a flash he darted into the dining-room, took off his apron, and put on his coat and Sunday bowler-hat, which were hanging on a peg. A minute later he was in the street.

"Monsier Hilaire!" shouted his wife.

He made no answer to her appeal which he considered belated, but hurried on. At the corner of the Rue St. Antoine he met Barkimel and Florent on their way to him, scared by the news of the day.

"We are dancing on a volcano," exclaimed M. Barkimel.

"Let's dance on anything you like as long as we dance," returned M. Hilaire.

He drew them away with him. That Sunday morning, in spite of the early hour, the streets were already thronged with an idle, anxious crowd ready to give ear to every rumor, easily stirred, and betraying their excitement by cries, clamor and song.

Troops were moved in readiness for every eventuality. Two battalions which had left their barracks to strengthen the Republican Guard at the Palais Bourbon, where the Commission of Inquiry was sitting, were loudly cheered. Flottard, the civilian Governor, clad in a magnificent uniform suggestive of that of a Commissary-General of the Army, and riding between two Generals, was cheered and hooted in turn. Vigorous fisticuffs were exchanged more or less everywhere. Special editions of the papers contained reports of the work of the Commission of Inquiry.

Notwithstanding the exceptional secrecy with which the Commission had shrouded its labors, it was known that it had resolved to demand at the sitting on Monday the suspension of Parliamentary privilege and inviolability in the case of over one hundred and fifty Senators and Deputies whose names were given and who were held responsible for Carlier's assassination. The list was headed by the name of Major Jacques de Touchais. . . .

But to return to Hilaire, Barkimel and Florent. On arriving at the Place de l'Hôtel de Ville they were so roughly hustled that they determined to make for the left bank of the Seine. But here they found the Sorbonne in a ferment, and to escape a cavalry charge were obliged to take a refuge in a courtyard. They then observed that they were on the premises of the Francs Archers Club and had lost M. Hilaire, who had suddenly disappeared.

Paris was crowded with clubs secretly supported by international Communists waiting for their hour to come. . . . Popular clubs had established their tyrannical influence in every district, and their spokesmen did not hesitate to declare that "the National Convention had done no good until it was dominated by the Commune." From that to advocating government by municipality was not far, not to mention that these clubs made it their business to send delegates to interview the Government, which was obliged to receive them. They presented their demands and resolutions, and even their denunciations, to the Government. From denunciation to indictment was not far either. . . .

M. Florent shook his head at M. Barkimel's lamentations.

"Whatever they do they won't come near the work of the Jacobin Club of despotic memory. The members of the Committee of Public Safety came to that club to take the people's orders, and obtained from it a list of suspects, profiteers and agents of Pitt and Cobourg, whom the Revolutionary Tribunal made it its business to send to the guillotine."

In reality M. Florent was shaking in his shoes. His argument was intended to depreciate the bravado of M. Hilaire, secretary of the Arsenal Club, and to surprise M. Barkimel by its erudition. But he began to be no more easy in his mind than his friend Barkimel; and it was he who first suggested leaving the courtyard where a mob orator was making a speech.

"Citizens, the people alone enjoy the privilege of freedom from error. The people must send Commissioners into the provinces. They must dismiss every General and replace him by a son of the people as was done by the French in '93. Soldiers must elect their own officers, and we shall no longer have to reckon with the adventure of a Major Jacques, a disgrace to the Republic. Citizens, the eyes of the world are upon you. You are the admiration of the universe. And it is the University and Francs

Archers Clubs that will save France and Europe
from the last efforts of tyranny."

"Let's go," whispered M. Florent, seizing M.
Barkimel by the skirt of his coat.

"Yes, let's go," shivered M. Barkimel. "The man
frightens me. He talks like a Bolshevist."

They turned towards the exit. They had lost
their safeguard, the worthy M. Hilaire, whose
friendly protection they valued above everything
else, and whose company they assiduously culti-
vated on account of his position at the Arsenal
Club. They came upon him again on the pavement
looking to right and left and seemingly in some
difficulty.

"Have you seen an old fellow with tinted spectacles, bent with age, a small tub of olives and peanuts under his arm? A little while ago he entered
the courtyard of the Francs Archers Club to say a
word to a couple of men standing near you. I ran
after him, but the two men hustled me and I lost
sight of him. I came back to see the two men, but
couldn't find them again either."

"What do you want the peanut dealer for?"
asked M. Florent.

"Well, to buy some peanuts from him," returned
M. Hilaire.

Suddenly he uttered a cry and slipped with surprising agility among a group of people. Barkimel
and Florent thought then they had lost him once
more. But they came up to him again on the quay,
and he signalled to them to keep quiet and say
nothing. Then they observed that he was following two persons of singular appearance and manner.

To begin with, these two men, judged from their

manner of walking with a roll and working their jaws as though they were chewing the inevitable quid of tobacco, were sailors. But their faces were without that look of simple good-humor characteristic of seamen enjoying themselves in town. Their entire personality exhaled something formidable, and at first sight they inspired little confidence. Finally, they spoke the language of hooligans.

Barkimel and Florent failed to understand what interest M. Hilaire could have in pursuing these redoubtable rascals, but they followed their leader. M. Hilaire listened carefully to what was being said ahead of him, although Barkimel and Florent were convinced that he understood the conversation as little as they did.

"My dear Jean Jean, Daddy doesn't seem to be having much fun to-day. He placed twelve peanuts on the table of the bloke speechifying at the Francs Archers Club."

"Twelve—that's one less than thirteen," returned Polydore.

"And in my opinion when a man receives thirteen of 'em he won't make old bones."

"You saw how pale the babbler turned. I bet you have a bloke there who wanted to get rid of Cravely, and Daddy wasn't pleased."

"Very likely. He's no longer in the know. He's just had five years in quod, and from what I can hear had nothing better to do than go back to the suburbs and find his old place in the Rue St. Margot. That's where Daddy found him."

"Yes, now he's got to run straight for the Major."

Suddenly they looked round, for it seemed to them that they were being too closely followed.

They cast so sharp a glance at Barkimel and Florent that they had neither the strength to advance nor to retire.

"Well, what's the matter now?" said M. Hilaire.

"Aren't we going to leave the quays soon?" asked M. Barkimel in a trembling voice.

"I suggest a little turn in the Bois de Boulogne before lunch," said M. Florent.

"Well, that suits me," said M. Hilaire at once, and in a couple of leaps was on the steps of an omnibus which had pulled up and in which Jean Jean and Polydore had entered.

The two friends followed, and were not a little dismayed to find themselves on the platform beside the two terrible sailors who this time glared at them with a grim expression on their faces.

"Haven't you a weakness for police spies?" said Jean Jean to Polydore.

"Not more than you have, old man," returned Polydore. "And I'll tell you a little story that'll make you split your sides."

"I know it," said Polydore. "It's about that fellow Gésier, who only had one eye and was told: 'Follow him day and night and use your eye.' "

"That's it. Poor Gésier! He followed me day and night. But he'll never use that eye again. Do you remember that kick?"

"What do you think! The police of every district can leave us alone. We're doing no harm. We are heroes! We were in the Subdamoun campaign. And we have been thanked by the Government."

"I'll tell you a good thing, Polydore. Suppose we give them a good dressing?"

"I'm getting out," said M. Barkimel, his teeth chattering.

"We'll get out at the next stop," said M. Florent, feeling very uncomfortable.

"So you're leaving me," said M. Hilaire aloud. "I thought you were going to have a turn in the Bois de Boulogne."

"I don't feel like it now," said M. Barkimel.

At the next stopping-place Barkimel and Florent hurried off the car. They were joined by M. Hilaire, who laughed at their fears.

"Well, you are a pair of cowards."

"I wonder what sort of pleasure you can find in listening to such an awful talk," exclaimed M. Florent after the car had noisily disappeared.

"Look here, my dear fellow," said M. Hilaire, who seemed to have some idea of his own, "I'll stand you a lunch in a little restaurant opposite Batignolles railway station which makes a specialty of calves' head, and you can tell me what you think of it."

"I love calves' head," agreed M. Florent. "Off we go."

About half-past twelve the three friends entered a restaurant standing at a corner of two busy streets. The room was already nearly full.

"Gentlemen," said M. Hilaire, who seemed to be looking for some one or something, "as this room is full we'll go up to the first floor, if you don't mind."

When Barkimel and Florent reached the landing they uttered a horse exclamation and shrank back. Seated at a table near the window opposite them were the two formidable sailors finishing their lunch. M. Barkimel was already dragging M. Florent by his coat-tails to the little spiral staircase when half the lanky body of M. Hilaire emerged into view.

"What's the matter, and what's all the row about?" he asked in a calm voice.

Jean Jean and Polydore had risen to their feet after throwing a bank-note on the table. They exchanged glances as they lit their cigars, and in their heavy silence appeared to be concerting by stealth joint measures to rid themselves for ever of the three interlopers who had been pursuing them since the morning.

Their intention had become so obvious, and the grunt which came from them as they advanced towards the trio sounded so appalling in the ears of Barkimel and Florent, that they began to cry out as though they were to be flayed alive. They made a rush for the staircase. M. Hilaire received them in his arms and at once explained:

"Gentlemen, you are, I assure you, under a strange misapprehension—accident has brought us here. These gentlemen are simply inoffensive citizens. One of them is my friend Florent, who formerly kept a stationer's shop in the Marais district, and the other is my friend Barkimel, who was an umbrella dealer in the same neighborhood. I have known them for fifteen years. They are incapable, as you can see, of hurting a fly, and it was enough for you to give them a look to cause them almost to faint in my arms."

"Then you, who are bragging so much—who are you?" asked Jean Jean in a harsh voice.

"I am M. Hilaire, proprietor of 'Hilaire's Up-to-date Grocery Stores,' purveyor to Major Jacques, at your service."

The statement at once made a salutary impression.

"You know Major Jacques?" asked Jean Jean in a milder tone.

"I should think I do know him! Why, we went to the same school, and I was for a long time in the service of the Marchioness de Touchais."

"You know the Marchioness de Touchais!" exclaimed Jean Jean.

"He knows the Marchioness!" repeated Polydore.

"Yes, and Mlle Jacqueline and Mlle Lydia and the whole family, and I am proud of it, believe me. If you are friends of theirs allow me to say: the friends of my friends are my friends. The day when you are passing my place and care to come in and drink the Major's health will be a proud day for the 'Up-to-date Grocery Stores.'"

"If that's the case let's have a drink now," said Jean Jean. "A round of drinks to the health of the Major!"

Feeling much easier, Barkimel and Florent warmly shook the rough hands of their newly found friends. They called the waiter. They drank, they clinked glasses. They shouted, "The Major for ever!" and after a last handshake and a last glance at the clock the two sailors took their departure. M. Hilaire darted to the window, and M. Barkimel said to M. Florent:

"Order the lunch, I'm famished. . . . Well, what are you looking at, M. Hilaire?"

"Why, at my two friends crossing the boulevard."

"Those shady-looking fellows seem greatly to interest you," M. Barkimel ventured to say, pulling M. Hilaire's sleeve.

"They would have had very good excuse for punching our heads, you know. We were following them all the morning," added M. Florent.

"I presume, M. Hilaire, you heard them mention this restaurant and played the trick of bringing us here without telling us."

But M. Hilaire, still at his post of observation, seemed not to hear them.

"I say, they are entering that splendid private house," said M. Barkimel, himself looking out of the window. "Upon my word, they're going in as if the place belonged to them."

The waiter came to relay the table. M. Hilaire turned to him and said:

"Tell me, waiter, who lives in that private house opposite."

"That private house," returned the waiter in a sepulchral voice, "belongs to Mlle Sonia Liskinne, and the gentleman getting out of the car to enter it is M. Lavobourg, Vice-President of the Chamber of Deputies, said to be her lover, a traitor to the Republic. . . . Have you chosen your lunch, gentlemen?"

M. Hilaire ordered what he wanted. Barkimel and Florent had lost their appetite.

CHAPTER X

THE PEANUT DEALER

LAVOBOURG sent in his name to Sonia. It was to be his first sight of her since his terrible conversation with Baron d'Askof. He had called at the house the day before at five o'clock, but was told that Sonia was out and would be dining in town. At eleven o'clock he had returned and was informed that she had a violent headache and had gone to bed and wished to be allowed to rest, but that he was to be told when he called that she relied on him to lunch with her next day.

Lavobourg spent the Saturday night without closing his eyes. He had not seen d'Askof again, but he continued to think of him and his disclosure. And he was no longer certain of anything.

He had no doubt that d'Askof had fallen in love with Sonia. He was perhaps actuated by jealousy. On the other hand, d'Askof had confessed that he was working for the Major only under compulsion and hated him. D'Askof had, perhaps, invented his horrible story of having surprised the two lovers to induce him to take a revenge which would play into his hands. He may, too, have spoken the truth. Lavobourg was so tormented by the thought of the truth that he was increasingly disinclined to believe in it.

"Good morning, Lucien."

Sonia had come into the room. She was clad for an informal luncheon at home in one of those de-

lightful fluffy frocks made up of a few chiffons
whose art consisted wholly in the fashion in which
she had arranged the folds round her beautiful
supple figure. She rarely called him by his Chris-
tian name.

"Lucien!" He stared at her.

"Let me set your mind at rest—all goes well,"
she at once said. "Nothing remains to be done
but a trifling formality which I will explain, and
soon all your apprehensions will be over. Come,
tell me everything you've done since I saw you
last."

"And you?" he asked abruptly. The retort escaped him involuntarily.

Surprised by his tone, she gazed boldly at him,
perhaps too boldly.

"What do you mean?"

"Yes, and you? For the last two days I have
been calling here, and for the last two days I have
been unable to see you."

"You have called here—you have been unable
to see me! You know quite well that you are in
your own house here. Why, you are imagining
things, my dear. I was dining in town, that's all.
Come, Lucien, seriously, what's the matter with
you?"

"Nothing. . . . Nothing," he said, taking her
hands and covering them with quick kisses.
"Nothing."

"And besides, I have been working with Jacques," she said gravely in her rich and sonorous
voice.

"Oh, have you?"

"Does that surprise you? Why do you say, 'Oh,

have you?' in such a tone of melodrama? Are you still jealous? You make me smile, you know, with your jealousy. Oh, my dear friend, if you knew how little I mean to him!"

"Yes, that's what you are always saying. But am I to believe you?"

He was smiling now. He refused to credit, he no longer credited, the awful story. Sonia was too candid, too sincere, and the face that was turned to him was too honest.

"Don't let's talk about these trifles," he begged. "Let's discuss politics. Am I soon to be in possession of the great secret?"

"At once—after lunch you will know everything. I have been instructed to tell you everything. We're going to spend a nice afternoon together. Here is the program of the day: Lunch in the little boudoir. At this lunch Jacques will be present, though no one will know it, d'Askof, who will come openly, you and myself. In the afternoon you and I will have work to do. In the evening you, d'Askof and I will dine in a restaurant. We must be seen in public, my dear. Afterwards we'll go to the theatre and at midnight sally forth to the ball in the Grand Parc, where we have taken a box. As we shall be seen enjoying ourselves until two o'clock, the Government will be reassured, perhaps, in the matter of the great conspiracy. At two o'clock you and I will return and meet Jacques here and help him to put the finishing touches to his work. And so we shan't leave each other until—until we have saved the Republic!"

"Does it not occur to you that you may have to fear some catastrophe?"

"Everything is possible, but I am not afraid of it."

"I admire your courage."

Baron d'Askof was shown in. Sonia went up to him and shook his hand with great cordiality and apologized for having to leave them together for a moment. D'Askof at once strode over to Lavobourg.

"Well?"

"Well?" repeated Lavobourg, casually opening a newspaper. "Have you any news?"

"And you?"

"I? No. I may tell you that I haven't opened a paper for the last two days, and I've given up trying to understand what is happening around me. I have tried to make Sonia speak. She has postponed letting me into the secret—indefinitely. I have tried to make you speak, too. You have yourself been more mysterious than all the others put together."

"It seems to me that there was one point on which I was not mysterious with you," returned d'Askof in a low voice, looking at Lavobourg with some surprise.

"Yes, I know," returned Lavobourg, bluntly throwing down his paper. "This business between Sonia and Jacques. I will tell you the truth, my dear fellow—I don't believe it."

D'Askof took a step back. Obviously he was not expecting such a change of attitude.

"So you think I invented the story. Well, we'll discuss it later. Hist! here she is."

Sonia came in again.

"Quick, children, let's go upstairs. The Major has arrived," she said delightedly.

They found Jacques in the boudoir and the table for lunch was already laid. Aunt Natcha was there to wait on them. The lunch began at first in intense silence. Lavobourg fixed his eyes on Jacques and Sonia. They did not look at each other and seemed entirely at their ease. At last the Major turned to Lavobourg:

"My dear Lavobourg, the goal is in sight. Everything leads me to believe that we shall succeed. In case of failure I will take the entire responsibility. Sonia will ask you to render us a little service later. It's a question of your signature. If the matter turns out badly you will be able to say that your signature was extorted from you by force and under a threat of death. I shall not contradict you. In case of success you will share my fortunes. We shall have a provisional Government consisting of a duumvirate. You and I will jointly exercise power."

Lavobourg could find nothing to say. He seemed applying himself to the contents of his plate, and yet he swallowed the food with difficulty.

"Well, are you deaf?" asked Sonia impatiently.

"No, my dear," he returned. "The Major knows that I am quite at his disposal and wish success to his efforts on behalf of the country. As to the risks, I am ready to take my share of them."

"Our poor Lavobourg has much more courage than any of us," said the Major with a laugh, "for at heart he is the least easy in his mind, but he will go ahead all the same. . . . It is well for you to know that certain newspapers, on my orders, have spread the most sinister reports regarding the in-

tentions of the Commission of Inquiry. I wished to
some extent to make an impression on my troops
before going into battle so that they might know
that their only salvation lay in victory. Baruch, the
President of the Senate, informs me that the state
of mind of the Senators is excellent, and fear has
overcome their last scruples. At the same time I
have good news of the Army. It is entirely with us.
It only depends upon ourselves to obtain its assistance. It will help us if we represent the law—even
if it be only for a quarter or half an hour. That
will suffice. Afterwards it will not draw back because we shall be in power."

"Tut, tut, that's all very fine, but I should prefer
to have the names of the Generals," said d'Askof.

"Don't pretend you do not know them," returned
Jacques. "My dear d'Askof, I have not yet promised you anything. You have been so useful to us
and shown such wonderful ingenuity in keeping
our secrets and our persons in safety that I don't
know what to offer you. It is quite easy. You may
have anything you wish. Is that not so, Lavobourg? . . ."

D'Askof beckoned to Lavobourg and after taking leave withdrew from the boudoir declaring that
he had not a moment to lose.

"Oh, allow me, I have a word to say to d'Askof,"
said Lavobourg at once.

He left the boudoir, closing the door on Jacques
and Sonia. Then d'Askof asked him to follow
him, treading softly down a short dark passage
which at the end ran parallel with the boudoir
wall. Here he pushed aside a curtain and pointed
to a chink in the partition to which Lavobourg

applied one eye. The scene that met his view was
not at first calculated to excite him. Jacques and
Sonia were both on their feet. Jacques was putting
some papers in his portfolio. Then they exchanged
a few unimportant words.

"And now to get away," said Jacques. "I must
put on my disguise again. . . . Good-bye, Sonia."

He bent with great politeness over the hand that
she held out to him. But as he drew himself up she
took his head between her hands and kissed him
full on the lips. He made scarcely any attempt to
resist her.

"Sonia you are mad—mad!" And when he recovered his breath: "And you promised me to be
sensible."

"Jacques, I adore you!"

"You know quite well that all this is forbidden
for a couple of days. . . . Good-bye till this evening."

Jacques disappeared through the small door behind the full-length portrait. Sonia remained motionless for some moments: "It's true, I am mad."
And suddenly she murmured: "I was forgetting all
about Lavobourg. Where has he gone?"

She found him in the smoking-room smoking like
a chimney.

"This place reeks of smoke," she cried. "I
thought you had given up cigars. . . . And do you
drink liqueurs now?"

Lavobourg lay stretched on a divan and had
ordered himself a liqueur brandy. He amazed Sonia
that afternoon by the good-humored alacrity with
which he yielded to her every fancy. He expressed
no surprise at anything, and on learning what was

expected of him at once set to work to sign the letters convoking the Chamber.

At six o'clock his man, in answer to a telephone message, brought his bag containing his dress, clothes. Sonia had laughingly told him that he was her prisoner and she would not allow him to move a step without her, alleging as a pretext that he might be needed at any moment.

Secretly he slipped a letter into his valet's hand telling him to deliver it to Hérisson. The man went away but returned almost at once. As he was about to leave the house the door was shut in his face and two unknown men somewhat rudely invited him to join them in a game of cards in the concierge's room.

"That's all right, Jean," said Lavobourg, taking back the letter and putting it in his pocket. "Go and have your game of cards and do nothing except what you are allowed to do. You are under Mlle Liskinne's orders to-day."

Lavobourg went to find the beautiful Sonia and told her of the incident without displaying the least ill-humor.

"You are quite right not to take offense, dear," said Sonia. "The order applies to everyone. There are secrets in this house. No one must leave it— without me! D'Askof will be here presently. Though I ask you to tell him nothing, unless it is absolutely necessary, he will not leave you either."

And as d'Askof happened to come in:

"Here is the Baron. Well, let's go. Where shall we dine?"

They dined in the Bois de Boulogne and then spent an hour or two in a fashionable theatre.

Wherever they were seen they created a sensation. To begin with, Sonia was looking her best, and then some admiration was expressed for Lavobourg, whom many persons believed already under lock and key.

No later than ten o'clock the Grand Parc and the supper clubs were seething with continuous excitement. Paris had started to plunge into a whirl of jazz and dancing. The crowd seemed to be giving itself up to the enjoyment of the moment, taking no heed of the terror of the morrow. Was the Republic to be wrecked? Was it to be saved? Meanwhile let them dance! And the fashions of the day, as in the worst period of the Directory, imparted to this medley the semblance of a masquerade. It was as though the tiers of boxes were filled with Floras, Hebes, Greeks, Orientals. But the most beautiful and fascinating figure that evening was Sonia, seated between Lavobourg and d'Askof excited as much by her presence as by their coming revenge.

When she appeared in the box and removed her cloak a murmur of admiration arose.

Among the throng staring at her with the most persistent attention were three persons seated at a table a few steps from the box. They were three respectable citizens obviously unaccustomed to the place. They seemed more shocked than enraptured by their surroundings, and Sonia's toilet in particular roused their unfavorable comments. One of them, in fact, stared boldly at the actress. She turned her head away and gave no further heed to these three idiots unaccustomed to pay court to a beautiful woman when she favored the chance wayfarer with a sight of her charms.

"Turn your head away, you shameless hussy," said M. Barkimel in an undertone so as not to be heard by any but his neighbors. "Blush if you still can at the scandal that you are causing by such indecency, but you won't make a respectable citizen lower his eyes."

M. Florent took a different view. He told him so flatly. The two friends continued to wrangle, and M. Hilaire, obviously irritated, suddenly rose, and begging them not to disturb themselves, stated that he would be back soon. He left the dance. It was the third time that he had sneaked off in this way.

"He is a mystery. I shall remember his evening out," declared M. Florent.

After M. Hilaire had left, a gentleman with a spreading beard, clad in a loose-fitting great-coat and soft felt hat pulled well over his eyes, sat down in the vacant seat.

"That chair is taken," said M. Barkimel.

"It belongs to one of our friends who is coming back and won't like to find his seat occupied," added M. Florent.

But say what they might the intruder did not seem to hear them.

"Are you deaf?"

"What's that? What's the matter? What did you say?"

"We said that this chair is engaged."

"No, gentlemen, this chair is not engaged. When a chair is engaged you put something on it, but nothing was on this chair. I shall keep it."

"Look here," said M. Florent with a dignity that excited M. Barkimel's admiration, "do you take us for a couple of idiots?"

"Yes, gentlemen," the man in the soft felt hat made answer.

Barkimel and Florent exchanged glances with gleaming eyes as though they were thinking of reducing this impertinent interloper to pulp, and then M. Florent with the same dignity said:

"Since you talk in that style we have nothing more to say."

"Quite right," said M. Barkimel.

The man imperceptibly moved his chair away from the table, drawing nearer the box occupied by the beautiful Sonia.

"He's afraid," said M. Florent.

"You sat upon him," said M. Barkimel.

Just then M. Hilaire returned and was surprised to find his chair gone.

"That gentleman took it from you," explained M. Barkimel.

"The devil he did," cried M. Hilaire.

At that moment the man rose from his seat and leant his back against the corner of Sonia's box, and M. Hilaire ran over and regained his chair, whereupon the man smiled.

"He never said a word. At heart he is a coward," said M. Barkimel.

"Not to mention the peculiar ways of the swanker," said M. Florent. "Look at him slipping in front of the box with his hands behind his back."

"If I were in the beautiful Sonia's place I wouldn't take any risks and let my wrist-bag hang down like that."

"Look the man is in front of the bag. Now he has passed it and the bag is gone!"

"Thief! Stop thief!" shouted M. Hilaire in a shrill voice.

The man was even now some distance away, creeping among groups of persons near the exit. M. Hilaire darted forward: "Thief! Thief! Stop thief!" he shouted again. He was at once surrounded, hustled, and even struck.

"What thief? What thief?" some one asked, raining blows on him.

Rescued by a municipal guard, he at last explained himself:

"A man ran off with Mlle Sonia Liskinne's wrist-bag."

Every eye was fixed on the actress's box.

"Have you been robbed of your wrist-bag?" asked the municipal guard.

"I? Why, I didn't bring a wrist-bag with me," she returned.

"But, hang it all, I was not dreaming," cried M. Hilaire, driven to exasperation. "A few minutes ago a wrist-bag, held in madame's hand, was hanging out of the box."

"The man is mad," said Sonia.

"When a person indulges in these sort of jokes he should confine himself to tap-room dances," said another.

"You are not accustomed to fashionable society," said a strange, muffled, harsh voice which seemed to come from the ground.

M. Hilaire gave a start. He saw an old man, almost bent in two by the weight of years, stealing from one place to another like a spectre, and leaving at most of the tables on the ledges of the boxes a few peanuts from the barrel under his arm.

"Ah, there's Daddy Peanuts!" came from various tables.

M. Hilaire had at last discovered the peanut dealer whom he was seeking. He was exactly as Mlle Jacqueline had described him. It was indeed the man in whom the Marchioness de Touchais had expressed so much interest. Therefore he forgot everything to apply himself to Daddy Peanuts, and he returned and sat down once more at his table watching every movement of the strange old fellow.

"That voice. . . . That voice. . . ." M. Hilaire said to himself. "I have heard it somewhere. But when? It was a very long time ago it seems to me—a very long time ago. Good! He is returning this way. Look out! He is passing the boxes. Now the people in the beautiful Sonia's box are beckoning him. But he doesn't care a hang. He's not going to hurry himself for her. . . . There! He is placing a pink paper bag in the box. But what's the matter with the beautiful Sonia? And the gentleman beside her with the golden beard—is he going to faint?

True enough Daddy Peanuts' movements created a sensation in the box. Sonia was at first amused by the eccentric old man, greeted by shouts and buffoonery on every side. Then she felt some surprise that the management of so flourishing an establishment should permit this miserable specimen in rags and tatters to appear in such luxurious surroundings.

"Oh, it would be no easy matter to prevent Daddy

Peanuts from going anywhere he wanted to go,"
said d'Askof. "He is known in all the night restaurants. He is the friend of all revellers and night
birds. I hear he has more money than one would
think to look at him, and by selling olives and
peanuts has been able to lay by a little hoard.
Many stories are told about Daddy Peanuts."

"I have been told that he belongs to the police,"
said Lavobourg.

"Very likely," returned the Baron. "Everything
is possible in that matter. But Daddy Peanuts
seems to me too old and broken-down for his services to be of any value. . . ."

"Would there be anything surprising in the police
using him to send out certain watchwords?" asked
Lavobourg in a low voice. "We ourselves have had
the same idea."

"Exactly," returned the Baron with a laugh. "I
got the idea of using peanuts one night on seeing
Daddy Peanuts dole them out to his customers
with his melodramatic air."

"Look, he is coming this way. Attract his attention."

Lavobourg called the old man, and d'Askof, with
a calm look and his mind at rest, seated at the back
of the box, watched Daddy Peanuts approach
them.

The poor old fellow came up without haste and
said to Sonia in his hoarse, hollow voice:

"Olives? Peanuts?"

"Peanuts," returned Sonia.

"How much?"

"I leave it to you."

The old fellow took a spoon and scooped up and poured the peanuts into a paper bag which he closed and placed on the ledge of the box.

Sonia could not repress a slight cry.

The bag was made of pink paper exactly like that which contained the famous list stolen from Jacques and returned to her in so unaccountable a fashion.

"Oh, that paper!" she said in a whisper, putting out her trembling hand.

"What is it, lady? Don't you like the peanuts?" asked the hoarse, hollow voice.

"Yes, yes," returned Sonia, quickly opening the bag.

Then she read on the paper: "Long live Major Jacques."

"Isn't this extraordinary?" she said to Lavobourg, pointing to the bag.

"I have slogans suitable for every taste. Daddy Peanuts doesn't care a rap for politics. I have slogans: 'Long live Major Jacques' and others: 'Long live the Government.' But no one will have those wishing long life to the Government. It's a pity, for I shall have some left."

"That'll do," said Lavobourg, losing patience.

"All right, I'm off," said Daddy Peanuts. "But I still have a few peanuts over—they are for the gentleman in the box with you, lady. Not the one who is so impatient, but the other—the silent one at the back."

The Baron held out his hand, smiling. The old man put a number of peanuts in it, counting them the while:

"One, two, three, four, five, six, seven, eight,

nine, ten, eleven"—at this number the Baron made a movement of surprise—"twelve"—his hand shook —"thirteen"—the Baron leant against the partition. . . .

Sonia and Lavobourg looked at him. He had become deadly pale.

"What's the matter?"

"Are you ill?"

"No. . . . Yes. . . . A passing giddiness."

"Well, let's go," said Sonia, rising.

She cast a glance at Daddy Peanuts, now chatting with the three men, who had stared so persistently at her when she entered the box.

"Lean on my arm, you seem in pain," she said to d'Askof. . . .

If the trifling incidents that marked Daddy Peanuts' presence in Sonia's box seriously stirred the beautiful actress, what can be said of the ever-increasing anguish with which M. Hilaire heard the old man's voice?

How it resembled another voice that was very dear to him in the long ago! A voice that he could never hear without a tremor, a voice that aroused in him every fear and yet every heroic impulse. . . . To be sure it could not be the same voice. It was without that terrible ring that caused the men between decks to tremble in those wonderful days when it issued orders for the general uprising and revolt of the convicts on the *Bayard*.[1]

What thoughts! . . . What memories! . . . O Book of the Past which he imagined would never again be opened! . . . So much blood wiped away

---

[1] See *The Floating Prison*, by Gaston Leroux. Translated by Hannaford Bennett.

by so much treacle in the "Up-to-date Grocery Stores!" Poor M. Hilaire! Pitiable Dodger! In the old days as thin as a lath and to-day as plump as a sausage. . . . He shivered in his Sunday clothes as formerly he used to shiver in the rags that covered his miserable form when he had to work hard to gain a little peace in this vale of tears. . . .

M. Hilaire, like everyone else, bought peanuts.

"I say, Daddy Peanuts," he said, overcoming the emotion that clutched at his throat, "do you know that I too sell peanuts?"

"What is that to do with me?" returned the old fellow in a disagreeable tone.

"Nothing, perhaps, but to me it means competition," explained M. Hilaire, wishing to be pleasant in spite of every rebuff.

"This gentleman is in the grocery business," interposed M. Florent.

"You needn't tell me that—it's self-evident."

"How much do I owe you, my good man?" asked M. Hilaire, greatly piqued.

"Have you been in the grocery business long?" asked the old man, pocketing his money.

"Over fifteen years," said M. Barkimel.

"Fifteen years!" repeated Daddy Peanuts. "The Commercial Exchange will have to look after itself!"

"Let's clear out," said M. Hilaire, whose patience was now exhausted.

But Daddy Peanuts caught the incensed M. Hilaire by his coat-tail.

"I'm sorry, my lord. But just tell me, do you sell cod in your shop?"

"Of course we sell cod. What then?"

"I mean the real, genuine article. Cod prepared in the Spanish way?"

At those words M. Hilaire staggered. Ah, how fond the *other* had been of cod prepared in the Spanish way!

While lost in bewilderment his eyes sought the figure of the peanut dealer who had disappeared, and his lips murmured to himself alone, so low that not a soul could have heard him, the fateful words beginning with a C and a B.

"Ché . . . Bi . . . Bi . . . Ché . . . Bi . . . Bi . . ."

Just then a great clamor burst forth in the assemblage. A man mounted a table and read in a loud voice an extract from the *Journal des Clubs*, the evening paper supporting Coudry; and M. Hilaire, despite the pitiful state to which the mention of cod in the Spanish way had reduced his ego, could not help hearing.

"Arsenal Club: Citizen Tholosée in the Chair: Report of this evening's meeting: Citizen Tholosée proposed and succeeded in carrying by a show of hands, amid frantic enthusiasm, a resolution calling upon all Clubs in Paris to unite in urging the Chamber to reimpose the death penalty in political crimes, and recommending the Government to erect the people's guillotine in the Place de la Concorde so that this place should be worthy of being called the Place de la Liberté. . . . At the conclusion of the meeting Citizen Tholosée carried a resolution suggesting that the first head to fall in this way should be that of Major Jacques de Touchais, a traitor to France and the Republic."

At once a confusion of shouts, cheers, insults and

fisticuffs ensued. Some cried, "Long live the Major!" others, "Down with the Major!" and others again, "Send Tholosée to a madhouse!" "Set fire to the Arsenal Club!" and what was more important to M. Hilaire, "Duck the Secretary!"

M. Hilaire, who had dropped almost fainting into a seat, found himself, as if by magic, alone. Barkimel and Florent had vanished. Then he was suddenly threatened by a hostile crowd.

"You are the Secretary of the Arsenal Club."

"I?" exclaimed M. Hilaire, and having a brain wave: "I can't even read!"

Unfortunately his pockets were crammed with newspapers, a fact that did not escape notice, and they were not exactly of that shade of political opinion appreciated by the Major's friends.

"Duck him! Duck the Secretary!" was shouted, and a couple of sturdy fellows made a movement to hoist him on their shoulders.

Suddenly a hoarse voice cried:

"Leave my friend alone, please. You're not going to do him any harm, I hope. That's the grocer who supplies me with peanuts for nothing."

"Ah, you should have told us so, Daddy Peanuts."

And they loosed their hold of M. Hilaire, by now more dead than alive.

M. Hilaire gazed at the peanut dealer beside him with unspeakable emotion. He could barely stammer two words in his gratitude, and even so he dared not utter them aloud. "Chér . . .Bib . . . Chér . . . Bib," he whispered with clasped hands and trembling limbs.

"Hush!" said the old man, placing a finger on

his lip. He made a gesture for M. Hilaire to follow him, and gave a hollow laugh.

"Oh, it's his laugh right enough. I recognize his laugh. You can't mistake a laugh like that. There isn't another laugh in the whole world like Chér . . . Bi . . . laugh."

From what infernal region had this ghost of the past returned? M. Hilaire, his body aching and his mind affected, not knowing exactly whether to rejoice or be dismayed by this miraculous encounter, followed the formidable spectre as it crept in the obscurity through the Grand Parc.

CHAPTER XI

AN HISTORIC NIGHT

HISTORY will record the Sunday night that preceded the daring attempt to set up a Dictatorship as among the great "historic nights."

Major Jacques's secret emissaries had informed his principal supporters that they must hold themselves in readiness that night for every contingency. In the Senate President Baruch had a long conference with Michel, Oudard, Barclef, and the big Jew Saroch. The latter told them that an effort to corrupt the patriotic and revolutionary integrity of Flottard, the civilian head of the military Government, had entirely failed.

"We shall know how to do without him," said Baruch to Oudard, breaking into lamentations. "The Major has promised me that at the decisive hour Flottard will not be allowed to leave his house."

Baruch was a wizened, obstinate, little old man who had learned to love the Republic with the staunch and incorruptible Republicans, and had sworn to wrest it from the hands of the revolutionaries and bring it back to the healthy traditions of the good old days when Government was all powerful. To this end he had not hesitated to unite his fortunes, for the time being, with those of a soldier whose assistance was absolutely necessary to him, but he declared to the great Republicans who were in the plot and feared the future while deploring the present, that since he was a party to it the "Republic had nothing to fear."

Jacques had sounded him with a view to his joining the Provisional Government, but Baruch, born artful, declined, preferring to remain at the head of the Senate and thus to safeguard the near future without rousing suspicion. At heart he considered that the reign of the Provisional Government would be of short duration, for the work of revising the Constitution would be carried through without delay, after which the great Republicans, once more masters of the situation, would be free to rid themselves of the temporary duumvirate with more or less good grace according to the attitude adopted by Jacques.

What was Jacques doing that night? Shut up in the mysterious and elegant little room in the house in the Boulevard Pereire with Frederic Héloni, he was giving his last orders to his faithful lieutenant and making his final preparations while

Cravely's police believed them both to be in the Avenue de Jena.

Downstairs in the main room of Little Buddha's Inn a regular bodyguard under various disguises was waiting for him fully armed—a bodyguard which was to escort him to the Chamber and defend him to the death against every attempt to kidnap him, the only danger to be feared from the treachery which he must needs provide against.

But the treachery was to arise from a source that he had not foreseen. It entered the house with Lavobourg on his return with Sonia from the Grand Parc ball.

The car had put down d'Askof at his own door. The unhappy man had excited Sonia's pity, but she was nothing loth to leave him for, she reflected, his part was played, and they had no further use for him. As she had remained seated between Lavobourg and d'Askof during the evening she felt sure that d'Askof knew nothing of the final arrangements which they had mapped out. Moreover, she had complete confidence in Lavobourg, and was glad to see him so resolved to go through with it at the decisive moment.

"It's done," she said on entering the boudoir. "My wrist-bag has reached its destination. The notices convoking the Chamber and Senate are being distributed now."

Jacques thanked her with a motion of his head, continuing to dictate to Frederic Héloni the proclamation which he was to take to the printers immediately the resolution was passed by the two Houses decreeing the revision of the Constitution and the meeting of both Houses in a National Assembly at Versailles. The proclamation was not to be published and posted throughout France until a telephone message was received from the Provisional Government at Versailles.

Just then a knock came at the little secret door behind Sonia's portrait. Jacques himself opened the door slightly, took a letter, reclosed the door, and opened the letter. It was unsigned and typewritten, but bore a number in the corner of the page, and Jacques at once said:

"It's from Mabel!"

He read the letter and then burnt it.

"Excellent. . . . Mabel tells me he is absolutely confident that all the troops at Versailles will follow him. At quarter-past five Mabel will be in a car at the corner of the Place de l'Etoile and the Avenue du Bois. He will wait until six o'clock for the order signed by the President of the Senate entrusting him with the defence of the National Assembly. As soon as he receives it he will set out for Versailles."

"Who's going to take the order to him?" asked Héloni.

"I shall, and I shall go to Versailles with him," returned Jacques.

"Who's going to deliver the President's order to you?"

"You will, Frederic. You will at once go to the Senate and place yourself from now onwards at Baruch's disposal. When the moment comes you will telephone from the Senate to me at the Chamber telling me what has happened in the Upper House. Finally you will bring me Baruch's order

for Mabel as soon as it is in your hands. Do you
follow me?"

"Yes."

"Well, good-bye, Frederic. . . . For if you do
not bring me that order we shall probably not see
each other again until we meet before a firing party
for our execution."

The two men embraced, and Frederic left the
boudoir. Lavobourg was smoking, stretched on a
lounge chair.

"Now that we are alone I may as well tell you
what I think of your proclamation," he said. "I
don't see much good in it."

"What do you mean?" asked Sonia, taken aback.

Jacques stopped and faced Lavobourg. He understood him no more than Sonia did.

"You were wrong, my dear, not to explain yourself before Frederic left," she said, mastering a feeling of ill-temper. "Now it is too late. What is
there in the proclamation to which you object?"

"Nothing—absolutely nothing. I consider it unnecessary—that's all."

"Why—speak out."

"I consider it unnecessary because within five
minutes you will have me assassinated as you had
Carlier assassinated."

Jacques and Sonia started up before him in the
same gesture of surprise and denial.

"Let me finish," said Lavobourg without con-
descending to notice the indescribable agitation
into which he had thrown them. "You will have
me assassinated or else . . ."

"He has lost his head!" exclaimed Jacques.

"Lucien, pull yourself together. Think of the

gravity of the hour, the importance of every moment, and don't talk nonsense," entreated Sonia distractedly.

"Or else," went on Lavobourg, calmly flickering off the ash of his cigarette, "I shall be called upon presently to preside over the Chamber, and as I have determined to do my duty, my whole duty, I swear to you that I will not open the proceedings nor close them until every Deputy has been summoned by me and is free to take part normally in the debates. You see, my dear," he ended, "your proclamation in these circumstances has but a relatively small chance of serving any purpose."

On hearing these words, so terrible in their simplicity, wherein was developed in the clearest language Lavobourg's plan of treachery, a plan which would destroy and bring their efforts to naught when they were in sight of the goal, Jacques and Sonia, who could no longer believe in the madness of this man, looked at each other in anguish, for they realized before he made his meaning clear that his treachery was an act of revenge for their treachery towards him.

"Unless you are a coward, Lavobourg," said Jacques in a hollow voice in which there was less menace than supplication, "and if you have retained some sense of your duty, I will not say towards me, but towards the country which expects its deliverance from you, you will come to the Chamber with me as was agreed and you will know how to silence your personal resentment, however intense and justified you may imagine it to be in this moment of madness, and help me to save the Republic."

"No phrases," exclaimed Lavobourg. "You

dream merely of strangling the Republic. Well, you'll get no assistance from me, and you must make up your mind that you will fail *because of me.* You may possibly do away with me, free me from a life which henceforward will be hateful because you have poisoned it for me. You know quite well what I mean. . . ."

"But we know nothing," cried Sonia. "I swear, Lucien, that your conduct is a mystery to me."

He did not interrupt her nor look at her but waited quietly until her lying and hypocritical protest was over. Then he went on:

"I shall at least have the consolation of destroying your scheme and ruining you." He gave a leer. "I shall rob you of victory. But we shall be quits —you robbed me of my mistress."

"That is false," burst out Sonia, standing erect before him. "And it's a deadly crime of you to think so. . . . Who told you this disgraceful story?"

"Oh, at least be as ashamed of it as your accomplice. Has he offered any denial?"

"That will do! This scene has lasted long enough," said Jacques, suddenly coming to an inflexible resolution. "I will kill you, monsieur."

Lucien sprang to his feet. He had spoken of his death but he had not believed in it. . . .

Jacques had left the room for a moment and now stood before Lavobourg with two swords in his hands. He threw one of them down.

"My death or Lavobourg's"—that was the determination to which he had come. "And if I kill him I will find another President, whatever he may say. But I haven't a moment to lose."

Thus he laid his plans.

Lavobourg was an expert swordsman. He made a rush on the weapon provided for him with all the more frenzy since he had feared for the moment that instead of a sword he would have had to fight with a dagger.

Sonia followed the shifting fortunes of the fight with such intense agony that she groaned with pain as though she herself was being run through by the blade whenever Lavobourg made a lunge at the Major. At one moment after a straight thrust by Lavobourg, who had the advantage of height and reach, she imagined that Jacques would be pinned to the wall, and fell on her knees crying:

"Don't kill him!"

But Jacques parried the stroke, struck up his adversary's sword, and, slipping under it, made a tremendous lunge at Lavobourg, which he avoided only by a quick leap in the rear.

Jacques, resuming the offensive, brought back the fight to the middle of the room, and the mortal struggle continued between the two men amid overturned furniture and Sonia on her knees, gasping for breath, watching with hope and terror the clash of the swords. But Jacques was too eager to make an end of it and Lavobourg grasped that fact. From that moment he changed his tactics. He knew only too well that every moment wasted deprived his adversary of his strength by lessening his self-possession, and he took advantage of the position to play a cautious game which would excite the Major's impatience.

It was for this that he was waiting. Jacques committed a serious fault in recklessly uncovering his guard in order to entice Lavobourg, and Lavobourg, by a solid stop thrust after withdrawing his arm, wounded him in the chest, but fortunately the sword glided off the breast-bone. Jacque's shirt was stained with blood, and Sonia threw herself between the two duellists with a heart-rending moan, but they roughly thrust her aside, and she fell half-fainting to the floor while they took up again their desperate encounter.

Jacques was wounded for the second and third time—in the forearm and face. Each of these blows diffused a rain of blood. His mind, as he fought, was obsessed by too many extraneous things. He was thinking of the Deputies now beginning to arrive at the Palais Bourbon, and feeling that unless he could finish the fight at once all was lost. The blood coursing down his forehead hampered him by obscuring his vision.

He uttered a cry of rage against the injustice of fate in waiting until the last moment thus to turn the scales against him on the very brink of success, and he threw himself on Lavobourg, driven back against the door of Sonia's room, with the fierce determination to risk a thrust in which there was danger of each running the other through. But suddenly the door opened and four huge arms seized and carried off Lavobourg as though he were a feather. Sonia had herself fetched them, and, breathing heavily, she closed the door on Jacques's bodyguard and their prey—the door through which hitherto love alone had entered but which now, perhaps, had opened to assassination.

That was Jacques's first thought when he grasped what had happened and the manner in which he was rid of an enemy whom he had succeeded in bringing down with his own hand.

"Don't kill him," he cried, shaking the door which the men had locked behind them.

"No, no. . . . They won't hurt him—he is our prisoner. Let me dress your wounds and go. . . ."

"You don't know them." And he shouted: "Jean Jean, bind him hand and foot. . . . Gag him, but I shall hold you answerable for his life with your own. . . ."

She pointed to the time by the Buhl clock on the mantelpiece. It was perhaps the only article in the room that had remained standing in the tumult of the battle.

Half-past four!

She drew him into the dressing-room and sought for the wound in his chest. The sword had grazed his ribs, and a great deal of blood had flowed from a hurt in no way serious. She quickly set to work to dress the wound, and he left it to her without uttering a word, for he was collecting his thoughts, laying once more the threads of his snare, loosened for a moment by a stupid interlude.

The cut on his forehead was merely a "muscle caught." He put some sticking plaster on it, drew a lock of hair over it in battle array, gave no heed to the cut on his arm, put on his coat, and hurried to the secret door, followed by Sonia, who gave him, as Lydia had done before, a warm kiss, shouted "Victory!"—and he disappeared.

CHAPTER XII

BARON D'ASKOF'S THIRTEEN PEANUTS

THE reader has not yet made acquaintance with
the home life of Baron and Baroness d'Askof in
their charming flat opposite the Square Monceau.

The most conspicuous figure of the family was
undoubtedly Marie Thérèse, Lydia's friend. She
was a brunette, with a golden rose complexion, a
slightly aquiline profile, a youthful brow expressive
of decision, and large, dark, singularly beautiful
eyes, lacking, however, in softness.

Marie Thérèse's mother was jealous of her daughter. The presence by her side of this beautiful child
who diverted men's adulation from her was beyond all bearing. It was the Baroness's second
marriage which, more especially, had broken every
tie of affection between mother and daughter.

Marie Thérèse could never see d'Askof without
saying something unpleasant to him. She considered him a coxcomb, conceited, disturbing, sly,
formidable. She failed to understand why her
mother allowed herself to be influenced by so inimi-
cal a character; and most of all she could not forgive the haste with which the new union had been
contracted after her father's tragic death. And
when she thought of this incident she scarcely dared
admit to herself that d'Askof was one of the hunting
party and had no scruples. Nevertheless a kind
of truce had been called between mother and daughter during the last few months. Marie Thérèse,
indeed, was now absorbed solely in her own affairs,

and these were summed up in her love for Frederic
Héloni. The young people had met at the houses
of mutual friends, and as Marie Thérèse attended
the same classes as Lydia the two girls soon shared
each other's secrets. . . .

That night Marie Thérèse was discovered by the
Baroness answering Frederic's letter. The altercation between them at once reached a high pitch.

"You tell me that Frederic hasn't a sou, but
d'Askof wasn't a rich man either when you agreed
to marry him. You say Frederic is after my money
. . . d'Askof has taken yours and perhaps some of
mine. . . ."

"I have known for a long time that you are my
worst enemy, and I will send you to a convent
until you are of age."

"Indeed, my dear mother, I would soon escape
from it, I assure you, and let all the world know
that your d'Askof murdered my father at a shoot."

The blow struck home, and Vera was so stunned
by it that she could not at first make any reply.
She cast a bewildered look at her daugher, and a
leaden hue overspread her features a moment before scarlet with fury. At last she recovered sufficient strength and breath to cry:

"Wretched girl! how dare you. . . ."

But it was too late, and her daughter threw in
her face:

"Too late, mother. You have by your demeanor
admitted it. You knew it. . . . You knew it. . . .
I simply suspected it, and you have just admitted it."

"I swear . . ." stammered her mother distractedly.

"Don't swear. Father will hear you. As you
hope to be saved, don't swear! You understand,
mother, that I am not accusing *you*. No, no, anything but that. But it was he who killed him. You
are as convinced of it now as I am. . . . And you
—oh, I don't want to see you again. . . ."

"And I—I have done with you," groaned the
Baroness. . . . "I have a daughter who raves and
makes imputations on her mother—accuses her stepfather—and hates me merely because I begged her
to take time to think before marrying a schemer."

"D'Askof is a murderer and Frederic is an honest
man."

"Let me tell you—let me tell you that you can
marry him to-morrow if you wish. You can please
yourself."

Just then a knock came at the door and the Polish
maid called her mistress. The Baron had come
in and desired to see the Baroness at once. Vera
gave a sigh, turned her distorted face to her daughter and shuffled slowly from the room. The door
was slammed behind her, and she had the feeling
of being thrown out like a dog.

D'Askof was waiting for her in his room. When
their eyes met they scarcely recognized each other.
Though she had become in five minutes ugly and
repellent, her George wore such a look of terror,
the piteous look of an animal hunted to the death,
that it was she who exclaimed first:

"What's the matter with you?"

"Look here—do you know what's happened?"

"No—tell me quickly."

"Well, my dear, I have received thirteen peanuts."

She stared at him as if at first she failed to under-

stand him, and then repeated with a look of stupor
on her face: "Thirteen?   What do you say?   Thirteen?"

"He himself counted them out to me," returned
d'Askof, sinking into a seat beside her on the sofa,
both stricken by an unspeakable, extraordinary
terror.

But this time she had forgotten the scene between her daughter and herself, and nothing mat-
tered to her but the thirteen peanuts.   She wound
her trembling arms round her George's neck.

"What have you done, my poor dear?" she asked,
looking at him as a mother might look at a son condemned to death.

He shrugged his shoulders:

"How do I know?   He will tell me, or get someone to tell me before it's all up with me."

"Hush! don't talk like that.   If you were certain
of it you wouldn't say it.   You know very well he
can't do without you.   You are too useful to him.
Last time he forgave you, and he will forgive you
again."

D'Askof shook his head:

"Last time he warned me.   He told me that it
would be the 'last time,' and you know when he
says a thing he means it.   Besides, what can I do?
There's nothing for it but to wait."

"My poor dear!   My poor dear!   Have you
made no attempt to get away?"

He smiled grimly:

"Where?   Had I not returned home direct I
should have been done for.   Have you forgotten
what happened to Bastard?   As soon as he received
his thirteen he tried to decamp.   Next day his widow

identified his body in the mortuary. No, you see, I have come back here."

"But shall we never get rid of this man?"

"Never."

"But will he never die? Will no one ever make an end of him?"

"Kill him? Why, death is his servant. If you only knew! I haven't told you one-half of what I know about this man, and I am ignorant of so many things that go to make up his power. You wish to be rid of him, but, unhappy woman, by that very fact you are wishing our ruin, for, take it from me, he has provided for every contingency, and he fears no treachery. One day he said to me: 'The day after my death, even if I die a natural death, it will be all over with you and yours!' "

"Oh, the torture of it! Will you never tell me, George, what you did to place yourself in this monster's power?"

"What I did. . . . He had but to open his hands and I fell into them. I wanted money and his hands were full of it."

"But where does he get all his wealth?"

"When a man is in possession of the world's secrets he is in possession of the world's wealth. . . . With his money he bought me, and he has me in his power—always. I have sold my body, soul, mind, heart and hatred to this man—yes, I have sold even the sacred thing, my hatred. . . . Listen, Vera, I must tell you things because who knows if to-morrow I shall be here to talk to you?"

"Hush, George!—you don't believe it, but if it were so I swear that I would know how to avenge you."

He stood erect before her in intense excitement. "Do you think you would, Vera?"

"I would kill him. I would strike him down in such a way that he would know I was avenging you."

"Is that what you call avenging me—cause the death of a man in the ordinary way?"

"Then what would you have me do?"

"You must let him live. . . . What torture, what slow torture will be his if you go the right way to work! . . . I will tell you certain things, and others explaining part of this man's secret you will find in a sealed letter that I will show you. . . ."

Just then a curious sound of whistling could be heard in the street. D'Askof stood up, scared, strode over to the window, lifted the curtain slightly and peered into the night, the impenetrable darkness of the square. Other whistles farther away could be heard seemingly in answer to the first. D'Askof let the curtain fall and returned to Vera shuddering.

"I am well watched," he said. "They are satisfied that while the blow is being struck to-night, and Subdamoun is burgling the Republic, I can't give him away."

An atrocious grin swept over his face as he thought of Lavobourg having to carry out that task alone.

"I am convinced that you have done idiotic things," said Vera, endeavoring to draw a confession from him. "Had you done nothing he would not be keeping an eye on you in this way, nor playing the game of terrifying you with the thirteen peanuts."

"Yes, I have done idiotic things," admitted d'Askof, lighting a cigarette, opening his liqueur stand, and taking out the decanter of vodka. "It was I who gave information to the police which enabled them to lay hands on Jacques's and Lavobourg's papers. You saw that they didn't remain long in Carlier's pocket, and the old man quickly got them back again—and how cleverly! It can't be helped. I lost my head! . . . When I think that that fellow Jacques is going to succeed—the whole country is waiting for him—men, women and the Republic itself are behind him! Oh, Vera, don't you think the whole thing is monstrous?"

"The extraordinary thing to me in this business, you know, George, is that you should show so much hatred for a man who has never done you any harm, and to whom at worst you should have been indifferent. You have never told me why you hate him like this."

"Yes, I have told you a hundred times. . . . Because everyone else admires him."

"Because Sonia Liskinne loves him," corrected Vera, suspicious and jealous.

Then he burst out:

"The moment is come to tell you why I hate him. I hate him because he is—my brother!"

"What do you say?"

"My first secret. It won't be the only one to-day," he added in a low, uneasy voice, "but listen —listen to what is happening in the street."

He hurried back to the window. Three whistles had just sounded anew. More shadowy figures stole quickly up to the garden railings, seeming to meet a small body of men who were running. And then d'Askof could perceive nothing more. Everything was blotted out in the darkness of the night. He dropped the curtain, went over to the writing-table, lifted the panel, and showed Vera a large sealed envelope ingeniously concealed therein.

"The letter I told you about," he explained in a whisper, letting down the panel which concealed the hiding-place.

Vera, staggered by his amazing disclosure, exclaimed:

"His brother! Then are you a de Touchais?"

"The elder brother," returned d'Askof, emptying his glass of vodka. "It is I who should be bearing the title of Marquis. It is mine—mine alone. But he has stolen it from me. Jacques has robbed me of everything. Now do you understand why I hate him?"

"No, I don't understand," returned Vera, shaking her head. "I know he had an elder brother who died in America—and unless you are that brother."

"I am."

"Are you not a d'Askof?"

"You never believed I was."

"I believed everything you cared to tell me—you know that. We women when we love ask only to be loved, and all else matters very little. There is but one crime in our eyes—unfaithfulness in the man we love. . . . Never mind that, dearest, tell me your story. Don't be afraid—because I love you just as you are. . . . You Jacques's brother! Why, you are not a bit like him."

"No, I am not a bit like him. I thank you for

those words. I believe he is a bastard—and it means that a bastard has stolen my position, my rank . . ."

"And your fortune."

"No, I myself squandered the fortune. I had to have my revenge, eh? . . . If you only knew how a boy, spoilt as I was by an unhappy mother, can suffer when he suddenly sees his mother's caresses diverted from him, a grown-up lad, and lavished on the new-comer, the little unexpected belated brother who all in a moment becomes the idol of the house! . . .

"But to cut short this early period of my life you must know that one fine day I went for him with a spade and nearly killed him. Then they packed me off, they banished me to England. From that day to this my mother and brother have never set eyes on me. They might meet, and even know, Baron d'Askof, but, you understand, Bernard— that was my name—is dead to them. I went from England to America, and there I squandered in business in general, and in one or two things in particular in which my brother's honor was involved, pretty well the whole fortune. . . .

"What my life at that time was you who know me can imagine. I stopped at nothing. I felt an unholy joy in knowing that every one of my new —let me say new contrivances—was striking a blow at them in France, rending them, ruining them; and I was dreaming in San Francisco of a final stroke which should dishonor for ever the name of de Touchais, when suddenly a miserable-looking old man called on me. . . .

"This poor old man—you recognize him—was *he*. It was the man whom every one calls Daddy Pea-nuts."

"But his real name—his real name," cried Vera.

"Don't ever wish to know his name. . . . You will not know it until I am dead. Then you will open the letter that I have shown you and learn definitely who he is."

"And you put yourself in this man's power?"

"Yes, and when he left my place with my signa-ture I knew that I had become the slave of one of those diabolical characters wielding sufficient power to influence the fate of the world."

"But who was he? In whose power had you put yourself?"

"When for the first time I was obliged to speak of the peanut dealer. . . ."

"It was the first time I saw you looking so pale and worn out. . . ."

"It meant that it was the first time I had roused his anger. And I had to confess to you, I had to tell you that my life depended upon this man, that he was the master of my secrets, the agent of a for-midable political league which in my hour of need I had agreed to join and which I was compelled blindly to obey. Now I lied to you when I spoke of a political league. The man to whom I sold myself is the King of the Convict Settlement."

"What do you say!" exclaimed Vera, more and more distracted. "What do you mean by the King of the Convict Settlement?"

"I mean that he is something like the head of the criminal classes of the world. Listen, Vera. . . . There have always been at all times—not only in fiction but in history—beings in every country who have found themselves at the head of the world's outlaws, around whom all those who have sold their souls to the devil have gathered together in the shadows—condemned criminals, outcasts no longer possessing the power to kill or rob without concealment because they have been caught once.   This prodigious gang, scattered and hidden in the underworld, disguised under false occupations or false names, submits to a leader, the King of the Convict Settlement.   *Le Dab du Pré,* as these bandits say in their own language.

"It is he who keeps the cash box, sends money when it is needed, collects it when the harvest is ripe.   It is he who in the supposed interests of all does away at his own sweet will with those who refuse to obey him.

"His men never fail him, his satellites never weaken.   Crime brings him new recruits every year. And his recruiting is done systematically. . . .   It is wonderful. . . .

"And who leads this army of evil?   He does.   Do you follow me?   He alone knows precisely what has become of his men, continues to keep an eye on them, imposes a tax on their gains and fears.   He helps and terrifies them in turn."

"But what made you agree to become a wheel in this awful piece of mechanism?"

"Oh, I was the principal wheel! . . .   He proposed that I should be his right-hand man.   It was the display of his power, made, Heaven knows, with such arrogance, that lured me on.   And then, my dear, had I not agreed there would have been an end of it.   I saw for myself that after such a pro-

posal he would not have allowed me to enjoy life
for long. . . .

"Moreover, as I told you, I had reached a crisis
in my life when all is lost unless the devil comes
to the rescue. He came! And in point of fact he
only needed one formidable, terrible thing from me."

"What do you mean?"

"I am coming to that, to the mystery of mysteries, which will be my third and last secret. He
needed my services only to build up the triumph of
my brother."

"That is what I find so impossible to understand,"
said Vera. "Why did he appeal to you, Jacques's
brother, to secure the triumph of Jacques, whom
you hate?"

"He wanted to punish me for my hatred. He
afterwards told me so himself. He wanted to penal-
ize me for nearly killing Jacques one day in a boyish
quarrel, and indeed he could not have contrived
a more subtle form of torture."

"But what is Jacques to this man?"

"I will tell you what he said to me one day in one
of those outbursts of ungovernable fury which made
this man such a formidable and hideous sight. It
was one day after I had declared that I had not
become a d'Askof to work any longer for the honor
of a de Touchais. He took me in his arms—in his
arms, you understand—but not to embrace me, I
can assure you. At first I thought he was going to
smother me. He held me as in a vice, and I feared
lest the vice should squeeze the life out of me. . . .
But suddenly he threw me with the force of a cata-
pult into a corner and spluttered: 'You will work
all your life at that job and others as well. . . .

All your life for having dared to touch a hair of Jacques's head—all your life for bringing sorrow to Cecily!'

"He did not say the Marchioness, but Cecily. If you only knew the tone of voice in which he spoke! I had never heard him speak like that before. And the wretch was shedding tears—yes, I saw tears in the eyes of the King of the Convicts! He walked away. The manner in which he spoke of Jacques and Cecily gave me food for thought. I have already told you that the Marchioness de Touchais, though married and a good mother, had not always lived happily with my father. Well, I began to look up this period of the de Touchais history. I got up the facts. . . .

"I made enquiries, exercising some caution, as you may believe. I reckoned things up, I made deductions, and I dared to draw certain conclusions. My mother, a Frenchwoman—her maiden name was Bourelier—a rich young girl, but belonging to the people, might have had, as the saying goes, a 'best boy' in the district before she married—some poor fellow who may have been madly in love with the young lady in the Villa de la Falaise. . . . She got married, became a Marchioness, and was as wretched as could be. The poor fellow during this time had 'been in trouble,' afterwards returning to the district. I am convinced that he saw my mother again. But how? Under what name, under what disguise? How did he manage to become friends with her? That is the mystery, the momentous, unfathomable mystery. And I cannot tell you more about that young man because here I come up against the secret to disclose which is punishable with death, but which you will find set down in my letter—if I am to die. . . .

"Well, Vera, it is in this fact that your power to obtain a startling revenge consists. You will have but to throw the name contained in the letter in Jacques's teeth publicly. He will fall never to rise again. And it will be the death of Daddy Peanuts. . . ."

"You believe then? . . ."

"I believe Jacques is his son. I not only believe it, I am convinced of it."

Once more d'Askof, breathing heavily, stood up, his limbs shaking under him. From the street the sound of a long-drawn-out whistle could be heard, a kind of tremolo, fantastic and ominous.

"The whistle of death," he murmured. "He knows when we are thinking of betraying him, and he tells us by that whistle of death how dearly we shall pay for it. But all said, he cannot make away with me. After my death he would miss the joy of making me suffer. He can't do without that."

Vera took time to think over all that she had been told.

"The extraordinary part is that no one has ever, if not denounced, at least put the police on him," she said.

"My dear child, denounce him to the police! People have denounced him to the police twenty times. Not only men of his own gang, but official informers and also respectable citizens alarmed by his behavior, and even policemen considering his movements suspicious—these people have waited on Cravely, the Chief of the Detective Service, and described the old man to him. Cravely, after thank-

ing them, has sent for Daddy Peanuts and said:
'Take care, Cartel, you are being found out. People are beginning to suspect you. . . .'

"But, my dear Vera, Daddy Peanuts forms part
of Cravely's police. He is his chief informer. He
has given him plenty of proofs of his usefulness.
He has betrayed plenty of ex-convicts who have
ceased to do his bidding. Daddy Peanuts is
Cravely's most valuable assistant. Do you know
what he is to Cravely? Why, a convict, called
Cartel, escaped from the penal settlement. Do you
see the point? . . .

"And don't you think it very clever, eh? Cartel,
sentenced to twenty years in the penal settlement
for swindling and attempted murder, returns to
France and offers his services to the Chief of the
Detective Department, and at once does such good
work that Cravely leaves it to him to keep watch
over Major Jacques! Thereupon Daddy Peanuts
furnishes Major Jacques with two stalwarts, Jean
Jean and Polydore, who stick to him like a leech,
and, moreover, served under him in Subdamoun.
. . . Well, Daddy did not hide from Cravely that
those fellows were themselves escaped convicts, and
on the plea of keeping watch on the Major they
are guarding him for the police, which they dream
of joining as a means of settling down. . . .

"And that will explain to you, my dear, why no
one laid hands on the two sailors, notwithstanding
their somewhat brutal intervention in the Chamber
when they rushed into the hemicycle to defend the
Major."

"Oh, it's very ingenious," exclaimed Vera, at last
convinced.

"Ingenious is the word, dearest. No! Nothing can be done against him. One can only count one's thirteen peanuts, listen to the whistle of death, and wait here for the lightning stroke which is perhaps to strike one down. Denounce him to Cravely! You can imagine how Cravely would laugh. There is but one thing that could prevent Cravely from laughing—if, for instance, he receive the letter which is here"—he pointed to the spot where it was concealed—"and you must take it to him, Vera."

"Why not at once?"

"Because we should have nothing to do but disappear. . . . Wait, therefore, until I am gone. This letter cannot save, but it can avenge me in the hands of a person who knows that once her revenge is effected she must die. . . ."

CHAPTER XIII

TO LOVE—TO DIE

THEY remained silent for some moments, and then Vera could not repress a disconsolate moan.

"What a terrible night," she cried, sweeping her hand over her distraught face, aged in a few hours by ten years. "Do you know what Marie Thérèse said to me before you came in? She accused you of murdering her father at a shoot."

"No!"

"Oh, how she detests you!"

"Well, of course she does if she thinks I murdered her father," returned d'Askof, coolly. "The idea scarcely surprises me, and I have often read

it in her black looks. But after all, she never put
it into words. What on earth came over her to-
day?"

"I caught her reading and writing love-letters."

"To whom? From whom?"

"Frederic."

"Frederic Héloni?"

"Yes. She is infatuated with that youth and
wants to marry him. At my first word of objection
she treated me to an amazing outburst, taunting
me with my second marriage and your crime. . . .
That is the word she used."

"Indeed. Never mind. What then?"

"Then I threatened to send her to a convent, and
seeing that she was up in arms I ended by telling
her that she could marry whom she pleased, for
after all I don't care one way or the other."

The Baron gave his most wicked smile.

"These young people are mad," he said. "The
sight of an officer's tunic turns their heads. Mlle
de la Morlière is in love with Jacques, Marie
Thérèse is in love with Frederic. It's very pretty,
touching, idyllic. If they only knew how these beautiful officers in reality are making game of them and
are only after their money!"

"Can you prove it?"

"I have the proofs in my pocket. Here they are."

D'Askof drew from his pocket-book the elegant
little sachet containing Jacques's letters to Sonia
Liskinne which he had picked up from the table
in the boudoir. He passed them over to Vera, who
could not conceal her delight as she read them.

"But this is all we want," she cried. "When one
reads these letters it is impossible to doubt the ties

that bind Jacques and Sonia together. And as for Frederic, here are three notes that are absolutely clear. . . . The foursome in the country, eh? Jacques and Sonia, Frederic and Lucienne Drice, the actress, and these words from Jacques: 'Fortunately, Lucienne was absorbed in Frederic and unable to hear our conversation.' Oh, the poor darlings!"

"Vera, I will lend you these letters. You must show them to Marie Thérèse, and Marie Thérèse must show them to Lydia. This is how you must set about it: Marie Thérèse is sure to ask you to leave them with her for a few hours. She is very religious. You will have to make her swear on the crucifix to return them after showing them to Lydia. You must make her swear, too, not to show them to anyone else. . . . Go now, Vera. I shall be waiting for you."

The Baroness did not need to be asked a second time. She gathered the letters together, put them in the sachet, and hastened to her daughter's room.

The interview did not take long.

The moment her mother was gone Marie Thérèse dressed, opened her door and listened. Hearing no sound, she slipped into the passage and thence to the entrance lobby. The key was in the door. Soon she was on the landing. Descending the stairs, she asked the concierge to open the door, and went out. An empty cab was passing the corner of the street. She hailed it, and gave the driver the address of the Marchioness de Touchais.

Some minutes later she rang the bell of the porter's lodge in the de Touchais's courtyard. The con-

cierge woke up and looked through the wicket. It
was half-past three in the morning.

"I must see Mlle de la Morlière at once," she
said, and as the man stood there dumbfounded, trying to understand, she went on: "If you won't let
me in, send her word by Mlle Jacqueline, but whatever you do don't disturb the Marchioness."

"Well, we'll see about that. Come in," he said,
half opening one of the wings of the carriage entrance, and closing it carefully again he added:
"Mlle Jacqueline gets up every morning at four
o'clock to go to Mass at St. Paul's, which is at five
o'clock. We shall only be taking half an hour from
her sleep. Please wait here."

Two minutes later he returned and beckoned her
to follow him. The aged Jacqueline, wrapped in a
long shawl, her eyes still swollen with sleep, stood
waiting at the door of her room apprehensive, bewildered.

"What's the matter?" she asked, showing her in.

"Let me go to Lydia at once, my dear Jacqueline."

"Hush! Not so loud. What is it? Heavens,
are you bringing us bad news? What makes you
come at this hour?"

"Calm yourself, Jacqueline, it's only my own
affairs. I don't want to go back to my parent's flat.
I want to put myself under the protection of the
Marchioness and my dear Lydia. If you only knew
how miserable I am, Jacqueline! Let me see Lydia
at once, will you?"

"Wait here. . . . I'll go and tell her. . . . What
a pity!"

She drew the shawl closely round her and left

the room. Soon she returned, and showed Marie
Thérèse to Lydia's room, and, telling them that she
had to dress for Mass at five o'clock, left them.

Lydia remained seated on her bed. She was unable to say a word when Marie Thérèse came in.
She stared at her without understanding, but feared
lest some terrible calamity had happened. Marie
Thérèse closed and locked the door. Then she
went over to Lydia, who could now see her deathly
pallor. She hadn't the strength to question her, and
Marie Thérèse said simply:

"I want to die with you."

"Are *they* dead?" exclaimed the unhappy child,
pressing her hand to her heart.

"No, Lydia, they are not dead, but they no longer
love us. . . ."

"Oh, was it to tell me this that you came here so
early?"

"Yes, and to show you this. You will be able to
say if it is really Jacques's writing. . . . I thought
I recognized it."

"And I recognize that scent."

Lydia turned over in her trembling hands the
sachet bearing Sonia's initials. Marie Thérèse,
losing patience, drew the letters from the bag and
ruthlessly read in a low breathless voice: "My
dear Sonia . . ."

She read them all while Lydia, stretched on her
bed, her great eyes filled with tears, stared at her.
And she wept for her shattered love, her young life
spoilt, for she knew that she would never survive
the blow. But it was to no purpose that Marie
Thérèse tried to get her to glance through the letters. She refused:

"I have no need to recognize his writing," she said. "I know his phrases. He used to tell me, too, that 'there was no one like me.' Marie Thérèse, how are we going to die?"

"I thought it would be quite easy," returned Marie Thérèse, gently placing her arm under her friend's head. "You have gas here, and we have only to remain in the room and turn on the taps."

"Yes, that's a good idea," said Lydia. "As it happens, Jacqueline always turns on the main every morning to make some coffee for herself before going to Mass. When she returns we shall certainly be dead if only we send her on one or two errands."

Marie Thérèse kissed Lydia affectionately, then, taking the sachet and letters, went over to the writing-desk standing in a corner of the room.

"What are you doing?" asked Lydia.

"I'm writing a message for Jacqueline. I promised my mother to return these letters to Baron d'Askof. I am going to put them in an envelope with the sachet and when Jacqueline leaves church she will take them home."

"Was it your stepfather who discovered the correspondence?" asked Lydia.

"Yes. It's the first time he has done me a good turn. Oh, and what else do you think I learnt to-night? I learnt that the Baron killed my father at a shoot. My mother knew it, and I told her so. She hadn't the strength to deny it—at any rate it was a very weak denial. So you can understand why I have had enough of life. . . . To live with people like that or risk being married to a—Frederic Héloni!"

"Don't let's speak ill of our fiancés, my dear,"

interrupted Lydia in her gentlest tones. "We were so much in love with them. I—I think I still love Jacques. . . ."

"Then let me die alone. You have friends. Jacques's family has adopted you, the Marchioness loves you as a daughter, and you can still be happy. But I have no one, and I don't love Frederic any more. . . . Let me die alone."

"Why do you say that, my dear? It is because I still love Jacques that I wish to die."

She had the strength to get up, drag herself to the desk, take the seat that Marie Thérèse after enclosing the sachet and letters in an envelope gave up to her. She opened a drawer, drew out a withered flower which she had placed in it the evening when Jacques first spoke the soft language of love to her —the flower whose perfume she had inhaled that evening as it lay in the button-hole of his dinner jacket—that evening when they had vowed eternal love. . . . She bent over the desk and wrote in a hand rendered almost firm by despair:

"You thought you loved me, but you loved only fame. It has kept me too long in expectation, and now you have forgotten me. Good-bye, dearest, good-bye for ever. I forgive you. . . . Keep this flower in remembrance of me as I was keeping it in remembrance of my love."

She signed her name and a tear-drop fell. She slipped the flower into the envelope, sealed it, and wrote: "To be delivered by hand to Jacques de Touchais, Avenue de Jena."

"That's done," said Lydia, passing the envelope to Marie Thérèse. "Take the letters yourself to Jacqueline and tell her to deliver them after Mass."

"Suppose I, too, write a line to Frederic," said Marie Thérèse, suddenly. "I want him to know one thing—that it is he who has killed me and I cannot forgive him."

She wrote:

"Frederic—You and Jacques by your conduct have taken away from us the desire to live. So good-bye, and may you be happy with those ladies. A last word of advice: Don't enter Lydia's room with a light."

CHAPTER XIV

CHÉRI-BIBI AND THE DODGER

M. HILAIRE followed the peanut dealer as he slowly started to walk along the quays. It could not have been far from three o'clock in the morning.

Strange forms suddenly appeared and disappeared in the darkness, brushing against Daddy Peanuts apparently in no way surprised at anything but jogging along steadily, his keg under his arm, with the aspect of an old woman returning home with her shopping. On the other side of the water strange sounds of whistles rang out as though signalling and answering each other. The night was ominous with mystery. M. Hilaire longed to be sleeping peacefully in his bed.

And yet he had just met Chéri-Bibi once more. It was Chéri-Bibi right enough. He could no longer doubt it; and his last words about cod prepared in the Spanish way with which in the old days he used to regale his friend positively confirmed his suspicions.

Chéri-Bibi, whom he had so greatly loved, whose death he had so long mourned, was still alive! How came it then that M. Hilaire's heart was not filled with an unspeakable joy? . . .

Chéri-Bibi, morally and physically deteriorated, was but a wreck of his old self. Truth to tell, M. Hilaire, in the depths of his inner consciousness, scarcely dared confess as much. Would it not have been better for Chéri-Bibi to have met an heroic and splendid death in the fire at La Falaise, in the smoking ruins of the de Touchais's house, or in the convict settlement when he returned to it, rather than come to life again before the troubled eyes of the Dodger—Hush! said M. Hilaire to himself —in the pitiable carcass of a peanut dealer?

"See how the poor fellow hobbles along!" apostrophized M. Hilaire under his breath. "It is enough to make one cry! He must be crippled with rheumatism. Why didn't he come to see me before? Of course, because he was ashamed. . . . I will make him a small allowance without telling Mme Hilaire. Poor Chéri-Bibi! . . . But where's he going? . . . Ah, we're entering the historic alley."

M. Hilaire recognized the historic alley. It was here that the Duc d'Orleans was assassinated in the days of the Armagnacs. . . . They were now in the Francs Bourgeois quarter, M. Hilaire's quarter.

When M. Hilaire came to the end of the alley, lit dimly by the pale gleam of the moon, he raised his head and saw Daddy Peanuts deep in talk with a youth wearing a peak cap over a little curl flattened down on his forehead, whose very appearance

caused M. Hilaire such unutterable repugnance.
"That's the sort of person he mixes with now."

The youth was standing between the shafts of a
handcart heavily laden with two sacks. The youth
had dragged the cart so far and was apparently
waiting for orders. It was then that Daddy Peanuts gave a shrill whistle which caused M. Hilaire
to hasten up from the semi-darkness as he used to
do in the old days when Chéri-Bibi called him for
some urgent piece of work. M. Hilaire did not realize the pathetic spontaneity of his gesture until he
was close to him. He reddened in the darkness, and
Daddy Peanuts began to laugh in disagreeable little
jerks, grinding his teeth, for they were all still sound,
between his terrible jaws.

"Well done, M. Hilaire!"

M. Hilaire gave a start and took a step back.
Clearly Chéri-Bibi would compromise him, and he
had a mind to whisper: "No names—I live in these
parts." But after what he had just seen it was unnecessary to tell Chéri-Bibi that he lived in that
quarter!

"We have never met because he starts off to sell
his peanuts at a time when I am going to bed."

"M. Hilaire, let me introduce you to young
Mazeppa, employed at a coffee house, where his
duty is to empty the dregs of brandy from the
glasses. Between whiles he does jobs for me. He
has just brought me a couple of sacks of peanuts,
and I will ask you to help me unload them for
Mazeppa is in a hurry and his boss wants him. Can
I rely on you, M. Hilaire?"

"Yes, yes. . . . Why, of course."

M. Hilaire did not know what to do with himself. It was very different when Mazeppa, after touching his cap respectfully to Daddy Peanuts, shook M. Hilaire's hand as though he were a real pal. . . .

Chéri-Bibi set him to work. With his assistance he had to lift up one of the sacks. He would never have believed that a sack of peanuts was so heavy. The extraordinary part was that he bent under the load while Chéri-Bibi lifted it without apparent effort. "Hullo," he thought, "he is not so worn out as I assumed."

Daddy Peanuts opened the low door of his cellar, for he lived here, and led the way.

"Mind you don't break your neck," he warned in his hoarse voice. "That once happened in this spot in days gone by to the Duc d'Orleans. It won't do to have the same thing over again. What? . . . Look out for the steps. There's ten of 'em to go down, and we are on the first floor!"

They were in murky darkness. M. Hilaire was sweating and puffing. . . .

"You're getting old, Dodger," grunted the old man.

"Hush!"

"Beg your pardon, M. Hilaire."

"Do shut up!"

"Well, what do you want me to call you?"

"Nothing."

A kind of roar broke forth in the darkness and M. Hilaire let fall his sack, which rolled down without him.

"Get upstairs!" said the voice.

M. Hilaire mounted the steps backwards as though to repel the attack of the shadowy figure.

He reached the level of the valley safe and sound. But the terrible form of the peanut dealer showed up almost at once in the moonlight. He was shaking with rage. He went over to the handcart, whose shafts pointed heavenwards as though in supplication, and with a simple effort and a "Ha!" of hideous pride, threw the second sack of peanuts on his back and, turning to M. Hilaire, pointed to the end of the lane where the wan light of a street lamp flickered.

"Beat it!" he ordered, and plunged into his cellar with the heavy burden of the sack on his shoulders, thrusting back with a contemptuous kick the door behind him, which closed and cut him off from his companion.

M. Hilaire hung about the door, shook the latch, gave vent to the most pitiable moans, and uttered words of infinite softness, for he was sincerely repentant. He understood Chéri-Bibi's wrath and his own unworthiness. And he begged forgiveness. "Chéri-Bibi, I am sorry," he wailed. "Open the door. . . . Open your heart to me. It's the Dodger imploring you. It's your servant, monsieur le Marquis, at your feet."

He was unable to continue his speech; emotion choked him, tears deluged his eyes, and he was certainly on the verge of collapse in his despair when the low door opened once more, a hand clutched him as he stood on the pavement in misery and remorse, drew him into the underground cellar, into this dark cave, where suddenly he felt himself in powerful arms that held him close to a heart beating fiercely to the rhythm of the noblest friendship —the friendship that can forgive! . . .

"My dear Hilaire!   Are you still fond of me?"

"Why, of course I am.   Ah, monsieur le Marquis!"

"No, no.   Call me Chéri-Bibi as in the old days."

"Why, of course I am fond of you, Chéri-Bibi—
I mean I have never been so fond of you.   My life,
all I possess is yours—they belong to you.   Command me as you did of old."

"Of old!   Oh, my Dodger of old!   There let
me cry, old man. . . .   Do you remember when
we walked down the sloping road to Dieppe for the
first time?   We arrived at Le Pollet, and I pointed
out the butcher's shop where I served my apprenticeship and learnt how to use the knife!"

"I should think I do remember, monsieur le Marquis.   How excited you were when you saw the
shop front.   You said: 'It's the same old place.   I
recognize the "bleeder" and the "gambrel."   Here
you can always get pork. . . .' "

"And when the Marchioness, my sweet and kind-hearted Cecily, used to wait for us and greet us
from the distance by waving her lace handkerchief."

"With one hand, monsieur le Marquis, for with
the other she held your boy in her arms!"

The revival of that memory was followed by a
silence charged with emotion.   Each was thinking
with regret of those days.

"Come, we must be sensible.   There, let me light
a candle.   Don't stir.   You might break your leg."

Soon a modest light shone in Chéri-Bibi's hand,
and he showed M. Hilaire round his apartments.
They were somewhat depressing, bare, musty.   Real
cellars!   Cellars with furniture of so crude a character   that M. Hilaire, who possessed a real Louis

Philippe mahogany bedroom suite, turned up his nose. He sighed.

"My dear Dodger, you think all this very poverty-stricken. That's because I haven't shown you everything. Come, now you shall see my riches."

He took a bunch of keys and opened a door hidden behind the wooden wall at the end of a damp passage. Then he lighted six candles. . . . M. Hilaire started back, dazzled.

The walls of this little cellar, now resplendent with light, were covered with portraits of a woman and child. But such wonderful portraits! Never even on the walls of Byzantine churches had so many jewels, pearls, necklaces been suspended with more loving care round an ikon of the Virgin and Child. They were portraits of Cecily in the happiest days of her beauty and motherhood, and of Jacques from babyhood onwards.

"Ah yes, I always said that you were a family man," exclaimed M. Hilaire, touched to the heart by the wonderful sight.

"I have never wanted anything but to live quietly with my wife and son as a good husband and father," returned the old man, "and it's not my fault if things have worked out differently."

M. Hilaire began to think that if all the jewels on those walls were genuine then the cellar contained a very respectable fortune.

"All the money I make goes in this," said Daddy Peanuts, answering M. Hilaire's unspoken thought.

M. Hilaire gave a start. He reflected that it could not be by the sale of peanuts that the old man was able to afford the luxury of presenting such jewels to his wife and son.

Chéri-Bibi stood entranced before the portraits.

"I never fail to give *these portraits* a little present on their patron saint's days and birthdays, and whenever I see a date in the calendar reminding me of some happy event in the good old days. . . . My dear wife, my dear son! . . . Look here, Dodger, I am going to show you something."

While speaking he opened a chest and went on:

"When I learned of his intention to join the army I was as proud as could be. . . . It was splendid. A de Touchais! A de Touchais must needs be a soldier—a dashing officer with a fine sword. . . . And I presented him with his first sword. There, you see his first sword! . . . Now I'm going to show you something else. Here's the cross of the Legion of Honor. I must tell you that I presented it to him long before the Government did. I sent the cross anonymously to his mother, explaining that one of her son's admirers would be glad if she would accept the gift and herself pin it on his breast. . . . You can imagine my thoughts as I waited for her reply. . . . Alas, the reply soon came. Cecily returned the cross, saying that she could not accept it from an unknown person. I didn't get over it for a week. . . . She probably regarded the cross as too costly. . . . Look at those diamonds. Ah, how sorry I was. My son is the cleverest, handsomest, strongest, of them all. . . . He'll hold the Republic in the hollow of his hand. He'll be a king. I am having a crown made for him in Paris by the best jeweller in the Rue de la Paix. . . . Besides, I'll tell you something else—something beyond expression. *I see Cecily every day.*"

"You see Cecily. . . . You see the Marchioness every day?"

"As plainly as I see you now, my dear Hilaire."

"But she never goes out."

"Oh, you know that, do you. Well, perhaps she is at home to me."

"She is at home to you."

"As you'll see, I am only joking. But there, stand on this bench, look through this little grated opening and tell me what you see."

"I see a garden in the moonlight with two old moss-grown stone benches, ivy-clad walls, and grass-grown paths—a cheerless little garden."

"It is not a cheerless little garden when she comes here for a walk. It seems to me then as big as the wide world," murmured Chéri-Bibi.

"Does she live there?" asked the Dodger. "I have called at La Morlière house sometimes, but I didn't know this side of it looking on to the garden."

"You see, my dear Dodger, since God gave me this little cellar window I can refuse him nothing."

"Who gave it to you?"

"God. He can ask me to commit every crime of which he stands in need. He is sure to get them done."

M. Hilaire, much easier now as to Chéri-Bibi's health, began to have a little less pity for him while feeling much of the terrified admiration of the old days; but after what he had just heard he could not entirely shake off a feeling of apprehension as far as he himself was concerned. Thus it was not without a certain agitation that he heard the question, though it was put in pleasant tones:

"And you, my dear Hilaire, what has happened to you?"

They were now back in the cellar, standing between a truckle bed, an old desk with three legs, and the two sacks of peanuts lying in a corner.

"Well, things have not been too bad," returned M. Hilaire with a somewhat ingenuous smile.

"What about Virginie? Is she still difficult to put up with?" asked Chéri-Bibi.

"Tut! Tut!"

"But after all she doesn't make you too miserable? As I brought about the marriage I should never forgive myself if she did. And then you know—you've only got to say the word—I'd soon send her to kingdom come."

M. Hilaire started to his feet in dismay.

"Heavens, monsieur le Marquis, don't lay hands on my wife."

"Come now, I don't in the least want to interfere."

"If anything happened to her she'd haunt me every night. I know her. . . . Oh, monsieur le Marquis, don't frighten me. What can you have been thinking of? Why, we've got on very well together since our last troubles. We are looked upon by the neighbors as a model couple. Now and then we have a little difference of opinion. But in every household there are moments of impatience."

"Of course."

"And as long as I do what she tells me and let her have her own sweet will she ends by giving way to me."

"Good old Virginie!"

"Oh, she has her good qualities. She looks after

the money. There's no one like her for keeping accounts. And she is faithful to me."

"And are you faithful to her?"

"I swear I am, monsieur le Marquis. I have never forgotten your principles in this respect, and I should have been the vilest of wretches had I not profited by your precepts and example."

"I am glad to hear it, friend Dodger," returned Chéri-Bibi seriously with obvious satisfaction. He had never jested on the subject of morals.

"But I must tell you my wife is so domineering— for she is domineering—that she has made me take up politics in spite of myself," said M. Hilaire, and he coughed.

"Well, my dear fellow, she was quite right. In these troublous times no one is entitled to refuse to interest himself in public affairs."

"Since that is your opinion I am glad that Virginie is at one with you," murmured M. Hilaire, wiping the beads of perspiration trickling down his forehead.

"So your wife wished you to take up politics? I suppose she is ambitious for you?"

"Yes, monsieur le Marquis," returned M. Hilaire, growing more and more embarrassed. "She wants to see me a municipal councillor."

"Well done! We will help you in that, I give you my word. It will be better than wasting your time in a club."

"O Lord, I hope he'll never know that I am the Secretary of the Arsenal Club," groaned M. Hilaire under his breath; and as he suddenly recalled the extract from the evening paper, read out at the ball in the Grand Parc—the extract that told of the work

being done that night and the passing of the resolution demanding the death penalty against Major
Jacques—he was seized with a sort of weakness.

"Come, Dodger, are you ill?"

"No, no. I felt a slight giddiness. I suffer from
it occasionally."

"You do yourself too well," said Chéri-Bibi.
"You must be careful. Do you live far from here,
my boy?"

"No, not very far. I might almost say next
door."

"Wait a bit! Ah, so that's it. The 'Up-to-date
Grocery Stores'! You, Hilaire, are the owner of
those splendid grocery and provision stores."

"That's my shop."

"I congratulate you. You have got on in the
world since you lived in the Rue St. Roch. . . .
Now, my dear Dodger, let's be serious, but first lend
me a hand in emptying these two sacks of peanuts."

With one movement the old man drew the truckle
bed towards him, disclosing a trap-door in the
brickwork floor of the century-old building. He
pulled back the flap. . . . A cold, damp current of
air swept into the wretched cellar and the guggle-
guggle of a kind of underground waterway could be
heard.

"Whatever you do, don't come too near. The
water flows into the deeps and is lost somewhere or
other in the catacombs—a waterway that appears
and disappears, plunges anew underground, carrying with it whatever is committed to its charge and
never giving it up again! . . . Let it have a few
peanuts, Dodger."

Chéri-Bibi's peculiar language was not calculated to reassure M. Hilaire.

"Look! Take hold of the sack by one of the ends as I am doing, lift it, shake it, and pull it back. There! As you see, it's easy enough."

The horror of it! Out of the sack, with a large quantity of peanuts, slid a dead body. And M. Hilaire recognized the fiery anarchist so full of life and ardor who that very morning was tempestuously orating from a table in the Francs Archers Club. M. Hilaire dropped the empty sack.

Chéri-Bibi with the tip of his boot rolled the body to the edge of the trap-door, it toppled over, and was lost to sight. A few seconds later a dull "flop" was heard—it was the end of that man!

It was in vain that Chéri-Bibi strove to obtain the Dodger's help for the second sack. . . . He stood like a statue of terror. Therefore Chéri-Bibi emptied the sack himself, and a second dead body slid out with the peanuts. This time M. Hilaire recognized his friend Tholosée of the Arsenal Club. He fell on his knees clasping his hands, affrighted.

Chéri-Bibi closed the trap-door with his foot. Apparently he had finished his work of death for that day. But he gazed with pity on the sorry object gasping for breath in a corner of his hovel.

"Why are you groaning?" he asked in a hideously calm voice. "What matters a few specimens of humanity? Come, stand up, Dodger. Summon up the heart and pluck of the old days. Look at me and don't trust to appearances. See, I am as physically strong and more terrible than ever."

While speaking the old man drew himself up, his

limbs unbent, his stature increased, his chest and shoulders and bust expanded in all their splendid fullness; the muffler covering his face fell away, and above the body of a Titan a head appeared, diabolic, glowing with the burning furnace of Chéri-Bibi's eyes—eyes set free for the nonce from their tinted spectacles.

"Why do you start back in fear?" asked Chéri-Bibi, proudly folding his arms across his chest. "You used not to be afraid of me, and your friendly talk was my one consolation in those hours of fatality. Come, get up, the hour has struck again! My services are still needed. . . . God seeing one day how much evil would have to be done so that good might come shrank from so great a responsibility and created Chéri-Bibi!"

He was like some monstrous, some prodigious spectre of the spirit of evil . . . and then it all vanished as if by magic. M. Hilaire saw before him only the mean-looking old man, who turned to him and said:

"By the way, M. Hilaire, how comes it that you haven't yet spoken of your duties at the Arsenal Club?"

M. Hilaire remained silent. M. Hilaire, who had already suffered so great a strain in the course of this historic night, was unable to utter a syllable. He was stifling.

"The Ar . . . the Arsenal Club. . . . It was not my doing. . . . It was Virginie who insisted on it. I was elected a member of the Club, put on the Committee, made Secretary, but I had absolutely nothing to do with it."

"What about your speeches?"

"Oh, my speeches. . . . Lord, my speeches," returned M. Hilaire, growing deathly pale. "They were harmless—quite ordinary. . . ."

"I beg your pardon."

"What, monsieur le Marquis, has anyone mentioned my speeches to you?"

"Why, I heard them."

"You heard . . ."

M. Hilaire fell in a huddled heap on the first step of the stairs.

"You want a little air now," said Chéri-Bibi. "Wait a bit . . . I'll open the door, and then we can go out. That'll do you good and me too. Besides, we're going to have a little turn together in the country. . . . See, the dawn is rising—the dawn of a beautiful day!   Off we go."

He drew M. Hilaire away with him, repeating some of the phrases of the speeches that had stuck in his memory.

"Citizens, have done with idle words, the time is come for deeds. . . . Let us demand the public prosecution of every person lifting his voice in favor of a hateful despotism. . . . And if necessary let the Government bring in a law by which suspected persons may be arrested. . . ."

"That's Virginie," gasped M. Hilaire.

"What, Virginie!   She wrote that speech for you!   Well, you can congratulate her on it.   Personally, I think she has worked our business very well."

"You—you think so?"

"When I heard you make that speech I said to myself: 'That's jolly smart.   M. Hilaire is master of the situation.   The Arsenal Club is on our side.' "

"Whew!" gasped M. Hilaire. "That's exactly what I said to myself, too—the Arsenal Club is on our side."

"In future," went on Chéri-Bibi imperturbably, "this terrible club may decide whatever it pleases; it can't do anything without us."

"Oh, it can't do anything without us. What a consolation it is to say that."

"We shall be in the secret of the gods."

"Of course," agreed M. Hilaire, gasping again.

"And what power will be ours when we come forward in the name of the Arsenal Club!"

"Nothing will be able to stand against us," murmured M. Hilaire tearfully.

"We shall know who are Major Jacques's friends and enemies for you, my dear Hilaire, must be a rabid supporter of Subdamoun."

"Rabid, monsieur le Marquis."

"In case *our* attempt against the Republic is not such a success as we hope, our exceptional position in your district will save us. Who dare suspect you? Your cellar will become a safe refuge for our proscribed friends. Here they will find security for the time being, for we may need such a place, and, after all, we must be prepared for every emergency."

"Hum! Hum!" said M. Hilaire, beginning to cough again.

"Put on your muffler," advised Chéri-Bibi prudently.

"Hum! Hum! . . . Of course, my cellar—my cellar is always there."

"Not forgetting that Mme Hilaire, from what you have told me, will be equal to the occasion. She will be entrusted with the job of providing these political refugees with food."

"Hum! Hum! . . . Mme Hilaire. . . ."

"Why not Mme Hilaire?"

"Well, between ourselves, it will be better to say nothing about it to Mme Hilaire."

"Don't excite yourself, my dear Hilaire," returned Chéri-Bibi in a kind tone. "For the time being we are only concerned with victory. And we're going, both of us, to complete the arrangements."

"I thought we were going into the country."

"Yes, to Versailles. That's where we're going to complete the arrangements for victory, but before taking the train you must provide yourself with fifty Members' Cards bearing the Arsenal Club stamp."

"Good heavens!" exclaimed M. Hilaire.

"What's the matter now?" asked Daddy Peanuts. "Does your conscience shrink from adopting such measures?"

"Not at all. On the contrary, I am very glad of the opportunity to do you a service."

"Then what's the trouble?"

"Well, the trouble is that I must go home to fetch them."

"Of course."

"If I go home my wife, I fear, will raise some difficulty about letting me out again."

"You must tell her that it's for the great cause, my dear Hilaire, and she'll let you do what you wish."

"Oh, you think so! You don't know her."

"Go, Hilaire, go. . . . Here's your magnificent

shop. This is not the moment to show cowardice. Go, old man, I'll wait for you."

It was a definite command. M. Hilaire did not wait to be told a second time, but with unspeakable dread approached the threshold of his imposing establishment. He opened the low door in the iron shop front with a trembling hand and closed it behind him.

Chéri-Bibi waited for him. At first nothing distracted him, and then he pricked up his ears as he caught a sound from the first floor that grew louder and louder. A certain tumult was taking place inside. He could clearly hear the smashing of crockery. And then the noise seemed to descend, to roll from the first to the ground floor with a tremendous clash. Heavy, dull blows resounded on the walls as if they were being bombarded with missiles. A window was broken, and cries, wails, entreaties rent the air.

"Mme Hilaire is waking up," said Chéri-Bibi to himself calmly, and he was beginning to pity his friend the Dodger when his attention was attracted by a kind of whining voice emerging from the ground at his feet. It was then that he saw at a window of the "Up-to-date Grocery Stores" famous cellars the dishevelled, distraught, bruised head of poor M. Hilaire.

"Quick! Help me to get out of this," he choked. "She's coming. . . . Quick! Save me!"

"Take my hand," said Chéri-Bibi, holding out his huge paw.

M. Hilaire clutched it with all his might.

"Up we come," cried Chéri-Bibi, pulling poor M. Hilaire out of the inferno and the cellar; and to the echo of Mme Hilaire's imprecations as she continued her search for him the two pals made off.

"Don't tell me you haven't got the Members' Cards," said Daddy Peanuts.

"I've got 'em," gasped M. Hilaire, rubbing his head. "There now, what a commotion. . . . What a woman. See what a sight I am. Isn't it awful?"

Chéri-Bibi gazed at M. Hilaire with a certain compassion; and indeed he was not pleasant to look at in the wan light of the morning. He was without collar or tie, the dicky of his shirt had been torn away, his blue Sunday suit was in rags, and his hat, of course, remained on the battlefield. M. Hilaire would not have gone back for it for a trifle.

"All the same," he said after a few minutes' silence, "I mustn't be seen in the streets, or even in the country, in this state. I look like a thief—or rather like a man who has been robbed."

"I will tell you what you look like," returned Chéri-Bibi. "You look like a club orator who has come up against a few hecklers paid by the opposition party. Keep your rags, M. Hilaire, if you don't mind."

They reached the corner of the street. M. Hilaire clutched Daddy Peanuts' arm:

"Hist—Mlle Jacqueline! Do you recognize her?"

"Sister St. Mary of the Angels," returned Chéri-Bibi in a whisper, steadying himself against his friend. "What an early riser she is. . . . I wager she is still going to church to pray for me."

"She's going to five o'clock Mass at St. Paul's."

CHAPTER XV

BRUMAIRE

ON arriving at the Palais Bourbon Major Jacques was at once approached by Michel and the patriot Lespinasse.

The three men engaged in a preliminary discussion while the Deputies, betraying every sign of anxiety, hurried into the Chamber where the ushers, notified at the last moment of the proceedings by the *questeurs* supporting the new movement, displayed their bewilderment.

"All goes well," said Michel. "They are in a deadly funk. If you succeed they will be grateful to you, but if you make a false step they'll throw you over. They have nearly all of them come here pretending to be intensely surprised. But after all, they say, they could not refuse to answer a summons sent out in the usual way. So you are warned! They will grant you everything presented to them in due form, and thus they will leave themselves a door for retreat in case of failure. The thing is to do things quickly. Oh, they would like to be at Versailles, and I don't deny that I would like it, too. They have not forgotten that Napoleon Bonaparte nearly failed to overthrow the Directory because he took two days over the job."

"The unfortunate part is that we shan't have Lavobourg with us," said the Major, calmly.

Had a thunderbolt dropped between the two Deputies the effect could not have been greater.

"What do you say! . . . No Lavobourg. He

must be coming. He ought to be here very soon."

"No, he isn't coming. He has thrown us over."

"So that's why you are so pale. But who is going to preside over the Chamber?"

Jacques was no longer listening to Michel. He was watching Lespinasse, who was shaking with impatience and anguish to see the whole thing fizzling out, since everything depended upon Lavobourg.

"Lespinasse, you have been a soldier and a good soldier," said Jacques, fixing him with a burning look. "You must carry out my orders as a soldier obeys his chief in war time."

"At your service."

"You must go to Tissier."

"The second Vice-President of the Chamber? He lives quite near here—that's quickly done."

"But Tissier refuses to have anything to do with it. I have sounded him myself," cried Michel. "He'll let things take their course—and keep to his bed."

"Hold your tongue, please." And turning to Lespinasse, he gave him a document from the Commission of Inquiry. "You will show him his name on the list of persons against whom a warrant for arrest is to be issued this very day. If he wishes to save himself let him come. Don't tell him that Lavobourg has left us in the lurch. Tell him, on the contrary, that Lavobourg will take the chair. . . . In short, bring him with you. With this document in your possession it will not be difficult."

"I understand," said Lespinasse. "I will bring him along willy-nilly. Rely on it, Major. In a quarter of an hour at latest we shall be here."

"You amaze me," exclaimed Michel, puffing

loudly, and wiping the perspiration from his wide forehead. "I would never have believed that Tissier, Pagès's friend, would be included in the Commission of Inquiry's list."

"It was not in it," returned Jacques calmly. "I added it myself, and to do so I imitated Coudry's handwriting, old man."

"A forgery . . . I say," exclaimed Michel admiringly. "You did not stop at forgery!"

"Don't let's waste time," returned Jacques. "Reassure those who are uneasy. Tell them Lavobourg has sent word that he will be here in five minutes. I will find out what's happening in the Senate."

He hastened to the telephone and was at once put through to Frederic.

Events had moved rapidly in the Senate. Frederic gave him the facts in a few words and explained the state of mind of the Senators. The proceedings had not taken long. The President brought forward a Bill for the Revision of the Constitution, a Bill drawn up by Oudard and Barclef, and it was passed without discussion.

"You know what I'm expecting from you," said Jacques, still at the telephone.

"Yes, the President's order entrusting General Mabel, the commander of the troops at Versailles, with the task of guarding the National Assembly. The President is about to draft it. I will bring it to you."

"I shall wait for you here. The Chamber will have finished its work within ten minutes. Let everyone make a start for Versailles."

"They won't set out until they receive the news

that the Chamber has also agreed to the Revision of the Constitution."

"They are about to receive it. . . . So long, Frederic."

Some twenty Deputies were standing near the telephone box waiting for him to speak to them. He told them that the sitting was over in the Senate and the Bill for Revision passed. A murmur of elation and enthusiasm spread to the Chamber.

What was Lavobourg doing? It was rumored that .he had betrayed them, and consternation, a chilling fear, swept in a moment through the groups seething with excitement in the hemicycle. But it was reported almost immediately after that the Major had deprived him of any power to do mischief, and each one exchanged a glance of renewed fear. That was going beyond the usual methods. That was departing from the regular course. They had no great love of that. And then suddenly cries, gestures of impatience, the banging of desks, an extraordinary nervousness broke forth. . . .

"Why not get it over? The whole thing could have been finished in ten minutes," exclaimed some. "Why disturb us at five o'clock in the morning for a debate at six o'clock?" And others began to play the innocent: "Why have we been summoned? What is it that we have to debate? The Revision of the Constitution? Why were we not informed? It is senseless. We know nothing. No one has told us anything. What does it all mean?" While others again exclaimed: "We are here because it is our duty to be here, but whatever happens we wash our hands of the whole proceedings."

Meantime Jacques waited in a fever of expectancy for the Vice-President, whom Lespinasse had undertaken to bring to the Chamber. As he stood looking anxiously down the pallid and deserted quays he was not a little surprised to see a taxi draw up alongside the kerb with Jacqueline seated in it. She alighted. She held two letters in her hand, but when the uniformed men stopped her at the entrance she handed her letters to one of them, pointing to the Major, already starting to walk towards her.

The letters were at once taken to him. One was addressed to him and the other to Frederic Héloni, and he recognized Lydia and Marie Thérèse's handwriting. At that very moment Lespinasse came along with Tissier. From thenceforward he became oblivious of everything but his mission. He grew confident now of victory if no time were wasted, and postponed as a matter of course the reading of "love-letters" until later. Tissier was deadly pale. Lespinasse had obviously shown him the list of accused persons in which he had read his own name.

"We were only waiting for you to save the Republic," cried the Major.

He drew him into the Chamber, where their entrance was greeted with murmurs of impatience. No one knew what was about to happen nor what to make of Lavobourg's absence. The advent of Tissier, who had always maintained friendly relations with Pagès, nothwithstanding the difference in their political views, seemed to indicate that the project had already leaked out and was ruined.

But Jacques, leading Tissier to the steps to the President's chair, said:

"Gentlemen, in the absence of our friend Lavobourg, the victim of an odius outrage by our adversaries, our friend Tissier will, as is his bounden duty, preside at this sitting which must determine the fate of the Republic."

Loud cheers broke forth. Oh, of course, since Tissier was in it they felt a renewal of confidence! Lespinasse helped him to the President's chair and Jacques darted into the tribune:

"Gentlemen, the Senate, the supreme guardian of our Republican liberties, has just set us an example by passing a Bill for the Revision of the Constitution and decreeing a meeting of the National Assembly at Versailles. Unless you follow the Senate at once in the only path of safety that remains to us it is the end of the Republic and Republicans. I denounce from this place the hideous plot devised against the country and our liberties by the fomenters of terrorism."

The rough and impassioned language of Jacques's speech readily inflamed his hearers, who had now heard too much to draw back. Amid a storm of cries, questions, applause, Jacques went on to read a violent indictment of the underhand intrigues of clubs and Communists in the provinces. Finally, after putting fear into their hearts by reading a list of suspects drawn up by the Commission of Inquiry, he ended by appealing to the courage and patriotic spirit of the Chamber. Not a single Deputy present asked for further explanation. The vote was carried. They held the pivot upon which the whole movement would henceforward turn. Nothing remained to be done but to set out for Versailles.

Just then Frederic Héloni arrived with the order signed by the President of the Senate entrusting General Mabel with the defence of the National Assembly. He was received with thunders of applause. They all considered themselves safe, delivered absolutely from a revolutionary reign of terror, the masters of a new regime. Legally, constitutionally, they were about to give France a new Government without danger to themselves since they had the army behind them.

"To Versailles! . . . To Versailles!"

Even now a few Deputies, learning what was happening from friends desirous of implicating them, came hurrying up on foot or by car, furious at having been ignored. If the movement in the course of the day only just beginning hung fire and seemed like failure it was these Deputies who would precipitate the failure and display the greatest rancour.

Jacques and Frederic were the last to leave the Chamber after shaking hands with some two hundred Deputies and instilling courage into every heart.

As they stepped into a car which was to drive them to the Place de l'Etoile, where General Mabel was waiting for them, Jacques thought of the letters handed to him by Jacqueline and meantime forgotten. He drew them from his pocket.

CHAPTER XVI

FIVE MINUTES

"I HAVE a letter for you," Jacques said, giving one to Frederic and opening his own. "This is, I should say, a delicate attention from our fiancées," he went on, but he did not finish his sentence. He uttered a dull exclamation, and Frederic himself, who had read his own letter, uttered a cry of pain.

"Pull up, driver!"

They informed each other of the contents of the letters. The sentence in which Marie Thérèse gave them the final advice not to enter Lydia's room with a light made a tremendous impression on them.

Héloni, who had become as white as a sheet, said no word. He knew how precious every moment was for the success of the *coup d'état* in which Jacques had enlisted the lives of so many good men. He waited with a terrible anguish at his heart Jacques's decision.

"The simplest thing," said Jacques in a voice that Frederic scarcely recognized, "would be for you to go at once to my mother's house and, after raising the alarm and learning how matters stand, join me at Versailles, but there are no taxis about —not a single taxi."

A frightful struggle was raging in Jacques's heart and conscience. Frederic gazed at him with dismay in his eyes. He clearly read in them the determination to order the chauffeur to proceed on his way— his chief's terrible heroism was visible in his eyes. It was a sentence of death to Lydia and Marie

Thérèse. Then, scarcely knowing what he did, he drew out his watch and said at haphazard:

"We may have five minutes. We shouldn't want more than five minutes."

"Let's go there then," roared Jacques in a desperate fury. He shouted the order for the chauffeur to drive to La Morlière.

They did not wait for the car to stop before making a dash into the house. The concierge saw two men rush past with all the more alarm as they nearly knocked him down on their way. Jacques was even now at Lydia's door.

"Lydia! Lydia!" he cried, shaking the door. "It's I, Jacques. . . . Open the door!"

"Marie Thérèse! . . . Open the door!" cried Frederic in a choking voice.

Then the two men took a sudden spring and threw themselves simultaneously against the door, which gave way. A horrible odor of gas swept into the passage and throughout the house. Jacques ran to the windows, shattered the panes, and, feeling faint, returned to Frederic, who was already carrying Marie Thérèse out. Jacques seized Lydia. . . . It seemed as if both girls were dead, for they lay inert in their arms. Jacques was shouting to the concierge to fetch a doctor when Cecily came up.

What new misfortune was knocking at her door? She loved Lydia as a daughter. Was Fate about to take her away, too?

The two girls were carried to Jacqueline's room.

"They tried to commit suicide," groaned Frederic.

"But they are still breathing," returned Jacques, hopefully.

Lydia opened her dimmed eyes and sighed.

"Air . . . more air," cried Jacques.

Marie Thérèse in her turn opened her lifeless eyes and Frederic could not restrain his tears. He had found the two girls locked in each other's arms as though they had met death with a chaste last kiss. . . . And he was utterly amazed by the tragedy of it, for it was not he who was to blame. The really guilty man implored his mother to save his fiancée's life.

Just then the doctor came in and applied the usual restoratives, but was unable to say at that moment whether their lives would be saved.

"We shall know more in another five minutes," he declared.

Jacques, who was on his knees before Lydia, rose to his feet and beckoned Frederic to come with him.

"Aren't you going to wait to know whether they will live or die?" asked Cecily, surprised.

"No, mother. We are confident, Frederic and I, that you will do everything in your power to save them. Good-bye, mother. We have no right to remain here another moment. We are expected elsewhere, and there, too, it is a question of life or death. As to Lydia and Maire Thérèse, when they can understand you, tell them that we still love them, and send us word at Versailles that their lives have been saved."

The car drove off at the same mad pace, but when Jacques and Frederic reached the Place de l'Etoile they looked in vain for General Mabel's car and the General himself. He was no longer there.

CHAPTER XVII

VERSAILLES

JACQUES looked at his watch.

"We are five minutes behind the time he himself fixed as the latest for waiting. It's our fault. We may, perhaps, overtake him on the road."

The car shot forward again like an arrow. It tore through woods, villages, plains. . . . On the way they sought General Mabel's car, but it must have already reached Versailles. The General had doubtless been told what had happened in the Chamber and Senate, and perhaps had already seen the President of the Senate.

The troops under his command, close on ten thousand strong, must have by now surrounded the Château. They passed several cars in which they recognized Parliamentary friends.

As the old Comte de Chaume pointed out Jacques to Warren, of the great motor-car firm of Warren, who had placed over twenty cars at the disposal of the Senate, he said:

"That fellow to-night will be on a lower level than Paillasse or above Epaminondes."

They reached Versailles not much behind time, but were dumbfounded on entering the Place du Château not to see a single soldier. . . .

What then had become of Mabel's army? Where then was Mabel himself? And where was the Sub-damoun battalion which ought by now to be in the Château courtyard? An indescribable confusion seemed to prevail there. The absence of regular troops dismayed the parliamentarians. A group of them made a rush towards Jacques when they saw him alight from his car.

"Well, what about Mabel? Where's Mabel? . . . We're waiting for him. We're waiting for you. What's happening?"

"Mabel is coming," cried Jacques. "Let's all take our seats. Where is the President of the Senate?"

"Why, he's waiting for Mabel. He's waiting for you. We can do nothing without Mabel."

As Jacques strode into the Palais due Versailles he ran up against Michel coming out:

"Mabel! . . . Mabel!" cried Michel.

"I've just left him. Take your seats," he shouted in the corridors. He acted as usher, furious at the sight of the discomfited, white-faced, flabby air of most of those present, no longer believing in success now that they were unable to see the promised bayonets.

Some Deputies were already shrugging their shoulders. Others regretted being there. Others again sneered at the elaborate care and attention taken by the President of the Senate who wished the proceedings to be held in the usual surroundings, and had given orders during the night for a canvas canopy to be erected in the left wing of the Château facing the Hall of Congress.

It was in the room usually reserved for Ministers on days of Congress that Jacques found the President with the Committee of the Senate and Oudard and Barclef. He left them again almost immediately. He met Frederic seated on one of the benches in red velvet frienged with gold in the vestibule ornamented by the busts of celebrated persons.

"Come," he said, "these fellows will do nothing without Mabel, and we don't know what has become of him. We must try to work things without him."

In the courtyard and square men ran up to him:

"Where are you going? Where are you going?"

"I have an appointment with Mabel. I shall be back in five minutes with the General and the troops."

He asked to be taken to the barracks where the Subdamoun battalion was temporarily stationed under the command of officers of the Colonial Army, upon whom he could make any demand. The officer who succeeded him in command of the crack regiment was Major Daniel, a friend who had served under him in the campaign. He found him in the barracks waiting impatiently for an order from Mabel which would place him at Jacques's disposal.

Daniel was surprised to see Jacques enter the barracks with Frederic, and drew him into a room.

"What's happened?"

"Do you know what's become of General Mabel?"

"No."

"Nor do I. But I have just told everybody that I left him a moment ago. Here is a decree signed by the President of the National Assembly charging him with the safety of the representatives of the people. The Chamber and Senate, exercising their constitutional prerogatives, have resolved on the revision of the Constitution. If Mabel were here he would tell you, for the matter was arranged with him, to call out your men and lead them to the Château courtyard and place your services at

the President's disposal. Will you consider that
you have already seen Mabel and thus carry out the
decree? In half an hour I shall be appointed head
of the Provisional Government, and I will take full
responsibility, whatever happens."

"Major, my life belongs to you," returned Daniel.
The two men embraced.

"Thanks, Daniel. Had you not agreed to follow
me nothing would have remained for me to do but
to blow my brains out. . . . Sound the call. And
march to the Château at once."

Daniel gave his orders. The barracks at once
became alive with the clatter of soldiery.

"That's not all," went on Jacques. "If you wish
to help me to see it through you will telephone to
the commanders of the various corps telling them
that you have received Mabel's orders to march to
the parade ground and the Château, and to pass on
the order which must be executed here and now."

"I understand. Anything you please. . . . Superior and subordinate officers are as impatient to
act as I am. We shall be running no risk with them,
seeing that they are covered by the decree signed
by the President of the National Assembly. Ah,
why isn't General Mabel here?"

"Recriminations are useless. Let us act."

Daniel hastened to the telephone. He came back
almost at once.

"Col. Brasin will march. . . . He asked for no
explanations, and says that he has but to obey
orders. But General Lavinge is surprised not to
have seen General Mabel, and wants something in
writing."

"Frederic, this is where you come in. You must

call on General Lavinge and show him the decree
signed by the President of the National Assembly.
And you must call at all the barracks and see all
commanding officers. Tell them that you are making this round on General Mabel's orders. I rely
on you to fire them with enthusiasm. . . .

"As to General Mabel, he is supposed to be waiting for them all in the Château. At the moment he
cannot leave the Assembly, where he remains at the
President's orders."

"Very good, Major. . . . With that order I will
get them to support us to the last."

"Wait while I give you a last order, for I shall
not be able to devote any further attention to you.
When you get back with the infantry this is what
you must do: place a cordon of troops twenty yards
from the Château walls. Three open passages in the
parade-ground will allow Deputies and Senators
and other authorized persons to enter."

"I understand."

"Frederic, they must not be able to come to us
later and say we refused admittance to any Deputy
or Senator. Do you see? You follow me? . . .
And yet, as we are already three-quarters of an
hour behind time, you must manage, without receiving any order to that effect, to prevent any
more obtaining admission during the next half-hour.
. . . All those who come along within the next half
hour will probably not bear you any good will. . . .
I am telling you things that I should have said to
General Mabel."

"I will act throughout as though he were here.
And I'll give all orders in his name."

"Go, and good luck, old man."

Five minutes later Jacques was loudly cheered in the courtyard of the barracks by the entire battalion under arms. An indescribable enthusiasm seized these men, and he had no need to explain what was required of them.

"Comrades, the moment is come to save France," he cried. "Forward! . . . Follow your leaders!"

At once the battalion marched to the parade-ground to the sound of bugles and drums, arriving as Colonel Brasin came up at the head of his regiment. The effect was startling. Jacques seemed more than ever the master of the situation. He had promised them soldiers. He was coming back with them.

When members of both Houses saw the khaki uniforms of the colonial troops on the one hand and the great-coats of the regular infantry on the other, they could not restrain an almost childish enthusiasm.

So it was true? They had succeeded. They represented law and order imposed by force. And it no longer depended on them alone to relieve the country of those factions of whom they stood in terror. . . . They could not believe their own eyes.

In the Hall of Congress the great Republicans, such as Michel, Oudard and Barclef, had at last made up their minds to bring matters to a head and chance their luck without General Mabel, whose absence was as disturbing and unfortunate as Lavobourg's. And they conceived the idea of replacing Lavobourg in the Provisional Government by Tissier, a staunch Republican, a friend of Pagès, who would not allow the Republic to be overthrown under the pretext of saving it.

When Tissier learnt of his nomination he was dumbfounded. In reality he continued to allow himself to be pushed forward by others, still unable to understand the course of events, forbearing to compromise himself by unnecessary speech, and seeming above all bored by being awakened so early.

Just then Jacques came hurrying up:

"I bring you five thousand men ready to die for you, monsieur le President."

The President entered the Hall of Congress accompanied by his escort. Just as Jacques himself reached the door he was not a little surprised to be saluted in military fashion by two stalwart ushers, magnificent in their chains of office. He recognized his faithful bodyguard, Jean Jean and Polydore, but needless to say did not stop to ask for an explanation. . . .

Deputies and Senators rushed in after him to take their seats. A wan glimmer pierced the glass window in the roof and threw an ominous light on a group of "doubtfuls" and "late comers" who did not yet know "if they supported the movement," and waited their time in an attitude of hostility. They said to those gathering round them:

"The law — the law must be respected. . . . Afterwards time will show."

The President rose in his chair and read the clause in the Constitution in accordance with which the National Assembly was gathered at Versailles for the revision of the Constitution. Nothing could be more legal. What more did the sticklers for legality require?

Jacques mounted the tribune:

"Gentlemen, you are the representatives of the

people, and you are here because in your heart and conscience you believe that the condition of affairs in which we are floundering cannot continue. It would lead at the end of three years to an unbearable despotism.

"We wish to see the Republic founded on equality, civil and religious liberty, and political toleration. With a sound administration all our citizens will forget the factions to which they belong and be permitted at last to be Frenchmen. Is it not shameful to see the country to-day terrorized by clubs and secret revolutionaries as in the worst periods of its history?

"It is time to restore to those who defend our native land the confidence to which they are entitled. If some of these factions are to be believed we ought to be looked upon as enemies of the Republic—we who have strengthened it by our labors and our courage. . . . Well, to-day once more we come forward to rescue you from the anarchy which is at your door and which if you delay will enter and obstruct your deliberations.

"France desires liberty for all men.

"The essential policy that confronts us is to revive in France the conception of government with the theory of ordered authority, a policy of continuity and that stability which the word State implies. . . .

"Enough of this jerry-built system which sinks into impotence at the first breath! It is only a Government, limited by substantial safeguards, but strong and independent enough to govern by other means than tyranny and violence, that can ensure peace at home and abroad. Gentlemen, it is your duty to debate this question and to modify the Constitution.

"But problems of such a nature cannot be determined in twenty-four hours. In order to investigate them you need complete tranquility. Therefore I call upon you in the name of France, in the name of the Republic, to appoint a Provisional Government until the labors of the National Assembly are finished—a Provisional Government which under the high authority of the head of the State whose personality we leave entirely outside this struggle, will be in a position to protect you from your enemies.

"Gentlemen, two men will suffice for this task, which we must hope will soon be fulfilled. . . . It is for you to select them. Select them quickly and carefully, for I can even now hear disturbances in the streets from the fomenters of disorder. . . . Let these two men be strong and united. . . . Choose an old Republican like Tissier and a soldier. You need a soldier. . . . But if you know a soldier, a more devoted Republican than I am—elect him!"

It was on these words that he descended from the tribune. A thunder of applause greeted his peroration, while at the same time a great tumult swept through the Place d'Armes, the courtyard of the Château, the Gallery of Tombs—also called the Gallery of Busts—and reverberated as far as the Hall of Congress.

It was caused by the appearance of a dozen Deputies of the Left, led by Mulot and Coudry. They were foaming with rage. . . . They brought with them a wild-eyed member of the Government, the unfortunate Taburet, Minister of Public Works,

the only Minister they were able to find in the course
of their hurried rush to Versailles. They had learnt
of the course of events through inevitable indiscre-
tions, and feared lest they should arrive too late.
Fortunately it was not so. They stated that Hérisson had lost his head and raced from Government
office to Government office like a man possessed.
It was said that he had bundled the War Minister
into his car, and both had arrived at Flottard's
office in a frantic state. . . . At last everything
gradually leaked out and Deputies rushed off to
Versailles from every side.

When Jacques saw the yelping crew burst into
the Hall of Congress he realized that this particular
dozen Deputies would be followed by others. He
went over to the door and said to Jean Jean:

"Go at once to M. Frederic and tell him not to
let anyone else pass through—you understand—
not a single person."

He returned to the sitting. Even now the struggle was beginning.

"You are thieves, assassins," shouted Coudry and
Mulot. "You are trying to subvert the Constitution—to assassinate the Republic. . . . But we will
prevent you. Assassins! Assassins!"

Lespinasse flew at Coudry's throat and Mulot
tried to separate them. Meantime Jacques, Michel,
Oudard, Barclef forced the pace. They had a majority; they would have to make quick use of it.

The President put to the vote a Bill backed by
twenty well-known Republicans, appointing a Provisional Government for so long as the deliberations
of the National Assembly lasted.

For a while certain astute Deputies thought that

they ought to take Jacques at his word and nominate another member with Tissier to form the Duumvirate, but at the last moment the wild uproar caused by the arrival of Coudry's men flung them back into Jacques' arms.

The President realized that not a moment was to be lost, and thus the idea of summoning a Commission which should hold a five minutes' meeting and return with a hurriedly dispatched report was shelved.

It would be necessary to proceed to the vote on the proposal at once and give effect to it there and then. The National Assembly in the exercise of its full powers was bound to take whatever steps it might think fit to ensure the safety of the State.

Those who wavered most would have asked nothing better than for the vote to be taken "seated or standing," but the President set himself against it. He feared these shirkers later on, and refused to allow the comedy to degenerate into farce. And besides, the entire authority of the *coup d'état* would be derived from an honest scrutiny of the voting papers and an ordered and public vote.

Once more, what had they to fear? They had only to let the democrats and their keeper Coudry roar themselves hoarse while the others recorded their votes. For the rest, they drew up without delay the names of thirty-six tellers whose duty it would be to scrutinize the voter and check the voting papers.

The nominal roll-call was begun. At the rate at which the vote was being taken the whole proceedings would be over probably in three-quarters of an hour, for the members hurried to the tribune

to record their vote and not a moment was wasted.
Fortunately there were absentees.   The rest all
wished to set up a Provisional Government, and all
voted for Major Jacques and Tissier to form the
Duumvirate.

It was then that Pagès, appearing from no one
knew where, burst into the Hall of Congress like a
jack-in-the-box.   His eyes were starting from his
head, his hair stood on end with horror at the outrage that had been perpetrated, and with amazement
at his own ignorance of the plot.   He pointed to
Major Jacques and shouted: "Outlawed!"

CHAPTER XVIII

OUTSIDE THE CHÂTEAU

OUTSIDE the railings of the Château, behind the
impassive troops not yet knowing what orders they
would have to obey, the entire town was congre-
gated.

To begin with, the people, awakened in such
extraordinary circumstances, had crowded to the
spot to discover what was taking place.   The most
contradictory rumors were current.

Members of the advanced clubs in the town
rushed up in search of information with vigorous
demonstrations of loyal revolutionism.   From every
suburb of Paris groups of citizens flocked to Versailles.

Public officials, too, arrived by train from Paris
with distraught faces and made their way to the
railings, where, like the rest, they were brought up

short by the soldiers. No position, no rank enabled them to pass the barrier.

Frederic had thoroughly carried out his orders in accordance with Jacques's instructions, and after the first body of Deputies from Paris had gained admission he closed every entrance. When the second batch appeared with Pagès at their head there was a pretty tussle.

Pagès, trailing his men after him, asked to see first Colonel Brasin and then General Lavigne. The two officers were inflexible. They had received their orders. They were there to make them respected. They were, in fact, there only for that purpose. And their orders were to allow no one to pass.

"Who gave you those orders?"

"General Mabel."

"Impossible; General Mabel has been arrested."

"Mabel arrested! What nonsense! He is in the Hall of Congress."

"Have you seen him?"

"No, but his orders were transmitted to us. That is enough, gentlemen. I am only a soldier and take no part in politics. I was ordered here with my men. I am here. I was to allow no one to pass. No one will pass. I obey my orders."

So saying he turned on his heel.

"He is mad," said Pagès between his teeth. "Come, all of you. We will manage to find an opening and get through."

They went away, but the rumor of Mabel's arrest spread, and the officers present, who had not seen their chief at all, began to discuss this extraordinary piece of news.

Brasin and Lavigne felt much less assured. Had someone in reality been making fools of them by issuing orders in General Mabel's name? They were now inclined to think so.

They determined to take no further steps without a proper written order, and regretted omitting to insist on this safeguard from the beginning; all the more so, they thought, for if General Mabel was indeed under arrest the affair would fail, whatever Major Jacques might do.

Echoes of the rumors reached the crowd. At certain windows in the square peaceable citizens, armed with opera glasses, watched attentively what was passing in the courtyard of the Château, and drew conclusions more or less contrary to common sense. Moreover, it was as though the whole capital was flowing in a stream into Versailles.

In the streets motor-cars clattered, dashed forward, sounded their hooters. Taxis crowded with patriots or revolutionaries, singing or shouting, blocked the avenues. Here and there free fights broke out. The amazing news of the *coup d'état* had roused the people of Paris from their beds at an early hour, hurried them into all sorts of conveyances, and brought them to Versailles, either as sightseers or partisans.

Many women of fashion and actresses arrived in cars clad hastily in anything that came to hand. The restaurants were flooded with visitors.

One well-known hotel was filled with a smart crowd, all the more densely packed since it occupied the best place for gathering the latest news, and it was almost impossible to go further afield.

Suddenly a man with his soft felt hat pulled over

his eyes and the collar of his great-coat turned up, crossed one of the rooms, and certain persons recognizing him, exchanged glances: "Lavobourg! So he is not in it!"

It was indeed Lavobourg who strode quickly into the courtyard. Here he encountered some twenty sturdy fellows with a hang-dog look about them, who had ordered a snack of lunch in company with cabmen and chauffeurs.

The waiters at first raised some difficulty, for they were little desirous of serving gentlemen who were not of the class of their ordinary customers. But a certain peanut dealer who was present said to the head waiter with meaning:

"You are very particular to hesitate to deal with the foremost patriots of the Arsenal Club. You are certainly now aware that these respectable citizens are friends of this gentleman here, who is the secretary to the committee of the Arsenal Club— in other words, my dear man, he is somebody, and in these times it is well to have friends in every camp."

The head waiter grasped the point and hastened to serve them with whatever they required.

Lavobourg seemed slightly taken aback to come upon such gentry in so smart a restaurant, but they quickly made way for a gentleman who doubtless had "an assignation with a lady." He passed through.

"No need for you to disguise yourself. You've been recognized," said the peanut dealer.

Lavobourg quickened his step. He made his way to a pavilion which was built in days of old for Madame la Pompadour. Some of its rooms led directly through French windows to the park. The door opened. A hollow exclamation was heard. The door was closed after him.

"He has the look of a traitor," said one.

"It seems he's a friend of Major Jacques," said another.

"Down with the Major!"

"Long live the social revolution!"

"Long live the Arsenal Club!"

One man among them remained silent. It was M. Hilaire. He could not help thinking, though he was surrounded with friends, of the serious disadvantages of taking an active part in politics which occupied so many hours that might have been profitably devoted to business. And then he was obliged to tell himself that Daddy Peanuts made use of his political influence and his club membership cards with an amazing freedom.

Who were all these persons? And in what way would Chéri-Bibi make use of them for the good of France as he maintained? Moreover, M. Hilaire was no longer unaware that within a few yards from him a most audacious *coup d'état* was being attempted and that, thanks to Chéri-Bibi, his own responsibility was involved to an extent impossible for him to estimate.

If to these troubles of a public nature he added the fact that he had little reason to rejoice after the conjugal scene which had introduced discord into the "Up-to-date Grocery Stores," M. Hilaire's dejection may easily be understood.

As he looked up, a prey to these lugubrious reflections, he was not a little surprised to descry on the open front of a café opposite the simple faces

of his two friends of the night before, MM. Barkimel and Florent, who at once rose to their feet
and took their departure as though they had not
seen him.

It was an extraordinary thing. What were they
doing at Versailles?

That indeed was what M. Barkimel was now
explaining to M. Florent, who did not yet know.

M. Florent, after the excitement of a particularly
stirring day and night, was sleeping the sleep of the
just when he was suddenly roused from his bed, at
an exceptionally early hour, by the unexpected appearance of M. Barkimel.

To all his questions M. Barkimel would only consent to answer:

"Get up!"

"But tell me why."

"Get up!"

"Are we in any personal danger?"

"We have a serious duty to perform."

"Then I am with you," agreed M. Florent, trembling with anxiety.

M. Barkimel carried him off to Versailles. He
seemed greatly preoccupied, and made no answer
to any of his friend's questions.

On reaching the town they were not a little surprised to behold a scene of which M. Barkimel,
however, claimed to have been forewarned.

"Are you in the confidence of the gods?" asked
M. Florent, taken aback.

"I knew there would be an attempt to subvert
the Republic to-day at Versailles, of course,"
bridled M. Barkimel, complacently.

"You knew all about it, and you bring us into this dangerous mob! What for?"

"We ought to oppose this attempt, M. Florent."

"But I have always heard you say that the heavy hand . . ."

"I? You are dreaming. And if I may have said that the heavy hand is sometimes necessary I have always held that it should be on the arm of a staunch Republican and not of a soldier of fortune, M. Florent."

"Really, you amaze me. How are we to oppose this attempt to subvert the Republic?"

"By keeping an eye on M. Hilaire, that's all. Now do you understand?"

"Why, less than ever. M. Hilaire has always been one of the most zealous supporters of the Revolution."

"Hold your tongue, M. Florent. Here is M. Hilaire. I will tell you presently what you must think about it. . . ."

"Listen," continued M. Barkimel a moment later. "This is what happened to me this morning. It was about five o'clock. There was a loud and per-sistent knocking at my door. I got up, thinking the place was on fire. I opened the door and found myself face to face with a gentleman very neatly dressed in black, holding his bowler hat in his hand, who said meekly: 'M. Barkimel, may I have a word with you, if you please?'

"I told him that one does not wake up people at that early hour. He answered that he was there in my own interests, and had something serious to confide to me on behalf of an important person who desired for the moment to remain nameless.

"I showed him in. I asked him if he minded my going back to bed. He sat down near me, and, suddenly placing his hand on mine, said: 'M. Barkimel, would you like to receive a decoration?' "

On hearing this last unexpected sentence M. Florent flushed crimson and then purple. It seemed as if he were about to choke—truth to tell he gasped for breath. At last he managed to splutter:

"It was some practical joker."

M. Barkimel in his turn flushed crimson.

"Why a practical joker?" he stammered. "The man spoke very seriously, and he proved it to me afterwards. . . . Why a practical joker?"

"Oh, nothing. . . . Go on," coughed M. Florent.

"Then I told the man," continued M. Barkimel, "that my greatest ambition was to be an Officier d'Académie."

"Of course," agreed M. Florent, turning pale.

"I asked my visitor: 'What must I do to attain this object?'

" 'You must be a staunch Republican and a faithful friend,' he answered.

" 'A faithful friend to whom?'

" 'Why, M. Hilaire, for instance.'

" 'Oh, well, that will be easy,' I said. 'I have always loved the Republic, and I won't lose sight of M. Hilaire.'

" 'Then keep in touch with him more than ever,' advised my visitor. . . . 'With a man like you,' he added, 'I will come to the point, for you are possessed of intelligence above the average. You must know then that the staunch Republicans of the Arsenal Club are very surprised at certain of M. Hilaire's words and deeds.

" 'They find him sometimes lukewarm and sometimes eccentric. They want to be sure of the secretary to such an influential committee. Now they are aware that he supplies the de Touchais household, the meeting-place of Subdamoun and all his aristocrats.

" 'Moreover, he ought to have been present at the Club yesterday, where he was expected, and where the most serious resolutions were passed against the dictatorial intrigues of Jacques I. . . .

" 'He failed to turn up. Why? And here is the most mysterious fact of all. One of the leading members of the Arsenal Club has disappeared—he did not return home last night. We have every reason to suspect some criminal outrage. I am referring to Citizen Tholosée, whom, perhaps, you know.'

" 'Yes,' I said, 'I know Citizen Tholosée—he is an honest Republican. I have often seen him with M. Hilaire, and been pleased to shake hands with him.' "

"What humbug!" exclaimed M. Florent. "You have told me a hundred times that that wild fanatic frightened you."

"It is exactly because he did frighten me," returned M. Barkimel, "that I shook hands with him with pleasure. It's better to be on good than bad terms with persons who frighten you."

"What then?" asked M. Florent sharply.

"Well, then it was agreed that I should keep watch on M. Hilaire 'for his own good.' "

"A nice thing indeed!" exclaimed M. Florent. "Are you going to play the spy now?"

"Come, M. Florent, calm yourself. I said 'for his own good'—so that he should come to no harm. . . . To warn him in time if needs be. And over and above this I shall receive the decoration."

M. Florent could not contain himself any longer. He stopped short, folded his arms, and said:

"What will you do with it—you a retired umbrella dealer?"

"I shall wear it in my button-hole," returned M. Barkimel. "And don't be angry, pray. I have other things to tell you. . . . This gentleman did not leave me at once. He said to me: 'You have a friend equally intelligent who is on intimate terms with M. Hilaire.' "

"Ah, he said that, did he?" returned M. Florent, now delighted.

"And he told me that his friend was called M. Florent, and that if he too liked to serve the Republic there would be a decoration for my friend Florent as well."

"Oh, I say!" exclaimed M. Florent, whose eyes became moist as he shook his friend's hand.

"Does that please you, eh?"

"M. Barkimel, it is always a pleasure to an honest man to receive a decoration, and, understand me, when this man deserves a decoration as I do. . . ."

"M. Florent, you shall be decorated. He said to me: 'He shall have the Mérite Agricole.' "

M. Florent this time staggered and became ashen gray in the face.

"M. Barkimel," he said, choking with indignation, "keep it! I won't have anything to do with

your leek. All very well for you, M. Barkimel, to
sell a friend for a decoration, but M. Florent will
remain plain M. Florent. Good-bye."

"Florent!"

"Good-bye, I say. I've done with you. You are
a wretch—and besides, your Republic is done for."

"The Republic done for! Anyway, it's not you
who will bring it down."

"It is on its last legs. You've always made me
laugh with your Revolution."

As M. Florent was just then surrounded by a
sympathetic crowd he turned to it, and pointing to
M. Barkimel, whom he no longer regarded as a
friend, cried:

"There's another man who believes in clubs and
revolutionaries."

M. Barkimel was at once set upon by a hostile
group, who did not let him go until he had shouted:

"Long live Major Jacques!"

M. Florent walked away with an unholy grin on
his face. M. Barkimel went back with a heavy
heart to keep an eye on M. Hilaire:

"I will never forgive him for this," he said to
himself.

M. Hilaire and his strange companions had not
left the hotel courtyard. The door which had closed
on Lavobourg was not reopened. As we have mentioned, when he entered the pavilion a hollow exclamation was heard.

"You did not expect to see me," said Lavobourg.

"No," returned Sonia. "What are you doing
here? More treachery?"

It was, in fact, Sonia who occupied at that critical moment Madame La Pompadour's pavilion.

She had secured the place the night before, aware of its facilities for communicating direct with the Château. But assuredly she had not expected to see Lavobourg.

Had the prisoner, then, been able to get rid of his bonds? Or had Coudry's men released him, for they must have already made a search of her house? She trembled for Jacques and his venture.

"Who was the first to play the traitor?" he asked in a hoarse voice. "It's all very well for you to talk —you who nearly had me assassinated. Oh, I knew that I should find you here—in this place. It is so convenient for lovers at Versailles. Do you remember?" he added with a jeer that almost ended in tears. "Ah, Sonia, you have lost all shame."

"Whatever happens, I ask your forgiveness."

"You do not need my forgiveness. I have had my revenge," he returned.

"What else have you done?" she asked in apprehension.

"I don't know if Jacques will succeed. . . . That is quite possible, but at least I shall have the consolation of having done my uttermost to bring about his failure."

She drew him before her, shook him by the shoulders. Her eyes were hard, her lips quivered, her hands tore at him.

"What do you say!"

"I've been to Flottard, the Military Governor of Paris, and warned him, and I'm pretty sure I was in time to enable him to do his work well. Before coming here I had the pleasure of hearing that, thanks to me, they were able to lay hands on General Mabel as he was preparing to leave the Place

de l'Etoile for Versailles to put himself at the head
of his troops. Mabel was arrested and thrown into
the Conciergerie Prison like a criminal."

She was no longer listening to him. It meant
that he had dealt them a terrible blow. She was
thinking only of how to warn Jacques, who must
certainly be unaware of it.

Just then the door gave way as if it had been
wrested from its hinges and a mob burst into the
room. It was Pagès's gang searching on all sides
for an entrance into the Château; someone had suggested this way to them.

Pagès bowed and made an apology, but suddenly
he and his men recognized Lavobourg and Sonia
Liskinne. There was no doubt in their minds that
these two were in hiding there to conspire against
the State. If the general rumor could be believed,
they were the leading spirits in the *coup d'état*.

"Here are our hostages! Here are our prisoners!
Subdamoun's spies!" they cried.

On the other hand they were in haste to make
their way into the National Assembly. As it happened members of the Arsenal Club came running
up and offered their services, which were accepted.
Sonia and Lavobourg were surrounded by these
sinister-looking persons speaking a fearsome slang.
They seemed to be under the leadership of a little
old man in whom Sonia recognized the peanut dealer
of the night before. He gave her, by stealth, a nod
of understanding and she breathed more freely
again.

But when one of their chance jailers returned
from the courtyard with the news that Major
Jacques had been assassinated she uttered a pierc-

ing shriek, while the little old man darted into the
park with the agility of a youth of twenty. . . .

CHAPTER XIX

"STAKE YOUR MONEY—THE GAME BEGINS"

LET us return to Pagès who, followed by a few
friends, the most violent members of his party,
had managed to gain admission into the Hall of
Congress by the staff entrance.

The Deputies behind him shouted repeatedly,
"Outlawed! Outlawed!" and other members of
the party under the vehement leadership of Coudry,
already at grips with their adversaries, took up
the cry, "Outlawed! Outlawed!" shaking their
fists at Major Jacques.

Up to that time the great majority of representatives had succeeded in thrusting back from the
hemicycle the fanatics of the Extreme Left and in
protecting the voting which was being continued
with the utmost speed, for the aim of the newcom-
ers was neither more nor less than to prevent the
voting—to render it impossible.

In the midst of the storm Jacques strove to divert
their fury to his own head. Meantime the voting
went on. He shouted. He orated. He excited his
opponents in a voice of thunder which they had
not suspected him to possess, and succeeded in
equalizing the effect produced by Pagès and his supporters.

"You are on the brink of a volcano. Lose no

time in extinguishing it," he cried. "Let us safeguard Liberty! Let us save Equality."

"Outlawed! Outlawed! Death to the Dictator!"

"The advocates of the scaffold for political opponents," yelled Jacques, "are gathering together their party and preparing to carry out their horrible schemes. Let us hurry! For my part I desire only to save the Republic."

"Outlawed!"

"I claim to have given sufficient pledges of my devotion to the country. . . . Long live France!"

With an irresistible rush Coudry and his followers reached Jacques and his supporters. The encounter became a scrimmage.

"Our liberty is being violated," cried Jacques to the President. "The voting should be declared over and the result read out. The country must have no further dealings with this gang of madmen."

But his voice was drowned in the din, and by this time more Deputies of the Opposition had arrived from Paris and entered the precincts, reinforcing Pagès, Coudry and Mulot.

The tumult increased.

"Down with the Dictator! Down with the tyrant! Outlawed!"

Had not two sturdy ushers stood beside him and sent those who came too near him sprawling with their fists he would have been torn to pieces. He was face to face with the most violent Communists who had stepped over the benches.

He felt as if a weight lay on his chest; his eyes grew dim. But the sound of arms was heard in the

corridor, and a platoon of colonial troops came to
the rescue of its chief in danger. A frightful disorder, an incredible uproar ensued. The voting
was stopped.

The President tried to speak but was unable to
make himself heard. Only the soldiers were able
to put a little order in the hideous confusion. At
last they released Jacques from the clutches of the
madmen by making a rampart of their bodies. He
was taken outside.

He appeared in the courtyārd ghastly pale, his
features distraught, his head sunk on his shoulders,
almost fainting, held up by two colonial soldiers.

Inside the building the revolutionaries, repeating
their battle-cry, "Outlawed!" turned their attention
to the President's platform and were now climbing
the steps. The ballot boxes were thrown down and
smashed. . . . And Deputies shook their fists at
the President, whose only hope was in the intervention of the regular troops, for whom he was
waiting. He declared the voting closed.

Let the soldiers come! Even now they could
save the situation.

From the courtyard, the Place d'Armes, the street
outside and the parade shouts went up: "To arms!
To arms!" The rumor spread that an attempt had
been made on the life of the idol of the day, and
a thousand voices clamored for the army to save
the nation.

But whose orders was the army to obey—the orders of its chief, General Mabel? . . . General
Mabel was nowhere to be seen, and rumor declared
that he was a prisoner. Would the army obey the
orders of the President of the National Assembly?

But rumor also declared that Ministers and members of the Government were hastening to Versailles and the President was to be impeached for violating the Constitution.

And Jacques? Were his fame and popularity sufficient to carry troops which had never come into direct association with him?

In reality Jacques could depend only upon his own battalion. After a moment of weakness he completely regained his strength and vigor. Men crowded about him. He asked for a horse. A captain surrendered his own to him.

He rode over to his colonial troops and was received with a storm of cheering. He asked for silence, and proceeded to denounce the revolutionaries in unmeasured language:

"They are villains—traitors to their country. . . . I was suggesting means by which the Republic could be saved and they attempted to assassinate me."

He wore a grim expression:

"Soldiers, can I rely on you?" he cried.

There was a thunder of acclamation, but the colonial soldiers alone were cheering. The other troops looked as if they were turned to stone.

Just then a body of Deputies emerged from the Hall of Congress bringing with them the President, who was on the verge of collapse.

It seemed as if the revolutionaries by their incredible violence and audacity, for they were still small in numbers, were masters of the parliamentary domain. Nevertheless the President had the strength to shout to the impassive soldiers: "Save the Republic! Drive out these sedition mongers!

The vote has been passed!   The Duumvirate has been proclaimed!"

"You hear the President's declaration," cried Jacques.   "I entrust my soldiers with the duty of liberating the majority of the nation's representatives.   Forward, my lads!"

He put himself at the head of the small column which marched into the Château.   The loud roll of the drums was heard, and the drummers marched into the Gallery of Busts, beating their drums continuously as the colonial troops swept through the Hall of Congress and expelled all those who clung there still and, like Pagès and Coudry, threatened to die where they were.

It was a formidable task, and the sight of the bayonets threw the revolutionaries into the most gloomy fanaticism.   They now thought that all was lost.   They held on to their seats, and the soldiers were obliged to take them in their arms and carry them out as though they were unruly children.

And outside the air resounded with tremendous shouts of: "Long live the Republic! . . . Long live Hérisson! . . . Long like Flottard!" while Pagès's voice could be heard yelling: "To the Orangery!   To the Orangery!   It can hold the entire National Assembly. . . .   Let us appoint a Committee of Public Safety."

Jacques darted into the courtyard to discover what had happened.   What had happened was that the game which he believed was won was in fact lost.   He was expecting Mabel, and it was Flottard, Mabel's chief, and Hérisson, the President of the Council, who had appeared: two men still representing the established Government while he represented merely an adventure that had failed owing to a delay—a delay of five minutes.

If he had only met Mabel in the Place de l'Etoile at the appointed hour! . . .

Tears of despair filled his eyes. What could his battalion do against the troops brought by Flottard, against the two squadrons of gendarmery moving at the other end of the courtyard in front of the infantry which had not stirred, which would never stir until a General, and a General who had the right, lifted his sword?

Hérisson had even now given an order to close every gate, every outlet. He was determined to allow no single person to escape. He would know how to avenge outraged liberty. And his first victim was indicated. It meant the arrest of Major Jacques. But it was no easy task in face of the battalion of colonial trops ready to die for their old leader.

It was the War Minister who stepped forward. He addressed himself to Daniel. He ordered him to hand over Major Jacques.

"Never, monsieur le Ministre, I am a soldier. I am not a policeman."

In the courtyard every eye was fixed on the tragic scene. Major Jacques, realizing that all was lost, folded his arms across his breast, and impassive, stern, stood waiting the last blow of fate. His companions in arms pressed round him and swore never to desert him, but to follow him to the end of the world.

"Daniel, the end of the world for me is the firing party," he said in a calm voice. "We have both done our duty, and you are sufficiently compro-

mised, my dear friend. Your fate, I fear, will
scarcely be more fortunate than mine. Hand me
over, Daniel."

"Never! Listen to the mutterings of my men."

"The game is up. I entreat you to let me pass.
I would have no unnecessary blood shed on my account. And you cannot imagine that I should
allow French soldiers to fight French soldiers. . . .
Good-bye, my friends."

Then Daniel took his sword and broke it across
his knee and strode over and threw it at the feet of
the War Minister and M. Flottard, the civil head
of the military government of Paris.

"Here is my sword and here is your prisoner."

Jacques took a step nearer. Two gendarmes put
the handcuffs on.

Meantime Pagès, Coudry and the extremist majority, assembled in the Orangery, appointed the
members of a Committee of Public Safety, and restored the death penalty for political offences.

CHAPTER XX

THE NEW TERROR

WHEN the first "tumbril" containing a group of
prisoners sentenced to death, hands bound behind
their backs, hair cut to lay bare their necks, emerged
on the quay from the gate of the Conciergerie
Prison, the immense hum of the populace that had
resounded from the river's banks since dawn that
morning was suddenly hushed. Paris became
silent.

It was two o'clock in the afternoon. The sun was pouring down like a furnace. Oh, the death penalty was no longer carried out in the dusk of early morn! Now it dealt its blows in broad daylight, and the procession made a sort of mourning retinue to the Place de la Concorde, once more called the Place de la Revolution.

The only difference was that the 'tumbril" was a motor lorry of forty horse-power. It was drawn by no worn-out hack, and a chauffeur drove slowly, very slowly, this lorry of death. Civic guards with fixed bayonets stood on this moving platform with the prisoners. Other guards, but these mounted guards, led the way and brought up the rear.

And blood was about to flow—a great deal of blood. "The Republic needs a little blood-letting or it is done for," said Coudry; and in spite of Pagès's efforts the National Assembly meeting in the Orangery at Versailles after the arrest of Major Jacques and his chief accomplices proclaimed the Republic in danger at its first sitting, and restored the death penalty for enemies of the State and the guillotine as a permanent structure in the heart of Paris.

It was in vain that Pagès, the great orator of the Extreme Left, raised his voice against a sanguinary law which would be a law aimed at suspects; it was in vain that he implored them not to "stain the robe of Republican victory on that great day," Mulot made answer that the robe was red and the blood on it would not be seen. The utmost concession that he was able to obtain was that prisoners should not be executed wholesale by machine-gun fire, and their trial should retain some appearance of legal form. Pagés who had carried a vote establishing a Committee of Public Safety, and been elected its President, was obliged to remain silent to avoid an immediate downfall.

For a fortnight the remnants of the National Assembly, organized into a sort of Convention, working day and night, passed law after law exceeding the worst memories of the Commune and even the first French Revolution. The Convention had no need to concern itself with the President of the Republic, who was ignored and on the first day resigned his office. Paris was split into sixty divisions, and the administration of these divisions handed over wholly to the clubs. In each division twelve Commissioners were elected, bound to render a daily account of their stewardship to their electors.

The chief function of these Commissioners was to bring the names of suspected persons before the Vigilance Committee elected by the Assembly in Versailles, and sitting in Paris. These suspects were sent before the Revolutionary Tribunal on warrants which were issued by the Vigilance Committee.

The members of the Revolutionary Tribunal, assembled in the great room of the Supreme Court in Paris, were selected by the Committee of Public Safety from a list furnished by the divisions, each division electing one of the members on this list. No appeal was allowed against sentences and executions were carried out within twenty-four hours. . . . Oh, the divisions had the game in their own hands!

They were the masters of Paris, especially since Flottard, the civil head of the military government of Paris, had caused arms to be distributed to them with instructions to train as large a number of civic guards as could be relied upon.

And while as far as possible they moved the regular army away from the great towns and massed it on the frontiers after issuing to the world a bombastic proclamation of peace, the Committee of Public Safety sent Departmental Commissioners into every district to organize, or attempt to organize, in the provinces the same system of divisions and civic guards.

A number of large towns dominated by extremists at once followed Paris; but in other towns a strong opposition became manifest which declared its intention to save France from revolution.

The Commissioners of the Committee of Public Safety complained that in these "centres of reaction" they could make no headway without appealing to the lowest elements of the population: "They do not believe in your power. They think your revolution will be short lived. Some sensational incident is necessary to galvanize the people."

The sensational incident occurred. It took the form of the first "tumbril." And in order to reach the Place de la Revolution it made the tour of the Boulevards.

At a corner of the extended Boulevard Haussman, in a room in the Café Werther, several leading lights of the day were gathered to observe, behind a raised curtain, the passage of the procession and the impression that it made. There was considerable argument and some uneasiness.

Coudry fulminated against the Committee of Public Safety and in particular against Pagés whom

he accused of moderatism. It was Pagés fault if
they had not raised Paris to white heat, and if they
had not organized the demonstrations which were
essential at such a time.

The rage of the young revolutionary only increased when Cravely, who came in to report upon
the position to Mulot, now a delegate of the Ministry of the Interior in Hérisson's place—there were
no Ministers now—expatiated blissfully on the
people's calm. They were both sat upon.

"Then you are satisfied! . . . True, the people
are calm. . . . They are nowhere to be seen. They
are hiding behind their windows. . . . Then you
think it is for this that we of the Vigilance Committee are working, do you!—to allow you to organize a procession in which those who follow it
seem to be mourning the victims of the Revolutionary Tribunal. Damn it all, we must make the
people gallop behind the tumbril. You must let
your rowdy element break loose. . . . But I see
only soldiers and civic guards. The Boulevards
ought to be crammed with the mob."

He stormed. He foamed at the mouth. Accustomed to his outbursts, Mulot shrugged his
shoulders, stroked his moustache, and sipped his
brandy.

Just then Pagès came in. He was very pale.

"Ah, here comes the bourgeois," greeted Coudry.

"The bourgeois is yourself," returned Pagès in a
serious voice, taking a seat and wiping with his
check handkerchief the icy perspiration that
trickled down his pallid forehead. "It is you who
bring about a bourgeois revolution and repeat all
the blunders of the bourgeoisie."

"If you don't like our revolution leave it," retorted Coudry.

"You terrify me, Coudry, you and your friends.
You are rushing us along a path the end of which
no man can see."

"That's the nature of revolutions, my dear fellow," returned Coudry. "I tell you again you are
trying to put too much system into the Revolution.
That will be your undoing. Ought not Subdamoun
to have been the first to pay the penalty? Ought
he not to have been sent in the first tumbril as a
fitting homage to him? What are you waiting for?
That is what the people of Paris do not understand.
You have given them his accomplices and you seem
to wish to spare the chief actor."

"Certainly I will give you Subdamoun, and even
his chief supporters, the Lavobourgs and other
traitors to the Republic," said Pagès, "and I am not
the man to delay their punishment for a moment."

"I am responsible for that," said Mulot, "and
you know quite well why. It is not to our interest
to hand them over to the executioner until we have
discovered everything about the plot. The prisoners may still be useful to us for confronting certain
suspects. Moreover, everything will soon be finished—at least I hope so. Don't you agree,
Cravely?"

The head of the Political Detective Service had
been for a tour round the Boulevards and had just
come in.

"The one missing man whom we want, and badly
want, is Baron d'Askof," he said. "Baron d'Askof
was the organizer of the whole thing at the beautiful
Sonia's house. Now, I'm pretty sure that we are

going to lay hands on him to-day or at latest to-morrow. We shall learn also the whereabouts of the de Touchais family, and before a couple of days are over the Marchioness and her adopted daughter, Subdamoun's fiancée, will be lodged with the Major in the Conciergerie Prison."

"What does Sonia in the Conciergerie Prison say?" asked Coudry.

"It seems that she is making merry. Yes, she holds receptions, and they play charades and forfeits."

"Rotten play actress," said Coudry with a look of disgust.

"I hear she was d'Askof's mistress. . . . As to d'Askof, I will give you a word of advice, Cravely. Try to hand him over bound hand and foot within twenty-four hours or I won't answer for you."

"Oh," said Cravely, turning pale, "I think I am pretty sure. . . ."

"Yes, what I am telling you is for your own good. I warn you that the Vigilance Committee and the Committee of the Detective Service have decided to ask the Committee of Public Safety for your dismissal and even an inquiry into your work if you have not arrested d'Askof by to-morrow night at latest.

"We on the Committee are convinced that he is the key of the whole business. It was he who was the essential intermediary between Subdamoun and all the others. . . . If you do not hand him over to us you are making yourself his accomplice."

"I have been telling him so for the last week," corroborated Mulot. "Though Cravely handed over at Versailles in the course of the day about a

hundred of Subdamoun's supporters, not all small
fry, and showed considerable zeal, and though he
is my chief representative, as he used to be Carlier's,
the Committee of Public Safety would have sacked
him before now had he not promised us d'Askof
and the Marchioness de Touchais."

"You shall have them," declared Cravely. "I
swear, gentlemen, that I am doing my utmost. I
am waiting here to see an agent who is to report
when and how he can arrest the Baron, for he is
still in Paris."

As he spoke three shrill whistles rang out in the
Boulevard. Cravely went over to Coudry at the
window.

"I really believe that that's my man," said the
head of the Political Detective Service in increasing agitation, for the thought of losing his position
and an inquiry into his work had completely staggered him. He drew aside the curtain and made
some sign. The next moment a squalid-looking
street urchin threw his cap into the air as he turned
his eyes towards the window, and after giving three
loud whistles, ran off.

"Is that young blackguard your agent?" asked
Coudry.

"No, that young blackguard is my agent's scout.
His name is Mazeppa, a hideous little beast who
has been very useful to us. He has just given me
the tip that it is important for me not to leave the
café, for the agent himself will be coming to see me
here at any moment." Then, lowering his voice,
he added: "I am anxious, M. Coudry, to satisfy you
and be useful to you and the nation. I have a tremendously extensive staff for the maintenance of

order. Every division is under arms, as you can see, and is lined up in every street. It is the people themselves who maintain order; they have to some extent been turned into soldiers and they cannot therefore join in demonstrations. But if you wish me to let loose my rowdy element I have them all ready at the Place de la Revolution."

"Your rowdy element!—we know them. There's no reason to bring them in as long as the streets remain quiet, otherwise we shall be accused of provocation," returned Coudry, drumming the window with his gnarled fingers.

"Well, I have a counter-demonstration some three hundred yards from here waiting the course of events. I will send them the order to make a clamor when the tumbril passes. . . . Here's my man," he added suddenly, and quickly left the room.

Coudry endeavored to pick out from the crowd which encumbered the pavements behind the double line of civic guards the man whom Cravely had called "my man," but saw nothing that could enlighten him in any way.

CHAPTER XXI

WHEREIN WE MEET OLD FRIENDS AGAIN

CRAVELY was stopped in the corridor by one of his agents, who had come to report progress. He took the opportunity to give him orders for the leader of the counter-demonstration: "Tell him that they must shout, 'Down with the murderers! Long live Subdamoun!' and let there be a scrimmage until you get to the Place de la Revolution, where you will let loose the rowdy element."

"What must these fellows shout?" asked the agent.

"Long live the Commune!"

"I understand," said the agent, knowing that his chief had just left Coudry, who was beginning to change his views towards the Commune.

Cravely went downstairs, but failed to discover the man for whom he was looking. He turned to one of the managers, who was no other than Lavobourg's late manservant. The ex-flunkey had been forced by hard times into the public-house line. But he could give Cravely no information.

"I am going up to the first floor," said Cravely. "If you see Daddy Peanuts tell him where I am."

"Very good," was the reply.

Cravely did not stand on ceremony with the manager, who belonged to the police—had turned informer—and escaped his master's fate by furnishing such particulars of Lavobourg's life as the Vigilance Committee and Detective Service required,

When Cravely went upstairs the manager dropped his napkin, and as he picked it up said to a customer, a curious-looking person, whose hair, beard, cap and general appearance suggested a student of the Russian revolutionary type, apparently dozing at a table on which lay the remnants of a frugal lunch:

"Look out!"

"What's that?" said the customer with a start, opening his heavy, short-sighted eyes behind his huge spectacles.

"Look out, Daddy is coming. He has an appointment with the head of the Detective Service."

The customer made a movement to slip away.

"Don't go. I assure you that no one will recognize you," said the manager, clearing the table.

"Oh, how can one tell with him," returned the other. "Anyway, time will show—it's worth risking it. If only the laundress would come. What can she be doing? She is more than half an hour late."

"It's not easy to get through the streets just now. . . . Look, here she is!"

And in fact a door at the other end of the café looking on to a back street had just opened and a little laundry-maid, wearing a cap over a wonderful mop of black hair, and carrying a large basket on her arm, came in, crossed the end of the room, and went down a staircase leading into the basement.

The manager left the room for a while. He soon returned and said:

"You are wanted on the telephone."

The customer rose from the table and also descended the staircase. But on the way to the telephone boxes a door stood slightly ajar, and he opened it, entered ,and closed it after him. He was in a small room serving as a lumber room for linen in which also laundry accounts were settled. He kissed the girl who stood before him.

"I thought you were never coming, Vera."

"That's a wonderful make-up," said the Baroness. "Had you not spoken I shouldn't have known you."

"I'm glad of that. Daddy is not far away."

"You don't mean it," she exclaimed excitedly.

Her husband calmed her.

"Oh, he hasn't seen me, he isn't here yet. He is coming here for Cravely, who is waiting for him in a private room; and I'm pretty sure, like you, he won't recognize me."

"No, but he will recognize me," said the Baroness.

"That's not certain, but don't let us waste time. Your last letter gave me some hope of success.

"As it happens, I shall probably be delivering her washing to-night."

"Then have you at last got the address where she is hiding?"

"Not yet. But the boss will have to give it to me. The Marchioness must be reduced to her last garment."

"Are you certain that you are dealing with the Marchioness?"

"Well, of course. The boss knows her linen well enough, I suppose—she has done her washing for years."

"Oh, if we only knew where she was hiding it would be a splendid stroke. If we had the beautiful Cecily and Mlle de la Morlière in our hands we should at once be able to ask whatever we liked from Daddy Peanuts."

"Meantime?" asked Vera.

"Meantime things are not too bad. Some of them are dropping him. I have ten of them under control at present. Ten notorious fellows who, like me, used to have a holy terror of him. . . . Well I have talked to them. I have made them see that we can't go on like this and had better take advantage of the present row to get rid of this friend who is exploiting us. And, upon my word, they, too, have given him up. With eleven of us together we shall make up a force that Daddy Peanuts will soon have to reckon with; all the more so as the fellow has been in a bit of a funk since the *coup d'état* failed. That fairly upset him.

"At first he took up his quarters in the courtyard of the hotel at Versailles. He managed to get civic cards, issued by the Arsenal Club, distributed to his pals. With those civic cards he could do what he liked. That was how he got Pagès himself to appoint him to take charge of the beautiful Sonia and Lavobourg.

"His object was obviously to bring about Sonia's escape and to denounce Lavobourg, who had betrayed Subdamoun too late to receive much consideration from the revolutionaries.

"Now it so happened that, concerned solely with the fate of Subdamoun, who had been arrested, Daddy forgot to give any order to his pals, and when he came back to look for these louts, as he calls them, they had surrendered both Sonia and Lavobourg to Pagès's men, who had come in search of them.

"That was how Sonia and Lavobourg came to be lodged in the Conciergerie Prison at once while Subdamoun was only transferred there in the night. Take it from me, Daddy doesn't know which way to turn."

"We shall never get out of the clutches of that brute," sighed Vera.

"What nonsense! Let dear little Jacques die on the guillotine and it will be all up with Chéri-B . . ."

The Baron was about to utter the name but had

ventured to pronounce only the first syllables when he turned pale and came to an abrupt stop. At that moment the door was slowly opened—very slowly. And the sham Russian student and the sham laundry-maid started back in terror. Daddy Peanuts himself came in and reclosed the door as softly as he opened it.

"Please excuse me, everybody," he said in a voice that was almost dead, "but you, Baron and Baroness, will certainly forgive my indiscretion when you know the cause that brought me here."

Never had he seemed so poverty-stricken, so pitiable. His shoulders were still more bent, and his miserable head drooped on his chest as if the segments of his spinal column had lost their power to support it, and swayed from side to side with a constant nervous twitching painful to the sight.

Vera retreated to the wall. She could not move a limb, hypnotized by the sinister figure that had loomed up before her. As to the Baron, he uttered a growl, his jaws set in an impulse of revolt, and between his teeth he cursed the malevolent fate that made him for ever the sport of this monster.

"I'm sorry," at last the old man gasped. "You must give me time to pull myself together. . . . I've been running. Just fancy, I was afraid of missing you and the Baroness, and as I like you both very much I should never have forgiven myself . . ."

"No more of this jesting, Daddy," broke in d'Askof in a blank voice. "How did you learn that we were here?"

He already suspected the ex-flunkey of giving him away.

"Well, it's like this," clucked the old man, "we patronize the same laundress. . . . Well, well, a little laundress in the Rue aux Phoques, my children, who does washing for all Daddy Peanuts's friends. . . . A very respectable business, don't you think so, my child?" he said to Vera.

D'Askof gave a gasp of admiration for this king of bandits.

"Even that!" he said to himself. "He even has the same laundress."

When it was a question after the grievous business of the *coup d'état* for them to escape alike the clutches of the new Government and Chéri-Bibi, it was at once the Baroness's laundress and Chéri-Bibi's laundress — Chéri-Bibi's laundress! — who offered them her services, furnished Vera with a disguise, and employed her as ironer—pending better times and Chéri-Bibi's orders!

Meantime the Baron had lived in the suburbs and passed himself off with others who, like himself, were traitors to the peanut dealer, as a Russian Communist. Well, that was another secret society which Chéri-Bibi could snap his fingers at, and d'Askof was prepared to bet now that old Zim, the proprietor of a public-house, who made them welcome and gave them meat and drink in his resort of artists, full of old pictures and bric-a-brac, was another of Chéri-Bibi's men. . . .

Chéri-Bibi for the moment gave his attention to the Baroness.

"You will presently go back to the shop, having done your errands. You will enter the laundress's office. The dear lady is waiting for you in the little study, where she keeps her books of accounts. She is waiting for you at the window. I prefer to tell you now so that you may not be taken too much by surprise when you arrive—she is waiting for you, hanging by the neck at the window."

The "little laundry-maid" began to sway in her chair, but Chéri-Bibi's tremendous paw kept her from falling.

"She has left a short letter on her desk, wishing her lover good-bye. In the eyes of the world the dear lady will have died over a love-affair. . . . Died of love at her age—she was fifty-two! But the brave never bring forward the excuse of old age—nor do fools. We who are clever, madame, know why this woman died. We have only to look at her tongue for that. When you go into the laundress's little study, look at her tongue. It is tremendously long. Your employer died because she had too long a tongue!"

Vera looked as if she were about to faint. D'Askof intervened, pale and grave. He could imagine Chéri-Bibi massacring them both as though they were dogs at the mere thought of the Baroness and himself suspecting Cecily's retreat. He realized that never had there been a more serious moment in the relations between himself, the Baroness and the peanut dealer.

"Now let us speak of the matter that I came to see you about, my dear d'Askof. You must lend me a hand to get Subdamoun out of prison."

"What do you want me to do?" asked d'Askof, digging his nails into his hands in his helplessness.

"What do I want you to do to get him out of prison?" repeated the old man, rubbing his huge hands. "Well, to do that it will be enough for you to go into it!"

"How do you expect me to go into the Conciergerie Prison?" asked d'Askof.

"There's a price on my husband's head. They are hunting him high and low," wailed the laundry-maid. "They will recognize him at once. Do you wish to ruin him? If that is what you want, say so, and have done with torturing us."

"How you love him!" said Chéri-Bibi gravely. "But I, too, am fond of him—because I need him. Therefore, don't be afraid. I will bring him back to you, dead or alive."

"Oh, Lord! Oh, Lord!" gasped Vera in tears.

"Besides, I will do the best I can, and Daddy Peanuts, you know, can do what he likes, particularly if his orders are carried out. If you will take my advice, dear lady, you will at once say good-bye to your husband and go straight back to the Rue aux Phoques without turning your head. Do you understand me? Without turning your head—whatever happens, whatever you hear, whatever is said to you. If you do that nothing will happen but what must happen in the interest of all of us, my dear Baroness."

Chéri-Bibi opened the door. The Baroness went out slowly, with her basket of linen on her arm. Tears trickled down her pale cheeks. She tried to speak, but it was beyond her power. Moreover, the door closed after her.

Chéri-Bibi was about to resume the conversation when the sound of an altercation was heard at the end of the passage, followed by the trampling of feet, the tumult of many voices, and suddenly a piercing cry:

"Stay where you are!"

D'Askof tried to throw himself on the door but Chéri-Bibi barred the way.

"Surely you heard her cry: 'Stay where you are!'"

"What's the matter? What's happened?" asked d'Askof breathlessly.

"I will tell you," replied the old man roughly. "But you see how difficult it is to deal with women. I told her to go right ahead, whatever she saw or heard. The first thing she did when she left this room was to cry out. . . . The silly fool! . . ."

"But why did she cry out?"

"Because she saw the passage full of detectives, who have come for you."

"What!"

"Don't get excited. They won't come in until I go out. It is understood that they will not interrupt our conversation. So you see, if I have to hand you over to Cravely it's entirely your own fault—you have only yourself to blame. . . ."

"I had Cravely's confidence," went on Chéri-Bibi, "but you and your friends have done your best to weaken it. You have warned him so often to beware of Daddy Peanuts that he hesitates now about working with me. And I have never needed his help so much as now that Subdamoun is in prison. . . . My dear fellow, I shall never completely win back Cravely's confidence until I have made him a present of Baron d'Askof. Do you grasp my meaning.

"You will hand me over?" he cried.

"So as to make sure of saving you, my boy—
you and Subdamoun. As you can see for yourself,
you can be of some service to me there, and believe
me it's a master stroke on my part. I wipe out at
once, let us say your inconsistencies, and make you
pay for them, and consequently I have nothing
further up against you. I save Subdamoun's life,
and it stands to reason yours into the bargain. . . .
Moreover, I win back Cravely's confidence. Come,
Baron d'Askof, you ought to congratulate me. . . .
And now, good-bye, and rely on me!"

D'Askof's frenzy, and his powerlessness to give
vent to his feelings, betrayed itself for a few moments in involuntary and confused gestures. But
after his distorted face had revealed the bitter
hatred that he bore for Chéri-Bibi and his rage at
being called upon to risk his own neck to save that
of a brother whom he would gladly have led to the
scaffold, he had to bow to the inevitable. In other
words, there was nothing for it but to submit.

"How shall we communicate in the Conciergerie
Prison?" he asked in a whisper.

"Through the Inspector of Prisons, an intimate
friend of mine, and the delegate of the Central Vigilance Committee."

"What!" he growled, at an utter loss. "The In-
spector of Prisons, the delegate of the Central
Vigilance, is your friend and you need me to rescue
Subdamoun from the Conciergerie Prison? . . ."

"You ass! . . . My friend has not yet been appointed to the position."

"When is he to be appointed?"

"Cravely will not appoint him until I have handed
d'Askof over to him. Do you see, my friend?"

"So that's the idea," was all he could say. . . .
Assuredly the boss was still the boss, and there was
no fighting against him! "All right—anything you
like," he added. "I am your man. Have me arrested when you please."

Chéri-Bibi gave a whistle and, picking up his tub,
opened the door and went out. In the passage some
twenty detectives were gathered. They fell upon
d'Askof, who offered no resistance, but quietly
submitted to the handcuffs. They dragged him into
the café. At the street door a taxi stood waiting.
He was bundled into it and driven off at once to the
Conciergerie Prison. . . .

The peanut dealer followed a man whose face was
beaming up the stairs leading to the first floor
private rooms. The man opened a door and pushed
the dealer into a small room, where pen and ink lay
upon a table. The dealer held a paper in his hand.

"I want you to sign this at once."

"Anything you please, Daddy Peanuts," agreed
Cravely. "But are you certain the plot is as serious
as you say?"

"Well, the whole prison is in it. It means prisoners murdering their warders—and they will be provided with arms."

"But suppose we transfer Subdamoun to another
prison?"

"Don't do that on any account. Nothing must
be allowed to leak out, and soon we shall have the
whole gang in our hands. But I must have an Inspector of Prisons who can be absolutely relied on."

"Do you answer for him? What must I say to
Coudry when I ask him to put the Committee's seal
on his appointment?"

"Say it's most urgent. Moreover, the man for the job is the same Hilaire, secretary of the Arsenal Club, who with a dozen friends kept Lavobourg and the beautiful Sonia prisoners in one of the hotel rooms."

"Ah, that's all right. . . . A capital idea. . . . Besides, he will do anything I ask him when I tell him that d'Askof has been taken. . . ."

Cravely signed the document.

CHAPTER XXII

M. FLORENT ON THORNS

As may be assumed, respectable citizens in those troublous times remained in their burrows like rabbits. But the rabbit that left his burrow least of all was M. Florent.

After the failure of the attempt to establish a dictatorship he returned to Paris in a state of consternation.

Truth to tell M. Florent's despondency was due less to the dangerous condition of the country, which, according to his own expression, was in the power of murderous demagogues, than to an unpleasant fear for his own personal safety. He bitterly upbraided himself for having without being forced to do so declared publicly in Versailles that the Republic was "on its last legs." Every one of his anti-revolutionary utterances at a time when the Revolution, in spite of his prognostics, was succeeding, seemed to him to be so many incalculable blunders.

M. Florent lived in a small flat on the fifth floor of an old house in the Marais quarter. It was his intention to shut himself up in it and to go out as little as possible, exercising the greatest caution.

He was on good terms with the concierge Talon, a cobbler, an honest man, who shared his political opinions and professed great contempt for supporters of public meetings. Therefore M. Florent hoped to get through, without overmuch difficulty, the worst days which, in his belief, would soon be over, for he still maintained that the whole tragi-comedy would collapse. Nevertheless, when at a corner of the street he encountered a mob waving swords and pikes he began to think that things were taking a turn for the worse.

A yelling crowd was pouring out of a military museum which it had plundered of its obsolete weapons, and as the screaming figures of women mingled with it, such as may be seen in old French prints of the time of the taking of the Bastille, M. Florent could believe that they were back again in those stirring times.

He was seized with an attack of weakness and took refuge in a porch to allow the mob to pass. Suddenly the street was filled with an immense crowd shouting: "Down with Subdamoun! Long live the Revolution!" escorting in triumph a number of prominent men of the day. M. Florent, thinking that he was possibly being watched, shouted at the top of his voice: "To the lamp-posts with all aristocrats!"

Thereupon a self-possessed gentleman, M. Saw, whom he knew quite well, for he used to lend him books from his circulating library when he was in business, and whose quiet manners and moderate opinions were the object of general commendation, said:

"M. Florent, there are no lamp-posts now."

M. Saw strode forward and mounted a passing bus. M. Florent flushed crimson. M. Saw was aware of his opinions and would certainly regard him as a weak coward. Disgusted with himself, he hurried away.

On reaching his flat he was struck with the furtive air with which Citizen Talon greeted him. Seated at the back of his badly lighted workshop wearing a dirty cap and fiercely hammering the sole of a boot, the concierge seemed to suggest to M. Florent's mind Simon the Cobbler. He thought it well to explain that he had been taking a breath of fresh air in the country and, having just returned, knew nothing of the latest news.

"All right," growled Talon. "But to-morrow you must call at the Arsenal Club and get a card of good citizenship, otherwise I shall be compelled to inform against you."

"You, M. Talon—would you do that?"

"Oh, I shouldn't mind. Representatives of the Club have been here. They are visiting every house. As times go, and seeing that the bourgeois are longing to overthrow the Republic, the least the people can do is to defend themselves. Between ourselves, M. Florent, let me tell you for your own good, it's high time you changed your opinions."

"Well, for my part I am only too anxious to live in peace," returned M. Florent in increasing anxiety. "You are quite right. . . . And I see as far as you are concerned you haven't hesitated either."

"How dare you," broke in Talon, rudely. "You don't know what you are talking about. You have never known my real opinions because I have always concealed them. But to-day it's an easy matter for me to show them. . . . As we are the masters we needn't make a fuss about anyone. . . . Look here, I admire the way they treated suspects in the time of the Commune, as it is called, in 1871."

"Don't talk to me of the Commune, M. Talon. . . . The Revolution gave us a Government. The Terror gave us a Government. But the Commune gave us nothing at all—it was simply brigandage— yes, plunder and arson."

M. Talon rose from his stool and strode fiercely up to M. Florent, who shrank back.

"The Commune was not a Government!"

He brandished on high his leather pricker as though it were a sword. M. Florent retreated, and with a trembling hand drew from his purse a twenty-franc note. He placed it on Talon's table.

"Couldn't you yourself obtain for me my card of good citizenship, M. Talon? You have known me for a very long time. You can answer for me."

"No, you have the reputation hereabouts of being a reactionary. I don't want to compromise myself," returned M. Talon, pocketing the twenty-franc note.

"All right. I'll go and see my friend M. Hilaire, the secretary of the Club, who knows my real opinions. No ill-feeling, I hope, M. Talon, and you can keep the twenty francs all the same."

He mounted the five floors to his flat, his limbs unsteady and his mind in a whirl.

"Reputation of being a reactionary!" . . . He had brought it on himself. Ah, M. Barkimel had been cleverer than he! He had never scoffed at the New Revolution. He had never turned it into ridicule. He had always lived in a respectful fear of the Extreme Left, so much so that when the Revolution broke out he who had always taken it seriously was quite ready to enrol himself among its warmest supporters.

M. Florent would never dare go for his card of good citizenship. Where would he find the necessary references? He was certain to encounter M. Barkimel's enmity, nor could he answer for M. Hilaire's friendship, for M. Hilaire must be greatly taken up in defending himself from the suspicion of members of the Club and the secret denunciations of the hateful Barkimel. . . . Oh, that man Barkimel—he would go to any length to get himself appointed an Officer d'Académie!

Next morning M. Florent succeeded in coming to an understanding with M. Talon, who brought him the newspapers. M. Talon received one thousand francs in consideration of which he pledged himself to declare that "he had not seen M. Florent." And so M. Florent would be missing. No one would have seen him. . . . Meantime he would live quietly in his flat on preserved food and cold water. That would last as long as it would last!

Our man lived in comparative safety for a fortnight. We say "comparative" because though physically he lived in safety, mentally he lived in mortal terror. From time to time M. Talon slipped a newspaper under the door and the news in it threw him into wild consternation.

The news from the Town Hall, the decrees of the Committee of Public Safety, the sentences of the

Central Vigilance Committee, Coudry's proclamations in the *Gazette des Clubs*—all these things staggered him.

"This Coudry—why, it's a repetition of Hebert and the newspaper *Père Duchesne!*" he said to himself. . . . "What did I say—we cannot begin the Revolution all over again. . . . Why, we are in the middle of it."

His knowledge of the history of the Great Revolution, knowledge of which he was so proud, enabled him to glimpse a thousand scenes, each more terrible than the other.

One morning he read an article which made him spring from his bed. The article was headed: "Men of Paris—Arise!" and it began: "Bloodshed, citizens, let there be bloodshed. We must amputate a limb to save the body. . . ." The article was signed "Saw."

"Saw!" gasped M. Florent. "That's the good-mannered man who used to borrow books from my library, and who reminded me the other day 'there were no lamp-posts now'—such a quiet and respectable gentleman. . . . Why, that's the limit. . . .

"After all," he went on a few minutes later when he had wiped the perspiration from his forehead. "After all, he is quite right. He does not worry about his past opinions. His present opinions are the only things that matter, seeing that they are the only ones that are of any use. One must know how to adapt oneself to circumstances. There are many people who begin as revolutionaries and end as reactionaries. Hang it all, one may very well begin as a reactionary and end as a revolutionary. Why should I be a bigger ass than Saw?"

And he conceived the idea of himself writing articles under a pseudonym and sending them to the *Gazette des Clubs,* wherein he would show himself a doughty lover of liberty animated by the true spirit of the great French Revolution with which he was so familiar.

As it happened he had kept some half-dozen volumes from his circulating library containing speeches by the chief orators of that period, and he unblushingly drew upon this sacred source. As was said by one of them—Danton: "Audacity, audacity, and for ever audacity!"

M. Florent displayed more audacity in his secret hiding-place than can be imagined, and doomed to the scaffold all those who could not at sight enumerate the Rights of Man, the catechism of every good citizen in every country.

His plan was to send in a few articles of this nature and, after he had become famous and safe, to introduce himself to the staff of Coudry's paper and disclose his identity.

The startling success of M. Barkimel's new politics, revealed in the public press, spurred him on, and he hoped to surpass his old friend in the uncompromising nature of his devotion to the cause.

And indeed what could M. Barkimel, with his inferior intelligence, have done to get himself nominated and elected by the Arsenal Club division as a member of the Revolutionary Tribunal?

M. Barkimel was a judge now! And M. Hilaire, the grocer, Commissioner for his division!

M. Florent's articles, carefully sealed, were delivered by M. Talon himself, who had received a second thousand-franc note and was more than ever convinced that a Reign of Terror was a good thing.

With what anxiety M. Florent every morning opened the *Gazette des Clubs* to see if his lucubrations were in it. But alas! he looked in vain for his masterpieces and his signature: The Old Cordelier.

Three articles had been delivered, and he had handed a fourth to Talon a quarter of an hour before, when a great tumult and the sound made by butt-ends of rifles filled the Rue des Francs Bourgeois. It was seven o'clock in the evening. M. Florent occupied the top floor, and ventured to put his nose out of the dormer window.

He descried below him M. Talon, accompanied by civilians, wearing their official red sashes, and an armed force. He no longer entertained any doubt that Talon, whom he had imprudently told on giving him the second thousand francs that he had no more money left, had informed against him in order to receive a reward.

Even now he could hear the tramp of heavy footsteps on the stairs and the voices of officers shouting their orders. M. Florent did not hesitate to creep like a cat over the tiles and, under cover of the gathering twilight, to steal from roof to roof. He all but fell and broke his neck a dozen times, but, reaching the open window of an attic, he entered and threw himself on his knees on the off chance. But the room was empty. M. Florent rose to his feet, opened the door and descended the stairs with as much composure as he could muster.

Fortune still favored him until he reached the ground floor, when he found himself in a narrow yard dimly lit by the lamps of a small cabaret, which he knew well, and in which he and M. Barkimel had been wont to treat themselves to tripe in the Caen manner, washed down by sparkling cider.

He would have to cross the yard to get away, and the window of the tavern, as it happened, was open. The room was full of diners, who were noisily drinking to the "success of the Municipality over the National Assembly."

M. Florent caught sight of M. Barkimel—of M. Barkimel, triumphant, wearing the insignia of his office; of M. Barkimel playing the part of leader, eating, drinking; of M. Barkimel treating the leading men of his division as though he were a great lord; of M. Barkimel who when he spoke was listened to! . . .

CHAPTER XXIII

SEQUEL TO M. FLORENT'S ADVENTURE

At that moment a great commotion arose in the cabaret. Loud cheers greeted a newcomer. M. Florent recognized M. Hilaire, who likewise wore round his waist a handsome red silk sash with gold tassels—the sash of the Commissioner for the division.

"What do you think has happened?" exclaimed M. Hilaire, hanging his sword and plumed cocked hat on a peg.

"Tell us, Commissioner."

"First, here's good health all round. I must tell you, my dear Barkimel, that it has to do with your friend Florent."

"Florent was never a friend of mine," cried Bar-

kimel indignantly. "I won't have you, my dear
Commissioner, give the sweet name of friend to a
bad citizen who ran away like the meanest coward
after joining with Subdamoun in trying to overthrow the Republic, and was always an infamous
reactionary. . . ."

"Just think, M. Florent is at his old tricks again,"
went on M. Hilaire. "As you know, we had a
meeting of Divisional Commissioners at the Town
Hall—a very important meeting. Under Coudry's
auspices we wanted to form an assembly of Commissioners of the Municipality from the united divisions with full power to save the Republic if the
Committee of the Municipality so ordered. You
will readily understand how far-reaching that might
be. But we must go to great lengths unless we wish
to be swallowed by the Communists, who look upon
us as rotten tradesmen. Coudry came in at the end
of the meeting, which was very lively, and when it
was all over, asked in a loud voice: 'Who is the
Commissioner for the Division?' I stepped forward. . . .

" 'Citizen Commissioner,' he said, 'I want you to
make a search of some importance. We have just
discovered the burrow of a dangerous reactionary
who, under the cloak of anonymity, sends the *Gazette des Clubs* horrible indictments of our Revolution. These infamous libels are signed: "The Old
Cordelier," and reach us by post. I have, for that
matter, had them set up in type so as to have several
copies on hand which can be read in the clubs, or
before the Revolutionary Tribunal, as evidence of
the audacity with which our enemies dream of
making us turn to the dark deeds of the past. . . .

" 'M. Verdier, one of my editors, at length discovered that the Old Cordelier's articles were posted
at the Town Hall. . . . We had this box kept
under observation, and so we were able to lay hands
on the man who posted the article, a man named
Talon, a concierge in the Rue des Francs Bourgeois,
and he at once confessed from whom he received
it. It is the work of one of his tenants, M. Florent.
In these circumstances we detained the man Talon,
and I rely on you, Mr. Commissioner, to arrest
Florent.' "

On hearing the story narrated by M. Hilaire, M.
Florent, we need not say, nearly died with horror in
the retreat in which he had taken refuge. His hair
stood on end. How came the unfortunate mistake,
of which he was about to be the victim, to arise?

"Well, he contrived to escape," went on M. Hilaire, filling his plate, "and let me tell you, between
ourselves, I should much prefer someone else to
arrest him rather than me, for after all he was a
good customer, and amused me with his old-fash-
ioned ideas."

"Ah, there's a decent, honest, good-hearted fellow for you," sighed M. Florent, and it occurred to
him that something was to be done in this direction.

"As for me, nobody knows what I am capable
of doing when it's a question of the public weal,"
declared Barkimel. And then, as if exhausted by
his heroic efforts, he made his excuses and took his
leave. Moreover, it was late, and the clubs and
divisions claimed their leaders.

By a lucky chance M. Hilaire, who, it is true,
was late in coming, was the last to go. He was

taking down his sword from the peg with a martial clatter of steel when a vague shadow leapt nimbly through the window from the yard and ran over and locked the door. M. Hilaire recognized M. Florent in spite of his parlous state. Therefore, instead of making a scene, he quickly closed the window.

"You!" he exclaimed. "Be careful. They are still searching for you in the quarter, and if they ever heard that I saw you and failed to arrest you I should be done for."

Florent made no answer. He dropped into a seat and uttered inarticulate moans.

"Poor fellow," murmured M. Hilaire. As we know, M. Hilaire was educated in the school of Chéri-Bibi and was full of noble and generous sentiments. "Poor fellow. What a state you are in. Eat and drink. Afterwards we'll see."

M. Florent did not wait to be asked a second time. When he had eaten his fill he said:

"You have a good heart, and I know you won't hand me over. You are not a knave like Barkimel, whom I advise you to be on your guard against."

"We have no time to speak ill of M. Barkimel," returned M. Hilaire. "Let's think about you."

"Before you help me to get away from here I want to safeguard you by warning you that Barkimel was ordered by the Arsenal Club to spy on you. He can ruin you—so take care. He suggested that I should keep a watch on you, but I told him that I refused to turn informer. That's why we fell out."

"You needn't worry yourself," returned M. Hilaire. "It is to him I owe the splendid position in which you see me to-day."

"How do you mean?" asked M. Florent, amazed.

"Why, it's very simple. Ordered by the Club to spy on me, as you say, he returned to the Club on the night of the *coup d'état* and made such an enthusiastic report on the manner in which I had acted during that difficult day, arresting with my own hands Lavobourg, the beautiful Sonia and their accomplices—acting, in short, as a true friend of the people—that the Club could find no better means of rewarding me than by appointing me Commissioner of the Division and presenting me with a sword of honor. . . .

"As far as he was personally concerned he managed also to present matters in such a favorable light that as he had apparently shared my risks and proved that he could take responsibility, it seemed to everyone that he deserved the congratulations of the Committee, and a few days later they nominated him a judge of the Revolutionary Tribunal."

"Oh I say, this is a bit too thick," exclaimed M. Florent, almost choking, "for he was only too willing to give you away. But he saw how he could turn your friendship to account, and that is why all of a sudden he showed such generosity. And here he is raised to the greatest dignity, while I, who had no ulterior motive in refusing to work secretly against you, am done for."

"No, you are not altogether done for," declared M. Hilaire positively.

"Thank you, M. Hilaire. My life is in your hands. I want you to find me some hiding-place until the unfortunate misunderstanding which has led Coudry to prosecute me is cleared up, for I have

never written any anti-revolutionary libels, I assure
you."

"Do you know where I can hide you?"

"In your house."

"Never as long as I live," returned M. Hilaire
with a grimace. "At my place people are for ever
coming in and out—a hundred people call at my
shop every day."

"Where do you suggest, M. Hilaire?"

"In Barkimel's flat."

M. Florent at first thought his ears were mis-
leading him, but M. Hilaire explained that he was
speaking seriously, and in the end M. Florent found
the suggestion extremely attractive.

"Oh, very well," he said. "That will be all right.
It's a very good joke. It serves him right. No one
will look for me in a flat owned by a judge of the
Revolutionary Tribunal, and I know his place well
enough to be able to hide without his suspecting
my presence."

"All the more so as he is rarely at home—a few
hours at night only. He tidies his rooms himself
in the morning and then sets out for the Law
Courts."

"Have you the key of his place?" asked M. Florent.

"He gave it to me so that I could send him in
some mineral water. I will execute this order myself, adding to it some preserved food for your use.
You must open the door to me, for you will have to
go there at once with the key. I will be off now,
but you mustn't leave here until you hear me
whistle twice. M. Barkimel's place is only a few

steps away. I'll talk to the concierge while you creep upstairs."

"What terrible times we live in!" gasped the ill-starred M. Florent. "But you are Providence itself for me. May I ask how Mme Hilaire is?"

"I believe," returned M. Hilaire, making ready to go, and passing his sword-belt under his sash, "I believe that I shall never again have occasion to feel angry with Mme Hilaire."

"Good Lord, is Mme Hilaire dead?" groaned M. Florent.

M. Hilaire did not wait to reply. He judged the moment opportune to slip into the street and begin to carry out the program which was to insure M. Florent's safety by secreting him in M. Barkimel's flat.

All went well, and thus at two o'clock in the morning M. Florent, hiding at the back of M. Barkimel's wardrobe, heard his old friend come in. M. Barkimel had no sooner closed his door than M. Florent, watching his movements through a little chink that he contrived to make in the partition, saw him with a weary gesture lay his candlestick on his bedside table and then sink into a reclining arm-chair with a deep moan.

He was no longer the proud M. Barkimel of a little while ago, the club orator, the implacable judge. He lacked the energy to pose before the mirror in his wardrobe. He was his natural self in the dreary privacy of his own room. He looked mean and cowardly again. He was once more the timid tradesman.

Suddenly he seemed to come to life again. He raised his head with a look of irritation, struck his

Louis Philippe table a resounding blow with his fist
and yelped fiercely:

"Am I to blame because they would not sentence
this Daniel to death? I warned the jury. I said:
"You'll see, that if you refuse Flottard this man's
head he will never forgive us.' But they wouldn't
listen to me. They sent Daniel before the Military
Court."

And he began to shout at the top of his voice:

"Guillotine them all!"

He must have been heard from top to bottom of
the house, and the tenants, aroused from their sleep,
would certainly be shivering in terror under the
bedclothes. M. Florent's teeth chattered.

"Well, how easy it is to be mistaken! He is a
wild beast," he thought.

He watched M. Barkimel, seemingly choking
with rage and revolutionary fervor, make for his
bedroom window, open it, and shout into the murky
darkness of the street:

"I never wanted to acquit anyone!"

In the face of this outburst M. Florent more and
more regretted M. Hilaire's idea to imprison him
with this tiger thirsting for blood.

M. Barkimel undressed without closing the window. In his excitement he omitted to notice the
somewhat cool breeze that swept in from the street,
while the draught produced a disastrous effect on
M. Florent, sweating for fear. He felt a tingling
sensation in his eyes and nose.

After a few moments' reflection M. Barkimel
closed the window and was preparing to go to bed
when a loud sneeze behind him made him start and
turn around in a panic.

The thin partition seemed still to be vibrating from this unexpected disturbance in the atmosphere, and M. Barkimel, wild-eyed, gazed at the things in the room as if he expected them to fall to pieces and bury him beneath their wreckage. At last, mastering as far as he could the terror which made the tassel of his nightcap shake, he gasped:

"Whoever is hiding there, show yourself if you are a friend of the people."

But no one moved, and a fresh sneeze emanating from the wardrobe, M. Barkimel in despair made a grab at his revolver, which he had placed in the drawer of his bedside table, and handled it so clumsily that a shot rang out with a deafening noise.

At once something rolled out of the wardrobe on to the floor. It was the quivering body of M. Florent, which M. Barkimel in horror recognized. At first he thought that he had killed him, and he drew back to the middle of the room and then to the door, when he observed that the body was assuming by degrees the posture of a man at prayer—knees on floor, hands clasped.

M. Florent was not dead; and he was imploring M. Barkimel's help.

M. Barkimel opened the door leading to the passage and, leaning over the staircase, listened for some time in the darkness of the night.

The more noise he made in his room the more the house seemed wrapped in slumber. It scarcely dared to breathe. . . . And a revolver shot in the night in such times was not likely to entice the curious out of doors. Far from it.

M. Barkimel returned to his room, drew his short figure erect, and struck himself on the chest.

"Monsieur, I don't know you," he said. "By what miracle you got here I prefer not to ask. And you may congratulate yourself on my lack of curiosity at such a time, for if I were inquisitive I might perhaps learn that your name is Florent and that you are threatened by the just laws of the country. Out you go—that's all I can say to you now."

With a proud and dignified gesture of command M. Barkimel pointed to the door.

"Very well," said M. Florent, beaten, crushed, making no effort to persist, fully convinced that he would never succeed in softening this stony revolutionist. "It was M. Hilaire, more generous than you, who gave me the key. . . . Very well . . . I will go, as you refuse to remember we were once friends."

"Where are you going?" asked M. Barkimel bluntly in a low voice, stopping M. Florent and closing the door.

"Who knows. . . . To the guillotine."

"Yes—guillotine them all," bellowed M. Barkimel. Nevertheless he made M. Florent sit down on his reclining arm-chair, and with tears in his eyes asked under his breath:

"Are you hungry, Florent—thirsty? Heavens above, how miserable you look. I feel sorry for you. You see where your opinions have led you. And what do you wish me to do for you now?"

"Keep me here," groaned M. Florent, embracing his old friend. Then they began to sob in each other's arms.

"Of course, I'll keep you here," said Barkimel, "but it will be no joke, you know. If ever you are discovered in this flat it will be all up with both of us."

"What terrible times we live in!"

"We live in glorious times," cried M. Barkimel in another outburst, "and up to now we have only seen the bright side of things. It is now that the Reign of Terror is really beginning—the Terror without which virtue is ineffectual."

"Hush!" whispered M. Florent. "People will know that you are talking to someone."

"Not a bit of it. They are used to my soliloquies. I strike terror into them with my soliloquies. Every now and then I get up in the night to frighten them. Ah, my dear fellow, what a job! But one must live, you know. They have made me a judge of the Revolutionary Tribunal. If I don't terrify the people hereabouts the people hereabouts will terrify me. And then I am afraid of spies. They plant them everywhere. They may be watching me in the dark; therefore I am never so bloodthirsty as when I am alone. In this way they know all about my real character."

"I will do whatever you like, my good Barkimel. . . . Ah, you haven't changed a bit. It is the times that have changed."

"Be quiet. . . . Listen. . . . I seem to hear something." Then in a resounding voice he went on: "As for me I shall reply to the weaklings of the Assembly: 'Gentlemen, a little bloodshed can only be remedied by a bigger one!' "

"Oh, hush! It's too awful. When you talk like that you make me feel ill."

"Well, and what about me? I frighten myself."

"Why, it's horrible."

"Hold your tongue. . . . I hear a noise in the
street. . . . Rifles. . . . Armed men of the division. . . . My God, I bet they are coming to look
for you."

M. Barkimel blew out the candle and both listened carefully. The sound of voices, shouts, military commands mingled with the sonorous rattle of
arms on the pavement and fists beating on the doors
reached their ears. . . .

"Open in the name of the law!"

"No, not that door but this one," insisted a
drunken voice. "I tell you he is here."

"Mercy on me, it's Talon's voice," groaned M.
Florent.

"The floor above. . . . In the judge's flat. With
his friend Barkimel. Take it from me, he is with
his friend Barkimel."

Barkimel pushed Florent into the wardrobe,
which had a sort of double bottom, and darted over
to his bed and rumpled the bedclothes. Then he
opened his door and shouted:

"What happened? What's the matter?"

"Come on, come on. . . . The little man was not
asleep just now. A light was in his room. It's a
certainty he is hiding him."

"Gentlemen, I am a judge of the Revolutionary
Tribunal. I assume from your shouts that you are
hunting for a man named Florent, whom I used to
know."

"He was a friend of yours," yelped Talon.

"Very likely, but he is not a friend now."

"He was seen to enter your flat."

"One thing I can assure you—he is not here."

"We are going to have a look."

The municipal officers proceeded to make a search in due form. They could discover nothing; but a shrewish woman accompanying the search party exclaimed:

"I believe I've got him. This wardrobe has a double bottom."

But by a miracle she failed to discover Florent in the wardrobe, for he was no longer there. Which way had he gone? How had he slipped out? M. Barkimel has since explained:

"Suddenly I grew even more pale and lay down on my bed with a sigh of weariness. I declared that I was exhausted, and this search would be the death of me. Now I had just felt someone stir near me, and it could only be Florent. Florent had crept between my two mattresses.

"How was it possible for him to breathe? ·Assuredly if the visit were long drawn out I should find him suffocated. And I was at once worried by the horrible thought that I should not know how to dispose of the body!

"At last the search party declared that nothing remained to be inspected but my bed. I thought I should have died on the spot. Fortunately, they were satisfied to examine the head and foot and to look under the bed.

"Afterwards they turned over the cushions of the sofas in my bedroom, dining room, and sitting-room. I thought they would never go. At last they had the hardihood to advise me to have a little sleep and wished me good night. They still remained for some time in the building and I lay on my bed without stirring a limb.

"The terrible part of it was that Florent did not

stir a limb either. Was he still alive? Was I lying
on my friend's dead body? Was there time even
yet to save him? I was in a state of horrible per-
plexity. At last I heard the street door close and
the hateful patrol march off into the darkness.

"I jumped out of bed and locked the door. Then
I darted back to the bed and dragged Florent from
it, but not without some difficulty, for while he lay
there he had endeavored to hold his breath as far
as possible and was almost stifling, unable to speak,
and in a bath of perspiration.

"I laid him in front of the window, which I
opened, and made him drink a glass of brandy. In
the end he came to himself and expressed his gratitude. He told me how terrified he had been and
how surprised at my courage in the presence of
these men, especially when they looked into the bed.
'Of course,' I returned, 'very few men would have
done what I did for you.' He admitted it, and I
gave him to understand that a second experience of
the same sort would be beyond my powers of endurance and that he could repay me in no better
way than by leaving the flat as soon as possible. . . .

"His face, as he listened to me, betrayed considerable dejection. All the same, he understood
me, forbore to argue, shook my hand, and went off.

"I quietly closed the door after him and I felt a
pang at my heart as I heard him cautiously descend
the stairs. It couldn't be helped! I was certain,
whatever happened, even if he were caught in the
house, to be able to maintain henceforward that he
had not been in hiding in my flat; and, in truth,
I had done enough for a man who had spent his life

246 THE NEW IDOL

in disagreeing with my opinions and in arguing with
me on every conceivable question. . . ."

CHAPTER XXIV

OF THE GREATEST DANGER INCURRED BY ALL
REVOLUTIONS

It was no easy task for poor M. Hilaire, acting
on Chéri-Bibi's orders, to persuade the de Touchais household to place themselves under his protection. When Cecily learned of the disaster to her
son, and Lydia knew that he was a prisoner, they
both declared that they desired but one thing—to
share the same cell and the same fate.

Fortunately, Marie Thérèse displayed sufficient
common sense for the three of them. Supported by
Jacqueline, she overcame Cecily and Lydia's last
hesitations, and the four fugitives, after leaving the
mansion, remained until the end of the day concealed in a covered stall kept by a man begrimed
with dirt who sold coal and wood.

At nightfall M. Hilaire took his party without let
or hindrance to a narrow lane, not far away, running at the back of his shop, where he possessed a
store-room in a basement leading to his cellars. . . .

The store-room was reached from the lane direct
by a low door, used in the ordinary way for the delivery of casks. M. Hilaire quickly picked the lock
and brought his four hapless guests down into the
store-room. Assisted by the coal dealer, in whom
he appeared to repose complete confidence, he settled them with some provisions among his casks and

made them as comfortable as circumstances permitted. The coal dealer lent them some mattresses
and sheets which they were surprised to find were
quite clean, despite the complexion of their owner.
At last M. Hilaire, after dismissing the coal dealer
and permanently blocking the door leading from the
store-room to his cellars, and enjoining the ladies
to barricade themselves in and on no account to
open the street door to anyone, closed this door and
hastened to his club to learn the latest news.

The news was unfavorable for the Major, but
favorable for M. Hilaire, who was presented with
his official sash as Commissioner for the division.

Now and again M. Barkimel, who, as we know,
had taken some considerable part in M. Hilaire's
appointment, said:

"Aren't you going home? Mme Hilaire must be
dying of anxiety. Just think, you have not been
home for the last two nights."

But M. Hilaire was in no hurry to go home. Indeed, it scarcely troubled him that Mme Hilaire was
dying of anxiety. On the contrary, it was the
thought that she was not dead of anxiety that disturbed him most. "I shall get it hot when I do go
home," he thought.

Suddenly he struck his forehead. They all
thought that he had found the solution of one of
those numerous social problems the discussion of
which caused such tumultuous excitement at the
meetings of the Arsenal Club, and they gathered
round him. And indeed it concerned something of
the sort.

"Can you tell me, my friends," began M. Hilaire
in a tone of the utmost secrecy, "what is the

greatest danger to which the Revolution is at the
present moment exposed?"

M. Hilaire's friends looked at each other with
puckered brows as if this poor Revolution was already at its last gasp, and as a measure of precaution they had been called together at that late hour
of the night to save it. But as in general they were
lacking in ideas they shook their heads in gloomy
hopelessness. Thereupon M. Hilaire resolved to
strike his great blow:

"The greatest danger to which the Revolution is
exposed comes from women."

He paused to weigh the effect of his words. His
audience exchanged glances open-mouthed. The
bachelors among them said: "Perhaps you're
right"; the married men kept silent so as not to
compromise themselves. They were waiting for
the sequel.

"It is certain," observed M. Barkimel, who had
some difficulty in holding his tongue, "that those
knitting women of the great French Revolution, for
instance . . ."

"Citizen Barkimel," interrupted M. Hilaire,
"don't speak ill of those knitting women. They
were ugly, but their very ugliness, by terrifying the
enemies of the nation, added to their punishment,
and the Revolution had nothing to complain of on
that score. I am referring to ordinary women, the
immense army of wives of us married men. I am
speaking of the women in our homes, the mothers
of our children, those kind-hearted and loving
housewives who make us return home after the
labors of the day so sweet to us. These are the

women who are a danger, a perpetual danger to the Revolution."

He broke off once more, and saw that his listeners were dumfounded and, as the phrase goes, hanging on his words.

"In truth," he went on with renewed vigor, "how often do we see citizens express surprise at some of the most harmless changes in the law? How often also do we see citizens advocating one day prompt and vigorous action and returning next day to propose amendments designed to destroy its efficacy and power? Why these changes of opinion? Why these waverings? Why this lack of courage which, I say again, may ruin the Republic! Citizens—a woman is at the bottom of it! . . . She is a creature of goodness, but also of weakness, and this weakness—oh, the pity of it!—by a strange phenomenon which it is absolutely necessary for us to guard against, is more potent than our strength. She reduces it to naught with her tears. She shatters it with a smile. She sometimes destroys it, I am bound to say, with a threat.

"My dear friends, you follow my argument. You now know why the greatest danger to which the Revolution is exposed comes from the wife at our side—yours, citizens, and—I don't pretend to be different—mine. When Mme Hilaire says to me: 'I don't like it. You can't have the heart to vote for it. You will not do that,' I am almost defenseless. Well, we must at one stroke liberate ourselves from this fatal domestic influence, greater than that which we have to fight against in our popular meetings. To-morrow I shall ask the Arsenal Club to carry the following resolution to be placed before the Parliamentary Committee: 'The wife of a revolutionary citizen refusing to obey her husband renders herself liable to the death penalty."

M. Hilaire ceased speaking and received a veritable ovation. The room almost shook with the appaluse of the married men; the bachelors, too, cheered, but with a smile.

"I intend to set you an example to-night," said M. Hilaire, seizing a piece of cardboard from an old calendar and asking for a sheet of white paper, paste, pen and ink. Five minutes later he displayed a placard on which he had written in splendid capital letters the dazzling sentence: "The wife of a revolutionary citizen refusing to obey her husband renders herself liable to the death penalty."

He put the placard under his arm and sent to the guard-house hard by for two civic guards, who arrived with fixed bayonets. He ordered them to follow him. Then, shaking hands with his friends with an excitement which they shared, for they all knew Virginie, he set out, supported by his guards, for his home, where Mme Hilaire, he believed, was impatiently waiting for him.

That night, however, she refused to open the door to him. He drummed vigorously on the iron shop front in vain. Mme Hilaire, entrenched within, declared from the open window of her room upstairs that "she refused to come down at that hour and be frozen to death, and M. Hilaire could go back again." She closed the window with a bang and M. Hilaire went away to spend the night in cabarets.

But he was raging within himself, and from the

manner in which next morning at eight o'clock he
approached the open door of the "Up-to-date Grocery Stores," carried his placard under his arm, and
led forward his two civic guards it was easy to see
that there was going to be trouble.

When he entered, after placing a warrior at each
side of the door, Mme Hilaire was in the cash desk.
As was her custom when she was in a state of suppressed fury, she did not even look up. She did
not see, nor would she condescend to see M. Hilaire,
who displayed across his waistcoat his wide sash
with gold tassels arousing the terrified admiration
of his assistants.

M. Hilaire at once went up to the cash desk with
as much courage as he could muster, which, it must
be admitted, was none too great. But he managed
to fix his placard to the woodwork of the cash desk,
despite his trembling hands.

Mme Hilaire could not as yet see it, but the shop
assistants were able to spell out the phrases, and
with a shudder immersed themselves again in the
handling of their bags of prunes. What was about
to happen? In Heaven's name, what was about to
happen?

M. Hilaire coughed, and in a voice that he strove
to render firm threw out this sentence to the echoes
of the "Up-to-date Grocery Stores":

"Have the \California apricots come?"

But the echoes gave forth no response. Every
eye was fixed on Mme Hilaire, continuing to add up
her figures.

"Am I speaking French or Greek?" asked M.
Hilaire, losing his temper. And he repeated:
،"Have the California apricots come?"

Then, not daring to look at his wife, he fixed the junior assistant with such a threatening look that the boy, keeping his distance, summoned up sufficient courage to say:

"I don't know, sir."

"Does anyone here know?" growled M. Hilaire fiercely.

Then the head assistant said:

"Yes, sir, we have received two cases."

"Has the macaroni also come? And what about the quarter pound tins of truffle scraps?"

M. Hilaire turned his back on the cash desk. He was conscious of the tempest rising behind him. A breath of the storm was wafted to him in these words:

"Scraps yourself! What does it matter to you what happens here after your behavior?"

It was M. Hilaire's turn to make no answer. He merely went over and took from a drawer in the cash desk the key of the store-room and stepped forward to the trap-door in the floor leading to the cellars.

"What are you going to do in the store-room? You've no need to go down there, and if you wish to do so, do me the favor to put on your cap and apron and take off that red dish-cloth round your waist."

"Mme Hilaire, I ask you to weigh your words," said M. Hilaire in a tone never before adopted in public towards his wife. "They are more serious than you think. I shall continue to wear this red dish-cloth, as you call it. It is the emblem of my new office. I have been appointed Commissioner for the Arsenal Division."

"A pretty Commissioner, upon my word! Just look at the face of this Commissioner. . . ."

"Appointed to see that the orders of the Assembly are respected," said M. Hilaire calmly. "Read this, madame."

As he spoke he pointed with the forefinger of his right hand to the placard hanging on the cash desk. Then he turned on his heels and went towards the trap-door.

It was too much for Virginie. She leapt rather than stepped down from her office throne and rolled towards the trap-door, at the edge of which she prudently came to a stop. Then she stood erect before M. Hilaire.

"I won't have you go down in that finery," she bellowed.

"That finery!" echoed M. Hilaire. "That finery has been forced upon me by the nation and henceforward will never leave me."

"Really I am sorry for you! Go to bed. You must want a rest after your orgies."

She made a movement to drop the trap-door, thus preventing M. Hilaire from descending to the cellars. But now thoroughly incensed and determined to go to all lengths, he took her arm and led her to the placard:

"The wife of a revolutionary citizen refusing to obey her husband renders herself liable to the death penalty."

But instead of being dismayed this resolute lady had the hardihood to burst out laughing, and tried to lay a sacrilegious hand on M. Hilaire's placard. The Grocer-Commissioner no longer hesitated to call his men to his assistance. The two civic guards ran up and on M. Hilaire's order made Mme Hilaire prisoner.

When she saw herself between two bayonets, hustled by fellows who looked as if they meant business, she changed color several times.

And just then the street resounded with a furious clamor, while a long procession of doubtful characters marched past, firing their revolvers in the air, waving their swords, acclaiming the first victory of the Revolution, and threatening with immediate death any citizen who refused to fly the red flag from his window. M. Hilaire showed his sash and was loudly cheered.

It was the Revolution stalking abroad. Never had Mme Hilaire seen it at such close quarters. She felt that it was not a matter to treat lightly, and that the placard might possibly be no idle fancy at a time when men could permit themselves every latitude. Then she burst into tears, thus confessing herself beaten.

"Put madame in the cash desk," ordered M. Hilaire.

The guards helped her to her seat.

"Until further orders she is in your charge," said the Grocer-Commissioner. "You are responsible for her behavior. If she stops making up her accounts and slips away from the cash desk you will have to give an explanation to me and the Club Committee, and we do not trifle with discipline. Stop crying, madame. Take this down—ten pounds of sugar. . . . ."

She wrote as she sobbed, blew her nose, sighed, wiped her eyes and mouth, her double chin puffed out with despair.

And every now and again when M. Hilaire's back was turned she cast her eyes on what he was doing, admired his new bearing, his confident movements, such as she had never seen before, admired the Commissioner with his sash, whom the customers greeted with such deference.   She was mastered. . . .

Where had he gone?   What was he doing in the dining-room?   One moment she heard him in the kitchen, and next he came back and went down into the cellars carrying a sort of hamper over which he had thrown an apron.   She wondered what was happening, and why he had taken the key of the store-room, which was entered only on Saturdays when their stocks of provisions or liquids were replenished.   She reckoned that he remained there nearly half an hour.

And it seemed to her that he came up with a strange look of gloom on his face. . . .   What was this new mystery?

After giving instructions to his chief assistant he left the stores and did not return until an hour later, when he was accompanied by a coal dealer carrying a sack on his shoulders, and both went down into the cellars.   The best of it was that M. Hilaire came up alone, leaving the coal dealer behind.

"It's the new coal dealer from next door," said M. Hilaire as he passed the cash desk.   "I have told him to put the sacks in order and sweep up the coal dust."

"But we shan't want any more coal until the winter, dear," Mme Hilaire ventured to suggest.

"A woman who can't see further than her nose

may think so, of course," returned M. Hilaire, "but a man who can foresee the almost immediate rise in prices will take his precautions."

"All right, dear."

"Oh, I was going to tell you—I have invited the coal dealer to lunch. That's the neighborly thing to do."

"Oh, my dear!"

She was almost choking. He had invited the coal dealer to lunch—he was indeed going off his head. She began to cry again.

"No blubbing," he said. "This is not the moment." I have four other guests."

She wiped her eyes.

"You might have told me so before. I would have got something special ready and changed my dress."

"That's all right. I like you to be reasonable, as you are now. But don't worry. Our guests are very ordinary people who will be quite satisfied to take pot luck, and there's no need for you to put on your best frock."

"Suppose they are all like the coal dealer!" she thought.

But she had no conception that she would see the arrival at midday of two sturdy market porters covered with flour, a hideous little imp wearing canvas shoes, and a distressful-looking old man, shrivelled and bent with age, whom M. Hilaire introduced as Daddy Peanuts.

Virginia grasped the position in a flash. M. Hilaire was taking care to keep on the right side of the common people. What a man! What a genius!

"Hilaire, I am very sorry," she said. "You can

tell those two gentlemen with bayonets to leave the shop. I will do anything you please."

He sent the two civic guards to their quarters after standing treat at the bar, and then kissed Virginie.

"Is it all over and done with?" he asked.

"Yes, Hilaire."

"Then go and join our guests in the dining room. All you have to do is to be pleasant. You will see that things will work out all right. I have got rid of the maid."

"Got rid of the maid!"

"Yes, she worried me with her chatter. In revolutionary times one has no use for maids. They misunderstand what is said, and they are the only creatures who give us away."

"You are right, Hilaire, all the more so as I was longing to give her notice. It's incredible the amount of metal polish she wasted. . . . But who is going to serve the lunch?"

"You, of course."

"What about the shopmen's lunch?"

"I shall give them five francs each and tell them to get their lunch outside."

"But you'll ruin us. . . ."

"They will be satisfied and won't listen at the door."

"All right," agreed Virginie, pensive.

The lunch passed off more successfully than she would have thought. These "poor people" behaved quite well, and their conversation did not overstep the limit. As the coal dealer had washed his hands, she considered that he had "very fine hands" for a man working at his trade. The others called him

"Monsieur Frederic," and appeared to have known him some time. Monsieur Frederic called the two stalwarts from the market Polydore and Jean Jean.

As to M. Mazeppa, the solicitor's clerk, and the peanut dealer, they seemed to form a party to themselves and did not join in the general talk, which fell upon the events of the day and the arrest of Subdamoun, on whom they piled up the vilest abuse.

Mme Hilaire spared no effort to be agreeable to her party. Observing that Daddy Peanuts looked depressed and was eating very little, she addressed a few kind words to him.

"How is business with you at present?" she asked.

"Well, madame," returned the old man in a tone of great dejection, "I must admit that trade is very bad."

Then he sat silent and Mme Hilaire was left to her thoughts. What a queer lot of people they were, anyhow! What strange guests. . . . Still, they would not, presumably, be sitting down at her table every day.

When she reached this point in her reflections and astonishment M. Hilaire confided to her that he had decided to invite Polydore and Jean Jean, the two stalwarts from the market, to stay with them, for they had had the misfortune that very morning to be turned out of their home by their landlord, a niggardly and foolhardy bourgeois, who expected to be paid his rent in these troublous times!

Mme Hilaire at first failed to grasp his meaning; the suggestion seemed to her so monstrous. When at last she realized that these two ruffians were to have board and lodging with them she rose to her feet. . . . She had seen and heard enough this time.

"Where are you going, dearest?" inquired M. Hilaire.

She went into the kitchen. M. Hilaire followed her.

"What is it?" he asked. "Have you broken anything?"

She gave vent to a gasp like the bellows of a forge, and at last said:

"Surely you are not going to give up our bed to them?"

"No," returned M. Hilaire calmly. "I shall put them in the cellar. They won't inconvenience us there."

"In the cellar, where all the wine—hams—sausages—provisions are! . . . In the cellar!"

To prevent herself from falling Mme Hilaire clung to the meat safe, which gave way, and M. Hilaire had to support both for a moment, which called forth one of the greatest efforts of his life. At last Virginie recovered her balance.

"I don't understand anything you tell me or what you are doing and I fear I shall go mad. Perhaps I am already mad."

Then, taking compassion, M. Hilaire kissed Mme Hilaire, who longed to bite him but after what had happened thought it more prudent to receive his caress with a smile.

"Don't try to understand, Virginie, and you will be happy."

Having said which he left her and returned to the dining-room and his guests, whose stations in life were so peculiar and whom Virginie did not know from Adam. But in the days that followed she out-lived worse things.

The dining-room became the bureau of a sort of council of war at which the fantastic peanut dealer, the little blackguard Mazeppa, the coal dealer, and the two freebooters, who never left the house, met at every hour of the day.

It was these two, Polydore and Jean Jean, who irritated Mme Hilaire the most. To know that they were in the house at night doing as they pleased was "more than she could bear," and "she was be-side herself."

The worst of it was that M. Hilaire himself con-tinued to take down to them what he called "a little snack for the night." And what a little snack it was! Chicken, early fruit and vegetables—in fact the pick of everything. It seemed like a bad dream! Moreover, she had received the order not to go down into the cellar.

"Now that a couple of men are living there, you understand, it's no place for you," M. Hilaire told her.

CHAPTER XXV

OF CERTAIN DISCOVERIES MADE BY MADAME HILAIRE AND THE RESULT

BUT a day came—it happened to be the day on which the first tumbril appeared from the Concier-gerie Prison—when Polydore and Jean Jean were absent from the house at the same time as M. Hilaire.

Virginie lit a lantern, opened the trap-door, and went down into the cellar to penetrate the mystery.

The place was in extraordinary confusion. Boxes had been turned upside down and some of them broken open. Wine had poured from the casks, saturating the ground as if it had been inundated by the waters of the Seine. A vat of light sparkling Anjou wine was empty. Half the contents of a barrel of red herrings lay on the sodden floor. A number of smoked hams had disappeared, or rather the bones that were left revealed that in spite of regular meals in the dining-room and M. Hilaire's nightly "little snacks" Polydore and Jean Jean had allowed their rapacious appetites to have full play.

Mme Hilaire, with her lantern, her sighs, and her hoarse exclamations, was pursuing her way amid the devastation when suddenly she heard the sound of voices from the far end of the cellar.

She came to a stand, trembling all over. Who was speaking?

She listened, but to no purpose. And yet she could not have been mistaken. The sound had indeed come from the back of the cellar, which was divided from the store-room by a wooden partition in which a thick door had been built.

Mme Hilaire had to place her hand on her breast to repress the loud beating of her heart.

She crept with infinite caution to the end of the underground passage. Two heavy casks had been placed against the store-room door to prevent anyone from entering.

Hush! . . . She could hear once more the murmurs of voices. . . . A gasp broke in her throat. It was a woman's voice! By the Blessed Virgin, M.

Hilaire was hiding some woman in the store-room.

Everything was now clear!

The snacks and delicacies taken down to the cellar by M. Hilaire were not intended for Polydore and Jean Jean, who, as she had ascertained for herself, unfortunately, had no need of these to fill their stomachs. No—all those delicacies were for a woman. . . . What woman? . . . M. Hilaire's mistress! . . . Damnation! . . . One of the upper classes doubtless, since she was in hiding like a suspect.

M. Hilaire had always shown a liking for women in high places. His devotion to the Marchioness de Touchais was often incomprehensible to Mme Hilaire. And M. Hilaire must indeed have been smitten with this woman in the store-room to have employed those two monsters to guard her, those two insatiable bullies who were costing him a mint of money and ruining his business.

In very truth that was the whole trouble. Was it surprising that she found him altered beyond recognition? It was this woman who had effected the change in him. It was on her account that she had so greatly suffered, on her account that she had been humiliated, threatened, turned into ridicule before them all. It was on account of this woman that she was no longer mistress in her own house. . . .

Well, time would show.

Determined to be revenged in startling fashion, and knowing that revenge is a dish to be eaten cold, she hastened to return to the light of day and to avoid the least scene.

Suddenly Daddy Peanuts appeared. M. Hilaire

had not yet come back.   Daddy Peanuts bowed to Mme Hilaire and told her that he had learned with pleasure on passing the Town Hall that M. Hilaire had just been appointed Inspector of Prisons.

"My congratulations, madam," he added.   "Every day your husband rises to a higher position, obtains a new office.   The Revolution is paying its respects to his great qualities of head and heart."

"Bravo!" agreed Jean Jean, who had just come in.   "We'll open a couple of bottles of champagne to celebrate it."

"Yes, and a flagon of old rum," added Polydore.

Mme Hilaire lowered her eyes to conceal the rage and hatred that possessed her.   These wretched persons were all in league with her husband.

At last M. Hilaire arrived and heard without undue surprise the news of his elevation to so important an office as Inspector of Prisons at a time when these places were full.

Vain as he was, he took naturally to his honors. A fresh piece of news brought by his friend the "new coal dealer," with the black face and white hands, seemed to affect him more.

A shiver passed through him when M. Frederic, with an emotion by no means assumed, told of his regret on learning some minutes before that his predecessor the coal dealer who had so kindly transferred his business—deal boards, lathing, coal—had been found dead that morning in the Rue de Turenne with a dagger in his back.

The worthy man had been for some time a friend of M. Hilaire's, and had, as we know, rendered him service on the day when he was engaged in finding the de Touchais family a safe place of refuge.   Was it not terrible for this man to be punished for those services by a stab in the back? Possibly he had let fall an indiscreet word in spite of M. Hilaire's explicit injunctions.

"Possibly that stab was merely a measure of precaution," said the abominable and frightful Chéri-Bibi.

Just then M. Barkimel appeared on the scene, pale and worn out. He had left the Revolutionary Tribunal and met on his way a colleague who had been present at the function in the Place de la Revolution and described how Tissier, the ex-President of the Chamber of Deputies, sentenced to death by Barkimel himself, had met his fate.

"There's no disputing," said Barkimel in a melancholy tone, "that it gives one a turn to think that one was instrumental in sending a man to the scaffold—a man who a little while ago was breathing like you and me, talking and turning his head round. . . ."

"Turning his head round! . . . Three cheers for turning his head round! You thought of that all by yourself—turning his head round! Of course, he can't turn his head round now," laughed the hideous Mazeppa, just come in.

Though M. Barkimel was aware of M. Hilaire's new custom of open-handed hospitality he had not hitherto met this new "pauper." He drew back in dismay. But Daddy Peanuts, seeming to wake from a dream, introduced the youthful Mazeppa to him. "My secretary," he added with an unexpected and grating laugh that scared the others more than anything else.

He was the first to enter the dining-room, and

they heard him laugh again—a terrible laugh. M. Hilaire's cheeks blanched. As to M. Frederic, the so-called coal dealer, he took his leave after apologizing to Mme Hilaire for being unable to accept her invitation to dinner that evening.

Mme Hilaire, rankling under her recent discovery, said to herself: "Play the farce to the end, my little men. We shall have the whole thing out shortly." And she went into the dining-room, giving her arm to M. Barkimel and ignoring the other guests.

"I don't know what has happened to Mme Hilaire to-day," came the rasping voice of Chéri-Bibi, who had already taken a seat at table like an ill-bred person, "but there is a look about her that suits her to perfection."

Mme Hilaire did not wince. Her turn would come.

The conversation fell on the news of d'Askof's arrest, published in the *Journal des Clubs,* and Daddy Peanuts expressed his surprise that the police should still be unable to trace the hiding-place of the de Touchais family.

"The beautiful Marchioness must be rather crestfallen," said Virginie. "She was so high and mighty that one scarcely dared speak to her. Where is she now? Perhaps she has found someone to hide her in a cellar, *as other people are doing.*"

On hearing this last sentence uttered in an aggressive tone the guests seemed for a moment to suspend their eating. Hilaire quivered with nervousness, which did not escape Mme Hilaire, and she rejoiced in his confusion with scarcely concealed malevolence. Polydore and Jean Jean exchanged glances. Daddy Peanuts told Mazeppa to go for a stroll and not to return until he whistled for him. Then he coughed, raised his tinted spectacles to Mme Hilaire, and said in a voice that trembled slightly:

"What do you mean? You ought to explain yourself."

"Explain myself," echoed this notable woman, her face radiant at the effect she had produced. "Need I explain myself? M. Hilaire knows perfectly well what I mean."

"I?" protested M. Hilaire with an air of innocence. "Why, I confess that I don't even understand Daddy Peanuts's surprise at what you say. Obviously the lady may be hiding in a cellar or garret."

"Cellar or garret, she'll get no pity out of me," exclaimed Mme Hilaire. "And if ever they nab the conceited thing and that affected Lydia and that old hypocrite Jacqueline I shall be the first to shout 'Hurrah!'"

"So you really hate her?" said Chéri-Bibi in a hoarse voice.

"I will explain . . ." broke in M. Hilaire.

"Shut up!" growled Chéri-Bibi. "Don't interrupt a lady. It's not done in polite society."

"Oh, on that subject we have never agreed," went on Mme Hilaire. "Though he now wins as many honors as he pleases he certainly regrets the day when he was a servant with these people. He told me so. He will not deny it. And he calls himself a Republican, a Revolutionist, and all the rest of it. I am only a woman of the people, but I feel more resentment."

"I've had enough of this," exclaimed M. Hilaire.

But Virginie continued her yelping:

"Not a bit of it. When he sees her he bows to the very ground. Upon my word, one might almost think he was in love with her. It's enough to make one sick, not to mention that Madame Cecily is no better than she should be. There was a great deal of talk about her at Dieppe when she was making assignations with the Vicomte de Pont Marie, even in church."

A pause ensued—all was silence. It seemed as if Mme Hilaire's words had struck M. Hilaire dead. He remained motionless, gave no sign of life. Suddenly the hoarse voice of the peanut dealer was heard:

"I can see that you don't like her."

"Oh no," exploded Virginie. "Look here, as I can't hope to have her as my housemaid, I have only one wish—to see her arrested, sentenced and guillotined."

The sound of breaking crockery seemed to emphasize the significance of such a wish. It was Daddy Peanuts, who had rolled under the table with his plate. He used often to eat under the table like a dog. He was generally quite comfortable, seated on his haunches on the floor, and as a rule joined in the conversation only by uttering a series of grunts. But this time no sound came from him. M. Barkimel broke the silence, which was becoming intolerable.

"Madame, you are a true citizen. I can tell you something that will please you—we are on the point of discovering the Marchioness de Touchais's hiding-place."

"So there is a Providence after all," exclaimed Virginie.

Something stirred under the table, and M. Hilaire, to show, perhaps, that he was not really dead, made a movement on his seat. Polydore and Jean Jean rocked themselves on theirs.

"Yes," went on M. Barkimel, "the thing occurred at the end of the sitting of the Revolutionary Tribunal. A young laundry-maid was brought before us. She was no more a laundry-maid than I am. In reality she was the Baroness d'Askof, the wife of Subdamoun's friend, who himself was arrested in the Café Werther.

"The Baroness d'Askof, whose fate we were to settle at once, and who naturally feared to be sentenced to death and executed to-morrow, asked us whether we would spare her life if she placed us in a position to arrest the Marchioness de Touchais, Subdamoun's mother.

"The public prosecutor took it upon himself to promise to agree to her request if her information turned out to be of real value. Then she stated that the laundress who had received and concealed her and dressed her up as a laundry-maid was the Marchioness's former laundress, and had recognized some of her things among linen recently sent to her by a customer."

On hearing these words M. Hilaire seemed to be about to faint, and then he uttered a piercing shriek. They were all seriously alarmed.

"Oh, it's nothing," he said. "It's over. . . . A slight heart attack."

The truth was that he had been bitten in the leg

by the thing under the table. He at once realized his blunder in sending among his house linen an article belonging to the Marchioness, and he realized also that if his blunder had the terrible consequences which would now have to be provided for it was not his wife who would be destroyed by the thing under the table but himself, Commissioner for the Division and Inspector of Prisons though he was.

M. Barkimel, failing to notice the dramatic interest which his story excited, went on:

"She gave us the name of the laundress in the Rue aux Phoques."

"Rue aux Phoques!" exclaimed Virginie. "Why, that's our laundress."

"The case was adjourned while we sent a Commissioner to make enquiries," continued M. Barkimel. "This officer soon returned and informed us that he had discovered the laundress dead, hanging from the fastening of the window. . . . Well, what do you think of that? Was not the matter getting rather intricate? He at first assumed that it was a case of suicide because a love-letter was found near the body, but afterwards he had no difficulty in reconstructing the crime. It was another blow struck by Subdamoun's friends, who must have been warned of our being on the track of the mother of their idol. These men stop at nothing."

"What did you do with the Baroness d'Askof?" M. Hilaire had the strength to ask, wiping the beads of perspiration from his forehead.

"We were on the point of sentencing her to death, since her information had been of no avail, when she told us that she remembered quite well the initials of the customer who had sent the linen in question. These initials are——"

M. Barkimel was unable to proceed. A terrific crash resounded in the dining-room. The heavy table, with all that lay on it—china, glass, knives and forks, everything—was overturned, and the table itself fell on M. Barkimel's feet. He began to cry out as if he were being flayed alive. In the midst of the confusion Daddy Peanuts apologized to Mme Hilaire for having risen a little too abruptly and thus stupidly caused the catastrophe.

M. Barkimel, greatly disgusted with a dinner at which he had found no pleasure and his feet were nearly crushed, took leave somewhat in the sulks, assisted by Mazeppa, who was told to see him home and look after him, "as if he were his father."

On a sign from Daddy Peanuts, Polydore and Jean Jean returned to their cellar, where their bed was waiting for them, alleging as a pretext that they were worn out with the exertions of the day, so that Daddy Peanuts and M. and Mme Hilaire remained alone in the dining-room. Mme Hilaire, who no longer doubted the identity of the visitor whom they were hiding, seemed ready to burst. Her face scarlet from the influxion of blood, her bosom raging, her arms akimbo, she waited for the word that should be the signal for the explosion.

Daddy Peanuts, after very carefully closing the door, said:

"I don't think that ass Barkimel has any suspicion or else he would not have come here to dinner for fear of compromising himself, nor would he have told us his story."

"I quite agree with you," said M. Hilaire, trembling in every limb.

"How should he have any suspicion?" began Virginie. "But personally I have nothing more to learn."

"Madame Hilaire," broke in Daddy Peanuts, seizing her wrists in an iron grip and forcing her back to the other end of the room. "Madame Hilaire, I like you because I cannot forget that you are the wife of my good friend Hilaire. Let me then advise you not to open your mouth so wide when you speak of your cellar. . . .

"Do you realize that M. Barkimel's blindness and stupidity are an untold advantage to him, seeing that he knows nothing of what happens to be in your cellar? . . . Those who discovered the fact have died from their knowledge. The coal man who preceded Monsieur Frederic died from it. Your laundress died from it!"

He let go of her. She fell into a chair in a state of collapse and stared haggard-eyed at the diabolical old man. Then he resumed in a slightly quieter tone:

"What can I do with you now, madame—now that you know this thing? It is a secret of which you are no longer the mistress. A gesture, a look may betray us. In these circumstances you see for yourself that you must disappear. . . ."

"O God, take pity on her!" groaned M. Hilaire, who was not a bad sort of man.

Virginie gave an agonising gasp.

"I will spare your life," said the old man after reflection, "but I say again—you must disappear. And the best way for you to disappear, in my interests and in every one's interests, is for you to go down into the cellar and be shut up there with the lady in question."

"Nev——" Virginie began but did not finish the sentence. A flaming black look scorched her last effort of resistance.

"You will be shut up with her, Madame Hilaire, and as this lady in the unhappy state to which for the time being she has been reduced needs little attentions you will give them to her. You will lavish them on her. You will be her servant—her humble and obedient servant. There is no menial work that you must stop at in your service. . . . I think I have made myself sufficiently clear. That is the best I can do for you."

He looked round and said to Hilaire:

"Please pack such things in a valise as Mme Hilaire may need for her little journey."

CHAPTER XXVI

IN THE CONCIERGERIE PRISON

The Conciergerie Prison at that time was used as a State prison and as a temporary lock-up for prisoners already sentenced.

M. Florent, whom revolutionary literature had ruined, and Baron d'Askof were taken there almost at the same time, so that they found themselves in the Record Office together, and were sent to a cell in which young Cazo, the ardent nationalist, had been incarcerated. M. Florent was in the slough of despair. He had been arrested at a moment when, at his wits' end, he himself was delivering an article, more inflammatory than ever, to the *Journal des Clubs*. He could no longer see any limit to his ill-fortune, and the beginning of his stay in this sinister place led him only too clearly to perceive the early end of it all without being able to understand the mystery of it.

As soon as he entered the prison he was unpleasantly impressed by the sight of the march past of prisoners summoned to appear on that particular day before the Revolutionary Tribunal, where the new judges appointed at the instance of Coudry and the clubs were waiting for them.

By this time some hard blows had been struck at the old bench of judges. All the same, they had not dared to lay sacrilegious hands on M. Dimier, the President of the Assize Court, an upright and conscientious judge, who plays but a small part in our story, but is of sufficient importance for us to pause a moment to set before the reader a portrait of him.

A notable case brought him into prominence. It was the trial of the "bandits of the North," who after plundering the province swooped down upon Paris when they learned that the city was in the grip of a revolution.

An amazing and reckless burglary at a museum enabled the police to capture the leaders of this formidable gang. Some of them had the cleverness to claim acquaintance with certain bigwigs of the Revolution and to threaten to prove it. Friendly political association was an exaggeration, but undoubtedly there had been unpleasantly compromising relations between them.

In short, two of the accused, Garot and Manol, would undoubtedly have escaped punishment had not M. Dimier, guided only by his conscience, set his face against it, and threatened the public prosecutor with a scandal.

On the other hand, Garot and Manol, seeing that they were not to be released, though the magistrate's examination was over, began to turn informer. They had been transferred to the Conciergerie Prison and were constantly demanding an interview with the Governor of the prison, who took down their statements and, like the honest man he was, made a report upon them and sent it to the proper authority. No attempt was made to interfere with M. Dimier, but the Governor was dismissed and succeeded by a dissolute person called Mathieu Talbot.

Capable of any low-down job, he understood the difficulty of some of his old friends, and hinted vaguely that as he was Governor, Garot and Manol would be able to decamp—the only way to avoid a scandal at the Assize Court.

When M. Florent passed through the guard-room he observed two narrow staircases, each leading to a tower on the first floor. In the tower on the right was the office of the Governor, and in the tower on the left was the office of the President of the Assize Court.

It was to this room that M. Dimier came from time to time to cross-question prisoners. This honest man, sound judge, good father, upright character, adorned with every virtue, was greatly respected, even by Chéri-Bibi himself, for at the beginning of his career he had expressed the opinion in his book on "Judicial Blunders" that it might well be that Chéri-Bibi, the criminal of world-wide notoriety, was innocent of the first murder for which he had been found guilty and sentenced.

M. Dimier despised M. Talbot, who had once come before him, and M. Talbot had a contempt for M. Dimier because he had come before him and been acquitted in circumstances that would have disgraced any other man.

M. Talbot was convinced, after the Garot and Manol affair, that he would "dish" M. Dimier, and rather too openly made a boast about it one night in a café. That very night as he was undressing he found in his coat pocket half a dozen peanuts in a paper bag on which was written: "Don't attempt to 'dish' M. Dimier." M. Talbot, who was ignorant of peanut language, failed to understand the meaning of the warning, which gave him food for thought for a few moments, though it did not keep him awake that night.

M. Talbot had a pimply face, red with erysipelas, and small grey eyes that never looked anyone in the face.

M. Dimier had a face as smooth as marble framed in a splendid white beard. His gaze was kindly with honest people, but hard when he was dealing with rogues.

Chéri-Bibi, who worshipped virtue in other people, would have died for him and not hesitated for a moment to send the shady M. Talbot to the grave if his interests ever so little constrained him to do so. We shall see that his interests prevented him from remaining neutral in this struggle in which M. Dimier was striving to confound two criminals,

the Governor of the prison was endeavoring to help
them to escape, and Chéri-Bibi was trying to turn
this difference to good account by substituting in
the escape Major Jacques and Baron d'Askof for
Garot and Manol. Without anticipating events we
may say at once that such was the peanut dealer's
scheme—a scheme to ensure the success of which
he had obtained M. Hilaire's appointment as Inspector of Prisons. This ruse alone would enable
him, he hoped, to save Subdamoun's life—the much-
loved son, for whom he would have shed the last
drop of blood in his veins, and the last drop of blood
in the veins of his friends as well as his enemies.

Subdamoun in his cell was watched with a wealth
of precautions. Four civic guards were always
present with him, and a platoon of twenty-five
others stood on duty at the door in the corridor. All
this, of course, without prejudice to a veritable garrison of men whom Talbot could mobilize within
five minutes—men who were constantly on the move
in the old prison and giving it an air of reanimation
that made M. Florent shudder in the very marrow
of his bones, for he was more and more confusing
this Revolution with its great predecessor, imagining
himself living a hundred and fifty years before.

Poor M. Florent! That Baron d'Askof, one of
Subdamoun's gang, and M. Cazo, longing to restore
the monarchy in France, should be in a prison cell
—he found nothing amiss in that. On the contrary
he considered it quite just; but that he who had
only taken part in politics once to eulogize the triumph of the cause and glorify the men of the day
under the pseudonym of "The Old Cordelier" should

be reduced to such misery—was that not inconceivable?

On recognizing among the new prisoners Baron d'Askof, whom he had met at the beautiful Sonia's house, young Cazo did not conceal his opinion of Subdamoun and his adventure nor his delight that it had turned out a failure since it had been attempted in the absence of his King.

D'Askof, in sullen mood and concerned mainly with his own affairs, made no answer and lay down as though to sleep, turning his face to the wall. The furious youth rounded on poor M. Florent.

"What are you doing here?" he asked roughly.

"Upon my word, I am going to ask the judges that," returned M. Florent in a low voice. "I have never conspired against anyone. I support Liberty and the Rights of Man."

The precious youth burst out laughing.

"Well, old man, it's all up with you," he said, "and you deserve it."

"What do I deserve?" asked M. Florent, gasping. "Explain yourself. Your laugh frightens me. Do you think there is any chance of escaping execution?"

"Not the slightest," roared Cazo. "Not the slightest, my dear sir."

"I have never done any harm to anyone."

"A man always does harm if he is not a royalist."

"To whom?"

"To France."

M. Florent bent his head. To be imprisoned with this young maniac filling the cell with his dangerously compromising rant was the last straw! Imitating Baron d'Askof's example, he turned his face to the wall and made a pretense to go to sleep.

A few minutes later, when the warders brought in some indifferent soup and a jug of water for the prisoners, the precious youth Cazo resumed his speechifying and continued well into the night. M. Florent suffered agonies. And when the door of the cell was opened with a violence that made him start, he really believed that his last moment had come.

In the gloomy darkness of the prison, dimly lit by a flickering light, a tall, slim form appeared wearing a red sash, followed by a bent, thick-set figure, from whose mouth the words "Commissioner-Inspector" fell at every moment. It was M. Talbot, the Governor, showing M. Hilaire over the prison. M. Hilaire, in the exercise of his new powers, had caused M. Talbot to be awakened so that he should accompany him on his nocturnal round.

M. Hilaire explained that having been warned by the Committee of the Town Hall of a plan of escape designed to save the lives of Subdamoun and Baron d'Askof, he was anxious to reassure the Committee that very night.

M. Florent shivered as though it were the depth of winter. He raised his trembling body with difficulty, while Baron d'Askof, still stretched on his pallet, looked round to see the Commissioner-Inspector, who was munching peanuts and carelessly dropped three on the Baron's face.

Three peanuts in the language of the King of Convicts meant, "All goes well."

D'Askof, having learnt something, and all the same not a little surprised to find Chéri-Bibi acting with such absolute confidence and audacity, again turned his face to the wall after declaring in answer to a question that M. Cazo's speechifying in no way disturbed him personally but on the contrary amused him, all the more so as "he has an extremely attractive voice."

M. Florent's teeth chattered, and when questioned in his turn was unable to speak.

"This man has fever," said M. Hilaire.

On hearing that voice M. Florent gave a jump and went down on his knees. He recognized M. Hilaire. He clung to his coat like a drowning man clinging to a straw.

"Hullo, M. Florent! What are you doing here?"

M. Florent lifted his hands above his shaking head in a gesture of supplication.

"M. Hilaire, you know me. You know I am incapable of doing anything that is not perfectly honest, and it is not for writing in the *Gazette des Clubs* that the Rights of Man . . ."

M. Florent was unable to get out any more. The Governor had already dragged M. Hilaire away.

"He is off his head," said Talbot, closing the door of the cell. "Men are like that when they have the guillotine on the brain."

CHAPTER XXVII

IN SUBDAMOUN'S CELL

On leaving d'Askof's cell, Commissioner-Inspector Hilaire asked to see Subdamoun. Thereupon Talbot, still accompanied by his turnkeys, walked with Hilaire to the cell occupied by Major Jacques. He dismissed the twenty-five civic guards keeping watch in the corridor bristling with a number of new iron gates.

A table and a chair had been placed at Subdamoun's disposal. He remained for hours and hours together seated in this chair with his arms on the table in an attitude of inscrutable meditation.

He did not even look up when his visitors entered.

They stood for some moments gazing at this absence of all movement. What were this man's thoughts? What was he expecting? Had he lost all hope? Was not his mind paralyzed by the terrible collapse of the structure built up upon such flimsy foundations? Was he thinking only that he was about to die? In the course of the inquiry, long drawn out for the purpose of presenting the revolutionary mob with the gift of the finest heads in the Republican, Agrarian and Nationalist reaction, he had uttered a few words that bespoke his complete detachment from it all.

Having once attempted to exonerate his accomplices and take the entire blame on his own shoulders, and observed that his effort would lead to no serious result, he said: "In the circumstances, take my head as soon as may be and ask me no more questions. . . ."

"I want to speak to the prisoner so that nobody may overhear us," said M. Hilaire to Talbot in an undertone.

"Against the regulations," returned the Governor.

M. Hilaire handed the Governor a document bearing the Committee's official stamp and Coudry's signature underneath the words: "Officials employed

in the administration of prisons are instructed to
carry out such orders as M. Hilaire, Commissioner
of the Arsenal Division and Inspector of Prisons,
may deem it necessary to make for the safety of the
prisoners and the well-being of the State."

Talbot reflected for a moment and said:

"Have you to speak to the prisoner on behalf of
the Committee?"

"If you are asked that question," returned M.
Hilaire, "I should advise you to answer that you
don't know. But between ourselves, as I am aware
that you are devoted to the Committee, I will say:
Yes. A secret mission connected with Hérisson,
who is said to have been sounded by Subdamoun
and perhaps Pagés—do you follow me? I know
that you and I have the same enemies, and I have
confidence in you. But mum's the word if you
value your head."

"Still, I shall make my report to-morrow."

"Of course."

"I can't allow you to speak to him without re-
cording the fact."

"You will record it."

"I must tell you that there is one order," went
on the Governor, still on his guard, "which I cannot overlook for it is peremptory, and the document
you have shown me does not cancel it."

"What is it?"

"The order that my men must never allow Subdamoun out of their sight day and night."

"Have I asked you to infringe that order? I
have something to say to Subdamoun. As long as I
am not overheard, that is all I ask. You have your,
responsibilities, I have mine."

The conversation passed quickly in a whisper in the doorway. Subdamoun, in fact, was to be kept continuously under the eye of his warders.

Talbot ordered the five civic guards to withdraw to the far end of the cell and stood with them. He made a sign to M. Hilaire that he could approach the prisoner.

Talbot, who was determined not to miss any movement of the two men, saw the Commissioner-Inspector bend over the prisoner and murmur a few words that seemed to produce some effect. Subdamoun looked up quickly, stared at his visitor, threw a glance at the Governor and the civic guards at the other end of the cell, and said aloud:

"Ah, it's you, M. Hilaire, Commissioner of the Arsenal Division."

"I am here in my capacity as Inspector-General of Prisons," returned M. Hilaire in a distinct voice.

"My congratulations," said Subdamoun. "The Republic is a good job as far as you are concerned."

"They don't seem to be very great friends," M. Talbot said to himself. "Their talk begins badly. Let's hear the sequel. He will be very clever if he gets anything out of him."

Nevertheless, M. Hilaire was by no means put out of countenance by the somewhat negative result of his first effort. He went on in a voice that M. Talbot could hear:

"From the beginning of the Inquiry you have acted in such a way as to inflict the greatest harm on yourself and friends. You are free to ruin yourself, but remember that if in this matter you were a little more amenable to reason those who are dear

to you would be grateful to you. I am here on behalf of the Committee of . . ."

M. Talbot could hear on more. M. Hilaire, however, went on talking in a whisper:

"Major, I am here to save your life. I only
accepted my present office to be of service to you
and yours. . . . You have heard that the Marchioness and Mlle Lydia are in a safe place. They
are in my house, in my cellar. I have a letter on
me from the Marchioness and hoped to give it to
you myself. That is impossible to-night, but I shall
find some means of letting you have it to-morrow.

"You will see from this letter that the Marchioness and Mlle Lydia are quite well, and they implore
you to have complete confidence in me and to do
whatever I ask you. In that case in three days'
time you will be free. The plan of your escape has
been maturely thought out. It is quite simple. M.
Talbot has decided to bring about the escape of
Garot and Manol, two ordinary criminals whom
we have won over to our side, and who will get
away some other time. You will change places and
clothes with them, and the Governor himself will
see you to the door. Be prepared, therefore, at
the least move, the least sign from me. . . ."

Apparently M. Hilaire's remarks had at last
roused Subdamoun, for M. Talbot saw him suddenly abandon the attitude of indifference hitherto
adopted, take his hands from his pale face, and
move his lips.

So Subdamoun was speaking! M. Hilaire had
succeeded in entering into conversation with him.
That was no mean feat! Subdamoun had answered

him. Still, the reply did not seem to be to M. Hilaire's liking.

"What you say is all very fine, but I do not intend to escape."

"What do you mean?"

"Have you given a thought to the many friends whom I prevailed upon to join me at Versailles and who followed me here? Can I save them too?"

"Well, that would be impossible, you know."

"You see, therefore, that I cannot escape. How could you suppose that after leading them to defeat I should desert them when they are about to die? I thank you for what you have done for my mother and fiancée. Continue to look after them. God will reward you. Tell them I shall think of them to my last moment, and strive on the scaffold to be worthy of the name of de Touchais. Tell my mother and fiancée all this. They will mourn for me, but they will understand and forgive me."

"It will kill them," said M. Hilaire, his eyes filled with tears.

"Would it kill them any the less if I behaved like a coward?" asked Subdamoun in a husky voice, placing his elbows on the table and his hands before his face.

M. Hilaire had no alternative but to leave the cell.

"Well, are you satisfied?" asked M. Talbot, accompanying him to the main gate.

"Upon my word, no," confessed M. Hilaire, "and I don't believe that those who sent me will have any reason to be satisfied either. This Subdamoun is more obstinate than one would have imagined."

When M. Hilaire found himself once more on the Quay de l'Horloge he looked about him. It was a dark, dismal, wet night. He made his way to the deserted front of a café. He had not been there five minutes when a poor old peanut dealer came up to him and asked him humbly to buy some peanuts. M. Hilaire, doubtless out of pity, bought a bag for a few sous.

"Well?" whispered Chéri-Bibi.

"Well—nothing doing. He refuses to escape. He doesn't wish to be considered a coward. He will die with his comrades. He has asked me to tell his mother and fiancée so."

The poor old fellow must have certainly been extremely ill, for he had barely handed the bag of peanuts to his customer when he sank to the ground in an inert mass. The customer darted forward and lifted him with difficulty, seemingly not without emotion. He whispered in his ear words that caused the hapless man to open his eyes at the moment when a well-dressed gentleman, protected from the shower by an umbrella, was passing. The gentleman stopped and asked in a compassionate voice why the poor peanut dealer had fallen to the pavement.

"It must be starvation," returned M. Hilaire.

The passer-by felt in his pocket and drew from his purse a ten-franc note, which he handed to M. Hilaire.

"Let him get something hot that will do him good," said the gentleman, and walked away.

Then Chéri-Bibi came to himself and exclaimed:

"Thank you, M. Dimier. God bless you!"

CHAPTER XXVIII

THE COURTYARD OF THE CONCIERGERIE PRISON

The number of political prisoners in the Conciergerie Prison increased to such an extent that only a few of them could be accommodated in separate cells.

After a time Subdamoun was the one prisoner with a cell to himself. The other prisoners were quartered together, and during the day showed themselves and met almost freely in the courtyard, which was to some extent in the center of the political cells.

M. Florent was singularly impressed by this courtyard, suggestive of a cloister, with its walls yellow with age and its stone table and fountain, round which a bevy of beautiful women with bare heads sat on straw-bottomed chairs and held court with the heroic charm of the long ago, while civic guards paced up and down with loaded rifles and fixed bayonets.

At this time the prisoners were allowed to join the ladies, thus men and women mingled together at the hour set aside for exercise. The artful ones at first expressed surprise at this agreeable indulgence, but in the end drew the conclusion that it was an artifice to stimulate conversation. They were convinced, in fact, that they were being watched, and that every word would be reported by spies to the infamous M. Talbot.

For the first few days, therefore, each and everyone remained on his guard, staring every stranger in the face, and suspicious of even a friendly word; but this constraint soon became unendurable to them all, and it was the beautiful Sonia herself who encouraged her "lady and gentlemen guests" to chat among themselves as freely at her "receptions in the Conciergerie Prison" as in her drawing-room in the Boulevard Pereire.

M. Florent had been a week in prison when he first set foot in this "select circle." A high fever had chained him to his wretched bed. D'Askof was a constant visitor, and regaled him with the latest gossip, which was not reassuring.

It was in vain that the Committee of Public Safety, whose President, M. Pagès, had resigned his office, sought to urge counsels of moderation on the Vigilance Committee; it was in vain that the remnants of the National Assembly, endeavoring to recover itself and react against this flood of revengeful fury, implored Coudry and his men "not to repeat the errors of the past." Coudry, applauded by every Division, seemed likely to become the master of Paris, and Paris was already antagonistic to Versailles.

Finally, to put the finishing touches to this ominous picture, the Baron told M. Florent in confidence that the Government of the Commune, as it was already called, would in all probability, in order to calm public opinion, imitate the famous September massacres.

"Oh, good Lord," mumbled M. Florent. "the September massacres! Is it possible?"

"Pah!" said the Baron in a tone of philosophy, "whether you die from a blow on the head with a pike or the guillotine it comes to the same thing, believe me. The annoying part is to die when you are not tired of life."

M. Florent was not tired of life, and Baron d'As-kof also found some degree of charm in it, especially since he had met the beautiful Sonia again in circumstances in which his love for that exquisite creature had assumed almost heroic proportions.

D'Askof was surprised at being kept in prison and seeing nothing more of Chéri-Bibi's messenger, the Commissioner-Inspector, to whose appointment he had so strangely contributed by his own arrest. The Baron ardently longed to be free in order to work for the release of his beautiful friend who, moreover, had received him with the most affectionate welcome.

Sonia knew nothing of the part played by him in the common catastrophe, but had she been aware of it she would have forgiven him all the same. Had she not forgiven Lavobourg who had betrayed them all?

"You committed a crime, dear," she said to Lavobourg, "but it was for love of me. . . . You may kiss my hand."

Lavobourg grasped her hand with sadness. D'Askof kissed it with passion.

When M. Florent entered the courtyard a brilliant crowd was assembled. The ladies and their cavaliers were playing a game of hot-cockles—an old game in which a person is blindfolded, and, being struck, guesses who strikes him.

Mme Tiffoni, Mlles Luciene Drice, Yolande Théry, whose lovers had already appeared before the Revolutionary Tribunal or were about to lose their heads on the scaffold—all these beautiful women of the Republic while waiting their turn to display their courage in public were striving to show in private their cheerful indifference to the fate that lay in store for them.

At that moment it was Lavobourg who was on his knees before Sonia, his head hidden in her lap, one open hand held out behind his back. And while the ladies made merry by giving Lavobourg, thus blindfolded, a sharp slap on the hand, Baron D'Askof, bending over the beautiful Sonia's shoulder, seemed less to be whispering to her than kissing her behind the ear.

Half the prisoners were in love with Sonia, and before being summoned by the Tribunal, from which they rarely returned, addressed love-letters to her which were read by all in common and helped to pass an agreeable hour or two.

For a couple of days they had been making fun of a M. Saw, who, like M. Florent, was arrested for sending to the most advanced newspapers violent diatribes adorned with all the figures of speech peculiar to the montagnards of the Convention. Like so many others, M. Saw fell in love with Sonia and told her so.

"Alas, madam, my love-affairs are not dangerous," he at once added, for he was a gentleman. "Having passed all my life among books, they are purely literary. In this way I have loved Madame Rolande, la belle Lucille, Thérèse and their circle, just as I love you who resemble them in mind and heart and surpass them in beauty."

Tiffoni, Luciene Drice, Yolande Théry clapped their hands. M. Saw rose to the occasion and addressed them with equally flattering compliments derived from his reading.

"Amuse yourselves," he said, "you will never amuse yourselves as much as those historic French-women. If only I had with me the *Memoirs of Mme Eliot* you would see what fun they had at Carmes Prison, the Conciergerie Prison and other places, and," he added with a touch of mischief, "it would perhaps fire you with more audacity and incite you to play other games than hot-cockles, puss in the corner and blind man's buff."

M. Saw was straightway called an old scamp, which was enough to induce him to apply for permission to lend Sonia certain volumes in his possession at home. He made a request for his warder to be authorized to go to his housekeeper for them in his spare time. The request was transmitted in due form to M. Talbot, who at once communicated with the Commissioner-Inspector.

"I find something most suspicious in this request,," said M. Hilaire, frowning. "Does not this anxiety to read at a time when M. Saw and Sonia Liskinne are about to appear before their judges conceal some hidden purpose? I will fetch the books myself and find out what it all means."

M. Talbot agreed with M. Hilaire, and thus next morning M. Florent saw the Governor and M. Hilaire enter the courtyard. M. Hilaire passed quite close, but did not appear to notice his old friend. He was carrying under his arm a volume which at once attracted the retired bookseller's attention. At the sight of this worn, soiled, nut-brown binding with its special tooling on the edge, designed by himself, M. Florent turned deadly pale.

M. Hilaire was now carrying the book in his hand, and M. Florent craned his neck in an effort to perceive on it the red label which had been his pride for over twenty years and bore the words: "Francs Bourgeois Library." But he failed to see the label, doubtless because it had been scraped off.

If only he could be certain that this book had been stolen he would perhaps have the consolation of learning before he died the name of the wretched creature who for years on end had been plundering his circulating library without rousing his suspicion and poisoning the last years of his association with trade and letters. When he reached this point in his anxiety and doubt his heart sank on perceiving his old customer M. Saw enter the courtyard, bowing to the ladies.

M. Talbot called M. Saw and told him that the Commissioner-Inspector had himself visited his home and examined his library, which showed deplorable taste and should by rights be confiscated. All the same, he had had the kindness to bring back one of the volumes, which he had glanced through and found unobjectionable. M. Saw could therefore lend it to the ladies for their amusement.

While the Governor was talking and M. Saw listening, M. Hilaire, wearing as usual his splendid red sash, went up to Sonia and, bowing, handed the book to her:

"You see, madame, we are not monsters. Amuse yourself while you may, and read the book quickly, for neither you nor I can tell what the future may hold for us."

"Thank you for the warning," returned Sonia, smiling. "I promise not to waste any time."

She at once opened the book and read aloud in a voice that she strove to render firm but which trembled slightly: "Memoirs of the French Revolution by Mme Eliot, translated from the English by the Comte de Baillon, with a Preface by Saint Beuve."

Obviously it was not the title that made her voice tremble, but rather that which she could read underneath: "Letters from the counter-revolutionary committees of Lyons, Bordeaux, Toulon, Marseilles, Lille, Nancy and Tours to Major Jacques, a prisoner in the hand of the enemies of the nation."

Not one of them, save Lavobourg and d'Askof observed her agitation.

M. Hilaire had drawn M. Talbot and M. Saw away with him to the far end of the courtyard and was holding forth on a subject that must have been extremely interesting but that history has failed to inscribe on its records.

As to M. Florent, he was less engrossed by the reader than the binding. He received a fresh shock on hearing the title, and no longer doubted that this book of "Memoirs," which had appeared in his library, was his property. If only he could get the book in his hands, even for a moment.

Slowly he stole towards the group of prisoners holding court round Sonia, but it so happened that Baron d'Askof left the party and strode up to him with a great show of friendship. He shook his hand.

"Is it really you, M. Florent—my dear companion in misfortune? How is it you made up your mind to venture out?"

M. Florent endeavored to withstand the Baron, who, while making him dizzy with his flow of language, led him into a corridor. He would not leave him. At last M. Florent said:

"Look here, all this does not interest me, but that book . . ."

"Oh, really. You are interested in some book. But what book?"

"Why, the book which the Commissioner-Inspector brought here from Saw's house at the request of that somewhat unscrupulous person."

"So you know M. Saw?"

"I should think I did know him! For over twenty years he was a subscriber to my circulating library, and I can see that a number of volumes are no longer in circulation."

"M. Florent, you have your wits about you."

"I don't know if I have my wits about me, but I should like to have my book. If Mlle Liskinne will lend it to me for a moment I will soon show her that these 'Memoirs' belong to me."

"If you really have your wits about you, M. Florent," said d'Askof, sharply, in a peculiar tone, "you will understand that you must not persist in asking for that book."

"Why not?" ask M. Florent, nonplussed.

"Because I have no liking for police spies," returned the Baron, taking M. Florent by the shoulder and glaring fiercely at him.

Feeling sure that he had made a considerable impression on M. Florent, the Baron turned on his heel and rejoined Sonia and her little group of friends seated in the middle of the courtyard while the other prisoners walked about near them.

Sonia quickly skimmed the pages of the letters to Major Jacques, which began: "Major! You are

the one hope of France, and yet we learn that you
have refused to take advantage of the only means
of escape which will save us.   You are not entitled to . . ."

Just then a certain uproar and the confused
sound of voices came from the other end of the
courtyard and attracted general attention.   Sonia
turned her eyes towards the tumult and beheld approaching her amid the throng of prisoners hastening up for a better view—Subdamoun himself.

His face was of a deadly pallor.   It was as though
another Lazarus had risen from the tomb.   But
under his funereal aspect he retained those wonderful lineaments which are the mark of a resolute
and noble character.   Alas, his one desire must have
been to conceal from the vulgar eye the despair of a
soul crushed by a too relentless fate.   It was in vain
that M. Talbot, leaning against a pillar in the corridor, and hidden by its shadows, looked for some
passing sign of weakness on the part of his distinguished prisoner.

That morning at breakfast time Subdamoun had
found in a piece of bread a scrap of paper bearing
a few words which had decided his conduct.   He
could not doubt that the message was an attempt to
induce him to go back on his refusal to countenance
any plan of escape, but out of respect for his mother
he submitted to her wishes.

Sonia stood up when she saw him, and her excitement was so intense that for once she was as pale
as he.   His first sad smile was for her.   Their eyes
met, and reawakened love brought the color to the
cheeks of the beautiful captive.

She could not restrain the impulse to throw herself forward almost in his arms. At that moment he was conscious of feeling something more than a guilty passion for her, and he admitted to himself that he was committing a crime in loving her. Poor Lydia! Did he therefore no longer love Lydia? Who could tell, or at least who could be sure of such a thing?

We trench here on one of those unfathomable mysteries of the human heart when it is assailed by two equally attractive but entirely different objects; and we may perhaps, especially in times of revolution, grant some indulgence to a man who would fain appreciate the virtue of one but lacks the courage to reject the allurements of the other.

In their embarrassment they did not know what to say to each other, and a child might have guessed their secret from their obvious agitation.

Fortunately, Baron d'Askof was there to save the position. He declared with noisy gaiety that they were all pleased to see Subdamoun once more. He asserted that from the first day only his presence was needed to enable them to fancy themselves at one of Sonia's private parties in the Boulevard Pereire, parties which lost nothing of their charm for being held "on the threshold of the scaffold."

"The scaffold," repeated Jacques. "That's true. My poor friends, will you ever forgive me?"

"We thank you," cried one of the old aristocracy. "We thank you, since it was impossible to live in these abominable days."

"It is not you who should ask forgiveness," interrupted Sonia, and she added in an undertone: "I have already forgiven in your name those who needed forgiveness."

While speaking she pointed to the hapless Lavobourg, looking a pitiable sight in his corner.

Subdamoun did not hesitate. He went up to him
and offered his hand. Lavobourg accepted the
friendly gesture without enthusiasm, for he had
readily forgotten the horror of his own political
treachery to remember only the deception of the
man who was willing to forgive him.

"Come, Lavobourg, we are all going to die. We
are all going to appear before the one great Judge.
Forgive me as I forgive you."

Lavobourg made an affirmative motion of his
head.

Sonia asked Jacques to sit down beside her, and,
convinced that no word that passed between them
would escape the ears of M. Talbot's secret police,
she was careful to tell him with an airy and affected
light-heartedness how she had employed her time
during her long hours of imprisonment.

"We are reading Mme Eliot's *Memoirs*. They
are very dreadful, but delightful. Look here, Major, it's your turn to read. . . . I am rather
tired. . . ."

She handed him the volume with a speaking
look that at once put him on the alert. He saw
that he held in his hand the key to the mystery
that had pursued him since the morning.

He carelessly opened the book and betrayed no
surprise when his eyes fell upon these lines: "Major, you are the one hope of France, and yet we
learn that you have refused to take advantage of
the only means of escape which will save us. You
are not entitled to . . ."

"Farther on," said Sonia. "I have already read that."

And bending over him so that he was conscious of her warm breath, her bare arm lightly touching him, she turned over the pages, and his eyes fell on these lines:

"If you set your mind on it, Major, nothing is lost. You may still save France. . . . You have no right to refuse. . . . You have no right to seek in death a means of shunning your duty."

The more he read the more perplexed he grew, and the more he felt his resolution falter.

Then at last he realized that it would be an act of veritable cowardice to shrink from the decisive struggle.

Sonia rivetted him with her eager eyes, in which Lavobourg and d'Askof read but love for him. But whereas Lavobourg betrayed only his dejection, d'Askof felt rising within him a wave of hatred and unspeakable jealousy. This brother, whom he detested, was robbing him of her smiles and the look in her eyes on the very steps of the scaffold. At the moment when he was certain of having won her completely, Jacques had but to show himself and she slipped from his grasp again.

Jacques closed the book and offered it to her, and she took the book and his hand and held them both in hers.

"Well, what do you say?" she asked with a meaning look.

D'Askof could see nothing but those hands, those clasped hands, and, mad with rage, losing his self-control, he was about to throw himself on the book and snatch it from them when he was forestalled by the unexpected intervention of a prisoner of whom, of a surety, no one was thinking.

It was M. Florent, who was impelled by the rights of property and the justice of his case to go so far, and, having seized the book, he shouted in a hoarse voice:

"This book belongs to me. I shall keep it."

The entire company, taken aback and not unnaturally shocked, stood up, but those who, like Sonia and Subdamoun and M. Hilaire, knew the value of the book quivered with dismay.

M. Hilaire hastened up on the heels of M. Talbot who, at a loss, at once demanded an explanation.

M. Florent did not hesitate to give it:

"This book is mine and I will prove it. It belonged to my circulating library. I have been hunting for it for years, and I can understand finding it here as I see my old customer M. Saw in the courtyard."

By this time M. Saw was face to face with M. Florent and tried to wrest the book from him.

"I bought it," exclaimed M. Saw with the boundless indignation of insincerity. "I bought it with my own money, and I will not allow you to call me a thief."

"I will prove it," stormed M. Florent. "There was a coffee stain in this book, and I will show it to you."

M. Florent was about to open the *Memoirs* before them all and, as the saying goes, "the fat would have been in the fire," when M. Hilaire thrust out his arm and in his turn secured the volume.

"I brought the book here and I will take it away," he said, more agitated than he wished to appear.

As to Sonia, she was almost fainting, and she had to sit down when she saw the book slip from the outstretched hands of M. Hilaire to fall into those of M. Talbot.

It was M. Florent who had pulled off that stroke.

"See—see for yourself if there isn't a coffee stain on it," he said to the Governor.

And this time he opened the book and eagerly turned over the pages.

M. Hilaire was as white as a sheet. Subdamoun stood with folded arms, prepared to receive this new blow of fate. D'Askof gave a leer. The few persons who, bending over the reader's shoulder, had been able to see or guess some part of the mystery, felt an anguished clutch at the heart. In another moment the trick would be discovered.

Suddenly a door slammed and a stentorian voice shouted in the courtyard: "Roll-call of prisoners to appear before the Revolutionary Tribunal," and the first name proclaimed was M. Florent's.

"Serves him right," said M. Saw, but M. Saw's name rang out immediately after, and M. Saw staggered in his turn and was obliged to clutch M. Talbot to prevent himself from falling. To rid himself of M. Saw, M. Talbot handed the book to M. Hilaire, who put it in his pocket.

No further attention was paid to the book. The Governor himself forgot about it. He busied himself after frantically shaking off M. Saw, who would not let go his hold, in ordering a bucket of cold water to be thrown over the apoplectic countenance of M. Florent, and then in lining up the wretched prisoners about to be taken before the Tribunal.

The douche brought M. Florent to himself. In

the end he was picked up somewhat roughly, and while the poor prisoners intended for the scaffold were being taken willy-nilly before the Tribunal the ex-librarian strove to explain to the warders and civic guards that he was the victim of a most grievous error. Though he was told to hold his tongue, he refused to listen to reason. In the end he was shouting at the top of his voice, in spite of blows from the butt-end of a musket, on the pretext that later on he would be unable to say a word before his judges owing to his timidity.

Sonia, in the courtyard, was herself again after her agitation, and, conscious that she was no longer under the eyes of Talbot, whom Hilaire was leading away, went up to Subdamoun and said:

"You see, dear, your duty is clear, and I am amazed that you should have waited until to-day to understand that."

"I thought everything was lost," he returned, "and I did not wish to desert you after bringing you to such a pass."

"Don't worry about me, I implore you," she said, stealthily pressing his hand.

"I shall not leave this place without you," he declared.

"I should look upon you as a child if you allowed such a consideration to stand in your way."

"It is because I love you."

"Great heavens," she murmured, and paused for a moment, for her heart seemed to have ceased to beat. He had never told her so before. "Hush!" she went on. "Are you not afraid of committing a sacrilege?"

I am telling you the truth, Sonia. It is you I love."

"The scaffold has no further terrors for me," she said, closing her eyes.

"The scaffold!" he said. "Let the executioner come and we will die together."

"Leave the prison," she urged. "Things cannot continue as they are, and you can put an end to them if you wish. Be a free man, Jacques. Promise—swear that you will."

"Yes, I promise. . . . I will be a free man so as to release you."

CHAPTER XXIX

IN WHICH M. FLORENT BEGINS TO REALIZE THAT SO FAR HE HAD NOT GRASPED THE IDEA OF THE SECOND FRENCH REVOLUTION

M. FLORENT might perhaps have continued the same conduct before the Revolutionary Tribunal, which would have been unworthy of him in his adversity, had he not on entering the room into which the civic guards had driven him with the butt-ends of their rifles recognized in the chief figure on the judicial bench M. Barkimel himself.

Truth to tell, chance or Providence had willed that M. Barkimel should be the Presiding Judge on the day when M. Florent was to be tried.

He was at once filled with a great hope, and thus, borne up by the thought that all was not yet lost, and realizing the disgrace that would be his if he paraded his cowardice before a man whom he had always regarded as his inferior, he managed to draw himself up with an air that was not without a certain dignity.

"Silence!" suddenly yelped a hideous fellow carrying a sword under his arm and acting as usher.

For that matter the entire company carried swords the prisoners excepted, of course.

M. Barkimel himself, in a grey suit, wearing a splendid sash, had a sword on his hip. He was seated at a table which bore various documents, an inkstand, pipes and bottles. Near to him were the assistant judges, and a dozen persons seated or standing formed the jury, two of whom were clad in jackets and aprons.

The Public Prosecutor, unkempt, from whose cruel upper lip drooped a heavy moustache, was seated in a corner on the right at a table laden with official reports.

Facing the Presiding Judge three men guarded a prisoner, seemingly in the sixties. Two civic guards went up to M. Barkimel and asked to be allowed to place before him a petition from the St. Sulpice division in favor of the old man before him, who did not seem to be a very dangerous character, but M. Barkimel, in the loud voice of a drunkard, which M. Florent had never heard before, replied: "Such requests are useless in the case of traitors," and he poured himself out a large glass of wine, which he emptied at a gulp with his eyes fixed on the Public Prosecutor as who should say: "Good health!"

"It's horrible. Your sentence amounts to murder," cried the prisoner.

"You all say the same thing!" exclaimed M. Barkimel. "It's getting on our nerves."

The respectable old man was shaken by a just indignation.

"Future generations," he exclaimed, "will refuse to believe that these crimes were committed in a civilized community under parliamentary government.

"A lot I care for future generations! Take him away," ordered M. Barkimel after consulting with a look the jury, who raised their hands for the death sentence.

The old man was quickly led out.

"Why, he is perfectly awful," thought Florent. "What a terrible judge, and how he drinks! . . . I must let him know I am here." And he coughed.

M. Barkimel at once looked up and observed M. Florent. He turned pale, and uttered a few incoherent words to the surprise of the assistant judges.

"Our President drinks too much," said one of the judges as he removed glass and bottle.

The habit of drinking wine at sittings of the Revolutionary Tribunal had arisen as a result of the great heat. At first water was supplied, the temperature of the Court being so stifling that the judges occupying the bench for hours at a stretch suffered real torture. Then lemonade was brought in. In the end each judge used to bring what suited his taste.

"At the National Assembly," one of the judges pointed out one day, "the representatives of the people are in the habit of sustaining themselves during their speeches with wine or spirits of their own choice—who therefore will have the heart to refuse a glass of wine to a judge needing all his courage

if he is to avoid being moved to pity by the hypocritical tears of the enemies of the people?"

But was it indeed excess of wine that changed M.
Barkimel's heart and made him turn pale and splutter for a few moments?

The Public Prosecutor did not share the mistake
of the assistant judges in this respect. He must
have caught the look that passed between the two
men; he must have been warned that some irregu-
larity in the administration of revolutionary justice
might occur that day; at any rate, he rose and
uttered these threatening words:

"If you, Citizen President, see no objection we
will now try the prisoner M. Florent. As the written evidence that I have had placed before the
Tribunal clearly demonstrates, he deserve, even in
the eyes of those most prejudiced in his favor, ten
times the death penalty."

M. Barkimel was conscious, from the icy tone in
which these words were uttered, that they were
aimed at least as much against him as M. Florent.
He realized that the moment was fraught with as
much gravity for the judge as the prisoner; thus,
collecting all his strength of mind, he managed to
overcome an emotion which might have been fatal
to him and declare in a hollow voice:

"I have no objection to the prisoner Florent being tried at once. Guards, bring him before me."

M. Florent was keenly alive to the hands that fell
heavily on his shoulder.

"I am innocent," he cried. "I am a staunch
partisan of the Revolution. You will not commit
the crime of sullying yourselves by taking my life.

I am confident that my judges will deal fairly with me."

M. Barkimel regarded this last sentence as horribly compromising. He at once said, frowning, without looking at M. Florent:

"To take the life of an enemy of the people is the one thing in the eyes of true patriots that gratifies them most."

M. Florent could not believe his own ears. Had M. Barkimel, in fact, addressed those words to him? He felt that his mind was in a whirl, and he feared lest he should lose his self-control once more and come hopelessly to grief.

"I am glad, Citizen President, to observe your readiness to deal with the prisoner Florent. Secret reports led me to believe that you were a friend of his and would make an effort to save him."

"I?" exclaimed M. Barkimel, placing his right hand on his heart, "I save an enemy of the people? Am I the man to do such a thing—I who have given in this place so many proofs of my patriotism?" And he added without looking at M. Florent: "For that matter, this man is not a friend of mine."

M. Florent's teeth chattered. He was not sure now that M. Barkimel would not drop him, repudiate him altogether.

"Secret reports," went on the Public Prosecutor calmly, "represent you as never being out of each other's sight."

M. Barkimel stood up. It seemed as if he himself were the accused. He raised his hand as though to bear witness to the fact that he was being slandered. Of course, he knew M. Florent, but to know a man and to be his intimate friend were two different things.

"I appeal to M. Florent," he exclaimed. "We have never been able to agree upon anything. Is that not so, M. Florent? I leave it to the prisoner's good faith."

"It is true that we have had a few little arguments," returned the prisoner as if in a dream.

"Admit, sir, that we have wrangled every day like fishwives. If you admit that you will be speaking the truth."

M. Barkimel was getting heated, for he was growing more and more convinced that the affair might be as disastrous to him as to M. Florent. Viewed in this light, the quarrels of days gone by seemed like so many crimes with which it was his duty to reproach M. Florent. He worked himself up at the recollection of disputes which might be of great use to him now.

"The prisoner should blush to describe as little discussions regular controversies in which I invariably did my utmost to uphold the Revolution."

"Would you venture to say that I attacked it?" asked M. Florent in a voice strained with anxiety, for he saw that he could no longer rely on his friend Barkimel or on his honesty as a judge.

"I should think I would venture to say so. You spoke of this Revolution, sir, only to ridicule it and compare it with the old French Revolution, which you called the great, the only Revolution—the Revolution that produced the giants of '93."

"That will do, Citizen President," declared the Public Prosecutor, who seemed to control the sitting. "You may sit down. Everything you say

corroborates the facts contained in the official report. This man—I speak of the prisoner—is un-
deserving of any pity, if pity could enter this Court.
Is that not your opinion, Citizen President?"

"Yes, that is my opinion," returned M. Barkimel
in a hoarse whisper.

And he allowed himself to drop into his seat as if
utterly exhausted. His right hand, which held a
pen, trembled to such an extent that the pen slipped
from his grasp and fell at M. Florent's feet. M.
Florent stooped and picked it up, took two steps
forward with a firm and easy bearing, and placed
it on the table before M. Barkimel.

"Thank you," said M. Barkimel, without looking up.

M. Barkimel's cowardice transformed M. Florent into a hero.

From that moment he surprised the Court by his
moral dignity, the clearness of his thoughts, and
the calmness with which he strove to defend a life
in such obvious jeopardy.

"Gentlemen," he said, lifting his head, "I am not
the man I am alleged to be. I may, indeed, have
chaffed the Presiding Judge about the Revolution.
If that is a crime you will say so and I am ready to
atone for it. But I venture to hope all the same that
you will be good enough to grant me my liberty, to
which I am attached by necessity and principle."

A few laughs greeted M. Florent's words. They
marvelled at his flippancy.

"It is the Public Prosecutor's turn to speak,"
fumed M. Barkimel.

"The prisoner before you is not an ordinary criminal," said the man with the heavy moustache after

his opening remarks. "We know that he is a friend of Subdamoun, and shouted 'Long live Subdamoun' at Versailles while the friends of the people were overcoming the seditious. Therefore it would have been easy to include him in the 'batch' of prisoners with Subdamoun at their head soon to be tried before you, and if we have not taken this course it is because M. Florent is, above all, a supporter of the policy of the Rights of Men."

"The Rights of Men! I have always upheld them," interrupted M. Florent, "and I should not be here had the *Gazette des Clubs* published the articles I sent them."

"Here they are! Do you acknowledge them?" asked the Public Prosecutor.

M. Florent admitted their authorship, and he was struck all of a heap when the Public Prosecutor went on:

"The wretched man confesses! . . . Need I read these infamous libels to you? They are the lucubrations of an old fossil whose mistaken ideals is a bourgeois Revolution. They preach the freedom of labor, in other words the abdominable tyranny of supply and demand. They extol the antiquated triumph of those who did away with the trade guilds and craftmanship, all those corporations friendly to industry which built up the old France and which the bourgeois Revolution of 1789 destroyed, to hand the citizens of every country over to the monopolists of international finance. With a stroke of the pen he condemns, therefore, the noble efforts by which our admirable labor unions have restored the Right of the olden time—that is to say the right of the State against the individual, against the hideous doctrine of the Rights of Man of 1789 which made us all equal, weak and strong, rich and poor alike without giving the one the means of defending himself against the other. In short, I accuse M. Florent, here present, of having with unimaginable cynicism sung the praises of a Revolution which our own is intended to suppress for ever and of which it desires to wipe out even the memory. I ask you, Citizen President, and you, gentlemen of the jury, if there can be a worse crime in these days than this? It is for you to say what punishment such conduct deserves."

Every eye was fixed on the Presiding Judge. M. Barkimel opened his mouth and was heard to say clearly:

"Death!"

Each member of the jury repeated the word: "Death!"

And staring wildly around him, M. Barkimel said:

"M. Florent, the Revolutionary Tribunal, after putting it to the jury, sentences you to death."

He called for some wine. As the civic guards were about to take M. Florent away, a disturbance arose at the back of the Court and M. Florent saw Citizen Talon, his concierge of the Rue des Francs Bourgeois, step forward.

"In the name of the people I ask to be heard," Talon said, showing a face distorted by every vice. "You have condemned the man Florent to death, and it serves him right. I was the one who denounced him to the police, but he is not the only guilty man here. I ask you all this question: Is not the man who hides a criminal of this sort and tries to help him escape justice at least as guilty as he is?"

"Of course. . . . Of course. . . . Quite right. Let's hear what he has to say," came from several voices.

"Does not this man deserve death?"

"Worse than death, because he encourages crime," returned the Public Prosecutor.

"Well, I denounce the man who concealed the prisoner. It was the Presiding Judge," yelled the concierge, pointing to M. Barkimel.

M. Barkimel put down his glass and turned a death's head to the concierge.

"I?" he exclaimed. He could say no more. A nervous twitching had seized him from head to foot.

"Yes, you. I saw my tenant Florent enter your flat. I told the civic guards. Your place was searched. They could not find him, but I swear he was there. The prisoner who was your friend, and whom you have had the cowardice to disown and sentence to death can have no further reason for denying the truth. Let him speak out—we will believe him."

The Public Prosecutor turned to M. Florent and invited him to say yes or no whether the Presiding Judge had offered him this criminal hospitality.

This time M. Barkimel gave a look at M. Florent. And such a look! All that remained of life was concentrated in that look. What a wealth of mute, cowardly, terrified entreaty lay in that glance. But M. Florent did not look at M. Barkimel. He raised his hand and declared:

"I swear that what this man said is false. I

swear that I have never been in M. Barkimel's flat
since the outbreak of the Revolution."

"Very well," declared the Public Prosecutor.
"The matter is settled. The witness will be arrested
for making a false declaration against a judge of
this Tribunal."

Loud cheers broke out in Court.

At that moment an elderly warder came forward.

"Monsieur le President, we have received word
from the authorities that the prison van is ready,
and if you have any condemned prisoners there is
an opportunity to take them away at once."

The Presiding Judge had no need to make answer.
The Public Prosecutor declared that M. Florent
could be handed over to the executioner. The civic
guards took him away.

On the evening of that day, which was filled with
so much excitement for M. Barkimel, presiding with
such impartiality at the Revolutionary Tribunal, his
colleagues were obliged to take him home in a taxi.
He seemed to be ill. Some of them suggested that
"he had had a drop too much." In stammering
and gloomy tones he thanked the friends of the people for kindly seeing him to his door.

When he was alone he tried to mount the stairs.
But he soon came to a stop and sat down on one of
the steps. His head seemed to be going round.

At ten o'clock that evening the electric light in
the staircase was switched off. He gave a deep sigh
and stood up. He was still shaking on his feet. But
he did not go into his flat. He went into the street
and, hugging the walls, made his way to the "Up-
to-date Grocery Stores."

 The street was empty, the shop-front closed, and

nothing suggested to the belated wayfarer that the inmates of this respectable house were not enjoying a well-earned repose.

All the same, M. Barkimel stopped at the low door and knocked on the offchance. M. Hilaire was their friend. M. Barkimel felt an imperative need to talk about M. Florent. The door was softly opened.

"Who's there?" asked M. Hilaire.

"Let me have a word with you," begged M. Barkimel in a voice of despair.

Then he stooped and passed through the door into the shop. He sat on a bag of nuts while M. Hilaire closed the door.

A small hand-lamp standing on the counter showed a faint glimmer in the spacious room. A light could be seen, too, in the dining-room, the sashdoor of which was closed. Nevertheless, the sound of someone stirring in this room could be heard.

"You may speak out," said M. Hilaire. "It's Mme Hilaire putting the things away. Have you brought bad news?"

"Yes," he returned with a gasp. "M. Florent is dead."

"Is that why you are in such a state?" asked M. Hilaire, almost with an air of indifference.

"I thought he was your friend as well as mine," said M. Barkimel, shaking his head. "But I can see there are no friends in these days."

"In revolutionary times it is a great difficulty to keep them," agreed M. Hilaire.

"It was I who sentenced him to death."

"Since you had to try your friend you were bound

to sentence him according to his crimes.   What offense had poor M. Florent committed?"

"He was a supporter of the Rights of Man.   Up to the last moment he bravely defended his opinions."

"You don't say so!   Supported the Rights of Man!   Why, the President of the Committee of Public Safety himself couldn't have saved him."

"But I—I ought to have given him a helping hand.   May his blood be upon my head."

"Well, I can't say anything more," declared M. Hilaire a little impatiently, "and you must go home to bed, M. Barkimel.   Come, good night.   Mme Hilaire is waiting for me. . . ."

At that moment a breath of wind, drifting in from outside extinguished the lamp in M. Hilaire's hand.   Only the panes of glass in the dining-room door remained lit up, and instead of Mme Hilaire's silhouette, M. Barkimel clearly observed the eccentric and terrible figure of the peanut dealer listening behind the door.

"Oh, you are still friends with that awful man. He will bring you bad luck, you see if he doesn't. Nothing good has happened to us since we've met him ,about everywhere."

But the little door had closed behind him and he found himself alone in the street.   Then tears came to his eyes and he was seized with a fit of rage against M. Hilaire for his shameful indifference to M. Florent's death.

"That man has no heart," he said to himself. "What's the use of telling me I've done my duty? It's no consolation to me to have done my duty."

Talking to himself in this way, he wandered

about all night like a drunken man. He could not have said what came to pass between the time of leaving M. Hilaire and reaching the Revolutionary Tribunal, where he arrived attired in his sash of office.

When he entered the Court, Talon, the concierge, who had denounced him the day before was on his trial.

M. Barkimel asked to be heard, and taking off his insignia of office and placing them on the table at which he had so often presided, he resigned his position as a judge on the ground of his unworthiness to hold it, acknowledging that he had in fact harbored in his flat an enemy of the people as stated by the accused. Then turning to the concierge he added:

"Let this man go in peace. He told the truth. Let me be tried in his place. I deserve the penalty of death, and I ask to be sentenced with no more pity than I have shown to the unfortunate prisoners who have appeared before me in this Court."

Shouts of fury greeted M. Barkimel's heroic utterance, and five minutes later he was duly sentenced to death as he desired and taken down to the temporary lock-up for condemned prisoners.

It was impossible to execute him that day, for the tumbril had already set out for the Place de la Revolution, but he was lodged in a cell which the warder thought was empty. The previous evening a condemned prisoner had been placed there too late to be included in that day's batch of executions.

When the cell door was closed and the sound of the turnkey's footsteps had died away in the corridor the forgotten man, whose eyes had become accustomed to the semi-darkness, exclaimed:

"Why, it's Barkimel!"

"Florent! So you're still alive!"

"That's not your fault."

"May be," exclaimed Barkimel, flinging himself into Florent's arms, "but it is also my fault that I am here. I felt so much remorse for what I had done that I asked to be sentenced to death to-day just as I sentenced you yesterday. And I shan't die happy unless you say you forgive me."

"We will die together," cried Florent, "and future generations"—M. Florent never lost an opportunity to call future generations to witness—"will look upon us as an example of true friendship."

Nevertheless, after this heroic outburst they began to condole with each other on their fate, regretting all the same, like respectable tradesmen, which they had never entirely ceased to be, having to die before their time.

CHAPTER XXX

IN WHICH M. HILAIRE HAS AN OPPORTUNITY OF
DECLARING THAT HONORS DO NOT NECES-
SARILY BRING HAPPINESS

PARIS learned all of a sudden that the trial of Subdamoun and his supporters, or rather such of them as were still left, was fixed for the next day. It was a blow struck by the Commune against Versailles, for the National Assembly, according to Coudry and the General Vigilance Committee, were

on the point of betraying the Revolution and playing the game of the reactionaries in the provinces.

All Subdamoun's friends, secret or avowed, were
in the plot. Therefore Coudry no longer hesitated,
on his own responsibility, to throw them the Major's
head as a challange. And on the evening of his
decision two thousand armed men were stationed
round the Conciergerie Prison and Law Courts.
He was afraid lest certain divisions might rise in
support of the Major.

It was six o'clock when Inspector-General Hilaire appeared at the wicket gate. He asked to see
the Governor at once. M. Talbot sent word that
he was waiting for him in the Tour de l'Ouest.

M. Hilaire seemed somewhat dejected. M. Talbot remarked on the fact. M. Hilaire gazed at himself in a small mirror hanging on the wall and
sighed.

"You are not so badly off," said Talbot, lolling
in an easy chair. "Suppose you were in my place?
Do you know that I haven't slept a wink since you
told me there was a plot to secure Subdamoun's
escape?"

"You will be able to sleep to-night. Two thousand men are in the street to keep guard, not to
mention your own little garrison, and to-morrow he
will be sentenced and executed. Why, if I were in
your place it is not the fear of Subdamoun breaking
out of prison that would keep me awake."

"What would keep you awake, pray?"

"Why," returned M. Hilaire, putting his mouth to
Talbot's ear, "simply my regret at having Garot
and Manol in my prison. There you have a couple
of tough customers that respectable people would

like to see sent to the devil. Their trial, you know, comes before the Assize Court at the beginning of next week, and their friends on the Vigilance Committee are in a considerable funk. Between ourselves, they are quite right, for there is no doubt the two bandits will turn informers."

While M. Hilaire was speaking M. Talbot changed color.

"Have you seen Coudry?" he asked.

"Yes," returned M. Hilaire. "He said to me: 'Your friend Talbot is a wonderful jailer. As long as he is the Governor there's no fear of Garot and Manol giving us the slip.'"

"He said that?"

"Well, yes. Those were his exact words. He added: 'That is a service the Republic will never forget.'"

Talbot gave a start, rose to his feet, and took up a position facing M. Hilaire.

"Is it my fault if they refuse to go?"

"Ah tush!" said M. Hilaire in ingenuous surprise, "why do they refuse to go?"

"Because they are not satisfied with any of the schemes that I have suggested to them."

"Deuce take it!" said M. Hilaire. "They are very difficult to please. After all, these fellows are right to take every precaution. An escape that failed would do for them for ever."

"They ask the impossible. They want a regular release. Something carried out in due form bearing my signature. The Governor's official stamp—a mere nothing. But what about me? What would become of me after a thing of that sort? I should be left in the lurch by everyone."

"Why?" asked Hilaire, suddenly stopping the irritating swing of his long legs.

"What do you mean—'Why?' . . . Are you making game of me? Because I alone would be held responsible."

"You would not be responsible for anything at all. Is not Coudry all-powerful?"

"Tut! Tut! That won't do. No, no, I have let these men know that they mustn't count on me for an affair of that sort. Hang it all, there are other ways. A wall is soon jumped over, a rain-pipe soon climbed."

"A bullet soon received."

"Those miscreants don't worry about bullets."

"You see that they do. Look here, my dear fellow, I am sorry for you—a man of your intelligence. I said again this afternoon to one of your friends: 'It's incredible that a clever man should allow himself to be stopped by such a trifle.' "

"And what did he reply?"

"That he was as surprised as I was. Of course, we are agreed that it would be difficult for a Governor of a prison to do *willingly* what these two fellows ask, but we fail to understand why you can't give way to *force*."

"Force?"

"Yes, Talbot. When one really wishes to give something and does not wish to give it willingly one allows it to be taken by force. Do you follow me?"

"Oh, that's absurd. How do you suppose they can take my signature by force?"

M. Hilaire laid one hand solemnly on M. Talbot's shoulder.

"It's not absurd, and it's exactly what will happen, my dear M. Talbot, or to-morrow you will cease to be Governor, and I wouldn't give much for your precious skin. At half-past seven you will ask to see Garot and Manol in your office. They will be brought here by their warders. They will state in the presence of the two men that they have a confession to make to you, but they wish to make it in private. You will order the warders to retire, waiting instructions at the foot of the staircase. When Garot and Manol are alone with you they will go for you. They will bind you hand and foot and gag you. On your desk there will be the necessary writing materials. And when they leave your office you will all be in order—you and the two prisoners! No one will be able to reproach you with anything. It will not be the first time that an escape has been made in such circumstances. It is almost a recognized method!"

"The warders at the door would never allow them to pass, even if their papers were in order. They would know what had happened. They would come to me for a confirmation of their release."

"They won't come to you for anything of the sort. Your two warders will be relieved by two others whom I shall bring along myself, and these men will be surprised at nothing, my dear M. Talbot, any more than the turnkey or the concierge. I shall be the only one to be surprised at the length of the interview in your room, and at supper time I shall come to disturb you!"

M. Talbot coughed, took a pinch of snuff, and stared M. Hilaire in the face.

"Have you spoken to Coudry about all this?" he asked after a pause.

"Well, you know the sort of man he is. I spoke to him about it vaguely as if the thing might happen to any Governor of a prison. He gave a smile. That is more than we want."

"Perhaps. Look here, I have an idea—which will prevent the affair coming as a surprise to anyone," said Talbot not without embarrassment, shovelling another big pinch of snuff into his capacious nose.

"What is it?"

"Our arrangement is not until half-past seven. I have plenty of time to make a call at the Town Hall."

"As you please," said M. Hilaire.

"I don't like the way you said that. Do you see any objection?"

"Well, if you ask my opinion, I think our friend would be none too pleased to receive a visit from you on the eve of a thing of this kind. There are malicious people about who might perhaps remember it next day." As he spoke M. Hilaire, with a doleful air, retied the knot of his sash. "Whatever happens, it's fixed for half-past seven, isn't it?"

"Look here, on further reflection I think it would be well to leave Coudry out of it," said the Governor.

"I agree with you."

"I know you are on very excellent terms with *them*. I can trust you."

"I believe your trust will not be misplaced, my dear M. Talbot. So it's fixed for half-past seven. Get everything ready on your desk. Have you a revolver?"

"Yes, in the drawer. I'll take it out to show that I was prepared to defend myself."

"If you take it out Manol and Garot, who have no scruples and are without weapons, might take it away from you! Give it to me. I will put it beside you when I come to see you after you are bound and those fellows are gone. That will make the thing more certain."

"You think of everything," said Talbot, handing the revolver to M. Hilaire, who put it in his pocket.

"Good-bye for the present, my dear Governor. I'll have a look at Manol and Garot and make certain that we understand each other."

After M. Hilaire's departure his anticipations were realized. Talbot left his office and soon afterwards the prison. Hilaire, who was watching him from behind a pillar in the guard-room, at once made his way to Baron d'Askof's cell and was shown in. D'Askof was alone. Their talk lasted ten minutes.

On leaving d'Askof, Hilaire paid a visit to Subdamoun's cell, where he distributed a few peanuts, amusing himself by cracking them during his inspection. Subdamoun was reading. On hearing mention of peanuts he looked up. Hilaire bowed to him and suggested with a laugh a few peanuts, as he had done to the warders. Subdamoun held out his hand. M. Hilaire counted out a certain number, and Subdamoun said: "Thank you."

Then the Inspector-General went to the part of the prison occupied by the cells, inspecting them thoroughly, remaining some time, however, in the cell in which Manol and Garot were incarcerated.

He returned to the guard-room and went upstairs to the Tour de l'Ouest. He knocked at the door of

the Governor's office.   Receiving no answer, he
went in, closing the door after him.   The room was
empty.   He looked at the clock.

"Talbot won't be back from the Town Hall for
another twenty minutes," he said aloud.

Then he walked round the room, casting his eyes
over everything.   There was no furniture—at least
very little.   A desk, some chairs, an arm-chair.   A
window, heavily barred, pierced the thick wall and
looked on to the quay.

Nothing in the nature of a surprise seemed possible in this bare room, whose spacious fireplace was
not hidden by any fire-screen.   At that season of
the year a fire was unnecessary.   The empty hearth
was as clean as the floor.

M. Hilaire stopped at the fireplace, turned his
back to it, and clasped his hands behind him.   He
seemed worried, and now and again a deep sigh
escaped him.   Doubtless he was looking back with
regret to the days when grocers played no part in
the conduct of State affairs.

Suddenly he quivered from head to foot—a peanut had fallen at his feet.   He seemed worried, and
still with his back to the fireplace said in an undertone, though no one could be seen either in front
or behind or round him:

"Everything is ready.   I've had a look at Manol
and Garot and given them the twenty thousand
francs, the revolver and the saw.   They'll break
out to-night through the courtyard.   The warders
will be taking them direct presently to the Visitors'
Room.   I have just came back.   No need to worry.
It's pretty well pitch dark there.   I shall take
d'Askof and Subdamoun there myself.   I shall stay

outside with the warders, who will be under my command. I have handed over the false wigs and beards to d'Askof. Our men will exchange clothes with Manol and Garot in the Visitors' Room. The whole thing will be done in a tick. Afterwards the warders will bring d'Askof and Subdamoun here to the Governor's office on my orders in the belief that they are in charge of Manol and Garot. Talbot has gone to see Coudry, who will read him a pretty lecture."

M. Hilaire finished speaking. He stooped, picked up the peanut, and ate it. As he was munching it his eyes suddenly fell on a letter which lay on the desk addressed to the Governor and marked "Urgent."

"Hullo," he said, "I know that handwriting," and without further consideration opened it. He ut-. tered a cry:

"Good God! It's all up with us!"

And he collapsed.

CHAPTER XXXI

IN WHICH CHÉRI-BIBI IS MORE THAN EVER IN THE GRIP OF FATALITY

AT the cry uttered by M. Hilaire a sort of fantastic gnome came crashing from the chimney and grew visible in the waning light whose shafts floated through the little barred window. The gnome leapt forward to M. Hilaire, still holding the ominous letter in his hand. It snatched the paper from him and read it. A sinister grunt accompanied the reading. And then it made a rush at M. Hilaire, who had dropped into a chair, shook him by the shoulders, and pulled him to his feet.

"Stand up, Dodger. Where did you find this letter?"

M. Hilaire pointed to the Governor's desk.

"Was it open?"

"No."

"Did you open it?"

M. Hilaire made an affirmative motion of his head.

"Then nothing is lost as the Governor knows nothing about it."

"Pah!" said M. Hilaire in a voice of gloomy despair, "he is bound to know about it since d'Askof has given us away." And Hilaire could not remove his eyes from the letter wherein he read:

"I entreat the Governor of the prison to come and see me in my cell at once without arousing the suspicions of any person and without, if possible, being seen by the Inspector-General. What I have to say is concerned with the escape of Subdamoun.
                                        D'ASKOF."

"We will do without d'Askof," snorted the gnome. "Come, pull yourself together, and I promise you everything will be all right."

"We can't do without d'Askof," said M. Hilaire in a doleful voice, shaking his head. "It is too late to work up a new scheme. It's a wash-out."

Suddenly M. Hilaire leapt aside. He felt the cold muzzle of a revolver on his forehead. Chéri-Bibi had straightened his back, and there was no doubt

the monster would have sent M. Hilaire to his last
account had he not on this occasion resolved to
recover his usual self-control. He fully understood.

"I am at your service, monsieur le Marquis," he
said at once, "as in the old days."

"Good. Listen to me," said Chéri-Bibi, darting a
look at him from a pair of scorching eyes. "Listen
and understand and act or I swear on Subdamoun's
life you shall never sell groceries again."

"On the day I met you after so many years, monsieur le Marquis," said M. Hilaire slowly, "I realized, amid the joy of our meeting, that I should
have to give up business."

"This is the last time I shall want you, Dodger.
After this I promise to leave you in peace."

"Oh, if you don't want me after this I doubt if I
shall want anyone either!"

"See how simple it is," said Chéri-Bibi with all
the deadly clairvoyance of a great captain who
changes his tactics on the field of battle. "Talbot
hasn't received this letter and won't know anything
about it. He hasn't seen d'Askof, and won't see
him. As soon as he returns from the Town Hall
he will come straight here. You will then start on
your job. When the whole five of you are in the
Visitors' Room—you, Subdamoun, d'Askof, Manol
and Garot—you will all go for d'Askof and do him
in. You will come out with Subdamoun only, who
will make up to look like Garot, and you'll get
through. When you reach the Governor's room you
must give out that Garot first wishes to speak to
him alone—and the trick is done. I will see that
it's a succes for no one shall come in here. Do you
follow me?"

"God help us," returned M. Hilaire simply. "If d'Askof kicks you may leave him to me."

"You can kill him, you know," said Chéri-Bibi, whose eyes gleamed with rage at the thought of the treachery that jeopardized his whole plan.

"I understand," returned the Dodger, who since he was to sacrifice his own life reckoned other lives as of no account.

"Have no more pity on the Baron than I shall have on the Governor of the prison," insisted the monster.

Chéri-Bibi stole towards the chimney. He went up, and suddenly emerged once more head downwards, his eyes below, while his lips above moved to say:

"That Talbot is a blackguard, and I shall take a real pleasure in sending him out of the world."

Then the mouth closed and the eyes also, and the head remained there, forming part of the architecture of the chimney, like some hideous gargoyle. Suddenly the Governor came in.

He rang for a light and a lamp was brought in. He sat down at his desk. His face was beaming.

"It's all right," he said. "Do you know where I've come from?"

"No."

"The Town Hall. Oh, I couldn't restrain myself any longer. Such a responsibility! On the plea that I had something urgent to say I saw Coudry, and without beating about the bush told him everything."

"He must have pulled a pretty long face."

"Not at all. He simply said: 'Try to avoid any

suspicion falling on you, my dear Talbot. That's all I can say to you.' "

"Didn't that put the wind up?"

"Yes, for the moment, but after I left him I thought it over and conceived a plan for averting any suspicion."

"What is your plan?"

"Well, here it is. . . . They must not spare me."

"They'll try not to," returned M. Hilaire, smiling all over his face in the semi-darkness.

"Understand what I mean. They must not handle me as though the thing were a joke. Manol and Garot certainly have some sharp instrument at their disposal."

"We'll find them one if necessary—but I believe as a fact they have something of the sort."

"They must make use of it."

"You frighten me."

"Blood must be shed. It will do if they stab me in my left hand. A great deal of blood will flow, and no one will dare suspect me. What do you think of my suggestion?"

"Well," returned Hilaire, "I think you are very plucky. But be easy in your mind. I will order these fellows to do the thing in such a way that it will never enter the head of anyone to suspect you of complicity in their escape!"

"Well then, that's agreed. . . . I will prepare the necessary papers and send for Manol and Garot. See on your part that there's no hitch of any kind, and send me, please, the officer on duty, to whom I have to give some orders regarding Subdamoun's trial to-morrow."

"Ah, we shall be able to breathe freely again when we are rid of all those fellows."

"You needn't tell me that! Good-bye then, my dear fellow, and let's hope we may both have good luck."

The Governor watched the Inspector-General leave the room. The door was no sooner closed than he left his armchair and began rubbing his hands with such unbounded glee that the gargoyle in the darkness of the chimney, still looking down on the scene in the Governor's office, felt a sort of shudder pass through him.

The Lieutenant on duty came in. He was blindly devoted to the Committee and generally on the best of terms with that ruffian of a Talbot.

"How many men have you in the guard-room at present?" he asked.

"About twenty," returned the Lieutenant.

"Well, you must send up ten of them at once fully armed. Send them quietly, without letting the Inspector-General know anything about it."

The Lieutenant left the room.

M. Talbot went on rubbing his hands. The gargoyle in the chimney was no longer the presentiment of a hideous smile; it had become a mask of agony and dismay.

It saw the ten civic guards enter. At Talbot's suggestion the Lieutenant lined them up against the wall so that persons entering the room covered by the door would not notice them.

"Very shortly two prisoners in charge of Hilaire and two warders will be brought here," said Talbot. "On a sign from me you will throw yourselves on them. If Hilaire and d'Askof come in you must make it impossible for them to do any harm. You mustn't hurt d'Askof. You will shoot down the other man—the man I will point out to you."

And Talbot, drawing the Lieutenant to the fireplace in front of the gargoyle, said in a low voice:

"Can you rely on your men?"

"Absolutely."

"Because the other man will be Subdamoun," said Talbot in a still lower voice.

"Good heavens! And must he be shot dead?"

"Coudry's orders. In these days we can never be sure of anything. It will be better to profit by this attempt at escape to make an end of him."

"How did you learn of this attempt to escape?"

"D'Askof found a way of letting Coudry know. They were to have attacked me and forced me to sign an order for their release. I have had a narrow escape. But whatever you do don't miss Subdamoun—what?"

"Leave that to me," returned the Lieutenant.

Talbot's head and throat and back were within reach of Chéri-Bibi's terrible hand. He had but to thrust out his arm and the man seized, throttled, dragged into the dark passage would have breathed his last in the arms of the demon. Never throughout his amazing criminal career had Chéri-Bibi been driven by such an intense longing for the throat of a man.

Alas! Chéri-Bibi only took life when he had no wish to do so!

His brain was in a hideous whirl, but the thought of the danger from which he must at all cost save Subdamoun reprieved Talbot. The gargoyle moved away.   Chéri-Bibi climbed the chimney with the agility of a monkey and a convict.

"Hilaire, Manol and Garot will take ten minutes to dispose of d'Askof in the Visitors' Room," he reckoned. "They've done that by now. Subdamoun must be fixing his make-up and putting on his false beard. Within five minutes they will be with the Governor and Jacques will be a goner."

But he had not wasted time. He emerged from the chimney like a jack-in-the-box. Fortunately, darkness had fallen.

From the street below rose the hum of soldiers talking together while waiting for the events of the next day and the hour when, after the trial, they would escort Subdamoun and his company to the scaffold. Chéri-Bibi could perceive the bivouac lights as he let himself down the side of the high chimney after twisting his rope round one arm.

All those soldiers in the streets—all those civic guards in the prison were concentrated against Subdamoun! All those armed men were brought together against his son—his son whom they would assassinate unless at this moment he could perform a miracle!

Like a cat he crept along the gutters overhanging the quay.

He mounted a gable, clambered to the top of his chimney as swiftly as he had descended the chimney in the Tour de l'Ouest. He fixed his rope, threw it down into the black pit, and himself slid down like an arrow.

He reached the fireplace and shot into the room. It was the room set apart for the President of the Assize Court for the examination, before their trial, of prisoners incarcerated for the time being in the Conciergerie Prison.

This room was identical with the Governor's office. Below it was the Barristers' Room, just as below the Governor's office was the Clerks' Room.

A flight of steps likewise led from the President's office to the guard-room. If Subdamoun and Hilaire took this staircase instead of the staircase leading to the Tour de l'Ouest they might yet be saved. In any case they could make an attempt to escape by way of the chimney and the roofs.

It no longer meant the peace and quietness of a legal departure! It meant a hue and cry, with all its hazards, dangers, sensations; but Chéri-Bibi, his brain on fire, believed that after all it was a chance worth the risk.

But he would have to get there in time to warn Hilaire. That was the crux of the problem.

Chéri-Bibi made a rush on the great door of the room at the head of the staircase.

Lord! the door was open. It was a minute gained. He quietly pushed it ajar. He was able to creep in the semi-darkness to the landing of the iron staircase. He lay prone, his bulk scarcely increasing the obscurity, watching the scene in the guard-room. Just then there was a considerable uproar which could not fail to assist his purpose.

He stretched his head over the stairs, seeking for Hilaire. He caught sight of him below, outside the door of the Visitors' Room.

He dropped a peanut at his feet, at the sound of which M. Hilaire at once looked up.

"Hist!" whispered Chéri-Bibi. "The thing has

failed in the Tour de l'Ouest, but come up to me in the Tour de l'Est."

Hilaire stooped, picked up the nut, cracked and ate it, signifying that he understood.

Never had Chéri-Bibi been so well served by circumstances. It really seemed as if, in his hour of need, chance had combined to rescue him from the abyss into which d'Askof had attempted to hurl him.

Knowing with certainty that he had been understood, Chéri-Bibi, who had projected himself over the well of the staircase, hanging almost entirely from a bar, the better to be heard by Hilaire, now regained his level on the landing and quietly slipped into the President's room, gliding along the ground like a snake. When he was inside he heard a voice in the darkness say:

"Bring a light."

Chéri-Bibi uttered a curse under his breath and closed the door.

He recognized the voice of M. Dimier, the President of the Assize Court. The fact that he had found the door of the President's office open meant that the President was paying a visit to the Conciergerie Prison and had just opened it, and while Chéri-Bibi was speaking to M. Hilaire had entered the Tour de l'Est.

Chéri-Bibi at once thought that the incident might possibly be turned to good account.

He could not doubt that M. Dimier had come to the office for the purpose of examining Manol and Garot on the eve of their trial. Therefore no one in the guard-room would be surprised to observe Hilaire taking the man whom they would assume to be one of the bandits to the Tour de l'Est, since the President of the Assize Court was waiting there to see him.

But what would happen when Subdamoun came face to face with M. Dimier?

At all costs M. Dimier would have to be made a party to the scheme.

We know in what esteem Chéri-Bibi held M. Dimier. He respected him as much as he despised the judicial bench in general for reasons known to himself.

Without any personal acquaintance with him M. Dimier had had the courage in a work on "Judicial Errors" to speak of his innocence of the first crime of which he was found guilty. Moreover, not only was M. Dimier an upright judge, but he was an honest man who could not fail to be sick at heart at the manner in which public affairs were being conducted, so much so that Chéri-Bibi ventured to think that when he was acquainted with the circumstances he would make no attempt to interfere with the escape of a man who was essential to the country if law and order were to be re-established.

Chéri-Bibi therefore went up to M. Dimier and in a voice that he strove to make friendly if not agreeable said:

"Don't be alarmed, monsieur le President, and whatever you do don't call out. I will explain what's going on."

M. Dimier, taken aback, perturbed, retreated a step, but recovering at once his habitual calm towards the mysterious figure who had closed the door, said:

"Who are you?"

"I am innocent, I am working for one who is

innocent," returned enigmatically the voice of the figure.

The answer failed to satisfy M. Dimier, who took a step towards the door.

"It's no use. You cannot leave until you have heard me."

"What do you want?"

"Your silence. You don't know me, but I know you. You are M. Dimier, President of the Assize Court, and you have come here to examine Manol and Garot. A man will be here presently who is neither the one nor the other, a man who is coming here to break out of prison. He will escape with me by way of the chimney which I have just come down. I ask of you one thing, one thing only— not to call out or shout or to take notice of his escape until it is too late to prevent it. This is quite simple."

M. Dimier allowed the man to speak in the darkness without interrupting him. When he finished he said:

"You say you know me. If you know me you must know that you are making a suggestion which conflicts with my duty. . . ."

"I am suggesting to you to save the life of a man."

"A criminal."

"No monsieur le President, this man is not a criminal. It is Subdamoun."

At the mention of this name M. Dimier gave a start which did not pass unnoticed. Chéri-Bibi said to himself: "He is saved!" and he offered no resistance when the door was opened and a man brought in a lamp. He felt, he knew, that M. Dimier would not denounce him. He was content to flatten himself against a corner of the wall, covered by the door, and he straightened his back when the door was closed again.

Chéri-Bibi no longer revealed the bowed figure of the peanut dealer when M. Dimier, lifting the lamp, scrutinized him in silence, but stood erect as Chéri-Bibi, in other words, with the stature of a giant.

"I am not a beauty," he said.

"You are frightful," returned M. Dimier. "Be off!"

"What?"

"I say—Be off! Go by the way you came. I have not seen you, I will not denounce you, I don't know you, and be careful that I never see you again— Go!"

M. Dimier quietly placed the lamp on the desk, sat down, and began to turn over his papers.

Chéri-Bibi remained standing. He was a a loss.

"I told you to go!" repeated M. Dimier with irritation.

"Go? But have you not understood me? I am here to save the life of Subdamoun."

"I understand that quite well, but it is not for me to allow any man's life to be saved. I am a judge, and my duty is to prevent the escape of prisoners, whoever they may be. . . . Do you hear— whoever they may be. You are not a prisoner — Go!"

A deadly silence ensued.

"If it were my father," continued M. Dimier, "I should either prevent his escape or send in my resignation as a judge."

It flashed through Chéri-Bibi's mind for a moment to cry: "Hush, he is my son!" but he thought

doubtless that such a confession would be no sufficient recommendation, and he kept his secret to
himself.

He sat down, for the President's words caused his
knees to give way beneath him. This last blow of
fate was too incredible. He had never expected
things to come to such a pass, for now he would
have to kill M. Dimier.

The necessity for this deed, which seemed inevitable, he could read in the proud and tenacious expression stamped on the judge's noble brow as
clearly as if it had been written in letters of fire.

Chéri-Bibi began to shake in every limb. M.
Dimier asked him why he was trembling like that.

"I will tell you," he returned. "Subdamoun was
to break out by the Tour de l'Ouest. The Tour de
l'Ouest is occupied by Talbot. I should have been
pleased to get rid of Talbot, who is a scoundrel, but
the thought that you . . ."

He came to an abrupt stop. M. Dimier, a little
pale, raised his head. He understood. He stared
at the monster seated before him, still shaking.
Chéri-Bibi's elbows and arms were twitching with
nervous tremors and his teeth chattered. That ap-
paling mouth wore an expression of fear. . . . And
yet that fear was hideously menacing.

"I could have handed you over a few minutes
ago," said the judge, thrusting his hand resolutely
towards the bell. Chéri-Bibi checked his hand.

"You will never know," he said in as kindly a
tone as was possible for him, "how much it costs me
to be disagreeable to you, M. Dimier. You wrote
a book which I shall never forget. You are perhaps
the one man in this world who ever had any pity

for me. One night when I fainted in the street from weakness you stopped and gave me alms. I admire and like you. Let me bind you hand and foot neatly, gag you nicely."

"That will do," said M. Dimier. "I have nothing more to say to you. And as you will not go I will hand you over to the police."

He rose to his feet and strode over to the door. Chéri-Bibi with one leap was on him and threw him to the ground. He gave a cry. But two hands clutched him by the throat. And as the sound of approaching footsteps could be heard on the stairs and not a moment was to be lost Chéri-Bibi pressed with all his might.

Chéri-Bibi rose from his stooping posture. He had taken the life of M. Dimier.

"*Fatalitas,*" he growled.

And he wept. . . . And then with a hideous gesture, sniffing, he wiped his eyes with the sleeve of his coat, shook his shoulders in readiness for the new work, drew a long breath, uttered intense "Ah!" of relief, and opened the door to Hilaire and Subdamoun, who hurried into the room.

They were just in time. A minute earlier and M. Dimier would have been saved and Subdamoun lost. Chéri-Bibi was sorry for his garrulity. The body had rolled under the desk. Chéri-Bibi blew out the lamp. Subdamoun observed nothing, and Hilaire learned of the necessity of the murder much later.

The door was now closed and bolted, and they were cut off from the horde of civic guards led by Talbot and the Lieutenant who, furious with rage at being tricked, attempted to break in, rained heavy blows on it, transformed themselves into catapults, and shouted for axes.

Subdamon could scarcely follow what was happening in the darkness, and he allowed himself to be lashed to a rope by a sort of fantastic giant who, bending over him, handled him with the greatest gentleness. M. Hilaire told him to submit himself to the operation.

The disturbing figure of the giant seen in a ray of moonlight climbed like a chimpanzee up the rope, and was lost in the huge chimney.

The Major grasped the fact that once on the roof his strange rescuer would hoist him up the chimney as though he were a package.

Meantime the blows at the door continued with renewed violence. It seemed as though it must be burst open. A savage clamor aimed at Subdamoun mingled with threats of death to M. Hilaire arose in terrible discordance.

Subdamoun, who was honor and courage personified, contrived to complicate still further that crucial moment.

He drew a knife from his pocket, cut the rope which bound him, and declared that he would not consent to mount the chimney unless the heroic Hilaire, to whom he owed his life, led the way and saved himself first.

M. Hilaire, as was natural, began to swear like a trooper.

"He would never forgive me for such a thing," he said.

"Who is 'he'?" asked Subdamoun.

"The Man up above," said M. Hilaire, attempting to refasten the rope round Subdamoun.

CHAPTER XXXII

CHÉRI-BIBI AND HIS SON MEET AGAIN

CHÉRI-BIBI, at the top of the chimney, hauled away at the rope. He could hear an unusual commotion at the foot of the tower. It seemed as if the civic guards on the quay were being warned from the Conciergerie Prison of the drama on the roof. Suddenly shots rang out and bullets ricochetted from the tower.

The position was critical. They must act quickly. Chéri-Bibi pulled at the rope and at last a head and then a body appeared. Chéri-Bibi seized it with fierce joy.

"It's me," came from the breathless and anxious voice of M. Hilaire.

A yell of fury ascended heavenwards in the night, and Chéri-Bibi hurled M. Hilaire down the chimney again.

M. Hilaire crashed to the bottom in a somewhat sorry state. His hands and face were bleeding and he complained of backache.

"There, what did I tell you," he said to Subdamoun, who deplored the result, and just then the door began to give way under the furious assaults upon it.

But the major had no time to condole with M. Hilaire. He was seized, borne down, tied up like a parcel by the demon who had descended from the clouds again, and hoisted up at the moment when the door gave way at its hinges.

Shots were fired up the chimney, but by a miracle they missed both the Man and Subdamoun.

More shots from the banks of the Seine greeted them as they emerged from the chimney. But here, too, they were missed. The Man took Subdamoun in his arms. He held him without roughness, almost with tenderness. He crept with him to the gutter of the roof.

"We are saved," he said.

Subdamoun did not believe a word of it, but all the same he marvelled at the Man's courage. Chéri-Bibi placed him on the side opposite the quay so as to shelter him from the volleys fired by the civic guards and the shots of certain warders of the Conciergerie Prison appearing at windows in the roofs.

The Man hooked the grapnel at the end of his rope to a gutter and let the rope hang downwards so that the lower end fell on another roof below. Then he put the rope in Subdamoun's hands. Subdamoun understood that he was to drop into the void. The rope swung with his weight. At last he reached a firm foothold.

The Man unhooked the grapnel so as not to part with his rope, rolled the rope round his shoulders, slid down a rain pipe with surprising dexterity, and was by Subdamoun's side before he could make a false step which might have proved fatal.

They were in almost complete darkness, and Subdamount could not understand how the Man contrived to see things around him which were indistinct to him, though he had some experience of keeping a look-out for danger.

A regular wilderness of roofs and shadowy places lay around. Chimneys loomed up suddenly like so many enemies lying in wait for them. Subdamoun could not restrain a start from time to time when taken by surprise. At last the Man said: "Don't be afraid," and then at once corrected himself. "I beg your pardon," he said, ashamed of advising a man like Subdamoun not to be afraid.

Subdamoun understood his meaning and was touched. He had not seen the Man's face in the darkness. He was sure he would not know him again.

To begin with he was not unduly surprised by this nameless devotion. He had observed on the battlefield the need which ordinary men feel to devote themselves body and soul to their chiefs. This Man was doubtless some obscure soldier in the great civic battle that Subdamoun was waging against established authority. Nevertheless the events on the roof could not fail to rouse his highest appreciation, not only of the strength but of the presence of mind with which the man disposed of every obstacle likely to impede their progress.

He led their flight so as to keep away as far as possible from the vicinity of the quay whence the shots came. And Subdamoun felt vaguely, as they traversed the twists and turns of the various roofs and gutters in which his strange guide was moving as though he were at home, that they were making for some specific objective.

A storm broke forth. Rain fell in torrents. The Man took off his coat, a sort of cape, and threw it over Subdamoun's shoulders.

Strange to say Subdamoun flung it aside with a shudder. The Man noticed his gesture and gave a groan.

"I am sorry," he said meekly.

"I don't want to deprive you of it," returned Subdamoun, picking it up and giving it back to him. "You need it as much as I do."

He was surprised at his own instinctive movement of repulsion. The Man did not persist.

Suddenly a flash of lightning blazed from one chimney to another. This time Subdamoun could see his rescuer's features. He leant for support on a slate behind him, filled with horror.

"He has the mug of a convict," he groaned.

Fortunately, the Man could not see Subdamoun's face or he would have read on it such a look of disgust that he might perhaps have fallen backwards to the pavement. The sound of a body of men moving about around them could be heard.

"Look out, men are on the roof. Lie flat on your stomach."

And in fact a number of figures appeared on a roof at their left. They were the helmeted shadows of firemen, who slid down between two gables and vanished the next moment.

The Man went off to reconnoitre, and saw the enemy again on the roof next to that on which he and Subdamoun were clinging. To reach their roof the firemen had thrown a ladder across which could be used as a footbridge.

They were creeping along this footbridge. Subdamoun, raising his head, could see them. Like shadows on a screen they stood out on the sky, lit by a blood-red moon which had just emerged from behind a heavy cloud.

The Man, after crawling along on hands and knees, stood up. He held in his hand the two ends of the ladder, and the human cluster were hurled in a screaming mass from a height of sixty feet into the court below.

The moon was veiled once more. All was darkness again. "It's horrible!" wailed Subdamoun like a child.

Suddenly the man stopped. They could hear the rush and cries of pursuers behind the roofs which they were climbing. They came to an attic. The Man tapped at the window. At the sound a head appeared.

"Is that you, Fanor?"

"No, it's Masson," was the reply.

The Man pounced on the head and pulled. The body followed, struggling. It was flung into space. Subdamoun shrank back appalled. The Man took hold of Subdamoun and placed him carefully in the room from which Masson had made so dramatic an exit. Then the Man in his turn climbed over and closed the window.

"Now, we must keep silence."

"What you did just now was murder."

"You don't suppose I did it for the fun of the thing," said the Man in a stifled voice, wincing at the reproof.

But Subdamoun was so overwhelmed that the Man seemed to think some explanation necessary.

"I don't know Masson. Oh, if it had been Fanor there would have been no trouble. I made a mistake in the attic. I am very sorry."

Subdamoun did not answer. They could scarcely see in the darkness of the room. They were like two blotches of shadow facing each other.

"Who is he?" wondered Subdamoun. And the

Man was in a state of consternation because he was conscious that his boy was angry.

"His boy!"

He had held him in his arms. Chéri-Bibi had held his son in his arms. . . . Oh, he had held him with all deference . . . almost tremblingly . . . and without daring to clasp him to his breast . . . his heart.

He felt how utterly unworthy of him he was.

The pride of the Republic in the arms of the pride of the Convict Settlement! He had profaned his son by holding him in his arms. He asked God's forgiveness, and thanked the Devil for it!

Suddenly Subdamoun said in a low voice:

"I want to know who you are."

Chéri-Bibi quivered from head to foot in the darkness.

"What is your name?" added Subdamoun.

"What does that matter to you? I am a detective in the Political Detective Service. I must not have any name."

"A detective in the Political Detective Service!" repeated Subdamoun, unable to get over his surprise.

"Yes. You should ask M. Cravely my name when you have succeeded. I work for him. I am no party to this business. I carry out instructions. Do you follow me?"

Subdamoun could not believe his ears.

"Are my affairs in such a satisfactory state that Cravely is with me?" he asked incredulously.

"They are very satisfactory if you do not get nabbed. The worst part is over. We have but to go downstairs. But first of all put on Masson's clothes."

"Who is Masson?"

"Masson, like his colleague, is a messenger in the Procurator-General's office," explained Chéri-Bibi-collecting from a bed standing in a corner of the attic the uniform and insignia of the unfortunate man and placing them before Subdamoun. "We ourselves are at this moment under the same roof as the Procurator-General's office, and it looks on to the Boulevard du Palais. We have but to go downstairs. I know the ins and outs of this house, and if we meet any inquisitive persons you must say nothing. You will follow me. Your uniform will enable you to go anywhere. In this way we shall reach without let or hindrance the Detective Department. I know a way which is perfectly safe."

"What about you?"

"Oh, they know me. Are you ready?"

Five minutes later Subdamoun and the Man went quietly down the staircase of the Procurator General's office. An indifferent light here and there illumined the spacious building, whose highly polished floors caused too loud an echo for Subdamoun's liking.

Subdamoun had a new surprise when the Man underwent a transformation and became a miserable old fellow with bent back and knock-knees. Subdamoun later vaguely remembered making his way through a narrow and damp passages, the doors in which were opened by the old man with a master key. Here they came upon detectives, to whom he gave some pass-word impossible to understand.

Then they both found themselves out of doors in the darkness of the street. The old man led the way, and, leaving behind him the sounds of the city, turned towards the quay and threaded his way through a deserted street. At the end of the street a closed car with lights out stood waiting. The miserable old man went up to it and opened the door.

"Will you get in, my Prince," he said in his rasping voice.

Jacques stepped in, and the old man closed the door.

The car got under way. There was no chauffeur, for it was driven from inside. . . .

"Here you are at last, Jacques!"

"Frederic!"

The two companions in arms had many questions to put to each other, but Subdamoun first wished Frederic to tell him something about the old man who had saved his life in such marvellous circumstances.

"He is a great friend of Hilaire. We can have complete confidence in him."

"It looks like it," agreed Subdamoun, shaking his head. "But what's his name?"

"I don't know. We call him the 'peanut dealer.' "

CHAPTER XXXIII

CHÉRI-BIBI MEETS HIS WIFE AGAIN

CHÉRI-BIBI watched the car drive away. When it was out of sight and he could no longer hear the throb of the engine he gave a sigh.

He walked away, and his mind turned to the work that he had still to do before he could go to bed. To begin with, though Subdamoun was out of prison he was not at the end of his difficulties; secondly, Subdamoun's mother, the admirable Marchioness de Touchais, was still in M. Hilaire's cellar waiting to be set free; thirdly, M. Hilaire himself was a victim in his turn of the enemies of the nation, and lodged in this Conciergerie Prison into which a gesture of ill-humor on the part of Chéri-Bibi had inopportunely flung him.

Was Chéri-Bibi to desert the faithful Dodger, the friend of his worst days? That would be very unlike him!

Suddenly he uttered a cry. It had flashed upon him that as M. Hilaire's real mission at the Conciergerie Prison was discovered the police would make a search of his house and discover Cecily there.

Chéri-Bibi started to run like a madman. Other people were also running in front, behind, and around him, without paying attention to him. The sound of shouting could be heard in the locality. Vivid flashes of light shot up on the right like sheaves of rockets, and he heard a voice say:

"The Up-to-date Grocery Stores is on fire!"

Then he cut a gap for himself in the crowd as straight as a cannon ball.

He no longer thought of anything but Hilaire's cellar and the stock of oil, petrol, and other spirits contained in it which would feed the flames, and in his mind's eye he saw the deified figure of the Marchioness de Touchais, eyes lifted heavenwards, like Joan of Arc at the stake.

As he turned the corner of the street he came upon, or rather collided with, the police cordon with such violence that they looked upon him as a lunatic who meant to throw himself into the flames.

Two policemen darted forward, but were quickly forced back by the heat of the fire.

The fire-engines, however, set to work throwing in the centre of the building great jets of water which sparkled and glittered, seeming to sustain the fire. Firemen on the roofs used their axes to cut away some of the beams.

The cellar in which the refugees were imprisoned was underneath the "Up-to-date Grocery Stores."

As we have already stated, this cellar could be reached by a low door, level with the pavement, which looked on to a narrow lane very little frequented, and used in the ordinary way for the delivery of casks. It was only with the greatest difficulty that this lane, masked by a veritable canopy of fire, could be approached. Chéri-Bibi, defying the danger, crept to a spot where no other man dared venture.

Just then he realized that the explosions around him were not caused entirely by the fire, for he was hit by a bullet which went right through his left hand. A firing party was shooting into the burning building from the opposite street. He just managed to rush into the shelter of a door when another volley was fired.

Then the door gave way under his weight, and he heard the well-known voice of his scout Mazeppa saying:

"This way, boss, if you don't like bullets."

At the same moment he found himself in the coal dealer's place.

The shop was beginning to burn, and two women lay on the floor choking for breath, half asphyxiated, while two men, blackened by the fire through which they had passed, were bending over them.

He recognized Lieutenant Frederic Héloni and Polydore, one of Subdamoun's redoubtable guards, to whom he had entrusted the care of the cellar when the Marchioness was shut up there with the other woman.

He threw himself on the ground, searching for Cecily. He found only Mlle Lydia de la Morlière and her friend Marie Thérèse.

"Where is the Marchioness?" he yelled.

"Jean Jean has saved her," said Polydore.

"Do you mean it?"

"You can be easy in your mind. We got here in time," explained Frederic.

"Is Subdamoun here?"

"No. He knows nothing. We drove to the place where we were expected. I saw Mazeppa there, and he told me that Hilaire's stores were on fire. I left our chiefs to their deliberations and hastened here without saying a word to the Major."

"Curse all liars," growled Chéri-Bibi, shaking his bleeding hand. "Where is the Marchioness?"

Polydore told him what had happened while Frederic continued his attentions to Lydia and Marie Thérèse, who were gradually coming to themselves.

"While we were running away from the fire they shot at us. I carried the young lady Lydia. Jean Jean took the Marchioness. We cut off in different directions to force the police to scatter. I saw Jean Jean with the Marchioness in his arms on the roofs beyond the stores. He was out of danger. When I got there I was too far behind him to pass that way. I came back here along the wall, knowing Mazeppa was waiting for me, and the coal dealer our Lieutenant, had brought the young lady Marie Thérèse here. Oh, you can be easy, boss, we looked after the ladies. Ask Mazeppa. Now we must think where to hop it, for it's getting as hot here as a baker's oven."

But Chéri-Bibi did not appear to notice the heat. No longer troubling about Lydia and Marie Thérése stretched on the floor, for whom the Lieutenant was doing his best, he asked, as though they were of no importance:

"Have they been firing on you long?"

He flattened the youth Mazeppa against the wall, and the young blackguard had to explain everything to him fully, while Polydore set to work to clear the far end of the cellar of the many sacks of coal that filled it so as to uncover a sort of underground passage leading to a court usually deserted, whence they could make their escape.

"Well, here's the whole story," said Mazeppa.

"It's a certainty, boss, we'll get our hair singed here. The coal dealer"—he pointed to Frederic —"when he left me told me to come to him in the Aveune Jena if there was the least trouble, and when I saw police and a gang of men of the Division . . ."

"What then?" growled Chéri-Bibi, fuming with suppressed rage.

"Well, I cleared out. Wait a bit, boss. These fellows had come from the Arsenal Club to search the place as Hilaire had helped Subdamoun to escape, so they said. They were not in the shop five minutes before they were exchanging shots with Jean Jean and Polydore, who had come up from the cellar to prevent them from going down. The shop assistants turned tail, yelling like mad. I said to myself: 'This is a wash-out. As I don't know where the boss is I'll go and tell the coal dealer.' I slipped out in less than no time to find the Lieutenant. I saw him enter the back door of the house where he was expected with Subdamoun. The coal dealer noticed me. He came out again and drove me back here with him in the car. He didn't waste any time, you bet. We did our seventy-five miles an hour. But things were pretty hot here. Furious at being kept out of the cellar, the police set the place on fire. . . . And the good ladies below were screaming. I heard Mme Hilaire's voice shouting for help as if she were being roasted alive. Poor Mme Hilaire! She was the only one we didn't bother about. . . . She soon stopped her noise. . . ."

"What about the Marchioness?" fumed Chéri-Bibi.

"Oh, the Marchioness! . . . We didn't hear her. She comes from a class that never makes a fuss, even if the house is on fire."

"Was she injured?"

"How should I know? How can I tell? Certainly when I saw her being carried off by Jean Jean she looked more dead than alive."

"If she is dead I'll do the lot of you in," growled Chéri-Bibi with clenched fists.

"But haven't I told you Jean Jean saved her. . . . Hullo, there she is!"

Chéri-Bibi leapt through the window. He, too, could see the Marchioness, or rather her quivering body, still being carried by the faithful Jean Jean. Chased on the roofs by the civic guards, and realizing that his retreat was cut off, he had been forced to return to the tottering walls of the burning building.

It was a tense moment. Jean Jean, as a last resort, was making for the lane in which he knew the coal dealer lived. But how was he to reach this haunt?

Though the fire at this spot had been decreasing in intensity for some time, it was an act of great daring on Jean Jean's part to risk bringing the Marchioness to the topmost floor window, for the flames were still reaching it from time to time.

Shots greeted Chéri-Bibi as he leapt out of the window, and civic guards rushed up from both ends of the lane, in spite of the intense heat. But the double rush saved our bandit. And indeed when the civic guards found themselves face to face they ceased firing lest they should shoot each other.

Chéri-Bibi seized the opportunity to finish his run and disappear into the inferno.

Then some of the guards made a dash for the coal dealer's shop, where they knew that the rest of the company had taken refuge.

The place was empty, but they discovered the underground passage by which obviously the three men had escaped with Mlle de la Morlière and Marie Thérèse.

After firing their revolvers into the narrow passage they groped their way forward and came upon two bodies stretched on the ground. They dragged them into the shop. One of them was Polydore, who had received a bullet in his back and seemed at his last gasp, and the other Lydia. With great difficulty they wrested from his grasp the poor girl, whom he had endeavored to save.

Lydia, amid the confusion and the light of the fire, came to herself.

"Good business," said the municipal officer. "Here is a prize! It's Subdamoun's fiancée."

Content with their work on this side, they ran into the lane again, now filled with the public, firemen and soldiers. There was a great crush, and some were scorched with the heat.

A loud and varied clamor went up, for a shot had hit the man carrying the Marchioness, and some of the onlookers protested against the civic guards being called upon to carry out such orders.

Jean Jean was certainly wounded. He clung desperately to an iron bar, twisted by the flames, the heat of which wrung a cry of pain from him.

But though he still held his burden he was swaying, and it seemed as if he must crash to the pavement with the Marchioness, when a raging demon appeared in the framework of the same window. This amazing being, thrown up by the fire as though he were the attendant spirit of the fire, appeared just in time to snatch the poor Marchioness from Jean Jean's arms as this victim of his devotion to the King of the Convict Settlement made his last pirouette and came smashing down into the fire, which sent up a veritable sheaf of fireworks under the impact.

Meantime the Man who had come out of the fire went back into it again. Flames and bullets whistled past his ears, a horde of civic guards above and around pursued him, a furnace was at his feet and an infernal canopy over his head—but Cecily lay on his heart.

Chéri-Bibi was in raptures. . . . Chéri-Bibi was in an earthly heaven.

In the midst of the furious battle that he was waging against men and the elements he thanked Heaven for sparing him for that great happiness.

To be sure that day meant something to him, an outcast from society, for on that day it was his lot to clasp in his arms those adored beings Jacques and Cecily.

Cecily his wife—his beloved wife whose unconscious form lay near his heart after so many years, so many years of mental torture spent in saying to timself: I will never go near her again!

He held her in his arms with the tenderness of a mother nursing her sleeping child. And his heart was burning for Cecily with an intenser fire than that conflagration—with a fire that would never be quenched!

Merciful heavens, the Man, with a sudden movement, availing himself of a curtain of fire, kissed
her!   Chéri-Bibi pressed his lips to the white forehead of that saintly woman in this temple of fire.

Chéri-Bibi shouted with delight, caught his
breath, snorted, danced with joy on the burning
bricks.   He appeared, disappeared, reappeared,
kissed his burden, held it heavenward, drew it back
to his heart, and leapt with it into some hole of a
garret into which the startled faces of his pursuers
peered without seeing anything.

Which way had he gone?   He alone, the King
of the Convicts, knew every road that led to the
underground haunt in the cul-de-sac where his dun-
geon lay.

*   *   *   *   *   *   *

Cecily swept her hand over her forehead as people
do when they wish to collect their thoughts and,
as the saying goes, return to life.   She remembered
the tragedy of the fire, and then her thoughts
harked back still farther.   Those eyes that wept
behind their spectacles, those poor horrible eyes
that pained and terrified her.   She had seen them
before.   She knew them now and murmured: The
peanut dealer!

It was the peanut dealer who had saved her
life and brought her there.   It was the peanut dealer
who had promised to save her son's life.   Whenever difficulties arose the peanut dealer invariably
appeared.   A shudder passed through her.   Why
—ah why?

She coud never think of this terrible rescuer

without a shudder. She called out to him though she feared him.

She feared him though she did not know him, and she could not bring herself to thank him. Who was he? What was his motive? Why was he watching over her?

He wore an expression of such terrible misery when he looked at her! Who could he be?

She wondered if he were not merely the presentment of her sick brain. He was perhaps the figment of her imagination.

She raised herself and stole from the wretched bed. A table bore a number of phials and basins, giving the place the appearance of a chemist's shop. She went beyond the table. She came to a passage, and at the end of the passage beheld a light in the distance.

Though the light did not allay her fears it attracted her. She went down a few steps and walked on. The light came from under a door.

The door was not closed. She pushed it open. Did she know what she was doing?

She uttered a cry of surprise. She found herself in a small cellar resplendent with light. A number of candles were burning in a magnificent candlelabrum. And their light fell upon the portraits of a woman and child. But such wonderful portraits! Not even on the walls of Byzantine churches had so many jewels, pearls, necklaces been suspended with such loving care round the sacred ikons.

She drew nearer. Then she saw the portraits clearly and recognized them. They were pictures of herself in the happiest days of her beauty and

motherhood, and of Jacques from babyhood onwards.

On a table resembling an altar an open casket
stood. A cross lay in the casket, a wonderful cross
of the Legion of Honor, set with pearls and diamonds.

Cecily recognized it. It was the cross which
she received one day as an offering to Jacques
from some unknown admirer but which she returned, unwilling to accept a gift of such value
without knowing the donor.

Little by little Cecily allowed herself to sink on
the steps of the altar where she and her son were,
so to speak, deified. She was more bewildered than
ever. More than ever she wondered why she should
be the object of such devotion. A strange feeling
of anguish came over her. She had never felt so
great a fear of she knew not what.

Suddenly her eyes alighted on a photograph, and
she dragged herself towards it. And she could not
restrain a cry: "The Villa de la Falaise!" And
indeed it was a photograph of the Bourreliers' villa
on the cliffs at Puys, near Dieppe, the house of her
parents, where she had spent her girlhood. The
photograph was taken from the garden.

She recognized the picture of herself standing at
the entrance of the garden talking to a butcher's
boy carrying a basket on his arm and obviously
taking orders from the young mistress of the house.

She remembered seeing this snapshot long ago
in the hands of Jacqueline, who later on became
Sister St. Mary of the Angels. . . . Cecily remembered it quite well. Yes, that was it! Jacqueline
had taken a snapshot of Cecily Bourrelier and

Chéri-Bibi. . . . Yes. . . . Yes. . . . the butcher's boy was Chéri-Bibi!   Chéri-Bibi!

She uttered the name aloud as the frightful truth
flashed through her mind.

She remembered that Chéri-Bibi loved her when
she was a young girl, though he had never spoken
of his love. She had seen him more than once with
tears in his eyes. Mercy of God, the eyes that
wept behind the spectacles of her rescuer were
Chéri-Bibi's eyes! . . . Chéri-Bibi the convict, the
King of Convicts. . . . She and her son owed their
protection to Chéri-Bibi!

The Marchioness de Touchais swooned once
more. She believed that she had fathomed the mystery. Poor Cecily! She had scarcely crossed the
threshold of it.

CHAPTER XXXIV

THE LAST TUMBRIL

FLORENT and Barkimel, who spent their time
in confessing their sins to each other and mutually
repeating the prayers for the dead, were greatly
surprised when the door of their cell was opened
and the warder flung into it with some violence the
Inspector-General of Prisons himself.

"M. Hilaire!" they exclaimed simultaneously,
uttering a hollow groan expressive of their united
misfortune, and offering him a hand.

M. Hilaire, recognized Florent and Barkimel, and
thanked Heaven for allowing him to spend his last
moments with such distinguished friends.

After indulging in sundry reflections on the truism that death makes all men equal, M. Hilaire thought it well to introduce a note of moderation into such gloomy philosophy by informing them that, for his part, he had not lost all hope of some improvement taking place in their prospects before long.

Expressing a severe condemnation of the Commune, he informed his friends that honest folk were rising in every part of the country to come to their assistance.

M. Florent did not wait for these encouraging words to be repeated before giving vent to a sigh of satisfaction. On the other hand, M. Barkimel lowered his head and remained silent so that his disconsolate attitude at last impressed M. Florent, and he asked the reason for it.

"M. Hilaire has spoken of 'honest folk,' and I know what he means by that. After playing the part which devolved on me in these evil days can I with any decency include myself among these 'honest folk'?"

"Of course, I understand your embarrassment," said M. Hilaire. "You have greatly distinguished yourself at the Revolutionary Tribunal!"

"Not more than you have in the Arsenal Club," returned M. Barkimel sadly but firmly, for he had possessed an innate sense of justice before he was appointed a judge. "And you must allow me to express surprise, M. Hilaire, that after making such violent speeches against the enemies of the revolution you should now rely on them to get you out of your troubles."

"That is because you are not aware," returned

M. Hilaire calmly, "that while I made those violent speeches openly I was working secretly for the counter-revolutionaries and have rendered them very conspicuous services."

"And you boast about it! What a shame!" exclaimed M. Barkimel, incensed by such cynicism.

"I am not boasting about it. I am merely telling you what I did, and what I did was not so very foolish. You served the revolutionaries because you considered it was in your interests to do so. I personally thought that two precautions were better than one, and that I should have more chance of saving myself by working for both sides."

"History will pass its judgment on you," retorted M. Barkimel, folding his arms.

"Don't let us waste our last few hours in argument," begged M. Florent.

The three friends had reached this stage when the door of the cell was opened and the warder called out their names. At that late hour they might at least have been allowed to have a last sleep in peace. What was happening?

The truth was that Subdamoun's escape had thrown the Communal authorities in disorder, and the Vigilance Committee determined that the trial of his accomplices shoud be proceeded with then and there so that their execution at dawn might to some extent conciliate their supporters ever ready to cry out that they were being betrayed.

The Vigilance Committee were so infuriated that no half measures would satisfy them. Nearly every cell was cleared. And so M. Barkimel was sent before the Tribunal a second time to be sentenced to death a second time.

"If I escape this time I shall be in luck's way," he said dolefully.

The large room used by the Revolutionary Tribunal was overcrowded with prisoners, closely guarded by men of the division with fixed bayonets. Some sixty victims named in advance were waiting the good pleasure of the judges.

Nevertheless, Baron d'Askof put a bold face on it. He knew the price the prisoners would have to pay for his treachery, and he rejoiced at the prospect in anticipation while gazing at Sonia Liskinne, who, for that matter, paid no attention to his airs and graces and proud bearing.

She was charitably devoting herself to the task of supporting and consoling an unhappy and beautiful young girl who had been thrown into her cell at the last moment.

The young girl was no other than Mlle de la Morlière.

Baron d'Askof's tortuous mind found matter for amusement in the uncommon sight formed by the two women, Sonia and Lydia. With what unholy joy he observed Lydia's pallor and despair, and with what a look of triumph he regarded Sonia, who could not fail soon to be his!

The trial passed quickly. All the prisoners were condemned to death except three. First, Mlle Sonia Liskinne, who could not believe her ears, and asked in a ringing voice to whom she owed "such a dishonor." She learned the truth when the Tribunal next acquitted d'Askof.

It was obvious that the Baron had acted the traitor and that it was to him that she owed such an outrageous act of clemency. The Baron grinned, but he stopped laughing when the Tribunal acquitted the Baroness d'Askof.

He had no wish to save her. He had, indeed, completely forgotten her, and in his plans for the future his wife found no place. Her acquittal was an act of "grace" on the part of the Public Prosecutor, desirous of placating a man who promised to make sensational revelations after the trial.

The Baroness had been sent for and brought into Court unobserved by the Baron, nor did he see her until her acquittal was announced, when she broke into a fit of hysterical sobbing, such as she usually reserved for grand occasions. As she was being carried out of Court the Baron swore like a trooper.

No further incident occurred, and the prisoners were escorted back to their cells again to remain there until the early morning.

Sonia continued to lavish attention on Mlle de la Morlière. At last her tears began to flow freely, and her paroxysm of emotion over her fate in itself afforded her some relief.

The two women exchanged a few friendly words over their terrible misfortune. In the hour of sorrow nothing can bring two women nearer to one another than the fact that they love the same man and fear for his safety. They fell into each other's arms. Jealousy was of no avail and fled at that supreme moment, and instead of rending they sought to console each other.

Lydia, reeling under the blow of her own sentence, had failed to hear Sonia's acquittal and believed that she was to suffer the same fate as herself. Sonia, on the other hand, refrained from telling

her the cruel truth. Moreover, she sincerely regretted her own acquittal, for the presence in Court
of M. Hilaire and his trial and sentence seemed
to indicate that Subdamoun's attempt at escape
had failed. It was rumored in prison that he had
been killed by the bayonets of the civic guards.

After a silence, as Lydia was still weeping, Sonia
said:

"Why are you crying? It was you that he loved."

Lydia gave a start, raised her eyes and shook
her head.

"No. You are too beautiful. When he came to
know you he never left you, and now that I have
seen you I can understand that."

She gave way to another fit of sobbing, and Sonia,
distraught, held her in her arms.

"Why, you are crazy, my dear. It was his ambition that led him to me, but he would have sacrificed even his ambition for you. We were friends
—friends for a day that was destined to know no
morrow, the morrow that belonged entirely to
you."

"Alas, I shall die without knowing that morrow.
Why did I not die on that wretched morning when
I tried to take my own life!"

"That morning, you poor girl, he tried to save
the country and failed because of your attempt to
die by your own hand," returned Sonia. "He gave
up everything to come to you. And the delay meant
the destruction of all his wonderful efforts. He did
not hesitate for a moment. You are an ungrateful
girl to forget. . . ."

"That's true," said Lydia in a weak voice. "That

morning he came to me. He gave up everything for me. I came to myself in his arms—in his arms."

She fell asleep at last murmuring "in his arms."

Sonia held her clasped for some minutes, listening to the breathing and the throbbing heart of that adored being condemned to die so young; then with infinite care she laid her on her pallet. She could hear footsteps in the corridor. She feared lest those sounds drawing nearer should awaken her. Anxiously she leant forward, but Lydia was sleeping, was sleeping now so soundly that she did not wake when the door of the cell opened and a police officer shouted: "Mlle de la Morlière.

"Here!" answered Sonia, and she strode out and joined the other condemned prisoners standing waiting between the bayonets of the guards.

The cell door was closed. Mlle Lydia de la Morlière still slept.

Afterwards it was assumed that the Tribunal had reconsidered its decision and sentenced Sonia Liskinne to death.

The condemned prisoners were prepared for their doom that morning in the guard-room. Only the sound of the scissors could be heard.

Sonia was facing a registrar's clerk whom in the past she had often "tipped"—a man endowed with a shy and poetic temperament.

His hands shook as he touched her bare neck and he could scarcely lift her magnificent hair. He hesitated to introduce his hideous scissors into that golden fleece and fumbled.

In her softest voice Sonia begged him to show

more nerve, for she wished her hair to be cut off as far as possible without being "spoiled."

"I want to make a present of it, so cut it off neatly," she said.

The clerk gave a gasp and followed her instructions, not without emotion.

"Am I so much to be pitied?" asked Sonia.

"Madame, if you do not wish me to be sorry for you, at least let me be sorry for those who will never see you again," he returned courteously.

His answer greatly pleased her, and she ventured to ask him to take her hair as a souvenir to the prisoner still occupying her cell.

The clerk promised to carry out her wishes, and at once took the precaution to move the golden treasure which had been entrusted to him to a place of safety.

Not far from Sonia, M. Lavobourg, the ex-President of the Chamber, was bending his head and shuddering at the contact of the scissors.

Hilaire, Florent and Barkimel were not uninteresting to contemplate. All they had seen in the Court Room was a jostling crowd. They came away from it suffering from the butt-ends of revolvers, which had terribly wounded their pride. They doomed to perdition a body which did not know how to respect its victims, and they regretted nothing so much as the fact that they would not be alive to witness the discomfiture which might have saved them.

As the last few touches were being put to their toilet they listened attentively to the remarks whispered in the semi-darkness of the Gothic hall.

Well-informed persons, whose shirt-collars had just been very neatly opened, declared that the reason why the Commune was "dispatching" them with such great haste was to be found in the ultimatum received the previous evening from Versailles.

It was stated that Coudry had massed two hundred guns on the Place de la Revolution on chance.

"We must resign ourselves to our fate and try to die like others with fitting dignity." Thus the two friends expressed themselves, mutually sustaining each other. When the shutter of the wicket gate was opened they hastily dabbed their eyes and concentrated themselves on keeping together.

Four tumbrils stood waiting in the courtyard. The three men were hurried into the first one. M. Barkimel helped M. Florent to get in, and next M. Florent helped M. Hilaire. M. Hilaire seemed preoccupied, paying no attention to his friends, but allowing his gaze to wander into the distance.

He was brought to attention by the sound of Sonia's voice. She stood next to him, and asked if it were true that Subdamoun was dead. M. Hilaire made answer that he hoped not, and that, to his knowledge, Subdamoun had a good chance of eluding his enemies.

Sonia changed countenance at these words and it would have been difficult to say whether from joy or sorrow—joy to think that Subdamoun was still alive or sorrow at having made so heroic a sacrifice of herself when she might have rejoined him.

Just then the outer wicket gate was opened and the grim procession started its progress along the quay.

When the first tumbril came out—it was a cart requistioned at the last moment the "funeral cars" themselves being full—a tumult of insults and curses went up against it. The tumbril contained the chief figures of our story.

Moreover, disorder, fighting, incendiarism, turmoil, singing, curses seemed that morning to have taken possession of the town and formed a sort of escort for these last victims of the new Revolution.

Beyond the flames on the river's bank, already consuming buildings age-old and hallowed by history, which had been set alight by a rabble let loose by the fury and incapacity of a committee of revolt beaten at the start, the condemned prisoners could hear the dull boom of the guns from Versailles, already on their way perhaps to liberate them.

At that moment, M. Hilaire was undoubtedly the most dejected of them all. But three hundred yards farther on he seemed to come to life again.

"There he is!"

And indeed it was the peanut dealer marching ahead of the first tumbril in the centre of a gang of men of blood and rapine. He seemed to be in a state of mad intoxication, and his blind frenzy delighted the hideous mob, which spurred him on with its laughter.

He threw his wares here and there, shouting:

"Eat these peanuts. The Versailles people shan't have 'em."

The cortège turned to the left as usual to reach the grand boulevards by way of the Boulevard Sébastopol. M. Hilaire had no eyes nor ears for anything but the fantastic old man brandishing on high his empty basket.

Assuredly he had good reason to count on Chéri-Bibi. Chéri-Bibi should have known better, of course, than to throw the Dodger down the chimney seeing that he had so fortunately reached the top, but his gesture of rage, pardonable in the circumstances, would obviously be redeemed by some startling plan to wrest M. Hilaire from the hands of the executioner.

M. Hilaire, however, was growing a little impatient as he saw the procession take a "short cut" —terrible words that flashed across his mind causing him to make a wry face—when his attention was attracted by a body of curious-looking bakers' boys selling cakes.

There were a number of pastry-cooks' shops in this quarter which enjoyed considerable prosperity, despite the troublous times through which they were passing. It was the custom to send out extra boys on public holidays to sell "hot cakes" among the crowd.

On this particular morning the number of boys was larger than usual, and their voices could be heard above the tumult. When the peanut dealer threw his empty basket in the air towards them they suddenly stopped.

After that M. Hilaire no longer doubted that the crucial moment had come.

The place was well chosen. The tumbrils were passing the foot of a flight of steps from which rose, one above the other, a number of old streets whose aspect had not changed for more than two hundred years.

A body of determined confederates could make an attempt with some chance of success to rush the procession from the steps and, by taking it by surprise, effect their purpose.

Hilaire tried to convey some hint of what was about to happen to M. Florent, but he had collapsed on M. Barkimel's shoulder. M. Barkimel himself seemed to be utterly exhausted.

Hilaire, glancing quickly round the cart, observed Sonia's beaming face and was struck by the brightness of her eyes.

He followed her gaze, fixed on a particular spot, and descried at a window overlooking the noisy crowd in the narrow cross-roads a countenance whose appearance caused him to utter a faint exclamation:

"Subdamoun!"

It was he right enough. Major Jacques was there, and it was obvious from his presence there that he was not acting alone. Assistance could not be very far away.

"That's a comfort," thought M. Hilaire, who had never seriously believed that he would die on the scaffold, or at least rejected the thought from his mind as particularly repulsive.

And just as his hope of deliverance put new life into him Subdamoun gave a signal whereupon a great commotion broke forth.

The bakers' boys, seemingly in command of the crowd, clambered up the balustrade at the top of the steps and rushed headlong to the causeway, followed by some hundred fierce-looking persons brandishing the most nondescript weapons. Shots rang out on all sides; civic guards fell; a desperate struggle was fought round the first tumbril.

Sonia watched with bated breath the shifting fortunes of the fray. She could see Subdamoun himself standing near the flight of steps directing the operations.

The civic guards, taken by surprise, were forced to retreat. A certain lack of decision betrayed itself in the movement of the cortège. The first tumbril became cut off from the rest.

M. Hilaire was seeking how to fling himself out of the cart. The peanut dealer had vanished. Suddenly M. Hilaire found himself clutched violently by the shoulders by a hand from outside.

He made no attempt to struggle, allowing himself to be carried off by this irresistible force. But the civic guard near him made a lunge at him full in the chest with his bayonet, or at least he aimed full at his chest, but the blow glanced under his arm.

As M. Hilaire toppled over, legs upwards, the man assumed that his thrust had struck home and ripped up his prisoner, and paid no further attention to him.

He had in fact other things to think about. The prisoners were like so many madmen, and though bound hand and foot, they fell with all their weight on their guards to prevent them from using their weapons.

The smallness of the space in which they were confined assisted their manœuvre, and some of the guards yelled with pain because they were bitten.

It is difficult to convey an impression of the confusion that reigned. The cries of the wounded and dying, of men trampled under foot, of mounted guards unhorsed, of the brigands of bakers' boys in whom a practiced military eye would have recognized many men from the colonial regiment devoted to Subdamoun—all these things created a deafening uproàr while the shooting of the guards went on apace.

All the same, the guards succeeded in reforming round the three remaining lorries, which were quickly driven towards the Place de la Revolution by a circuitous route.

It was assumed that the first tumbril was permanently in the hands of the assailants. For a few minutes, indeed, they held the upper hand. A wheel came off and its human freight rolled to the ground, with the exception of Sonia and Lavobourg, who instinctively clutched the rail nearest where they were standing. It was this movement that brought about their undoing.

Florent and Barkimel fell to the ground with the others. It was this movement that saved their lives.

They remained for a while stretched on the cobbles, and no more attention was paid to them than if they were dead.

The first tumbril was stranded against the pavement. Subdamoun, who had joined the fray, was preparing to dart forward, and Sonia might well believe that she was rescued, when the peanut dealer pushed him roughly and he stumbled and fell. Chéri-Bibi held him for a while on the ground, and at that very moment a volley of rifle fire blazed out.

It came from a party of soldiers under the command of General Flottard himself. Had not Chéri-Bibi prevented Subdamoun's rush forward he would have been literally shot to pieces.

After that there could be no question of continuing the fight. Civic guards made a grab at the two remaining prisoners, Sonia and Lavobourg, and forced them into a closed car that had been abandoned, and Flottard himself mounted the box-seat and took the wheel.

He swore to drive his victims to the guillotine himself, and set off at a moderate but safe pace, escorted by two hundred mounted guards. No further incident occurred on the way to the Place de la Revolution.

And so destiny willed that at that supreme hour those two beings who might have hated each other should be united in death.

Their eyes met, and the light of forgiveness shone in them.

"Let us say a prayer," said Sonia.

They both prayed.

"Forgive me as I forgive you."

"I loved you, and it is for you to forgive me," said Lavobourg.

Shouts of fury migled with curses greeted them as they mounted the steps of the fatal platform. All those who remained faithful to the old regime, now more than half defeated, seemed to have met there while the sound of the guns from Versailles continued to draw nearer.

"If we had been brought here an hour later . . ." began Lavobourg.

It was obvious that he was about to add "we might have been saved," but he had no time to finish his words, for the executioner's assistants seized and threw him on the trap and the guillotine fell.

Sonia turned away her pale golden head. The shouting for a moment ceased. Then Sonia heard a sob from someone in the crowd.

"He is here," she said to herself.

And she drew herself up to her full height, seemed still lovelier, and presently the executioner was to behead her. . . .

It did not take long. Her head fell among the other heads in the horrible basket. . . .

CHAPTER XXXV

THE BEST OF FRIENDS MUST PART

THREE weeks afterwards the revolutionary outbreak was but a memory.

It had been suppressed with no less dispatch than it had itself shown in satisfying its lust for universal destruction.

The victors took care to refrain from the excesses that followed the overthrow of the old "Commune." They were the first to set their faces against reprisals and further executions; they spared the lives of the hostages in their hands; and they set about the restoration of the ancient buildings which fanatics had started to burn down.

Coudry's men were allowed to decamp abroad, and Coudry himself was able to cross the frontier.

The National Assembly was to be succeeded by a newly elected Parliament, whose business it would be to revise the Constitution, and meantime Subdamoun was elected President.

The house in the Marais quarter assumed its normal aspect. Jacques found his mother at home. She had been taken there in circumstances still wrapped in mystery to her and them all.

After all, she and her son and his betrothed had escaped with their lives, which was the main thing. Frederic Héloni, too, had come to live in the house as well as Marie Thérèse, his betrothed, and they might all have been quite happy had not Subdamoun, upon whom fortune seemed to smile, worn a look of deep depression which grew darker every day.

Lydia did not venture to question him. Like the Marchioness and Frederic, she assumed that the tragic end of Mlle Sonia Liskinne was responsible for his gloomy demeanor.

And yet Subdamoun had never mentioned Sonia's name even to Frederic, nor had he made a pilgrimage to the house in the Boulevard Periere, which remained closed and was treated by Parisians when passing it with every mark of respect as if it were a tomb.

Life had assumed its former aspect in that quarter. Only the shutters of one shop remained closed —Little Buddha junior's famous cabaret. No one knew what had become of its proprietor. After the arrival of the troops from Versailles his forbidding face was no longer seen.

About two o'clock on that particular night two dark forms, hugging the walls, drew nearer to each other. The first, seemingly the shorter and shrivelled up, came from the fortifications; the second walked down from the Rue de Rome and crossed the iron bridge. They reached the cabaret door almost simultaneously and with one accord came to a stand.

The neighborhood was deserted. The shorter figure began to pick the lock, the other kept watch.

At last the door opened; the two men slipped into the cabaret, and the door closed behind them. A dark lantern cast a ray of light, and Chéri-Bibi said:

"Sit down, Dodger. I'll have a look round."

"If anyone is here he must be dead, for there isn't a sound," returned the Dodger.

The Dodger heard Chéri-Bibi's shuffling footsteps mounting the stairs from the room at the back; he heard doors being opened and closed above him: then a silence followed, and Chéri-Bibi appeared once more.

"I have had a look round as far as Sonia's house. Everything is quiet. We can talk."

"What's happened to Little Buddha?" asked the Dodger.

"I was going to ask you that!"

The Dodger coughed: "May I ask you, monsieur le Marquis," he said, "why you chose to meet your servant in this God-forsaken spot and at this late hour when honest grocers have long been in bed?"

"I didn't want to compromise you, my dear Dodger," returned Chéri-Bibi, sitting down opposite his pal and patting his hand.

"You are very good, monsieur le Marquis."

"Call me Chéri-Bibi as in the old days. The voice of a friend is sweet to hear."

The Dodger shrank back a little. He had no love for these exhibitions of feeling from the man who for so many years had never ceased in reality to be his master. What demand was he about to make on him now? Was it not understood that everything was over and done with? Had not Chéri-Bibi said to him with a sigh after rescuing him from the executioner: "It's all right now, my dear Dodger. You deserve to live happily and in peace. Our adventures are finished."

Chéri-Bibi rose from his chair and walked away in a curious state of excitement. He returned with a bottle of old brandy and poured out a glass for the Dodger.

"How's business with you?" he asked in a friendly voice.

"Well, it's looking up again slowly," returned the Dodger. "But we sadly miss poor Mme Hilaire."

"Are you still without any definite news?" asked Chéri-Bibi in a tone of sincere pity for the Dodger.

"Oh, yes. I know what happened, and that's what is grieving me," said M. Hilaire, sighing. "It's a great calamity. There's no doubt she's dead."

"Good heavens, you don't say so!"

"It's a certainty she was burnt alive, poor child."

"Don't take it too much to heart, Dodger."

"The only things I found were the half-charred part of one of her boots and her 'bun' of hair almost burnt. The rest of her made up a very small quantity of ashes which I reverently collected in an urn and placed on the marble top of my bedside table. Such a good woman, monsieur le Marquis, and what a head for business! It's awful. Believe me or not, I spend the time before my urn bewailing her loss."

"You'll end by getting the blues," said Chéri-Bibi, pouring out another glass of brandy. "You see, when sorrow comes in through the door it soon fills the whole house. If I were in your place I'd have a change of scene."

"Look out, we are coming to it!" thought M. Hilaire. "What's he going to suggest now?"

"I agree with you," went on Chéri-Bibi, "your wife was a superior woman and you'll never find another like her. Without her you'll go bankrupt to a certainty."

"Come, I say, don't let's overdo it," the Dodger ventured to say, regretting his too lavish display of conjugal grief. "Hang it all, I am a man."

"Do you mean that? Don't forget that your political opinions must have made a fair number of enemies for you in your neighborhood."

"Well, I've done good service to everyone about here," protested the Dodger.

"It's a thankless world."

"So I am not asking for anything out of the way. I only had two friends—Barkimel and Florent. They have been swept away by the storm. I shall know how to console myself, though I should like to see their cheerful faces in the morning for a glass of white wine as an appetizer. . . . As for my other customers, they will turn up as they did in the past, for the world, monsieur le Marquis, will always go where they can get the best goods. There you have the secret of business—there's no magic in it."

"In spite of the loss of your wife, I see that you intend to stick to your groceries."

Hilaire grew pale, but he mustered up his courage.

"Yes, with your permission, monsieur le Marquis."

"All right. I have nothing to say," said Chéri-Bibi, rising.

The Dodger was beside himself. He gave a gesture of childish rage.

"I don't know what stuff you are made of, but

I feel the need, at my age, to settle down and live quietly and be respected, I deserve it, and if you will allow me to express my opinion, you, too, monsieur le Marquis, should be content with what you've done. Take care lest a final blow should destroy the whole beautiful structure."

"It's wisdom itself that speaks through your lips," snorted Chéri-Bibi, "and you chatter with such eloquence that I don't wonder at your success at the Club, but I must tell you one thing—unless I pull off this last coup it's all up and everything else will be useless."

"You are perhaps fancying things—in the past you sometimes had such fancies."

"Don't talk like that," yelped Chéri-Bibi, holding the Dodger's wrist in a grip that made him cry out. "No, no, I never fancied things. . . . I never took life unless it was absolutely necessary."

M. Hilaire shrank back and his cheeks blanched.

"Then is there still some one who stands in your way?" he asked in a trembling voice.

"Two!"

A silence ensued between them. It was M. Hilaire who broke it first.

"Upon my soul, it's a great nuisance," he said, slapping his thigh.

"All the same, I am not forcing you to anything, M. Hilaire."

"Well, monsieur le Marquis, you see I am all attention. It's a great nuisance, but I'm all attention. What's the trouble, anyway?"

"It's like this," said Chéri-Bibi after a few minutes' reflection, "Subdamoun is depressed."

"Why should he be, in Heaven's name?"

"He is depressed because his life was saved by a man whom he doesn't know, and this man in order to save him killed M. Dimier, an honest man, and several others besides."

"Pah! Subdamoun is a soldier. Why should he even trouble about that? These are mere trifles. Besides, I don't see how we shall make him less depressed by killing a couple more! That would only, on the contrary, if I understand you aright, increase his depression."

"Subdamoun is depressed to death," returned Chéri-Bibi harshly, "because he has been tormented by a number of letters, anonymous letters, which follow him everywhere, some of which I have intercepted. These letters tell him that in all this business he has been merely the tool of the greatest bandit in the world, and offer to give him proof whenever he likes, and the name of the man."

"Whew! that's a pretty big offer!"

Chéri-Bibi put his hand on the Dodger's lips.

"Hold your tongue. . . . These letters contain particulars of this man's intervention, and draw the conclusion that unless Subdamoun himself gets rid of him or denounces him to the police as he deserves, he must be regarded as morally the accomplice of a murderer."

"Did Subdamoun at once believe all this?"

"No, at first he refused to believe it. It seemed to him, of course, inconceivable. Then in order to get at the facts Subdamoun asked the Detective Service to send him Daddy Peanuts. But Daddy Peanuts was nowhere to be found. After the Revolution was over Daddy Peanuts disappeared. 'He must be dead,' said Cravely. And I believe Cravely is right!"

"Well, you certainly promised me that he should die," said Hilaire.

"Look here, nothing will bring Daddy Peanuts to life again, and you may take it from me that Chéri-Bibi would rather die himself than allow Subdamoun to hear of certain things."

"Does the writer of the letters know as much as all that?" asked M. Hilaire with a catch in his breath.

"The writer knows everything."

"It's d'Askof!" exclaimed Hilaire.

"No, it's not d'Askof. D'Askof is dead by my hand as a punishment for his treachery. It's his wife. I recognized her handwriting."

"The Baroness! Damn it all, why isn't she dead?"

"Because I don't know where she is. It's just that. And she knows everything. Her husband must have told her everything. Before he died he was but a quivering mass in my hands, for I kept him on the rack, but he had the strength to shout out my name: 'Chéri-Bibi,' and also, 'Subdamoun is the son of a murderer. . . .' You see, Hilaire, how very simple it is. His wife is avenging his death. That's where I stand. . . .

"Nothing, however, is lost. Fortunately, she has not yet put everything in writing. . . . She wants to see Subdamoun and tell him herself the main things, and in order to prove that the peanut dealer was mixed up with the *coup d'état* and directed the whole affair from the outset, she is bringing with her a witness whose allegations it would be impos-

sible to refute. You can guess who that witness is
—Little Buddha—and she has promised him at the
same time to reveal the name of the man who made
away with his father. I, too, promised Little Buddha to disclose the name, but you will understand
why I was in no hurry to do so."

"What a rotten business! Then it's necessary to
do away with Little Buddha as well?"

"Of course. But where are they? You see, as
they are lying low they are taking their precautions.
They must be hiding in their burrows like rabbits.
They will only come out to tell my son: 'Chéri-
Bibi is your father!'"

Chéri-Bibi stood up in the semi-darkness a prey
to extraordinary excitement.

"Yes, their days are numbered," said M. Hilaire,
quietly seeking to appease him. "But how is the
thing to be done?"

"Oh, that's very easy. They have made an appointment for to-morrow night."

"How do you know that?"

"I never leave the Morlière's house. I am living
with Cecily, with my son; I am living side by side
with them, among them. They are searching for
me high and low. I am there! Subdamoun is having a search made for me in the provinces. . . . I
see him coming, going, living, breathing. The folds
of a curtain, a piece of furniture, a little shadow, the
cellar, the attic—anything, everything that can hide
a person is my home. I see what he is writing, I
rummage among the remnants of the letter that he
has received, I hear the orders that he gives. I am
the most happy and most miserable of men and I
know everything. Their house is my refuge and

my lair. And in this house I have worked out my plan for to-morrow. It was the Baroness who fixed the fatal hour and insisted upon a meeting in his house. She thinks that she will be entirely safe there. She is convinced that she will be better protected there than anywhere else. She will enter the house openly, and she imagines that she will come out of it again avenged, having at last struck to death father, mother, son. . . . And she will have Little Buddha with her. She asked Subdamoun to reply to her under her initials through the agony column of a newspaper, and he did reply to her. She has reckoned on everyone but me. You see for yourself, Hilaire, how easy it all is. I don't know where they are to-day, but at nine o'clock to-morrow evening they will be in the small drawing-room of the Morlière's house, where Subdamoun will meet them."

"Yes, it's very simple," agreed M. Hilaire in a muffled voice.

"Just one word more and I have done. Be at your place to-morrow night at eight o'clock. Mazeppa, who of course knows nothing of all this, will call for you from me, and you must come along with him. . . ."

Nothing more was said, and they left Little Buddha's cabaret with the same stealth and caution as they had entered it and, after shaking hands, took leave of each other in the darkness of the night.

On his way home M. Hilaire could not help saying to himself: "As the job is so easy, why does he need my assistance? He will make short work of the Baroness and Little Buddha."

Such being the trend of his reflections he at last convinced himself that his presence could only be a hindrance.

During the rest of the night and the following day the very simple nature of the job weighed on his mind like an obsession. A preliminary announcement in the morning papers describing the Government's clemency towards the misdeeds of the past and the complete amnesty that it intended to grant to its enemies on condition that they severed all connection with revolutionary proceedings; the peaceful and stable aspect of his shop with its rows of jars and boxes; the freedom from agitation of his little staff eagerly serving the various customers—all these things combined to persuade him of the futility of jeopardizing his personal liberty so happily and recently recovered in an adventure of such simplicity.

He took a sheet of paper headed "Up-to-date Grocery Stores" and wrote to Chéri-Bibi in his best handwriting:

"Monsieur le Marquis,

"I am exceedingly sorry to be unable to keep our appointment. I have received an order from the Prefect of Police to attend his office at half-past eight to-night without fail. I am afraid there is some unpleasantness in store for me, and it will be better for me to know where I am at once, if only in your interests. Detectives are keeping watch from the street on my movements. I wish you the best of luck."

At eight o'clock he went out, after giving the letter to his head assistant with his instructions:

"A youth will call for me at half-past eight. Tell

him I am not in. He will then buy a small ball of string. Give him the string and this letter, and ask him to take it once to his employer."

Mazeppa received the latter at half-past eight and returned to Chéri-Bibi, who was waiting for him in a small café near by.

Chéri-Bibi read the letter:

"There's no doubt every one is deserting me," he said with a sigh. "Very well, I'll do the job myself."

CHAPTER XXXVI

AT HOME

THE dinner hour in the de Touchais household was half-past seven. On that evening the meal which passed almost in gloom was over at eight o'clock.

Marie Thérèse was dining in town with a school friend, and Frederic Héloni availed himself of her absence to turn the conversation to the difficulty of arranging his marriage to a girl whose mother could not be found.

Subdamoun, who disliked any mention of the d'Askofs now that he knew that the Baron had betrayed his confidence, did not open his lips. Thereupon Frederic rose from the table, took leave of the Marchioness and Lydia, and said he was going out for a stroll.

He forbore to shake hands with Subdamoun. He resented his strange inertia at a time when, to his mind, he ought to have proclaimed himself the happiest of men.

After Frederic's departure Subdamoun rose in his turn, stating that he would be working throughout the night. He had given instructions for two persons whom he was expecting to call to be shown into the small drawing-room, and he asked that he should not be disturbed.

He went to his study. Lydia moved closer to the Marchioness, who saw that she was in tears.

"Lydia, my dear child . . ." sighed Cecily.

"It can't go on like this," said Lydia. "It is more than I can bear. He is too miserable. I must speak to him. He does not care for me any more. His thoughts are only of her. He is living on her memory."

"You must have a little patience, Lydia."

"I hate myself. I ought not to hide from him any longer the sacrifice she made for me. For his sake, and above all for her sake, I ought to tell him. She died for me. She died in my stead. Alas, why did she make me this gift of life? I would never have accepted her sacrifice. . . . But as it was made it is right that he should know about it."

"He would never, perhaps, forgive you for it, my dear Lydia."

The Marchioness at once regretted allowing these clumsily expressed words to slip out which, however, explained her conduct and the care with which she treated the confidences that Lydia was ever ready to share with her. On hearing the unfortunate words she gave a cry:

"Oh, you see for yourself he is not in love with me," she said, rising. "I will go and tell him everything."

From the tone in which Lydia spoke the Marchioness saw that it would be useless to argue with her.

"Go then and make him still more miserable," she said.

Lydia groaned but did not look round. She went to her room and came away from it carrying a small box. She did not knock at Subdamoun's door. She opened it and walked in.

Subdamoun was in his study, his head buried in his hands. He did not hear her come in. She walked the length of the room, stood before him, placed the box on his table, went down on her knees and waited.

He looked up and saw the kneeling figure, the sweet face bathed in tears.

"What are you doing here, Lydia?" he asked gently.

"I have brought you Sonia's hair," she said with a sob, opening the box.

The lustrous, living gold of the dead woman's hair shot forth its radiance. He rose trembling.

"What did you say?" he stammered.

"I said I have brought you Mlle Liskinne's hair," she repeated weakly.

He came over to her in time to support her and, faint though he was himself, saved her from sinking to the floor. And as she rested half unconscious in his arms:

"How good of you, Lydia. I love you for doing this. You may believe me, Lydia."

He pressed his lips to her forehead, which gave her new life. But he still gazed, haggard-eyed, on the hair that he dared not touch."

"Take it. It belongs to you. I give it to you,"
she said.

The sacrifice fulfilled, she recovered in part her
strength. He took the gift and his hands stole over
the silken wonder that he had so recently caressed.

"Do you mind?" he said. "She was a faithful
friend and gave her life for me." Tears prevented
Lydia from replying. "Poor Sonia!" he went on.
"Oh, Lydia, you deserve my utmost gratitude for
giving me such a moment as this. Her hair!
Where did you get it, Lydia?"

"She gave it to me before she died."

"How do you mean?"

"We shared the same cell."

"You have had it in your possession all this time
and waited until to-day! . . ."

"I am, I know, to blame, more to blame than you
think, dear," confessed Lydia, lowering her head
under the half-expressed reproach from those beloved lips. "I thought to myself that if I gave you
her hair and told you the circumstances in which it
came to me you would perhaps never forgive me."

"You frighten me."

"I assure you that I am not to blame for what
happened. I swear that."

"But what did happen?"

She told him the story, and with a sob exclaimed:
"You must always love her as I shall always pray
for her." Then she collapsed, worn out.

Jacques uttered a dull cry, but he checked himself in his vain regrets. To regret that one was
dead, was not that to regret that the other was
living?

He looked at the frail child who had so greatly suffered and so heroically come to him to say: "You must always love her." He bent over her and took her in his arms.

"You are worthy of her, Lydia. It is I who do not deserve the love of two such women. . . . Take away this relic of her. It belongs to you. We will never part with it."

Lydia took from him this token of a love in which she found it hard to believe. . . . And as she rose bewildered, dazed, not knowing whither to turn her steps, Subdamoun said to the Marchioness, who had come in quietly and witnessed the end of the scene:

"This box will be as sacred to you, mother, as it is to us, because it contains the hair of a woman who sacrificed herself to save the life of my promised wife."

He led Lydia up to his mother. The scene might perhaps have been prolonged had not the man-servant come in to tell him that two persons were waiting to see him in the small drawing-room.

CHAPTER XXXVII

THE SMALL DRAWING-ROOM

"Very well," said Subdamoun in a different voice. "Ask them to wait."

He begged his mother and Lydia to leave him. The tender feeling of a moment before was gone, giving place to an excitement which he vainly strove to control.

While the two women stood in amazement at the

change in him he made a gesture for them to go and sat down at his desk. He endeavored to become a master of himself again.

The enemy was in the house, for obviously it was an enemy who had come to make such a disclosure, an enemy to the death.

He had no wish to allow his fears to be seen before the game was played. He must, from the outset, treat the enemy as impostors, for his one last hope lay in the whole thing being an imposture.

Yes, he determined to believe that they were about to lie to him. And he would show a calm assurance in the presence of such a conspiracy.

Unfortunately his reflection on certain events of the last few days rendered it extremely difficult for him to maintain the necessary self-possession.

He would rather have found himself in the African desert amid the treachery of wild tribes than in that peaceful old house where two persons were waiting for him in the small drawing-room.

He had chosen that room, sometimes used by his mother in the daytime as a room of rest, because it was at the far end of a passage and they would be able to talk in peace without rousing the attention of any inquisitive listener.

Subdamoun opened a drawer, took out a revolver and loaded it. He put it in his pocket, and then began to pace up and down the study. He made an effort to think out some plan of campaign. It was to no purpose.

Suddenly the door opened and he found himself confronted by his mother, seemingly no less agitated than himself.

"What's the matter, Jacques?" she said. "As I

passed the small drawing-room, the door being ajar,
I heard a voice say: 'Is he going to keep us waiting
much longer?' I recognized the voice. It was the
Baroness d'Askof speaking."

Subdamoun, on his guard, managed in part to
conceal the excitement which the mention of that
name occasioned.

The Baroness d'Askof! So she was the enemy!

He thought of the many deeds that the Baron
could have done, or caused to be done, in his name
while they were conspiring together, and inwardly
quailed. In what deep waters was he floundering?

"Why have you not more confidence in me?"
went on the Marchioness. "I feel certain that some
great danger hangs over you."

"You are mistaken, mother," he returned. "I
have an appointment with the Baroness d'Askof
because we have to settle certain matters connected
with the past, but I am in no danger."

She stood motionless. He made a movement of
impatience.

"You ought to get some rest. Besides, I have
asked you to allow me to see these people without
worrying yourself about them."

He had never spoken to her in such a tone before. She was more than ever perturbed.

"You are not yourself. During the last few days
you have altered beyond recognition. Usually you
have such complete control of yourself, but you
cannot disguise your uneasiness. Why don't you
trust me? I have always looked upon these d'Askofs as bandits."

"I, too, have considered them as utterly unscrupulous," agreed Subdamoun.

"Ah, there you are giving yourself away. Well, refuse to meet these people. They mustn't be allowed to come to this house again. . . . We must break with them."

"It is for that very purpose that I must see them. Besides, you forget that this interview with the Baroness may be useful in assisting the marriage of Frederic Héloni and Maria Thérèse."

"Don't say any more. How can you put forward such a pretext! Marie Thérèse will wait if necessary until she is of age, and if it were nothing more than that I would see the Baroness myself. The look on your face frightens me, and I am frightened on your account."

He clenched his fists, and then at the sight of the grief on his mother's face he relented.

"Listen, mother. Things being what they are I must have done with them, and I will tell you everything briefly. These people have come here, it seems, to prove to me that in the matter of the *coup d'état* I was merely the tool of a murderer, and they're going to tell me that murderer's name. So you see I must receive them."

Cecily made no reply. She was at the end of her endurance. All her terrors, all her forebodings, all her suspicions, since it had been brought home to her how assassination had helped her son, the vague but terrible image of the man who had saved her life, the haunting memory of her captivity in the underground cellar where a loathsome slave grovelled at her feet; above all, the name, the deadly name, revealed by the photograph in the little temple with its relics of the past, the name that little children in France had learnt to fear like that of an ogre or the wolf-man—all these things rose up before her and enveloped her in a demoniacal whirl that paralyzed her mind, scorched her eyes, deafened her ears—her ears still ringing with the sound of those tragic syllables: "Chéri-Bibi! Chéri-Bibi!"

She put out her arms.

"Don't go there. . . . Don't go there."

She caught hold of him. He shook her as though she were the obstacle, forgetting that she was his mother, and she gave a gasp without losing her hold.

"Don't go there. . . . Don't go there."

At the thought that she should try to prevent him from getting at the truth Subdamoun darted forward in a frenzy, dragging her with him, and thus they reached the door of the small drawing-room, which was now closed.

Here he came to a stand and listened. She, too, mastering the delirium that was taking possession of her, drew herself up and listened. They could hear nothing but the loud throbbing of their hearts.

Suddenly he decided to open the door, and they entered the room.

A light softened by the shades over the electric bulbs was diffused over the middle of the room leaving the rest in shadow.

They were amazed. The room was empty.

"Gone!" exclaimed Subdamoun. "Why have they gone?"

And the fact that these people whom he had expected to see were no longer there increased his dismay.

As he approached the middle of the room his

foot slipped on the carpet. He stooped forward.
His hand touched the carpet, and he looked at his
hand in the light.

He uttered a cry—his hand was red. . . .   It
was blood! . . . His hand was red with blood.

He fell on his knees and stared—stared at the
pool of blood flowing towards the window.

Here, near the window, he picked up a hat, an
ordinary, common battered felt hat, and a little farther away a bag, a wrist bag, an elegant reticule,
open and bloodstained.

He stood up, his face pale, his eyes starting from
his head.

"Murder has been done here. . . .   Call . . .
Call the servants. . . ."

The Marchioness stood there open-mouthed, her
eyes filled with horror, her hands trembling, her
cheeks livid.

"*He* has murdered them. . . . Again *he* has done
murder."

Subdamoun was beside himself. . . . Who was
he?

"I want to know. . . . I want to know."

He was near the partly open window overlooking
the garden. The window creaked slightly as it was
blown back by a light breeze.

He thought that the criminal had fled through
the window with his victims. With a violent movement he flung the window still wider open and leapt
into the garden.

In the moonlight he could see before him a man
bending over the air-hole of a cellar and forcing
something through the aperture.

At the sound made by Subdamoun in leaping into

the garden the man turned round. And Subdamoun recognized his rescuer, the man who had helped him to break out of prison, the man who had killed M. Dimier and so many others. He drew his revolver and ran towards him.

The man saw that he would not have the time to slip into the cellar and he fled with incredible rapidity. He made mad rushes here and there to escape Subdamoun's revolver. . . .

"Hands up or I'll fire!" shouted Subdamoun. But the man again silently eluded him and made a dash for the window through which Subdamoun had come. Then he sprang through the window into the house.

The small drawing-room was empty. He tore across it like an arrow, mounted a staircase leading to the first floor, and saw on the landing the Marchioness, who was vainly endeavoring in a lifeless voice to rouse the servants.

At the sight of the frightful apparition she fell on her knees.

"Hide me, Cecily," said Chéri-Bibi.

And he went into her room and closed the door.

"Hide me, Cecily!" The Marchioness uttered a cry. That voice and that intonation when he said "Cecily!" And then that supreme cry for assistance from the man who had been her playmate as a child and who years ago, when she was a young girl, gratified her every caprice—and that way of saying "Cecily!" like the Marquis after his return from a long absence abroad, made her shudder to the very marrow.

When Jacques appeared on the landing in his turn she said in answer to his furious questions:

"No, I have not seen him."

She went into her room. She could not see him.
She did not know where he was hiding.

"Stay where you are!" she cried aloud.

Jacques's footsteps could be heard coming nearer.
He opened the door of his mother's room. His revolver was still in his hand. He was fuming with
rage and discomfiture.

"Where are the servants? Isn't there a servant
in the place? One would think they were all the
accomplices of this man."

His mother made no answer. She was kneeling
on a prayer-stool. Subdamoun left the room and
continued his frenzied search. He went into Lydia's
room. She was sleeping more soundly than usual
from the effects of some narcotic—the result, doubtless, of Chéri-Bibi's precautions.

While Subdamoun was out of his mother's room
no word passed between the Marchioness and the
man in hiding; there was nothing between them
but her prayers.

Jacques returned to her.

"That man is a devil and he saved my life."

"Yes," she said, rising from her prayer-stool.

"Did you suspect that?"

"Yes," she answered once more.

"But this is a most horrible catastrophe. We
don't know who this man is.

"Yes, I know him," she said.

"You know him?"

"Yes."

He started up. He forced her into a seat. He
shook her. She made no resistance.

"Have you known him long?"

"Yes."

"His name."

"Chéri-Bibi."

He gave a start. His brain reeled. But for the tragic look on his mother's face he could have believed that she was mocking him and had herself gone mad. He was the protégé of Chéri-Bibi, of Chéri-Bibi who had murdered both his grandfathers! . . . Chéri-Bibi! . . . Oh, that terrible name! He had heard it all around him when he was a little boy. He had been brought up in a place that rang with the story of his crimes—in a house stained with the blood of his victims. He knew that Chéri-Bibi's crimes at that period were past counting. When he went near the butcher's shop in Le Pollet his governess used to stop to tell him the story of the butcher's boy who first learnt in that shop how to use the knife!

He called to mind how they refrained from talking of him when the servant, dear Jacqueline, afterwards Sister St. Mary of the Angels, was near, because that sainted woman was the monster's sister.

Suddenly Subdamoun burst into a fit of wild laughter.

"Come, come, surely not. . . . What does it all mean? Chéri-Bibi has been dead for many a long year."

"No."

"But you yourself thought he was dead."

"Yes."

"When did you learn that he was alive?"

"When I learnt that the peanut dealer and he were one and the same person."

"How long ago was that?"

"Only a few days."

"Why did you not denounce him to the police?"

"He saved your life."

"Why did he not murder me instead of his other victims?" exclaimed Subdamoun.

"And me, too, alas," wailed Cecily in a' hollow voice. "Yes, you are right, Jacques, a thousand times right. There is no one in the world more wretched than we are through that monster. I have not denounced him to the police, but I execrate him. I would rather have died by his hand than know that we owe our lives to him."

Subdamoun stared at his mother. She spoke without looking at him, with strange force, despite her physical weakness. He was more than ever at a loss.

"But tell me the why and wherefore of all these murders committed by him round about us? What was the object—why? That is what I should like you to tell me, mother."

Cecily did not lower her eyes. She spoke like a clairvoyant who divines things that are hidden from ordinary mortals.

"I have had many afflictions in my life, Jacques, but I have just learnt that the greatest of all was to have been loved long ago by that little wretch. . . ."

"You!"

"Oh, he never told me so, but alas, I know it all the same. A Chéri-Bibi dare not speak openly of love to a good woman, but he may love her se-. cretly."

"And his murders are the tokens of his love for her!"

Subdamoun flung out his brutal retort and then lay prostrate on the sofa. Suddenly he looked up.

"Put in writing all you know of this man. I have but one object in life, and when I have accomplished it we will go away. I intend to find Chéri-Bibi and hand him over to the police."

Jacques had scarcely finished speaking when a cupboard door opened and the man stepped out.

"Here I am," he said, folding his arms. "I am ready to go with you. Hand me over to the police."

Subdamoun still held his revolver and instinctively aimed at him.

"Or shoot me," added the man.

"That would probably be the best thing to do, but not in front of my mother," said Subdamoun, thrusting aside the Marchioness, who clung to his arm.

"Wherever you please."

"Jacques, let this man go," cried Cecily in a strained voice. "Let us never see him again. Let him disappear as we will disappear ourselves."

"Oh, this man and I have a few mysteries to unravel," returned Jacques, opening the door, adding to Chéri-Bibi: "Be good enough to come down to my room."

The man went out and Subdamoun followed. The Marchioness could scarcely stand. She made no attempt to follow them. She had accomplished a superhuman effort in hiding the monster. Fate must take its course. . . .

The door was no sooner closed than it was

opened again and a vague form entered the room. It seemed to her that she was in the throes of some hideous nightmare. She was no longer surprised at anything. She came back to reality on hearing a voice say:

"I beg your pardon, madame, but I must have a word with you here and now."

She recognized the form. It was that of M. Hilaire of the "Up-to-date Grocery Stores," who regularly supplied the household with provisions.

CHAPTER XXXVIII

CHÉRI-BIBI AND SUBDAMOUN

SUBDAMOUN sat in his study listening to Chéri-Bibi. At first there was a short, sharp exchange of words between them. Confronted by the incredible audacity of the monster Jacques seemed ineffective.

"Yes, monsieur, I dared to act without asking your permission. What have you to complain of? You are not responsible for anything. You know nothing. And no one will ever be any the wiser if you are sufficiently clever to continue to remain ignorant. Hang it all, you were a combatant in the Great War. Lives are lost in peace as well as in war. For many long years I have worked secretly for you, saving you from every disagreeable necessity, taking upon myself the most hideous tasks. You have had the honor and the fame. . . . And for a long time I have got rid of all your Dukes d'Enghien! You have had but to march forward in the name of justice, and you have known no other course. . . . Thereupon you threaten to shoot me. What is that to me so long as I have succeeded? . . .

"But have I succeeded? That is the crux of the question. Are you going to shoot and then denounce me, that is to say, denounce yourself? Have I worked so hard only to see the country return to a state of anarchy from which I rescued it by placing at its head an honest man against whom no one can breathe a word of reproach? Think it over! You are not a child. Great heavens, you have returned from an army in the field. The military eagle never begot a tame dove! . . . You understand me. . . . You will end by understanding me."

"I understand that you are a murderer," said Subdamoun in a harsh voice, wiping with the back of his hand the perspiration that trickled down his forehead.

"A murderer!" repeated Chéri-Bibi. "What do you mean by a murderer? Can you tell me that? . . . Oh, I know the definition. A murderer is a man who wilfully puts a fellow-being to death. . . . Suppose I tell you that I have always had the intention to save my fellow-being, and that my intention has most often led me to kill him. I couldn't help that. Formerly I used to say *Fatalitas!* Now I hold my tongue and believe in the good God, the good God of my boyhood, who chastizes the wicked by my hand. I am not responsible for that."

"M. Dimier was an honest man and an upright judge," said Subdamoun, more and more aghast at the monster's frightful theories.

"M. Dimier was my friend. I would have given my life to save his life. I took his life to save yours.

You must know that I have never taken life but when there was no alternative. A man is not a murderer when he takes life only if there is no alternative!"

"No man had the right to kill another except in self-defense."

"Since my earliest boyhood I have been in a state of self-defense against society which has never ceased to attack me. . . . Another man might have borne malice. I have forgiven society. I have done more than forgive it. I have dreamed of reforming it, of working to make it better and more fit to live in under a leader of my own choice. And whom did I choose? You! And yet you do not seem in the least flattered. You have a look of disgust on your face. You turn round and say to yourself: 'To think that such a man supported me!' Why, my dear young sir, if you had not had that man behind you, you would have had no one in front of you to admire you and say: 'What a fine fellow he is! What a brave man! He's the man for us. Everything he touches succeeds.' Everything you touched did succeed. Without my help you would not have been returned at your first election."

"My opponent was the victim of a motor-car accident," declared Subdamoun, trembling with anguish though he endeavored to assume a brave front.

"Yes, a necessary accident."

"Oh!" groaned Jacques, clutching the butt-end of his revolver.

"Would you like me to recall the many fortunate accidents in your brilliant career?" asked Chéri-Bibi, walking round Jacques as if to exasperate him still further until he either confessed himself beaten or made an end of Chéri-Bibi.

"I know all about these 'accidents,' " he went on, "because I was at once your guardian angel, the chief of your detective service, your minister of justice, your hangman and your scavenger. You have no cause to complain. I ask you in return either to take advantage of these 'accidents' or kill me. That is a simple and definite proposal easily carried out. . . . I have done my work and I am ready to disappear. . . . You will never see me again. But if as a result of to-night's little affair you must, like a simpleton, send in your resignation and give up the game after it has been won, then kill me I entreat you."

Subdamoun laid his revolver on the table, sat down, took a sheet of paper and began to write.

Chéri-Bibi drew nearer. Subdamoun thought that he was about to seize the revolver. He made no attempt to prevent him. He was on the brink of the abyss. Now that he had heard the truth he asked only to be hurled into its depths.

He believed in righteousness. A man had come to him and said: "Your righteousness is built up on my crimes." Therefore he, too, asked only to die. Truth to tell he was a good fellow, a brave soldier, but not a great leader of men.

Chéri-Bibi looked over his shoulder and watched him as he wrote. With his huge paw he checked his hand as he was about to add his signature.

"Are you going to send in your resignation as President of the National Assembly? Are you going to tell the nation that you are retiring from public life? Why should you?"

Subdamoun rose to his feet.

"Because I will not be the child of your handiwork."

"Nothing can now prevent it."

"I renounce the heritage and in proof of that you must die."

"You will avenge *your* victims," sneered Chéri-Bibi, folding his arms and standing erect, impassive before him.

Subdamoun picked up his revolver.

"I shall shoot you simply because you murdered my two grandfathers. . . ."

But a hand interposed. It was the Marchioness, who had come in with the look of a madwoman and in her pallor seemed as if she were already about to descend to the tomb.

"Don't kill him—he is your father!"

Chéri-Bibi uttered a stifled exclamation. The Marchioness broke into mad laughter.

Subdamoun shot himself in the head.

EPILOGUE

Fortunately the wound was not fatal, and the adventure as a whole ended more satisfactorily than might have been expected from the tragic events related in the last chapters.

The skill with which Chéri-Bibi adjusted every difficulty contributed in no small degree to make life endurable to the sorely tried de Touchais family.

Subdamoun's letter of resignation was sent to the

National Assembly through the agency of the peanut dealer himself, who with a heavy heart gave up all hope of political fame for his son. The de Touchais mansion was closed, but that was an incident that caused no surprise seeing that Subdamoun had declared his intention of retiring from public life to enjoy a well-earned rest.

He was moreover, lauded to the skies and more than ever looked upon as a great figure. His conduct was compared to that of Cincinnatus, who after saving his country laid down his dictatorship to return to his farm.

But, truth to tell, if his disappearance from the scene caused rejoicing it was first because his popularity was so great that some feared lest he should monopolize all power, and secondly because others who knew him best judged him on his real merits which were not, as a section of the public would have fain believed, transcendent. His great courage as a citizen and a soldier had for the time being created the illusion that he was another "little corporal" returned from Egypt.

In reality he was no politician. He affected to have a great contempt for accidental circumstances, and yet he allowed himself to be mastered by them. He endeavored to appear hard and unfeeling, but at heart he was a sentimentalist. He was made to carry a redoubt and to lose his heart. He was unable to resist the beautiful Sonia, and his weakness precipitated disaster, but he had the good sense in the end to choose an honest wife, and it was this commonplace happening that saved him.

When he recovered from the scalp wound inflicted by his own hand he beheld only the white arms of

Mlle de la Morlière. Poor Cecily, who had more than once during her chequered life all but lost her reason, again escaped this disaster on seeing her son, who she believed was dead, restored to health again. It was an event that was bound to wipe out the memories of the past.

They all rose with new strength of mind and an ardent longing for peace and happiness in the oblivion of the country in some corner of France unknown to the world and politics such as may still be found in the more remote provinces.

·   ·   ·   ·   ·   ·

Two months have sped by since the events recorded in the last chapter.

On the saloon deck of a magnificent liner which had just set sail from Havre for the West Indies two passengers were seated in deck-chairs exchanging a few words before retiring to the luxurious cabins which Chéri-Bibi had engaged in order to render the voyage more agreeable to his friend the Dodger.

"We are no longer young men, my dear Hilaire," he said. "Certainly as far as I am concerned I still feel bubbling over with almost superhuman life and energy, and I know that you have plenty of 'pep' in you, but now that we are on our way to America and I have no fear of awakening regrets that might have kept you in France I shall not be sorry to hear the real reasons that induced you to leave the paradise of the 'Up-to-date Grocery Stores' to follow the fortunes of your old friend Chéri-Bibi, the Marquis, in some new hell upon earth.

"Tut tut!" said M. Hilaire after coughing to hide

him embarrassment. "There can't be any better reason for my conduct than the friendship that I have always felt for you."

"But that doesn't do away with the fact that you left me in the lurch on the day when I made a last urgent appeal for your unbounded devotion!" returned Chéri-Bibi.

"I will say again, monsier le Marquis, that it was remorse for my unpardonable cowardice on that day which has led me to give up everything for you just as it made me haste to join you in the Morlières' house by way of the underground passage, though I failed to arrive until the whole thing was over."

"And it ended very badly," growled Chéri-Bibi. "Had you turned up sooner I should have been able to get rid of the mortal remains of the noble Baroness and dear Little Buddha and clear out myself without being seen by that son of mine, Subdamoun. To think of that young muff indulging in the luxury of shooting himself because he learnt that I was his father! Isn't it enough to disgust one with working for one's children? . . .

"Oh, I was still capable of one honest sentiment —the feelings of a father, and the whole thing has estranged me, I can tell you. But by what light from above, by what revelation of a divine but cruel Providence, I should like to know, was Cecily able to suspect that Chéri-Bibi and the Marquis de Touchais were in days gone by one and the same person? Had it not been for that revelation I should have been done for."

"Yes," agreed the Dodger, "seeing that you were silly enough, saving your presence, not to stop him. It was indeed the will of Providence. Let us bow once more to Providence, which was pleased to direct our footsteps. We are but wisps of straw in its hands! For my part I believe that the Marchioness was able to recognize you by certain intonations in your voice which must have recalled to her mind some unforgetable moments of the past."

Thus spoke M. Hilaire, who was very careful not to disclose to Chéri-Bibi that he was the medium of that Providence which sprang so glibly to his lips, for he would not on any account have confessed that he had reached the house in time to see Chéri-Bibi enter Subdamoun's study with Subdamoun following, revolver in hand. M. Hilaire had at once grasped that something untoward was about to happen, for he felt sure that Chéri-Bibi would make no attempt to defend himself.

Consequently he had resolved to divulge to the Marchioness the frightful secret, the infernal mystery of the duality and unity of the Marquis and Chéri-Bibi, as the only means of averting patricide.

Chéri-Bibi's life, therefore, had been saved, but since as a result of M. Hilaire's bold initiative Subdamoun had attempted to commit suicide and the Marchioness had nearly lost her reason he was by no means eager to make a boast about it.

Moreover, it was not only on this point that he had concealed the truth. When he declared that he was impelled to accompany Chéri-Bibi to America because of his deep friendship for him and his remorse for refusing to lend his assistance, he was lying.

In the end he gave the real reason without appearing to attach any particular importance to it.

"I shall never forget," went on M. Hilaire after

a silence, "the sweet tones in which you used to speak to the Marchioness. When you uttered the word 'Cecily' you spoke volumes. Certainly yours was a model household. I cannot say as much for mine. Life in my house became an inferno."

"What are you trying to tell me, M. Hilaire? The last time you spoke of Mme Hilaire it was with tears in your voice. You were inconsolable over your loss."

"It was because I thought she was gone."

"Then is she still alive?"

"The truth is that on the day when I last spoke of her I thoroughly believed that I should never see her again. The half-charred boot and 'bun' of hair that I discovered made me weep over what I assumed was her tragic fate, and I was returning sorrowfully through the Rue de Roi d'Italie to the 'Up-to-date Grocery Stores' a little after nine o'clock that night when I observed coming towards me with outstretched hands and a smile on their faces—you will never guess to whom I refer—my good friends Barkimel and Florent.

" 'Hullo!' I exclaimed, 'have you come to life again? Look here, we must have a drink at my place to celebrate this happy meeting.'

"So we made our way to my stores and meantime they told me how they escaped the guillotine and how carefully they kept in the background until quiet was restored. Suddenly M. Florent said:

" 'Our first thought on returning to this neighborhood was to call on you, in spite of the lateness of the hour. Your shop-front was down but the door was still ajar. But we didn't care to go in because of Mme Hilaire. . . .'

" 'That's very good of you,' I said. 'Of course, I am very sorry she lost her life but that need not prevent us from having a drink together.'

"Barkimel and Florent stared at me as if they thought I was mad.

" 'Bah! the things you say! But you always did love your little joke. Mme Hilaire has never looked better. . . . She fills the cash desk!'

" 'What do you say?'

" 'What's the matter?'

"I was no longer listening to them. I ran straight off to the stores and cautiously glanced through a chink in the door, and as a matter of fact saw Mme Hilaire looming formidable behind the cash desk vigorously expressing to the shopman in charge her annoyance with me for still continuing my bad habits.

" 'He ought to be ashamed to be out at this time of night,' she said.

"Great heavens, monsieur le Marquis, that is the very thing I said to myself. I was ashamed to be out at that time of night—so thoroughly ashamed that I didn't go home at all!"

"You are a bad husband," returned Chéri-Bibi, smiling broadly behind his tinted spectacles. "A bad husband! I see everything now. It is to escape the conjugal hearth, M. Hilaire, that you are good enough to accompany me to the other end of the world."

"If I only knew what we are going to do when we get there!" M. Hilaire ventured to say to change the conversation.

"Well, I will tell you that, M. Hilaire, notwithstanding the great contempt that your matrimonial conduct arouses in me. After what has occurred in France I begin to feel disgusted with Republics. I know that in distant lands they need an Emperor. What would you say to Chéri-Bibi—Emperor?"

"I should say that there is no dignity that Chéri-Bibi may not aspire to," returned M. Hilaire with enthusiasm.

THE END

www.ingramcontent.com/pod-product-compliance
Lightning Source LLC
Chambersburg PA
CBHW020832030726
47496CB00001B/207